HOLD ME CLOSER, NECROMANCER

LISH MCBRIDE

SQUARE
FISH

HENRY HOLT AND COMPANY
NEW YORK

To my mother:
my anchor, my buoy,
and my star to sail 'er by.

ᑯᖕᗡ

SQUARE
FISH

An Imprint of Macmillan

HOLD ME CLOSER, NECROMANCER. Copyright © 2010 by Lish McBride.
All rights reserved. Printed in the United States of America by
R. R. Donnelley & Sons Company, Harrisonburg, Virginia.
For information, address Square Fish,
175 Fifth Avenue, New York, NY 10010.

Square Fish and the Square Fish logo are trademarks of Macmillan and
are used by Henry Holt and Company under license from Macmillan.

Library of Congress Cataloging-in-Publication Data
McBride, Lish.
Hold me closer, necromancer / Lish McBride.
p.   cm.
Summary: Sam LaCroix, a Seattle fast-food worker and college
dropout, discovers that he is a necromancer, part of a world of
harbingers, werewolves, satyrs, and one particular
necromancer who sees Sam as a threat to his lucrative
business of raising the dead.
ISBN 978-0-312-67437-3
[1. Supernatural—Fiction.   2. Magic—Fiction.   3. Dead—
Fiction.   4. Werewolves—Fiction.   5. Identity—
Fiction.   6. Seattle (Wash.)—Fiction.]   I. Title.
PZ7.M478267Hol 2010   [Fic]—dc22   2009050768

Originally published in the United States by Henry Holt and Company
First Square Fish Edition: May 2012
Square Fish logo designed by Filomena Tuosto
Book designed by Tim Hall
macteenbooks.com

10 9 8 7 6 5 4

DEAD MAN'S PARTY

I stood in front of today's schedule still holding my skateboard, still drenched from the ride over, and still desperately wishing that I hadn't dropped out of college. But wishing wouldn't erase *Sam* from the counter slot and rewrite it under the grill slot. No matter what, my job kind of sucks, but on the grill it sucks less. On the grill, you don't have to handle customers. Something about the fast food uniform makes people think it's okay to treat you like crap. Personally, I'm always polite to anyone who handles my food. There are lots of horrible things that can be done to your meal before it gets to your plate.

Maybe I could switch? No, the schedule told me Ramon worked grill today. Nothing short of fifty bucks and a twelve-pack would have made him switch, and I didn't have either of those. I groaned and leaned my head against the wall.

Someone walked in after me and slapped me on the shoulder. "Should've stayed in school," he said.

I recognized Ramon's voice without opening my eyes. Not surprising, since I'd known Ramon since sixth grade. I wasn't shocked by his lack of sympathy, either.

"You didn't drop out, and yet you're still here," I said, rolling my head to the side to look at him.

"What, and leave my man Sammy all alone? What kind of friend would that make me?"

"A smart one."

He laughed and tossed his black hoodie on the coat hooks, trading the sweatshirt for an apron. I did the same, but with much less enthusiasm.

Ramon was the only person who called me Sammy. Everyone else called me Sam, even my mom, except when she was pissed and did the full-name thing.

I signed on to my register slowly, glad that nobody stood at the counter waiting to be helped. While the manager, Kevin, counted and checked my till, I stared at the pictogram of a burger nestled between similar representations of shakes, sodas, and fries on the front of my register. I wondered why humankind seemed so dead set on destroying all of its accomplishments. We draw on cave walls, spend thousands of years developing complex language systems, the printing press, computers, and what do we do with it? Create a cash register with the picture of a burger on it, just in case the cashier didn't finish the second grade. One step forward, two steps back—like an evolutionary cha-cha. Working here just proved that the only things separating me from a monkey was pants. And no prehensile tail, which I wish I had. Oh, the applications.

My name is Samhain Corvus LaCroix, and I am a fry cook.

I tried to take some pride where I could. If I was going to be a dropout loser, then I was going to be the best dropout loser. That pride came with some complications because it always depressed me to spot anyone, short of a manager, working fast food over the age of eighteen. I didn't look in any mirrors until I got home and out of my uniform. It was better that way.

"There you go, Sam." Kevin shut my till and wandered off. We had a bet going to try and guess what it was he did in his office. Frank was pretty sure he was into some sort of online role-playing game, Ramon thought he was planning to take over the yakuza, and Brooke was convinced that he had a crippling addiction to romance novels. These all sounded plausible, except for Ramon's, though he insisted he had proof, but I didn't think Kevin could be that interesting. He probably just slept. Kevin also had the misfortune of sharing his name with my biological dad, so Ramon referred to our manager as the Lesser of Two Kevins. I slapped on my name tag and settled in.

I had my mom to thank for my name. My dad took his sweet time showing up to my birth, and in an uncharacteristic moment of spite, she named me Samhain just to tick him off. Apparently my dad wanted to name me Richard or Steve or something. But Mom got there first, and since I happened to be born on the happy pagan holiday of Samhain, well, there you go. I'm just lucky I wasn't born on Presidents' Day. She might have named me Abraham Lincoln, and there is no way I could pull off a stovepipe hat.

To retaliate, my dad started calling me Sam, since he said *Sowin*—which is how Samhain is pronounced—sounded funny.

Their divorce surprised no one.

The Plumpy's crowd was in a lull, so I watched Frank, the

other counter jockey, triple-check his condiments, napkins, and the rest of his fast food accoutrements. Frank was younger than me, and so he still had a little enthusiasm for his work. Brooke, Ramon, and I had all started a pool on how long it would take for this place to suck the life out of him. If he cracked next week, I got ten bucks. Brooke had this week, and she was doing her best to get Frank to break early.

Brooke left her station at the drive-thru window and sauntered over to the milkshake machine. I wasn't much older than Brooke, but she was young enough and tiny enough that Ramon and I both spent more time protecting her than ogling her. Not that we couldn't do both, really. I just felt a little dirty after. But I couldn't help my programming, and Brooke looked like a cheerleader in a dairy commercial: bouncy blond ponytail, clear blue eyes, and a wholesome smile that could turn any guy into man-putty. Frank didn't stand a chance because, although she tended to be a sweet girl, she could be devious when she wanted something. I probably wouldn't get my ten dollars.

Brooke finished pouring a large strawberry shake, snapped the lid on, and turned to look at Frank while she took a long sip from the straw. He ogled. I watched as she slid her hand over and flipped the machine's off switch. Frank manned register one and was responsible for the milkshake machine. He missed the tiny movement, his eyes intent on her lips as they wrapped around the straw. She sauntered back to her station, and I wondered how long it would be until Frank noticed the machine was no longer chugging behind him. If she kept on the offensive, Brooke would have him in tears before the weekend.

After about two hours, a dozen surly customers, and a minor shake machine malfunction, I decided to take a quick break. Frank could mop up shake mix and man the counter. Sure, the mess might make him crack early, but if I helped him, he'd never learn. And really, wasn't learning more important? I saluted him and hopped over the mess, stepping out back with Ramon. On the way, I grabbed my broom and the doorstop so we could leave the back door open in case someone needed to shout for us.

Ramon had quit smoking a year ago, but he never let that get in the way of a good smoke break. I had never smoked in the first place, but that didn't keep me from taking one, either. And since the rain had finally vamoosed, nothing stood between us and a decent game of potato hockey.

It is a relatively straightforward game. You get a medium-sized potato and two brooms, designate the goal areas, and you're ready to go. Today Ramon defended the garbage bin by Plumpy's back door, and I defended a shiny silver Mercedes because, according to Ramon, it represented the privileged white aristocracy of America trying to keep the Latino man down.

"Our duel," Ramon said, spinning his broom like a bo staff, "will represent the struggle our nation's currently engaged in."

"Please, we both know you're just going for home team advantage."

"You wound me, Sam. I can't help it if your crackerlike oppression gives me the better playing field." He did a quick hamstring stretch. "Suck it up."

"Fine," I said, "then I get the handicap."

"Sam, you're Texas. Texas always gets the handicap."

"I'm Team Texas again?"

He grinned, rolled his shoulders, and wiggled his arms, loosening them.

I gave up and nodded at the Mercedes. It looked old and expensive, especially in our parking lot. "Shiny."

Ramon snorted. "Classic. Check out the gullwing doors."

"Fine. Classic Shiny."

Ramon tossed an empty Plumpy's cup into the Dumpster. "Sometimes, Sammy, I question your manhood."

"A car is to get you from place to place. That's it."

Ramon shook his head at my ignorance.

"Whatever. Just try not to dent the car, Team Mexico."

"It's Team South America," he said.

"You do know that Mexico is in North America, right?"

"Yeah, but I have the whole continent behind me." He held up his fist dramatically. "They support their cousin to the north." I laughed and he dropped his hand back down. "And it's that guy's own fault for parking in our lot so he could sneak over to Eddie Bauer or Starbucks or whatever."

UVillage was an open-air shopping orgy that sat behind Plumpy's restaurant. Between the Gap, Abercrombie, and not one but two freestanding Starbucks, the place attracted a certain clientele that rubbed Ramon the wrong way. Mostly because UVillage had its own parking structure but their customers still parked over here because it was slightly closer. I didn't know why that pissed him off. He didn't like Plumpy's either. Maybe it was the principle of the thing. I was more disgusted than annoyed by the effort put forth by people just so they didn't have to walk ten extra feet.

I leaned down to tie my shoe, the leather pouch around my neck sliding out from under my shirt. I slid it back in without really thinking about it. A habit born from years of repetition. Personally, I didn't think UVillage was totally awful. Some of the food was good, and I found it hard to hate the bookstore. Of course, the bookstore contained the *third* Starbucks in the complex.

"Whatever," I said. "Game on." And I rolled the potato into the center.

Brooke came out to watch after Ramon scored another goal, making the score a depressing four to one.

"Ramon, order up," she said. She reached for his broom. "I'll pinch-hit in your absence."

"And leave Frank all alone up there?" he asked.

Brooke grinned deviously.

"That's my girl," Ramon said. He had already lost the bet, so he was now considered a free agent and worked to aid both of us. The important thing, he felt, was that Frank crack, not who won. Ramon handed Brooke his broom and walked inside.

"The devil in pigtails," I said.

Her grin widened as she adjusted her stance.

"Okay," I said, "but we're switching sides."

Brooke straightened up and sighed. "Fine, I'll be Texas."

I could be a man and admit that Brooke was much better at potato hockey than me. I didn't know what sports she played in high school or if she just worked out, but she was a better athlete than I was. I didn't even skateboard very well. My board could move me from point A to point B okay, but I couldn't really do anything fancy on it like Ramon, so I didn't feel the least bit ashamed in asking for the home field advantage.

We crouched down, brooms ready. I saw the faintest twitch around Brooke's eye before she flipped the potato into the air with the tight-packed bristles of her broom. Then she leaned back and gave it a whack with the handle. I blocked it from the garbage bin, barely, but only by slamming my own body into the bin's green, chipped side and taking the spud directly in the chest.

I squinted at her. "Dirty move."

"My brothers played lacrosse."

We both hunkered back down, eyes never leaving each other as the breeze pushed the gray clouds overhead. I blocked out the chatter from the shoppers in the distance and the sounds from the kitchen behind me. Then I tried to duplicate Brooke's move.

I didn't have any brothers who played lacrosse. Hell, I didn't have any brothers, period, though I'm pretty sure my little sister, Haley, could've given Brooke a run for her money. My lack of skill meant that my shot had force behind it but little aim.

The potato flew so far to the right that Brooke didn't even

try to go for the block. I got the point, and Classic Shiny got a broken taillight.

Brooke picked what was left of the potato off the ground, walked over to me, and threw it in the bin. "Game over," she said.

I stood, stuck to the spot. "In retrospect, the choice of goals might have been poor."

Brooke grabbed a wad of my shirt up by the neck and pulled me to the door. I felt the leather cord holding my pouch snap. Brooke let go with a "sorry" so I could snag it. "They shouldn't have parked there," she said, motioning toward the car. "Besides, that's what you get for being Texas."

I kicked the doorstop out and held the door open for Brooke. "I hear Austin's nice." I shoved my broken pouch into my hoodie pocket as we walked back in.

We were slammed for the next hour as the dinner rush invaded Plumpy's. We were busy enough that the Lesser of Two Kevins actually popped out of his office for a moment to tell us he was too busy to help. Not a useful gesture, but his concern was noted by all. I supposed we were lucky. Lesser Kevin usually only surfaced for Armageddon-level events. Actual Kevin never surfaced at all.

Finally, the people trickled out, and the place became ours again. I wandered toward the grill while Brooke made Frank mop out the newly puke-spattered Plumpy's Fun Zone. Brooke leaned against the counter, watching Frank and keeping an eye on the few straggling customers. Ramon and I started a rousing game of "Guess What I Put in the Fryer."

I closed my eyes and leaned against the back of the shake machine. There was a fairly large plop and a hiss from the fryer. "Pickle," I said.

"That's uncanny, Sam," Ramon said.

"Not really. I just helped Frank get the bucket out of the walk-in."

"Damn," he said.

After the pickle, a bun, one set of tongs, a spoonful of mayonnaise, and a hat, Ramon ran out of ideas, and I decided not to eat the fries here anymore. I stared at Ramon's spatula.

"Thou shalt not covet thy neighbor's spatula, Sammy."

"I'm pretty sure that's not in the Bible," I said.

"How do you know? Have you ever read it?" He slapped a chicken burger on the grill.

"Not really, but I'm still pretty sure that's not in there."

"Trust me," he said.

"Fine," I said, "what version, then?"

"The King Ramon version. Spatulas are considered very sacred in the King Ramon version."

I folded my arms across my chest. "Well, I'm not Christian, so I can covet. I can covet like a fiend."

"Won't get you back on grill, flame-boy," he said.

So I'd caught the grill on fire a few times. Okay, more than a few. Lesser Kevin had to remove the smoke alarms when I cooked. "I can't help it if grease is flammable. Besides, it's not like it hurts the grill."

"And what about last time?" Ramon asked, flipping the chicken burger onto a bun and placing it on a tray.

I handed the tray up to Brooke. "You're referring to the Plumpy's kids' meal incident? A lot of crap over a few boxes. Water under many bridges."

"Sam, the toys ignited and exploded melted plastic onto your apron, which also burst into flame."

"That's what fire extinguishers are for."

"The little girl at the counter started to cry because she thought you were going to immolate."

"Immolate?"

"You looked like the Human Torch, man." Ramon made an explosion-like noise and scraped something off the grill. "Flame on, Sam. Flame on."

I waved him off. "Psh." And since my arm hair had totally grown back, no permanent damage had been done.

"Besides," he said, pulling out a hotel pan full of precooked bacon, "can I help it if the grill responds to my raw Latin heat? You skinny white boys cook the burgers, but I make love to them."

"That's disgusting," I said.

In the last hour before closing, I crouched under a table with a putty knife and chipped old gum away. I led a very exciting life. Brooke was going to make Frank do it, so I offered before that could happen. Instead he got to sweep, and I was that much closer to winning the pool. Brooke sulked behind the counter, blacking out teeth and drawing mustaches on the people pictured on our tray liners. There were no customers, and the only sound besides the scrape of my putty knife and Frank's sweeping was Ramon, who for some reason hummed show tunes while he cleaned the grill. Right then it sounded like "Luck Be a Lady." He danced too. Ramon was a triple threat.

As I ran the putty knife along the wood-style plastic of the table, I wondered why people would pick this as the final resting place for their gum. Seriously, we had garbage cans, trays, wrappers—hell, they could stick it on Frank—so why always the table? While I considered this, I heard the door swing open. The sound wasn't loud, but I hadn't expected anyone else to come in so late on a weeknight. Especially with what appeared to be dress shoes. Plumpy's caters to the sneaker set. I tilted my head so I could peek out.

The man seemed to be of average height, but since I was lying on the floor, it was hard to tell. Everyone looks tall from that angle. I twisted my head so that I could follow him with my eyes, and as he got closer to Brooke, I decided that he must be just about an inch or two shy of six feet. He was skinny too. No, lean. But he gave off the impression of being much bigger than he was. His shoes weren't like anything I'd seen in a department store, and his charcoal suit looked expensive. He held an old-fashioned doctor's bag in his left hand and a piece of potato in his right.

Shit.

He held the potato out to Brooke. "I'd like someone to explain this," he said.

The guy had a preacher's voice, smooth and rolling, worn with use.

That voice sent a shiver of unease down my spine. I froze

under the table, not even daring to bring my arm and putty knife back down.

Brooke looked at the man, her eyes cool, her body language saying casual indifference. She pointed one dainty finger at the man's right hand. "It's a potato," she said.

The man didn't respond.

"You know, a kind of tuber? Grows in the ground. Almost killed Ireland. Any of this ringing a bell?"

I could see Brooke's face and the pink fingernail polish she was wearing as her hands gestured at the man.

"I know what it is," he said.

"Then why did you ask?" Brooke rested her hip on the counter and crossed her arms.

The man didn't move, but I saw his grip tighten on the handle of his bag.

I stayed motionless under the table, even though my arm was starting to get tired from holding the putty knife up. I didn't know why Brooke wasn't scared of the man, but my guess was that being the only girl raised alongside a bunch of gigantic, lacrosse-playing male siblings had more than one benefit. When she first started going to shows with me, I'd insisted on staying close to her, afraid she might take a rogue fist from the mosh pit or get swallowed by the sweating mass of the audience. That was until I saw her split the lip of an overly affectionate drunk at an all-ages show at El Corazón.

Brooke doesn't scare easy. Wish I could say the same about myself.

The man took a deep breath. His grip relaxed around the

handle of the bag. I could only see the back of his head, but I bet his anger never showed up on his face. "What I want to know is why it was in the broken taillight of my car, which was in *this* parking lot."

Brooke put her elbows on the counter and cupped her chin in her hands. "Oh, I love riddles," she said. She kept her eyes wide and innocent, her pink lips straight. Her blond ponytail slipped forward, and she absently twirled the end of it with one finger. Brooke had long ago mastered the vapid look. "I give up. Why did you put a potato in your taillight?"

"I didn't. It was there when I got back."

Brooke's eyes got a little round. "Oh, a mystery." She straightened back up off the counter and let the vapid look fall away. Her eyelids drooped a little, and her lip quirked up at one side, pure devilish disdain. "Well, then I'll just get Shaggy and Scooby, and we'll get right on it, mister."

The man laughed, and I couldn't help thinking that it was the most joyless sound I'd ever heard.

Ramon sauntered up from the back, drying his hands on a towel. "Is there a problem here?" He'd asked Brooke but kept his eyes on the man.

The man held up the potato. "I found this in my shattered taillight."

Ramon shrugged. "I don't know anything about it."

"I'd be grateful if I was you," Brooke added. "Your car could have been impounded for being in our lot. That's why we have signs posted every two feet saying 'for Plumpy's customers only' and 'park at your own risk.' We aren't a parking garage, we're a dining establishment."

"That serves potatoes," the man said softly. He set the remnants down on the counter.

She shrugged one shoulder. "A mashed potato taillight is getting off easy."

The man pushed the offending spud closer to Brooke before straightening up and squaring his shoulders. He inclined his head. "The manager, if you will."

"He's busy," Ramon said. We all knew that Lesser Kevin wouldn't come out of his office unless it was closing time or the building was burning to the ground.

Ramon's eyes flicked down to where I hid under the table. His eyebrow raised just a twitch, and I shook my head frantically. I didn't know who the complaining man was, but he scared me. The primitive part of my brain screamed *predator*, and I believed it. With predators, if you move, if you're seen, you're eaten, and this man in his expensive but understated gray suit could swallow me whole.

Ramon looked back at the man, but it wasn't fast enough.

I watched the man glance over his shoulder, just a short peek down to me hiding under the table, before he returned his attention to the counter.

I let a breath out slowly and tried to stop my hands from shaking. He hadn't really seen me.

Then he jerked back around.

His footsteps echoed in the empty restaurant as he headed my way. I scooted farther under the table, but I could feel the uselessness of the action already. The man leaned down, grabbed me by my Plumpy's T-shirt, and dragged me into the open. I heard Brooke and Ramon shout something, but I couldn't make it out. All my attention was focused on the brown eyes of the man in front of me. Lean as he was, he held me up by the shirt with little effort. Hanging like that was awkward, so I grabbed his wrists for balance. I felt a cold snap of electricity, like frozen static shock, and I immediately released his wrists.

"What," he said slowly, "do you think you're doing here?"

"I work here." My lips felt cracked and dry all of a sudden.

He tightened his grip on me and pulled me closer. Not really a place I wanted to be. I swallowed hard.

"Not here, fool. Seattle."

"I live here."

His face got even closer, and I grabbed at his wrists again. The shock was still there, a chill crackling up my arms, but I held on anyway. Unpleasant, but I didn't want to let him get his face any nearer to mine. The man's voice dropped to a low whisper. "You live here and you haven't petitioned the Council?"

"Huh?"

"When you moved here, you should have contacted us, asked permission"—he looked down at my name tag—"Sam."

Oh, good, he was crazy and scary. What an awesome combination. I let go of his wrists with one hand and leveraged myself back enough so I could pull my T-shirt out of his grip. I dropped to the floor, knowing full well that he let me do it.

"I have always lived here," I said, enunciating each word in that peculiar way people do when speaking with the insane. I straightened out my shirt. "I was born here, and I've never heard of any Council."

"Impossible," he said. "I would have known." His face was an odd mix of concern and disdain.

"Perhaps my mother forgot to send you an announcement." My hands shook. I shoved them into my pockets. At least that way the shaking would be less visible.

"Is there a problem?" Lesser Kevin had finally come out of his office.

I didn't look at him, thinking it best to keep my eyes firmly on whatever threat this man represented. My body still wanted to run screaming in the other direction, but I held it there anyway. I couldn't quite figure out which would be the safer choice.

"No, sir," I said, "no problem."

A moment passed as the man stood, eyes still locked on me, face unreadable. Then he grinned; the smile unfurling slowly on his face reminded me suddenly of the old Grinch cartoon they show on TV every year during Christmas. It's much creepier on a human face than on an animated one. He reached over and restraightened my shirt.

"No," he said, "just a misunderstanding." As the man turned toward Lesser Kevin, his face lit up, changing the smile to something lighthearted and normal. "A case of mistaken identity. You know how it is."

Kevin looked confused. "My employee tells me you had a complaint about your car?"

Behind Kevin, Frank cowered, his eyes wide, broom still firmly in hand. He gave me a little wave.

The stranger shook his head in dismissal. "No, no. It's not a big deal. Again, a simple misunderstanding." He walked over and shook Lesser Kevin's hand. Kevin still looked sort of apprehensive, but he didn't seem to be having the same problem touching the stranger as I did. In fact, the contact seemed to relax him. "Thank you for your time. I appreciate it."

He turned to leave but nodded in my direction on his way out. "Sam," he said, like he was my friend, but it wasn't friendly. It was ominous, like when my mom spoke my name in public with that tone that meant I was going to get an earful once we were alone.

2

WELL, AIN'T THAT A KICK IN THE HEAD?

I leaned my skateboard against the wall so I could zip up my hoodie. After the weird events earlier, closing time had seemed a little anticlimactic. Ramon still did his usual tricks to try to get a laugh out of me, and I forced a few smiles, but I felt too distracted to really pay attention to any of it. We made Frank do most of the actual cleanup. He didn't complain, just went about wiping, stocking, and mopping until the place was ready to go.

What the hell had crazy Classic Shiny car guy been talking about? What Council? I'd have marked him off as nuts, or eccentric since he drove an old Mercedes, except for the memory of cold electricity running up my arms. He'd asked about my birth. Well, where I'd been born. Maybe I should call my mom.

Ramon flicked off the lights, and Frank, Brooke, and I filed out. "Anything going on tonight?" Ramon asked.

Frank cleared his throat and pulled out a stack of DVDs from his messenger bag.

Ramon grabbed them. "*The Beastmaster, Dragonslayer, Conan the Barbarian*. Frank, I'm sensing a theme."

"Sweaty guys in loincloths?" Brooke asked.

"I'm secure enough in my sexuality to enjoy a good barbarian movie," Ramon said, holding up the *Conan* DVD so Brooke could see the glistening Arnold on the front. "It's Frank I'm worried about."

"You're so funny. Just funny, funny, funny all the time," Frank said. "You should be a comedian." He held his hands out as if he was envisioning a marquee. "Ladies and gentlemen, Ramon the Obnoxious."

"That's redundant," Ramon said, handing the movies back to Frank. "All comedians are obnoxious."

"Well," I said, "I know what we're doing tonight."

Brooke scoffed. "Huh-uh, count me out, boys."

"Really?" I asked. "These are the most girl-friendly movies we've watched in weeks."

"Please," she said, "I've seen *Conan*. He throws a chick into a fire."

"Yeah," Ramon said, "but she was asking for it."

"Nice." She huddled into her jacket and pushed her purse toward her hip. "I'll see you guys later, okay?" She flashed a grin at us and waved before walking to her car.

Frank watched her, looking like he might drool. I just wanted to make sure she got to her car okay. Tonight had made me a little paranoid. But she climbed into her blue VW Beetle and drove away, honking and waving as she left.

We all turned and walked toward Frank's white Jetta. I didn't live too far from Plumpy's, so I'd ridden my skateboard to work. Ramon didn't have a car. He usually found it much easier to force me to drive him everywhere in my Subaru.

Frank opened the trunk so Ramon and I could throw our boards in. I reached up to shut the trunk door and caught a movement in the shadow of a nearby building. A man was walking toward me. A big man. Of course, I'm not that tall, so a lot of guys make me feel short. But I think this guy would make most people feel puny. He was tall, muscle-bound, and man-pretty. I bet he spent a lot of time in the gym standing in front of the mirror checking his abs or bouncing his pecs. He was also tan and moved like one of those guys you see in the commercials for the military where they're climbing rock walls and running down beaches. The kind of dude you don't want to get in a bar fight with.

He moved up close to me, not totally in my face, but definitely in my personal space. I was beginning to see a pattern emerging. I could see Frank and Ramon watching.

"Are you Sam?" he asked.

The way today was going, I didn't really want to answer. But I also couldn't think of anything else to say, so I said, "Yeah."

"I've been sent by Douglas Montgomery."

"You say that like I should know who that is," I said.

He grinned at me—not so much a grin as a flash of teeth. "You should."

"Yeah, well, I don't," I said.

"Then I guess you should find out."

"No, I'm good. My dance card is full, but I'll check with my secretary. Ramon?"

"Booked," Ramon said.

I fixed on the big guy's brown eyes and tried not to flinch. "Tell your boss to get back to me in a few months." Then I did something stupid. Well, something stupid besides shooting my mouth off. I turned my back. A sound came from behind, a bit of a growl, low and deep, and then my feet left the ground as he clobbered me with a fist that felt like an SUV. The jolt of pavement followed, a hammer blow before I started to roll. I curled my arms to cradle my head. I skidded along the parking lot, grateful for my hoodie and jeans, knowing that I would be hurting soon anyway. Another strike hit my back, and whatever it was, it hurt like hell. Like sharp, burning hell.

A hand grabbed me by the sweatshirt and lifted me up. I spun like a top, and the grip shifted to my throat. Not good.

The man loomed in front of me again, looking pissed. He pulled me in close, right up to his face. His nostrils flared in and out as he breathed, as if he were taking in all the smells around us. His pupils dilated. Probably from an adrenaline rush. I didn't think this guy had the best self-control. I held still, ignoring the aching of bruised muscles and the burning in my back. What had he done to me?

I hung there and tried my best to radiate calm. Fear would only make it worse, I was sure of it, and I couldn't get angry because this guy could wipe the floor with my carcass. So I dangled there in pain, pretending to be calm, and waited for him to make his next move.

"You even smell a little like him," he said, his voice going throaty.

Disturbing. Was it good to smell like someone else? I reached out cautiously and put my hands over his, leveraging for a bit of breathing room. "Like who?" I choked out. Buff Guy had a fierce grip.

"Like the grave," he said, not really answering my question. "Like cold death."

"Thanks," I said. Creepy, creepy, creepy. I didn't add that he smelled like meat. Not that I could. Apparently, choking helped me keep my mouth shut and mind my manners. I wished he'd put me back down. Or that Ramon and Frank would rush him from behind. Then he'd have the opportunity to strangle all of us. I needed to get bigger friends.

"And blood," he said. "You smell like blood."

My pulse began to speed up despite my attempts to stay calm. This huge guy was talking about my blood, and he looked really, really happy about it. But I wasn't going to just hang here and die in the parking lot of Plumpy's.

I yelled in his face with all the air I could get and grabbed tighter onto his wrists, kicking whatever was in reach.

He laughed, but I kept kicking.

Then I heard Ramon yell, "Duck!" I did my best, but with his meaty paws around my throat, it was more of a leaning motion.

There was an unholy cracking noise as Ramon whacked him in the head with a skateboard, breaking it in two. The guy's hold loosened as he turned to evaluate the new threat, and I pushed away from him with all I had. For the second time in as many minutes, I hit pavement.

I heard a car engine and turned to see Frank backing up his beat-up Jetta and coming right at us. I rolled out of the way. The man didn't move as Frank drove at him, just cocked back his fist and punched the rear of the car. With his freaking *fist*. And he stopped the Jetta cold. While he turned his scary grin on Frank, I got to my feet and grabbed for the door. I slid in at the same time as Ramon.

Frank froze, staring at the back of his car.

Ramon slapped him to get his attention. "Drive!"

Frank slammed his foot down on the pedal. There was a screech and a jerk, but then we were driving over a small concrete divider and pulling onto the empty street. I kept my eyes on the man who now held Frank's rusty bumper in his hands as we drove away. I watched him toss it over his shoulder like it was made of paper.

"Seat belts!" Frank's voice held an edge of hysteria.

I stopped watching the man and curled into my seat, grabbing the seat belt and slipping it on. The motion made damn near every muscle and joint in my body scream, and I had to arch so my back wouldn't touch the seat.

Ramon turned as he clicked his own belt and eyed me. "You okay, Sammy?"

"What the hell is going on, Ramon? Did someone paint a target on me at work?"

"Right now I'm kind of worried about that freaked-out dude back there. You think he was all jacked up on PCP or something? I mean, he tore off Frank's damn bumper!"

"Rust problem? Adrenaline rush?" I threw out the ideas, though I didn't really believe any of them. That didn't keep my brain from searching for some kind of explanation.

"I don't know," he said, "but whatever it is, I don't think it's over."

"Me either." I closed my eyes and tried to find a somewhat comfortable position to hold myself in, only to realize that there wasn't one. Frank would need a new bumper and Ramon a new skateboard. I'd have to assess my damages when I got home. At least Brooke had left before anything had happened to her.

THESE ARE A FEW OF MY FAVORITE THINGS

Douglas shifted to the left, delighting in the warmth of the soft leather. Few things on this earth were as heavenly as leather seats. If that kind of luxury was a sin, he'd happily dance his way into hell.

He looked out through the dark in front of the house, letting his eyes get accustomed to the lack of light. The Beetle he'd been following idled in the driveway, and he watched as the girl got out. She pulled out two bags of groceries, balancing one of them on her hip as she shut the door. He would let her enter the house, get settled. It gave him time to prepare. His phone beeped as he turned it off. After Michael's failure with Sam, he would know better than to call Douglas again. Still, he didn't want his phone to ring at an inopportune time.

Michael would have been a better choice for this mission. But since he'd botched the earlier assignment—and a simple messenger job at that—Douglas decided to handle the matter on his own. If he couldn't trust Michael to put the fear of God into that boy Sam, he couldn't trust him with this. A delicate touch would be needed to sort this mess out.

Douglas sighed. The adage was true: It was so hard to find

good help these days. Not that he cared about Michael smacking the boy around. Violence certainly didn't bother Douglas. No, what bothered him was Michael's lack of finesse. He'd simply escalated the violence too quickly. Douglas had meant to try to woo the boy first, lull him into complacency. Then, if Sam didn't come around, well, time for plan B. But he hated having his hand forced.

He also hated surprises. Douglas chewed absently on a thumbnail. How could he have missed another necromancer, even one with so small a power? It wasn't like they grew on trees. And if he'd missed the boy, what else had he missed? Douglas shrugged off the uncomfortable thought and tried to concentrate on the things he knew for sure. If he'd discovered him earlier, Douglas could have planned better. He could have molded the boy in his image, coaxed his power out instead of using brute force to do the job.

Douglas watched as the girl unlocked the front door. No use debating what could have been. The gloves were already off, and now he was going to have to give a very ungentlemanly kind of warning. Pity, that. Still, a necromancer left unchecked could create all sorts of trouble. Best to put him in his place now.

The little parasite had to be lying. How could he not know? It wasn't like necromancy was a power one could ignore. Douglas could remember seeing his first spirit when he was quite young.

𝔇ouglas hadn't really understood why he was at his grandmother's house. He just knew that he was to be quiet and that he had to wear his itchy clothes. He yanked at his collar for the third time, and his mother took her hand off her swollen belly, grabbed his fingers, and pulled them away from his shirt. She glared at him and went back to fanning herself. He opened his mouth to argue, but out of the corner of his eye he saw Auntie Lynn frowning at him, so he snapped his mouth shut and looked at his feet, trying to make himself small.

Douglas was bored. He wished there were children to play with. The adults were busy crying and talking, and if they did come over, it was to greet his mother. He spotted a tray of cookies. With a sideways glance at his mother, he leaned slowly toward the table. Mother was busy talking to someone, her fan doing little to dry the sweaty curls around her face. Douglas made a quiet getaway and headed over to the cookies. He looked for gingersnaps, his favorite, and shoved one in his mouth while hiding a few others in his pockets. He took one last cookie and turned, nearly bumping into a sad-faced little boy. Douglas spoke around the cookie.

"Hi, Charlie," he said, spraying a fine mist of crumbs everywhere. Douglas quickly looked around. No one noticed the crumbs. If they did, he wouldn't be let into the parlor ever again. This was what his mother called a "nice room."

Charlie waved feebly at him. His skin was a little pale, and Douglas was surprised to see that Charlie wasn't wearing his itchy clothes.

"Your mother's going to whup you if she finds you in here

in your pajamas, Charlie." But Charlie just shrugged and motioned to the living room. Douglas brightened. "You wanna play trucks?"

A while later, Douglas's mother came into the living room and asked him what he was doing. "It isn't right," she said, "making a ruckus at a time like this."

"I'm sorry, Mother," he said. "I was just playing with Charlie." His cousin looked a little guilty, but he looked a little sad, too. Douglas felt bad. He didn't mean to get Charlie in trouble, especially for still being in his pajamas. "It's my fault, Mother. We'll be quieter."

The color faded from his mother's face. "What did you say, baby?"

"I didn't mean to get Charlie in trouble." He stared at the floor, stuck his lower lip out, and tried to look contrite. If he got the look right, he might avoid his talking-to. "I was being too loud."

His mother sank slowly to the floor. "Honey," she said gently, "do you know why we're here?"

"I promise to be quiet."

She shook her head and reached out, clutching his face in her hand. "No, I meant, do you understand why we're here today at Grandma Montgomery's?"

Douglas stared back at her.

She rubbed at some dirt on his cheek before letting go of his face. "Dougie, Charles got sick. Real sick." She paused. "He's, well, he can't play with you anymore. Charles has gone to heaven."

Douglas looked at Mother. Her face was open, honest. She wasn't fibbing. But he could still see Charlie right there. She was wrong. But Mother was never wrong. He stared at her, trying to figure out what to say.

"What?" Confusion pushed away the honest expression on her face.

Douglas pointed over to Charlie, who sat three feet away from her in his blue-striped pajamas. "He's right there. See?" His mother looked, but he could tell she couldn't see anything.

"You can't see him?" Douglas peeked at Charlie, who shrugged at him and pointed back at the trucks. His mother patted his head, worry clouding her eyes. She didn't believe him. Douglas felt the rotten sting of disappointment. He watched as she got up and went to find his father. Douglas went back to his trucks.

His mother's skirt had no sooner whisked out of sight than his auntie Lynn calmly strode over. "What's your cousin wearing, Douglas?"

Douglas frowned at the question. "Blue-striped jammies," he said, all the moisture leaving his mouth. He was a little scared of his auntie Lynn. The air around her always felt cold. "You're not going to tell on him, are you?"

"No, child, I'm not going to tell." She reached over and brushed his cheek with the tips of her fingers. Douglas froze. He couldn't remember the last time he'd been touched by Auntie Lynn. He didn't like it. She smiled at him then and turned the gesture into a light pat. Douglas liked that smile even less.

A few days after the funeral, Auntie Lynn offered to take Douglas away. His parents hadn't argued much. They talked it over for a few days, mostly at times when they thought Douglas was sleeping. He couldn't believe they were even considering it. He'd expected his mother to instantly refuse. When she hadn't, he thought his chest might cave in. What had he done? Then, for the first time, Douglas realized his parents were afraid of something. They were afraid of Auntie Lynn. And now they were afraid of him.

One week after the funeral, he packed his suitcase.

He cried at first, but in the end, it had all been for the best. Auntie Lynn explained that people like him were rare. They had to be trained—he had to be trained—and his aunt could do that. Left alone, she said, their kind could destroy themselves. Go crazy. Destroy others by accident. She helped him understand how useless his parents had been, how weak, and by being with them, how weak he was by extension. Auntie Lynn made that part very clear. Without her, Douglas would be nothing. Through her, he might become something. Someone.

She taught him everything: calculus and etiquette along with Sun Tzu, Aristotle, and Machiavelli. As he followed Auntie Lynn around the country, he began to understand something else: he wasn't the only one who was afraid of her. When Auntie Lynn walked into a crowded room, the people parted like the Red Sea he'd heard about from the fat preacher in church, though they didn't seem to know why they were doing it. Douglas didn't think it was because Auntie Lynn was close to God like Moses was. The avoidance seemed unconscious, like pulling back from a snake that has suddenly appeared in your path. On some deep level, people recognized her as a predator. Douglas thought it might make more sense for her to blend in better. It's easier to get prey if they can't see you're a predator in the first place. But he kept that to himself.

In time, he learned all about the family curse. That's what she called it, a curse. Yet she said the word lovingly. Of course, by then, Douglas understood. The curse had brought her all of her wealth and had kept her alive for a very, very long time.

By his sixteenth year, Douglas had learned all his aunt could show him. While most boys his age were chasing skirts, he practiced summoning and speaking to spirits. He could raise the dead. He'd grown powerful, much more so than she. She'd started to figure that out, toward the end. Unfortunately for her, Douglas had fully grasped her lessons concerning ruthless practicality, and he'd noticed that his teacher had grown overconfident. Sloppy. Auntie Lynn never tasted the sedative in her sherry, and she didn't wake up when he slit her open and stole her gift. As he'd knelt there, covered in her blood, his hand lolling to the side but still holding the dagger, drunk on her power, he couldn't help but think she'd be proud. He'd become the perfect pupil.

Douglas was no longer weak.

Well, Douglas thought, he'd clean this mess up, too. After all, he was number one. He was Council, and Sam had no right to be here. Douglas had to teach the boy how to get his gift under control. The last thing he needed was to give the Council an excuse to remove him as leader, and a rogue necromancer was a very good excuse. If training didn't work, he could just kill him. Both plans had their merits. If it all worked out, Douglas would have another servant at his beck and call. And if not, well, he still had Auntie Lynn's knife. He'd also had decades to perfect the ritual. With all the prep work and fumbling, it had taken him almost an hour to steal his aunt's powers. Repetition and practice had honed that time down to twenty minutes, and that's if the victim fought. Sam's power was almost too insignificant to even bother with. It would be far easier to kill him quickly and leave him in the woods somewhere. But, as they say, every little bit helps. Waste not, want not. Douglas grinned.

First, he had to show the boy he meant business. Well, he'd already done that, hadn't he? Michael may have gotten ahead of the plan, but the message he sent was clear. Still, Douglas didn't want to overestimate Sam's comprehension. The public schools these days weren't known for fostering independent thought. He'd have to send him something more personal.

Douglas got out of his car where he had been sitting—brooding, really, if he could admit it to himself—and shut his door quietly. He crept up the last bit of drive toward the blue Volkswagen Beetle he'd seen earlier at Plumpy's. He peeked into the carport, looking for anyone else who might have pulled up earlier, but the Volkswagen sat alone in the driveway. He smiled, singing snatches of a Julie Andrews song under his breath. The soundtrack was one of his favorites, and he often played it at home. Happily humming, he changed a few key words. *"People in terror groveling before me, these are a few of my favorite things . . ."*

Douglas slid past the Beetle and went in to collect his package.

4

BROWN PAPER PACKAGES TIED UP WITH STRING

I lived in a small one-bedroom apartment that I couldn't really afford. When I rented the place, I justified it because I could easily ride a bike to UW's campus from there and still be nowhere near Frat Row, which was the one place in Seattle I hoped never to live. The neighborhood was nice, with a lot of trees and a small park. And despite the faded gray exterior of my building, the inside of the apartment wasn't bad.

Once I became a dropout, my flimsy justification vanished along with my student loans. I was forced to rock the Top Ramen lifestyle that is envied by so many. Now, as I stood in my hallway, I took comfort in the quiet of the building and the fact that I had always helped Mrs. Winalski with her groceries, so that when she spotted me coming out of the elevator scratched, greasy, dirty, and already bruising, she didn't immediately call the police. Sometimes, you had to take the few small comforts life offered you.

"Sam, honey, you look filthier than a hot tub in a brothel."

"That's kind of gross, Mrs. W," I said.

She eyed Ramon and Frank behind me, her finger wagging

between them. "Your little boyfriends didn't beat you up, did they?" she said. "Sam's a nice boy, and if he won't call the cops on you two, I will."

"I'm grateful," I said. "I really am, but I'm neither gay nor a victim of domestic violence."

Mrs. Winalski dug around in her purse for her keys and made a harrumphing noise. "You worry me, Sam. I'm seventy, and I get a hell of a lot more action than you, boy. You're young—take advantage." She clasped her keys in one hand and patted her short, steely hair with the other. "How do I look?"

"Great. Knock 'em dead, Mrs. W." Mrs. Winalski had been widowed fairly young. She'd told me she'd spent a lot of time caring for her sick husband before that. I think she'd been making up for lost time since his death. On Tuesday nights, she sang karaoke. Wednesdays, she coached a local roller derby team. I wasn't sure what a roller derby coach did, but I wanted to go just to see her screaming obscenities from the sidelines. Come to think of it, she went out almost every night. Mrs. Winalski did not screw around when it came to her free time. She made me feel old.

"You're a good kid," she said. She waved behind her as she walked toward the elevator. "See you later, boys, and don't wait up."

I waved back and opened my door, flicking on the light and looking around before stepping in. I was still a little jumpy after the attack. Frank and Ramon followed me.

"She seems nice," Frank said.

"Dude," Ramon said, "did your seventy-year-old neighbor just order you to get laid?"

"What can I say? She worries." I tried to sound light-hearted, but I think it came out tired instead.

Out of habit, Ramon leaned to put his skateboard by the door. There was a dirty smudge on the wall because he always put his board in the same place. He sighed. "You owe me a new board, Sammy." His hand started to shake as he stared at the spot. "Not that I'm complaining. You know." He went silent for a moment, eyes locked on that empty space. "Board well spent."

I agreed to replace the board, even though we both knew I didn't have the money. Maybe I could just loan him mine for a while. In the morning. After the night I'd had, I planned to sleep with the damn thing. Skateboards made a great weapon in a pinch, as Ramon had proved earlier. I should get a bat. A big metal bat. And a dog. A giant, creepy-man-eating dog. With rabies. Who was I kidding? I couldn't afford myself, let alone a dog. To be honest, I couldn't afford the bat.

I slumped down into my ratty plaid easy chair, not even bothering with the footrest. I hissed when my back hit and had to sit a little forward to alleviate some of the pain. I felt exactly like a brothel hot tub, and it was not a pleasant feeling. Ramon kicked off his shoes and flopped onto the couch while Frank walked through my small apartment. I could hear him methodically checking my closets and under my bed. He caught me watching him as he exited my room, and his face flushed.

"Just checking," he said. I didn't want to think what for. I felt stupid for not doing it myself. Maybe I could blame the stupidity on shock. Frank picked at the hem of his shirt. "Shouldn't we take you to the hospital? Or the cops? We should go to the cops."

"And tell them what?" I snapped. "That a man said weird things to me and then another man tore off your bumper? Plus, we almost ran him over. No, I don't think so." I rubbed my face with the palm of my hand. "The cops will just say your decrepit bumper fell off or something."

"But you were assaulted!" Frank continued picking at his shirt. If he kept it up, he wouldn't have any shirt left. "And he started it."

"To be fair," Ramon said, plumping up the couch cushion behind his head, "we did assault him back. And it's not like cops can tell who hit who first." He settled into the couch. "I don't think they can, anyway."

"But." Frank looked pleadingly between the two of us before giving up with another mumbled, "Assaulted."

"And I'd like to not get more assaulted," I said, rubbing my temples. Cops scared me a little. But the Classic Shiny guy scared me more. On the way home I'd sorted through the night in my head and come to the conclusion that the beat-down had been directly related to the evening's earlier events. That Classic Shiny guy must have been the Douglas Montgomery that the big guy mentioned. It made more sense for the two bizarro incidents to be connected than for them to be isolated. Either way, laying low sounded pretty good right now.

"I agree with Sammy," Ramon said. "I think telling the cops on these guys would just make things worse."

"But—"

"Think about it, Frank. If you were a cop, who would you listen to, us or the guy in the fancy suit with a busted tail-light?"

Frank collapsed into a chair, looking even more defeated than a second ago. "So you think it's connected? The fight with the other guy?"

Ramon clapped him on the shoulder. "You think it's not?"

"I'm taking a shower," I said, standing up before Frank got his second wind. That's all I wanted, to wash today off me. Actually, there was a long list of other things that I wished for, but I'd settle for a shower. Ramon was antsy to talk about earlier, I could tell, but it would have to wait.

The quiet of my bathroom was comforting. It was nice to have a moment to myself, to let everything catch up. Unfortunately, since my bathroom was more like a glorified closet, thinking was about the only thing I could do easily. The beige sink was only an arm's length from the toilet, and I had to close the door to get into the shower. Sometimes it was good to be scrawny. A fatter Sam wouldn't have been able to fit in my bathroom.

I examined my face in the mirror and was surprised that Mrs. Winalski hadn't called the cops anyway. Bruises were already surfacing on my face, and a wicked-looking patch of scratches covered my cheekbone. Grease from the asphalt covered my shirt. What wasn't greasy looked shredded, and my name tag was ripped clean off.

I tried to remove my shirt. Blood made it stick to my back, though, so I pulled it off with a quick jerk that I regretted instantly. I twisted a little so I could see my back in the mirror. Long, bloody furrows went from my shoulder to the bottom of my rib cage, like I'd been pawed by a giant cat. I'm sure all the blood, dirt, and bruises made it look worse than it actually was. Or, at least, that's what I was hoping.

I threw my shirt into the trash and crawled into the shower, letting the water run until it went cold. But getting clean didn't help much. Before the shower, I was scared, tired, and confused. Afterward, I was all those things plus cold and wet.

I pulled on a clean pair of boxers and jeans and went out to rejoin the others. Frank was huddled over my computer in the corner, one hand on my skateboard, and Ramon was idly flipping through his biology textbook and taking sips out of the flask I'd gotten him on his last birthday. All the curtains were drawn, and they'd pushed my easy chair against the door. Welcome to a night at Casa Sam, where our parties are legendary. I cleared my throat.

"Um, one of you is going to have to bandage this for me," I said, though the choice was simple. Ramon might have some idea as to what he was doing, since he had gotten an A in biology. Besides, he had patched me up after the many, many times I'd wrecked my board. Frank was . . . Frank. I wasn't not quite sure what that qualified him to do.

Ramon went to the cupboard for my first aid kit while I took a seat at the kitchen table. Most guys my age didn't have first aid kits at all, much less one like mine. No Neosporin, aspirin, or rubbing alcohol. My mom wasn't against Western medicine per se, but it wasn't her first choice. Ramon had been around my family enough that he knew what the various jars and powders were. Frank, however, had not. He left the computer for a few moments to come watch, proving that even he felt the basic red-blooded male's attraction to gore and violence.

"That smells good," Frank said, picking up a jar Ramon had pulled out. "What is it?"

"Tea tree oil, cloves, whatever. They're natural antiseptics. Sam's mom's a hippie."

"She's an herbalist," I said. "She's made the same bottles for you and your family." And a bunch of other people. My mom had a small shop where she sold natural herb mixtures. She also had a Web site. You could buy the stuff Ramon was cleaning my back with for $12.99 over the Internet at HerbaceousPlanet.com.

"Yeah, that just means she's good at it. No patchouli stink and half-baked Frisbee days for her." Ramon finished cleaning my back and handed me the jar so I could get the scrapes on my front while he set about the bandaging.

"I'm a little worried about these scratches, Sam," he said. He'd been calling me Sammy since we were little, and he tended to drop the *y* only when he was being serious, which was rare.

I wasn't worried. We'd cleaned them well, and I didn't think they would become infected. I'd just have to keep an eye on them. I was more worried about how I got them.

Ramon seemed to follow my train of thought. "Did either of you see a knife or anything?"

I set the bottle of salve down on the table harder than I meant to. "No." I took a deep breath, trying to release some of my tension. "I was too busy getting my ass kicked." My voice shook a little, so I cleared my throat. "How about you guys?"

Frank shook his head. Ramon ripped off a piece of tape and handed the roll to Frank. "I didn't see anything, but he was moving fast. Real fast." He placed the tape on my back, wrapping it around toward the front. "But if I didn't know better, I'd say you were attacked by an animal," he said.

"They look like claw marks, don't they?" I said. The quaver came back into my voice. I needed to snap out of it. Going into shock wouldn't do me any good.

"We should call the cops," Frank said. Ramon and I both turned and stared at him. Frank shifted his weight from foot to foot, seemingly uncomfortable with our full attention.

"No," I said, shaking my head and wincing. You never fully appreciate how many muscles are attached to your back until you injure them. "No cops. Ramon is right. It looks like I was attacked by an animal." I slowly moved out of the chair. "I don't feel like getting laughed out of a police station. And I really don't feel like pissing these people off any more than I somehow have."

Frank blinked at me.

"This was a warning," I told him. "I'd hate to see what they do when they're actually mad."

Frank looked a little crestfallen. "Oh."

I clapped him on the shoulder. "Don't worry. I know you're trying to help."

"And you did," Ramon said. "That was some mean get-away driving."

Frank smiled.

Ramon collapsed into one of the chairs. "You sure you've never seen either of those guys before?"

"Nope." I grabbed a few beers out of my fridge and tossed two to Ramon and Frank. I leaned my side against the counter and popped the top on mine.

"I mean," Ramon said, taking a sip, "I've seen you piss people off, but usually you have to open your big mouth first."

"I know. It's a conundrum." I drank most of my beer in silence, racking my brain. I didn't recall seeing those guys before, and I think I would have remembered them. People who drag you around by the neck tend to stick in your memory. I also couldn't remember saying anything to warrant any of their behavior.

My brain stalled. I was too tired to think anymore, and my body ached with every movement. What I needed was sleep. The rest of the mess I'd sort out in the morning. And if something attacked me again that night, well, then I guessed I wouldn't have to worry about anything else. But I was still going to sleep with my skateboard.

"You guys do whatever," I said, "but I'm going to bed." I checked the deadbolt on the front door and made sure the easy chair fit snugly against it. It didn't make me feel much better, but any little bit helped. Frank crashed here a lot, and Ramon lived on my couch, most of his stuff either staying in the linen closet or in boxes in his mom's garage. He couldn't quite afford his own place—Ramon gave a good chunk of his paycheck to his mom—but he could afford my couch. Ramon I understood, but Frank? Sometimes I wondered if his parents ever noticed he wasn't coming home most nights.

I went to my room and shut the door. My room isn't what I'd call a haven. Right now it's more like ghosts of Sams past. Random textbooks from my first—and only—year of college gathered dust in the corner. I'd tried different classes in school, but nothing ever really grabbed me. Most people felt lost after high school. Sometimes I felt like I'd never really been found in the first place. I didn't have the heart to get rid of the textbooks, though I wasn't quite sure what to do with *Chemistry 101*, *English Literature: 1800s–1900s*, or anything else I had in that pile. I guess if someone attacked in the night, I could wing the books at them.

The textbooks sat next to several milk crates full of old vinyl. Some were purchased from thrift stores, but the bulk of my collection came from my father, Haden, when he died. He had a fascination with the Rolling Stones that I'd never really understood, going so far as to have "You Can't Always Get What You Want" played at his funeral. Every time I hear the song now, my eyes blur and I feel like I'm back in the cemetery, my little sister's clammy hand in mine. I smell the wet earth, see the Astroturf flung over it, trying to hide the reality. I can even see the flowers in my mom's hand, her white knuckles gripped around the stems, crushing them. And each time, the pain is fresh.

Careful of my back, I grabbed a shirt off my floor and swiped dust off the tops of my records. I couldn't see any, but it didn't hurt to be careful. Then I tossed the shirt onto my growing pile of dirty clothes.

I'd never looked forward to sleep so much in my life. I turned off my light and crawled under the blankets. Before I closed my eyes, I reached over and turned on the record player by my bed, a gift from my mom and sister. The last one had crapped out, so my sister, Haley, had found this fancy new one—it could handle records, CDs, you name it. Most people have moved on to digital. But I couldn't afford it. Besides, there was something about the hiss and pop of old records. I took last night's Paul Simon record off and replaced it with a Get Up Kids album. I didn't like to stick to one thing too long. When it came to music, I was omnivorous.

Sleep didn't come as instantaneously as I'd hoped. The evening kept playing out in my head. I kept hearing the man's voice, his implied warnings and threats. They scared me a whole hell of a lot more than the guy who wiped the floor with me. Bullies are easy to understand and outthink. I'd dealt with bullies aplenty in school. But the other guy? He was full of unknowns.

I reached over and turned the bedside lamp on before sitting up and swinging my legs to the side. I swallowed a few Tylenol tablets. My mom may not have been a big fan of Western medicine, but I sure as hell was, especially when it came to things like painkillers.

I dug around in the pockets of the dirty jeans that I'd left on the floor. My fingers found worn leather, and I pulled my pouch out. I ran my thumb over the stitched silhouette of a crow, a single shiny black bead for his eye. My mom usually left her medicine bags plain unless she really thought someone needed a little something extra. I was used to seeing the crow. My mom had long ago decided it was my totem animal, whatever that meant.

I opened my nightstand drawer and dug around. There, under a gaming magazine and next to a slightly dusty pack of condoms, was a spare piece of cotton string. It would have to do until my mom could fix it. I tied the string to the broken bits of hemp cord, slipping it over my head when it was done. If I was ever going to sleep, it was time to bring out the big guns, and my protection bag was a big gun.

My mom had made it for me when I was really little and kept having nightmares. I had been convinced that there were spirits in the house. Instead of dismissing my ideas like most parents would have, she had gone into her workshop and come out with this small pouch. She'd tied it around my neck, telling me never to open it because that would let all the magic out.

"What's it for?" I asked.

She smiled and smoothed my hair back. "For protection," she said. "You leave that thing on, and you'll have nothing to worry about."

"It'll keep the bad dreams away?"

"Yes." She hesitated, her brow knitting in thought. "It's the herbs. Remember when I explained aromatherapy to you?"

I nodded.

"It's like that, sweetheart. When you breathe, the fragrance of the herbs goes up into your sinuses and into the deep centers of the brain. Your brain responds by releasing chemicals, which correct the problem. Understand?" I didn't, not really, but her word that it would work was enough for me.

She put me back into bed, tucking the blankets around me, her long strawberry blond braid slipping over her shoulder. I gave her braid a little tug, like I always did.

She'd told the truth, too. The bad dreams did go away. When I got older, I tried leaving it off, sure the nightmares were gone for good. I'd convinced myself that I'd made them go away, not the pouch. They came back, though, stronger than before. One night Mom found me screaming and crying, my sheets wet with sweat. She'd put her arms around me, and I'd clung to her, a shaking and whimpering mess. I kept my eyes shut as she rocked me and told the bad dreams to go away. I echoed her softly, mumbling "go away" over and over until I felt my mom slip the cord of my pouch back over my head.

"Promise to never take it off again," she said. "It's medicine against the dreams."

I promised, but wouldn't let her go. Finally she'd helped me into dry pajamas and bundled me into bed with my sister. Then I'd slept like a baby. After that, the pouch stayed on, every day, every night.

I flicked off the light and rolled back into bed.

I woke up to a sharp knocking noise. I jerked and fell out of bed. Quite a present for my aching body. I lay there taking deep gulps of air, trying to breathe the pain away. I crawled slowly to my nightstand and swallowed a few more Tylenol.

There were no windows in my bedroom, so I had to sit up and read my clock to figure out how angry I should be at my visitor. Eight A.M. I hated whoever woke me up. Had they come an hour earlier, I would have also hated their families and any household pets. The sharp knock came again, so I hauled my ass off the floor and went to answer it.

Ramon had slept on my couch while Frank had camped out on my somewhat questionable carpet. Their heads popped out of their blankets, but neither made a move toward the knocking. I checked the peephole, but no one was there. Was that good or bad? Ramon helped me move the chair, and I peeked out the door. Still no one. I looked down. A square package about the size of a soccer ball sat on my front mat. It was wrapped in brown paper and tied with string. There was no postmark or markings that I could see. Maybe it was a bomb. Not a good start to my morning. I picked up the package and went inside, gesturing for Frank to shut the door and move the chair back.

I placed the package on the table, taking the seat in front of it. While I examined it, Ramon abused my coffeemaker in his morning hunt for caffeine. Technically, it was Ramon's coffeemaker. He'd bought it and set it up on my counter so he wouldn't have to walk to the nearest place every morning. Not that it was a far walk. You can pick any spot in Seattle, close your eyes, spin around, and odds are pretty good you'll be pointing at some sort of coffee shop, hut, or shack when you stop. Some stereotypes are true.

I stared at the package. The only clue I had was the brown paper and the string. Who wraps things like that anymore?

And my extensive knowledge of bombs told me that since the package didn't tick theatrically, I could rule that out.

Ramon sat on the floor, back against the wall, waiting for his coffee to brew. I untied the string, pulled the paper away, and stopped. The package felt cold, and I don't mean refrigerator-frosty. This box gave me the same chilly electric feeling as the man from Plumpy's. Not good.

"What's wrong?" Even half asleep, Ramon had noticed my pause. I shook my head at him.

"Nothing. Just paranoid, I think."

I opened the box, then quickly dropped it and scrambled up onto the counter, making very dignified shrieking noises. Ramon stared. Frank came into the kitchen just in time to see the box bounce onto its side and its contents roll lazily out. Ramon tried to back up, but he was already against the wall. Frank managed a quick hop back as Brooke's head rolled to a stop in the middle of the floor. It had been severed cleanly at the neck, making her ponytail appear longer as it trailed behind like the tail on a grotesque comet. I couldn't see any blood. In fact, the wound looked cauterized, which didn't make it any more pleasant.

Nobody said a word.

Nobody except Brooke.

"Ow, cut it out, you guys!" Her blue eyes popped open and swung around until they found me. "Ugh, so not cool. Really, Sam. You don't just drop somebody's head. Especially a friend's. Like being stuffed into a box and bounced around for an hour wasn't bad enough."

I screamed and grabbed a butter knife off the counter. I'm

not sure what I planned to do with it, but in the meantime I held it in front of me just in case Brooke suddenly grew her body back and attacked. I mean, if she could talk, what was stopping her from leaping up and gnawing piranha-style on my ankles? Once a severed head talks, life's possibilities seem endless.

Frank ran and hid in, I think, the bathroom. I heard some crashing noises that sounded like stuff being knocked around in my shower, anyway. Ramon slid behind the easy chair and hugged it, keeping his eyes on the head at all times. I think he'd stopped breathing. I crouched there, unmoving except for the shaking of my brandished butter knife, and stared at the head of a cute girl resting in the middle of the dirty linoleum of my kitchen floor. For some reason, I had the irrational thought of asking Mrs. Winalski whether or not this counted as having a girl in my apartment.

"Hey guys, show some chivalry here," Brooke said. "This floor is cold and ugly, and it could seriously use an introduction to a broom. Or a mop."

I closed my eyes. Had to be my imagination. There was no severed head on my floor. I opened my eyes. Brooke was still there, only now she looked disgusted with all of us. Frank ran in from the bathroom and started throwing assorted toiletries at her. Ramon continued to hug the easy chair.

"Frank." A small bottle of mouthwash bounced off her forehead. Brooke didn't yell, but she used that sharp tone some moms get when they mean business. "Cut it out."

Frank responded to the tone immediately, clutching the remaining shampoo bottle to his chest but not throwing it.

He breathed heavily instead, nostrils flaring and eyes a little wild.

"Stop it before you pass out," she said.

Frank stopped but didn't let go of the shampoo bottle.

Brooke turned her gaze back on me. "What are you going to do with that, perform snippets of *West Side Story*?"

I put the butter knife down. I was still freaked out of my mind, yes, but over that lay a thin patina of shame.

"Sam, if you don't get off the counter and free me from this humiliation, I will gnaw your damn ankles right off!"

Body or no body, it was still Brooke. Only Brooke could be so bossy at a time like this. I climbed off the counter and reached down for her head, stopping to ask, "You're not going to bite me, are you?"

"In your dreams, slacker." Her lip curled. "I don't know where you've been. You're probably as dirty as this floor." Then she squinted her eyes shut and yelled, "Now, pick me up!"

I gently placed my hands on the sides of her head, arching my palms so they didn't touch her hair. I almost dropped her again. Brooke's expression could have frosted the surface of the sun. I manned up and got a better grip, lifting her head and placing it on the counter next to the coffeemaker.

"Ew, Sam, come on," she said, her tone full of exaspera- tion. "I am not an appliance. Look, I know this visit isn't ideal, but I've had kind of a crappy night, so how 'bout taking me into the living room, 'kay?"

I picked her up again, trying not to poke her in the eye, and placed her head on the plaid easy chair. Frank skittered over to a spot on the living room floor, cuddling the shampoo to his chest all the while. Ramon sat on the couch, and I took a seat on the coffee table.

"What, um, happened?" I couldn't think of a gentle way to phrase it, so I just asked.

Ramon threw a pillow at me. "Dude, leave her alone. Let her catch her breath. . . ." He fidgeted. "You know, if she can. I'm sorry, Brooke, I don't really know how to handle . . . this."

"That's okay, Ramon. Frank, breathe."

Frank straightened up, eyes popping, but his breathing did slow down.

"I don't know, Sam." She shook her head and almost rocked off the chair. I rushed forward and propped her back up. "Thanks." She looked around the room, searching, though I'm not sure what for. "One minute I was watching *Mansquito* on Syfy, which was as awful and intriguing as it sounds; the next, it had gone to commercial and I was like I am now."

Frank perked up. "You were killed because you watched *Mansquito*?" He paled slightly. "Oh, man, I watched *Mansquito*. Do you think I'm next?"

We all turned and stared at him.

"What? Brooke's head is sitting in your easy chair and we're talking to it, and you're looking at me like *I'm* crazy?" He squinted his eyes shut and huddled around the shampoo bottle.

I looked back at Brooke. She was staring at my *Hellboy* poster like she hadn't seen it a thousand times. Her lip was trembling. Freaky or not, severed or otherwise, Brooke was my friend.

"Don't call her *it*, Frank." I nudged him with the toe of my shoe, hard. "Shut up and take it like a man. She's still Brooke. You're lucky to have her, head or otherwise." I nudged him again. "Now apologize."

His cheeks went red. "Sorry, Brooke."

"That's okay," she said with a sniff.

The silence was awkward. "So you didn't see anyone come in the house? Didn't accidentally take a bunch of painkillers and then fall on a knife?"

"I don't know, Sam. I think I felt a hand on my shoulder, but I'm not sure. Then . . . nothing." She pushed out her lower lip in thought. "Well, nothing until I woke back up and I was, you know. This."

The edge of her neck appeared so clean and straight that it looked as if the rest of Brooke was hidden in my chair, like we had cut a hole in the plaid so she could hide in there for a haunted house stunt.

Brooke cleared her throat. The noise snapped me back into the moment. I had been staring like an ass.

"So, um, Brooke, can I get you anything?" I asked.

"Water would be super, actually. Thanks."

I filled a small glass for her, grabbing a Plumpy's emblazoned straw as an afterthought.

Brooke took a sip and thanked me. I resumed my seat on the coffee table and set her glass to the side. Where did the water go? Come to think of it, how did she clear her throat?

"So . . ." I drifted off because, honestly, I couldn't really think of anything to say. Next time a talking head ended up in my easy chair, I would have all sorts of points of reference, but at that moment, I was completely at sea.

Brooke saved me from an extremely awkward pause. "Sam, I'm supposed to give you a message." She stopped to puff a strand of hair out of her face, which completely blew my mind. Where did the air come from? She had no lungs.

"Well, I was supposed to give you a message, but ass-face said he couldn't trust me to get the stupid thing right, and I was like, well, *duh*, like I'd want to do anything for you anyway. I mean, he cut off my head! What a douche bag. Like I'm supposed to turn into his little messenger girl just because he brought my head back. I mean, I would have been *all* alive if that psycho hadn't killed me in the first place—"

"Who gave you a message?"

She stared at me in exasperation. "The guy who woke me back up. Geez, Sam, get with the program here."

"Brooke," I interrupted, "I don't mean to be rude, but what message?"

"Oh," she said, "it's in the box."

She kept talking to the boys as I went over and searched the empty container. Tucked into the corner was a piece of expensive-looking stationery that had been folded in half. All it said in a loose sprawling cursive was "Two o'clock, Woodland Park Zoo, Asia exhibit. Come alone, or I'll send another message."

I flipped the note over. "There's no signature," I said.

"Not surprising. Talk about zero manners," Brooke said. "Martha Stewart would so bitch-slap that guy. And it would most certainly be a good thing."

Carefully, I collapsed onto the couch next to Ramon and handed him the note. I closed my eyes and leaned back, head resting against the wall. "I am so screwed."

"Ugh, you are such a baby," Brooke said. "Try being just a head for a little bit. Then you can complain."

5

SHE'S A LADY

Brid woke to the taste of blood and the scent of wolf. Normally a comforting smell, but now it made her uneasy. If they were close enough to smell, they should have been close enough to reach out and touch, or at the very least, call with her mind. But Brid could tell she was alone, and with the heavy musk of wolf around her, that shouldn't be.

She tried to sit up. The world became tilted and queasy. She put her head back down on the cool surface of the floor. Squashing the flood of panic, she willed herself calm. First, the facts. She could panic when she knew what kind of mess she was in.

It hurt to open her eyes, and she felt dizzy. A concussion? The blood in her mouth didn't taste fresh, so whatever had hit her had struck a while ago. She should have healed a concussion by now. But she hadn't, so either she'd taken on more damage than she knew, or something was interfering. Her stomach burned, her throat felt torched, and then she smelled it. Aconite. She'd been drugged, then. Drugged and beaten. Not good. And cold. Damn it. She'd been drugged, beaten, and stripped. That did not bode well at all.

Brid rolled quickly onto her side and retched for what felt like a very long time. When she thought she could manage it, she sat up. She leaned against cold bars and opened her eyes.

Bars. She'd been put in a cage. She touched the floor. Iron. Being enclosed in the stuff would keep her from her swords. She could, however, just as easily bend the iron like it was wicker. Sometimes it was good to be a hybrid. She stood up, reaching for the bar closest to her, and frowned. There at the top were runes done in silver, the wards drawn with a cold fire. She felt the chill of the symbols with the tips of her fingers and frowned. Somehow, someone had built a cage not just for a werewolf but specifically for her or someone like her.

Shit.

And then it hit her. The wolf smell. Her eyes burned with a red flame, fueled by hatred as the name slid between clenched teeth. "Michael." Then she smiled. Flip the situation on its side, and this could become a chance at revenge. Things were looking up.

She studied the room. It seemed she was being kept in a basement, no windows, solid concrete floor and walls. The cage only took up about a quarter of the space, but it was a big area. Manacles were attached to a few of the walls, some of which bore the same silver-drawn runes that were on the cage. Unpleasant. And sitting in the corner was a heavy wooden table with restraints that she didn't like the look of. Another table stood against the wall behind her. On it glass beakers were neatly arranged next to a Bunsen burner. Someone had hung a small chalkboard next to the table. Brid didn't recognize any of the symbols on the chalkboard. The lighting was bright, fluorescent, bathing everything in stark reality.

All in all, the basement looked like someone couldn't decide whether he wanted a torture chamber or a laboratory so he'd made both. Every scent she got felt tainted with death, incense, and old blood. Enough blood that Brid felt that the sooner she got out of here, the better. The drain in the floor wasn't giving her delighted butterflies either. There was something disturbing about this particular basement having an easy-rinse floor.

The only other things she could see were a few shelves piled high with old books and what she thought might be a small refrigerator under the stairs. She could hear the soft whir of a motor, and the size looked about right for a mini fridge.

Brid stretched, feeling a pleasant pull through her body as she did. She walked closer to the bookcase to get a better look. The books on the shelves were old enough that most of the leather bindings had lost their print. The few words she could read made her stomach twist. They looked like grimoires, but not like any of the ones Brid had seen before. Admittedly, she hadn't seen many, and most of those had been in the hands of witches who avoided black or tainted magic.

Brid stilled. She heard voices above her, both male, one the grinding bass of Michael. The other soothed her ears even though she didn't recognize it. The stranger sounded angry, but that smooth voice still rolled around in her mind, lulling her. Brid fought to keep her muscles tense. Usually if someone you didn't know used those tones, they meant to ensnare you in some way. Quickly she curled up on the floor, trying to appear relaxed and dozing. Brid wanted to hear as much as she could.

"I don't understand why you're so pissed." That was Michael. "If you didn't want me to do it, why'd you build the cage?"

"Your actions were premature. Premature and stupid."

"What's the difference? You got what you wanted, right?" Michael sounded sulky. Brid suppressed a grin and kept listening.

"I wanted a hybrid," the other man shouted, "not the heir to the damn throne." His voice quieted. "No one in Brannoc's line—I thought I made that perfectly clear."

A mumbling noise from Michael, then, "A mutt is a mutt."

Brid heard a thump, and a whimper from Michael. When the man started talking again, his voice grew soft enough that even Brid had to strain to hear it.

"The difference, Michael, is that I will be first on Brannoc's suspect list. The difference is, we wanted someone they wouldn't notice until much later." Brid heard another thump and whimper. "The difference is that you took a perfectly respectable plan and pissed all over it."

"I'm sorry. I didn't—"

"You never do. I will clean up your mess, but—and I will say this only once—do not become more trouble than you are worth."

The voices quieted. The man wanted a hybrid from one of the weaker families. Less noticeable, easier to handle, that was the implication. Well, if he thought stealing one of the others would have gone by without notice or care, then he was ignorant of how the pack functioned. Even before the attempted coup, a missing member would draw attention. After the coup, security was tight, and the weaker members drew the most attention when they vanished. Predators always cull the weak before the strong. The other hybrids were younger than her, mostly. Kids. The pack wouldn't take that lightly. And her father would hunt down anyone who took one of his own. And "own" extended far beyond his offspring.

Whoever the other man was, he'd never been pack.

Brid heard the slide and click of several locks from the top of the stairs, then muttering. Did the man have the door booby-trapped? Footsteps sounded on the stairs.

"The bitch was sniffing not two feet from me," Michael said. "What was I supposed to do? Hide?" He snorted. "I was upwind. She'd have run straight to her freak family."

"Please stop yammering, Michael."

There was an audible click as the werewolf shut his jaws.

Brid cast around in her memory, trying to pull out her last action. She'd been jogging in the park, burning off some excess energy. One of her dad's conditions for her to stay in the city was that she had to exercise every day. Gyms reeked of sweat and cleaning supplies, and if she wasn't careful, people noticed her. Especially when she lifted weights. So she usually ran. If she didn't, she'd have to change more, and that was harder in an urban setting. But she hadn't seen Michael in the park. She'd stopped when a strange smell had hit her. She remembered jogging in place, trying to catch it. Then she'd pretended to tie her shoe. After that . . . nothing.

The stranger spoke again, this time much closer to the cage. "You were lucky. I heard the last time you scuffled, this slip of a girl wiped the floor with you." Brid could hear a faint trace of amusement. He was provoking Michael.

Brid heard Michael spit. "She cheated."

"How?" the stranger said, laughter definitely in his voice now. "By being better than you?"

Michael growled as he walked up to the bars. He grabbed Brid by the neck, pushing her body farther into the cage before pulling her back and slamming her into the bars. She let him do it. Even with limited movement, the force of it hurt like hell. But the drug made dodging chancy, and this way a piece of him was in the cage. Her turn.

Brid grabbed his arm and bit down hard before pulling back with her head. A chunk came free, and Brid rolled to the center of the cage. She opened her eyes. She spit the chunk of flesh out of her mouth and onto the floor, an insult Michael was sure to get. Wolves did not waste food, not ever. Only humans killed for sport. By refusing his flesh, she was implying something unsavory about Michael. Like weakness.

Michael howled as he yanked his arm free. Blood poured down. He ripped off his T-shirt and held it to the wound, glaring at her the whole time.

Brid smiled at him, wide and toothy, like a yearbook photo. She knew how that smile would look coming from a mask of blood—his blood. Even naked, injured, and locked in a cage, she had gotten the best of him, and he knew it.

He came at the cage again.

"Michael," the stranger said, the command in his voice

absolute. He was not imposing physically. Medium build, not too tall. Dark hair cut in a Caesar style. He had pale skin, as if he didn't go out much and didn't care how he looked at the beach. Clean-shaven with a good mouth and solid jawline. Even his nails were spotless and well kept. Brid realized that everything about the man should have added up to handsome, and yet he didn't appeal to her. Something about him turned her system off. He emanated power, though, and Brid suspected that attracted more than enough women to keep the man company.

Michael stilled at the man's tone and glared at her. "Mongrel bitch," he spat.

Brid sighed and pulled her knees up to her chest, rolling her eyes at his childishness. Just the kind of action that she knew would piss Michael off.

Michael's lip curled back, showing his teeth. He was still trying to dominate her even now. No matter how many times she'd won, he just kept on trying. But he wasn't the dominant wolf here, she was, and she let that knowledge show in her face. Michael broke first. Brown eyes turned away, and a single earthy-brown curl dropped onto his forehead. Not for the first time, Brid wondered why the goddess had wasted such beauty on a total ass-hat.

The man leaned against the wall, content for now to observe the argument.

Michael kept his eyes averted. "I should have been next in line."

Brid released her knees and leaned back, palms on the floor. "Please. You were by no means second on the list. Or third."

She mused on that. "Maybe in the top ten, but barely." Michael had always relied too heavily on his biceps while ignoring his brain. Brid watched the muscle clench in his jaw. He'd never been able to understand that in wolf packs, were or otherwise, it wasn't always the biggest who ruled. Strength didn't mean much when everyone was strong. Her brothers could change all the tires on her dad's truck without a jack.

She didn't flinch as Michael launched himself at the cage, angry and thinking only of her throat in his mouth, she was sure. She clucked her tongue at him. "That's no way to get what you want. Go ahead, open the door. Who knows, with all the aconite you've given me, you might even stand a chance."

Michael slammed his fists on the floor and howled, spittle flying from the corner of his mouth. The other man walked up behind him and placed a hand on Michael's shoulder. Instead of reacting like Brid imagined he would—taking the guy's hand off at the wrist—Michael actually calmed, his brown eyes softening and losing their focus. Interesting.

"I think," the man said, "that now would be a good time for a constitutional, don't you?"

Michael nodded his head absently. Then he got up and walked out the door.

Brid couldn't remember Michael ever acting so docile, even before he'd gone rogue. Only a pack leader should have had the power to subdue him like that, and even then it probably would have taken longer. Brid made no outward move; she kept her position open and unconcerned, her brain filtering through all the information she had, and each thought placed the man in front of her higher up on the fear scale. Michael had the potential to cause problems, but Brid didn't fear him. She'd kicked his butt too many times for that. The man in front of her, however, was cause for concern. Lots of concern.

He pulled up a wooden chair. The hand-carved filigree made it look old and expensive, but he kept it in the basement. He took off his dove-colored suit jacket and hung it carefully over the back of the chair. He used the same care to settle himself into the seat when he was done, smoothing nonexistent wrinkles out of his pant leg as he sat. Finally, he folded his hands in his lap and made eye contact with her.

Most people aren't able to maintain eye contact for more than a few seconds without feeling uncomfortable. Even fewer can do it without speaking. This man managed to do both with seemingly no problems. Brid had always secretly believed that people looked away because they took the "eyes as windows to the soul" thing too seriously; she wondered if the man across from her had much of a soul to worry about.

Her nostrils flared slightly as she scented the air around him. It was faint and hiding under the smell of all the old blood in the room, but she could just make it out. He'd cleaned up, but the hint of fresh copper and salt spoke to her senses. He'd most likely killed, and recently.

Apparently, the man had finished his evaluation of her. "Are you comfortable, Ms. Blackthorn?"

"I'm naked and in an iron cage."

"Yes, my apologies about that," he said. "I understood werewolves to be an unself-conscious bunch."

Brid gave him her yearbook smile. "I don't give a rat's ass about whether or not you can see my nipples, but you do have me on a cold iron floor, which is uncomfortable, to say the least."

"Again, my apologies, but I can't just let you have free run of the place. That would be"—he paused and pursed his lips—"problematic."

"Nice euphemism."

"I try. Bridin—may I call you Bridin?"

"Could I stop you?"

He tutted at her like an old schoolmistress. "Let's try to maintain a little civility, shall we?"

She shrugged her shoulder.

"Do you know who I am?"

"I could take a few guesses," she said. In fact, the list of who the man could be was pretty short. The power, the blood, the cage. Very few could do these things. She'd never seen Douglas Montgomery because her father hadn't taken her to Council meetings yet, but she was willing to bet serious money that the man in front of her was the head of the Northwest Council. The fact that he held that position told Brid quite a lot. Other Councils, if they even had a necromancer, weren't led by them.

"Then why don't you take one?" he asked, amusement filling his voice.

"If you insist," she said. "Mr. Montgomery."

"Excellent. Now that we're acquainted, let's get down to business, as they say."

"Is this where you tell me your evil plan? I just want to

know if I need to get comfortable." If her comment angered him, Brid could see no sign of it.

"Sorry to disappoint," he said. "Here is what I will share: If all goes well, you'll be free in a few days. Meals and such are contingent on good behavior." He smiled, completely without warmth. "Essentially, Ms. Blackthorn, if you're a good girl, then you needn't have any worries." He stood up to leave, clearly feeling their discussion was finished.

Brid didn't agree. "Well, then, I'm afraid we have a problem, Mr. Montgomery."

He pulled on his suit jacket and checked his cuffs.

"I am a lot of things, but a good girl isn't one of them. Neither is stupid. You don't plan to set me free." She'd been raised to lead and had learned that some prisoners could be released and some couldn't. Brid knew she fell into the couldn't pile. The thought chilled her. She'd either escape or, failing that, hope that her pack found her in time.

He straightened his jacket.

"I'm dangerous to keep, yes, but I'm worse to let go."

Douglas laughed, a hollow booming sound that made Brid's spine want to straighten. "Why, because your pack will track me down and kill me for what I've done to you? I thought more of you, Bridin. Your father doesn't have the clout to challenge me."

He moved slightly when he said that. The thought of her father seemed to make him a little uncomfortable. Good. Bridin leaned her head to the side and flicked her bangs out of her face. "Oh, I wasn't talking about politics. No, I'll kill you myself for the whole kidnapping thing, that's a guarantee. But this—" She waved at the cage, palm up. "Once it gets out that you've built a cage that can hold me? One that can hold my father? There aren't any good reasons for why you'd create such a thing. No, every were and shifter in the world will be on you for this. You're a dead man, Douglas."

Douglas smiled and gave her a short bow before marching back up the stairs. "It has to reach the public for your prediction to come true," he said. "And I don't foresee that happening."

"You don't think I'll tell when I'm released?" The last word came out sarcastic.

His answered with a twisted-sounding chuckle. "Have a lovely evening." He flicked out the lights.

Brid heard the door shut and several locks click. His footsteps faded. Once they were gone, she stood up and shook herself, loosening her muscles. She stretched, walked around the cage a few times, then settled back down into a ball on the floor, the most warmth and comfort she could expect. When she'd relaxed herself, she began to cycle back through all the information she'd gotten so far. She'd find a way out. She just hoped she found it soon enough.

6

SWEET DREAMS ARE MADE OF THIS

The aconite gave her fevered dreams. Bits of memory floated up, one conversation blurring into another until she was just seeing pieces of what had happened. In the dreams, at least, she was out of the cage and back in the familiar meadows of her home.

She remembered circling her brother Sean, waiting for him to make his move. The smell of crushed grass underfoot reached her nose, and her blood soared. The anticipation of the fight was almost better than the fight itself. Almost. He feinted to the side. Instead of lunging at him immediately, she paid attention to the smaller muscle movements telling her which way Sean was actually going. The slight motions were clear to her, despite the darkness. She let him grab her, rolling with it instead of fighting, which took him by surprise. They both hit the ground with a bone-rattling thud, Brid absorbing most of the impact. She used it and her legs to jettison Sean fifteen feet through the air and into the base of a tree.

"I," said Sean, remaining prone on the pine-littered soil, "have got to learn how you do that."

Brid grinned, wiping blood from a new gash on her

forehead as she jogged over to help him up. She assessed his injuries quickly, popping a dislocated shoulder back into place with a sharp jerk and thrust of her wrist. Sean yelped.

"Easy."

"I am easy." She smacked his nose before he could make any off-color remarks to that. "Daddy would have made you wait."

The aconite burned again, and the scene jumped.

She didn't have time to duck, only to grab on and twist to the side and hope she fell with an advantage. They rolled several feet, Brid ending up on top, her hand against Sean's throat.

"Point," Bran said. He nudged Sean with the toes of his boot. "You have to be more aware of your surroundings." He lifted his boot and pushed Brid off Sean. "And you have to be careful when you do that. A bigger guy could toss you off."

"I wouldn't use it on a bigger guy." Brid dusted herself off.

"Or you could be too focused on the position and not notice an accomplice."

Brid shrugged. "It worked, didn't it?"

Bran shook his head. "You need to think these things out more."

Sean got up off the ground and put his arm around his sister's shoulders. "Leave it," he said.

"But she needs to remember," Bran said, frowning.

Brid gave Sean a one-armed hug.

"Hard to forget when you remind her every ten seconds."

Bran's frown loosened. "You're right." He leaned forward and kissed Brid on the forehead. "Sorry, sis."

"Me too," she said.

Sean hushed her. "Shut it. You'll be a great *tánaiste*."

It always amazed her how one word could pack so much weight. *Tánaiste*. Next in line, heir, one step away from being *taoiseach*. "You both sound so sure."

Bran nodded. "You are what the pack needs." He flicked her nose. "Besides, I will always be here to bail you out after you screw up."

Brid cocked her eyebrow. "You gonna back that up?"

Bran held up his hands in surrender. "Not today. Dad's just spent an hour making me practice in the dark."

"You need the practice." Her father came out of the darkness. He held out his hand. "Speaking of which, it's not yours yet." He motioned, and Bran returned the ancient bow to his father. Brannoc took it lovingly, then closed his eyes, willing the bow away. To Brid it appeared as if the bow was there one second, then gone the next.

"We'd better head homeward." Brannoc began to walk out of the clearing and into the woods, Bran a step behind him. Sean fell in with Brid, following a few steps after.

Brid watched the back of her father as he slid between the trees. "I wish he wouldn't make Bran practice. Not yet." Animals traveled quietly in the woods beside them, the tiny movements obscured by shadow. "Does he have to prepare him so soon?"

"Even Dad won't live forever," Sean whispered. "Mom didn't."

"I know," she said, "but I like to pretend that Dad will."

The scene blurred again, her mind picking out another night.

"Ooooh, them's fightin' words," Brid said. She dropped into a crouch. Sean mimicked her, pacing slowly to the side. They circled each other, all smiles suddenly gone. This time Brid advanced first. She dropped low and kicked out at Sean's ankle. He moved back and she missed. He ran forward before she could recover, knocking her over. Brid spent a second with her face in the dirt before she was able to twist around. After a few moments of grappling, they ended up in the same position they'd been in before, with Brid pinning her brother down using her knees.

She heard the slightest rustling to the right of her, and she knew it was Bran before she saw him. As it was, she barely managed a half turn before he knocked her over. Bran held her restrained for only a second before letting her go. He didn't have to press the fact that he'd won. They both knew it. He helped her up, dusting her off at the same time.

"Sorry," he said. "Dad insisted."

"It's okay," she whispered. She felt stupid. Brid hated feeling stupid. It was a useless, unhelpful feeling.

Brannoc joined them. "That's enough for today." He looked at Brid, and his face softened. "Why don't you boys go back to the house? Check in with your brothers and see if everything's okay?" Sean and Bran nodded and left, Sean throwing an apologetic look at his sister over his shoulder.

The woods grew quiet as her brothers' footsteps moved

farther and farther away. Brannoc let the silence hang for a few minutes, crossing his arms and giving Brid time to process her mistakes. As he always did.

"Do I need to apologize?"

Brid shook her head.

"Did Bran?"

Brid felt her eyes begin to water and hated it. "No," she said, shaking her head. "He was right to do it—you both were. I was overusing the move. He knew it. I knew it." She felt tears roll down her cheek and hated that too. A *tánaiste* should know better. Her father wiped her cheeks with his knuckle.

"So why did he say sorry, then?"

"Because he knows I hate to learn my lesson."

Brannoc grabbed her shoulders. "And because he knows you'll be too hard on yourself."

"It was a dumb mistake."

"And one much better made on the practice field, don't you think?"

"I can't make mistakes like that anymore, Dad." She felt her anger leak into her voice.

Brannoc laughed. "What, just because you're next in line now, you can't screw up?"

Brid looked at him. "When I'm *taoiseach*, mistakes will get people hurt."

Brannoc let go of her shoulders and brushed her hair out of her face. "You aren't *taoiseach* yet. That wonderful responsibility still lies with me. Worry about that when the day comes. Hopefully, it will be a long time." Brid opened her mouth, but he silenced her. "You've got to stop putting this pressure on yourself. Although I applaud that you're taking the position seriously, if you keep beating yourself up over small errors in judgment, you'll never make it to pack leader. Mistakes are our best teachers."

"I thought pain was the best teacher."

"Pain is a good teacher, not the best. You've got to start seeing your new position like a practice field. Mistakes are better made here and learned from than when they can actually hurt you."

"Yes, Daddy."

Brannoc leaned down a little and looked her in the eye. "Is that all that's bothering you?"

Brid didn't bother trying to hide it. Lying to her father was next to useless, and he'd keep picking at it until she started talking to him. She looked toward the archery range, even though the forest blocked it from view. All she could see was the occasional patch of stars and moon in the sky whenever the trees gave way.

"Ah," her father said. "You're wondering if I made the right decision."

She looked him in the eye and nodded.

"I'm positive I chose correctly."

"I didn't just win by default? We're pretty evenly matched."

"You and Sean?"

"Not funny, Daddy."

Brannoc put an arm around her. She leaned into him, taking in his smell along with the sharp tang of pine. "You did not win by default." He hushed her anticipated follow-up question. "I know what you're going to say, and yes, it was a factor. But it was not the only factor, and that's all you need to know for now."

"Do you think he's disappointed?" She kicked absently at a pinecone.

"Secretly relieved, I think."

"I hope so."

"How's school going?"

Brid let him change the subject. She was as done with it for now as he was. "Good. Hectic, but good."

"You getting enough to eat? Running all the time like we talked about? Watching your stress levels?"

Brid smiled. "You know, for an Alpha, you sound a lot like a mother hen." He pulled on her ear. She leaned away with a giggle but returned to the circle of his arm. "I'm fine, Daddy. I'm not going to hurt anyone."

"I'm more worried about someone hurting you."

They turned the bend in the trail, and she caught sight of the house. As much as Brid loved the city, loved going to school, she missed her home. The smell of pine and grass. The quiet broken only by blue jays or crows. No one but her pack for miles. She smiled at the warm glow of lights and watched as a few children chased one another in the yard. They whooped and hollered, excited voices carrying as they play-fought across the lawn. An adult ran up, herding them inside for dinner.

She closed her eyes, concentrating on smell and sound. Lingering on the threads of Bran and Sean as they mixed with her father's scent. Home. "Natural daddy stuff," she said, opening her eyes, "to worry about me at school, but I could take on the football team without too much trouble. I'm surrounded by humans all the time. Who would hurt me?"

Her father didn't answer, just pulled her closer.

The drug did funny things, jumbling past and present in her mind. Thoughts rushed forward sharp and clear, only to fuzz and dissolve as soon as she grabbed them. She floated in and out of herself, not sure what was memory, what was dream, and what was happening right now.

Douglas placed two fingers against Bridin's wrist, feeling for the flutter of her pulse. Slow and steady. He nodded at Michael to open the cage, choosing to carry her to the wall himself. Recent experiences had taught him that it was best not to lead young Michael into temptation. Unless, of course, it suited Douglas. He propped her up, eyeing Michael carefully as the were pulled on his gloves and closed the manacles. Once she was secured, held only by her thin little wrists, Douglas let her body sag.

He placed his own hands over the runes carefully etched into the manacles. They were skillfully made. Money well spent. He smiled and pushed his will into the runes, invoking them into being, painting metaphysical silver over the cold iron. Closing his eyes, he went over the lines in his head, making sure each one was in its place, each node of power where it should be. Precisely crafted runes would count for nothing if he invoked them poorly. Hastily drawn symbols begged for flaws in the work. Flaws were unsafe. Worse, they were sloppy, and he was anything but.

Michael slipped off his gloves and pulled up a chair. He spun it around backward, like he was in study hall instead of seated in front of a girl strung up in chains. Douglas thought the look on Michael's face would have been the same either way. He eased into his own chair.

"So what are we doing, anyway?"

Douglas pulled on latex gloves. "*We* aren't doing anything." He pulled out a sterile needle, a syringe, and a few vacuum-sealed tubes. "What *I* am doing is trying to make the best out of your mess." He held the capped needle in his teeth as he settled a tourniquet around Bridin's arm. He felt for the vein. Once he found the soft bump of it, he inserted the needle. The tubes made small popping noises as he slid each in turn into the syringe. Blood spurted, quickly filling up several tubes. Douglas held a cotton swab over the puncture as he removed the needle and tourniquet. Unhampered by the all-around dampening effect of the cage, the wound quickly closed. He put the blood vials into the small fridge under the stairs. He'd study those later.

He went to his bookcase, passing several older notebooks on his way to a fresh one. New subject, new book. Organization, Douglas felt, was a virtue.

With a fountain pen, he filled in the date on the first page, how much blood taken, how much aconite given. Then he drew a small chart for results. Admiring his work, he was amazed at how much fountain pens had improved since his youth. Even more elegant now in their maintenance and execution. He handed the notebook and pen to Michael, tempted for a moment to purchase a few ballpoints for the were.

Between the were and the pen, he was more concerned about replacing the pen.

Douglas rolled up his sleeves carefully once his hands were free. He pulled out his old athame, the double-edged dagger he'd taken from his aunt, and tested its edges with his own thumb. There were few things he liked more in this world than that knife. Everything about it was so delightfully familiar, from a dried spot of his blood on the blade to the way the groove on the handle bit into his palm. He smiled at it, using a thumbnail to chip off the speck of blood.

Then he got his ruler and stopwatch. "Please write 'athame' in the far left column." Douglas placed the ruler close to Bridin's spine. "We will be starting with a six-inch incision, shallow." His eyes never left his work. He sliced along the side of the ruler, making sure it went the full six inches, neither more nor less. He clicked the stopwatch and leaned back slightly. Though no doubt slowed by the aconite, Bridin's wound still healed at a remarkable rate. Once the skin had fully repaired itself, Douglas stopped the watch. He read off the numbers to Michael, who dutifully wrote them in the journal.

"Impressive," he whispered.

Michael grunted, not looking up from the paper.

Douglas ignored Michael's lack of scientific interest and placed the ruler on Bridin's back once more. "Seven inches." He waited to hear the scratch of the pen.

Then he brought the knife down.

7

I'M GONNA KEEP MY SHEEP SUIT ON

$\mathfrak{D}$ouglas ignored the CLOSED sign on the newly painted door of the Tongue & Buckle and knocked, knowing full well the door would open for him. He waited politely, hand clasping his wrist, as though he could stand there forever.

The door opened a sliver. "Can you not read, sir?"

If he hadn't known to listen for the slight Irish lilt in the voice, he might not have caught it. He adjusted his cuffs and waited for Aengus to get on with it.

"Was your mother neglectful," Aengus asked, "or just too busy with the milkman to be bothered?"

"They don't have milkmen anymore, Aengus. Not commonly, anyway."

A muffled curse came from behind the thick oak door before it was hastily opened. "My apologies, Douglas," he said. "Didn't realize it was you." He sounded more annoyed than contrite.

Douglas nodded at him anyway and stepped into the dimly lit pub. The Tongue & Buckle looked like it had been around longer than Seattle. The tables and chairs were finely carved, without padding, and stained with age. Worn in the way only well-used and well-cared-for furniture could be. Most people thought the bar was a quality reproduction of a rustic Irish pub. He knew it was the real McCoy, though he hadn't yet figured out how Aengus's family had gotten it here. He also knew better than to ask. Most fey wouldn't give you a straight answer if they could help it. Aengus wouldn't lie—he couldn't—but he'd do a damn fine job twisting the truth.

As soon as he was fully inside, a large, thick man leaned out of the shadows, hands ready to pat Douglas down, despite the early hour and the CLOSED sign. Aengus shrugged at him before slipping behind the bar. From the look on the fey's face, Douglas decided this was more of a test than any real worry that he was sneaking in weapons. He held his arms wide for the guard and indicated that he'd agree to the search. After all, he had nothing to hide, nothing this caveman would find anyway. The man hesitated and looked over at his boss. It appeared that neither of them thought Douglas would give in this easily.

"Go on, Zeke," Aengus said. "He's promised not to bite." The fey filled a heavy pint glass with stout, automatically grabbing a bottle of water for Douglas.

"Yeah, well, I didn't promise," Zeke said.

Douglas smiled benignly at Zeke, who grunted back. Benign was the best he could manage. He'd given up trying to look innocent a long time ago. He could mimic the face, but something around his eyes gave him away, so he no longer bothered.

Zeke leveled a stern glare at Douglas, who met his gaze easily. The bodyguard grunted again. "Smile all you want, but keep your hands to yourself."

"Why?" Douglas asked. "Afraid?" He said it mockingly, though Zeke didn't rise to the bait. Douglas raised his estimation of the bouncer just a touch.

"Not my job to be afraid." Zeke patted him down firmly, but in a way that told Douglas Zeke didn't feel the need to prove himself, at least not physically. "My job is to protect this bar, that man"—he jerked his head toward Aengus—"and the guests." Zeke's hands sorted through Douglas's pockets, blue eyes never breaking contact. "After that, I look after myself." He knelt and motioned for Douglas to take off his shoes. His eyes flicked between the shoe and its owner as he examined the soles for anything dangerous. He handed them back to Douglas. "A wise man doesn't overestimate himself." He stood and stretched to his full height. "But he doesn't underestimate the little guy either."

"Are you a wise man?"

"Wise enough to not let you touch me." He stepped away from Douglas.

"Then you're on your way," Douglas said softly.

Zeke nodded and knuckle-tapped the sign posted behind him, which read NO FIGHTING, NO STEALING, NO DEALING, AND WE HAVE THE RIGHT TO THROW YOU OUT ASS FIRST AT ANY TIME—MANAGEMENT. "Hope you enjoy the Tongue & Buckle, sir," Zeke said before he folded back into the shadows by the door.

Douglas followed Aengus into the back room. He couldn't

help but notice that, much like his bodyguard, Aengus kept a healthy gap between them.

$\mathcal{S}$ome people found Council meetings to be tedious. Douglas never had, but of course he held the gavel, metaphorically speaking. He did not, however, sit at the center of the crescent. He preferred to sit at the end of the table, where he could keep an eye on everyone present. Naturally, Brannoc sat at the other end, presumably to keep an eye on Douglas.

Douglas wondered who Bridin took after, her fey hound father or her were mother. Douglas couldn't see much resemblance between Brannoc and the girl back home in the cage. Not physically. They both held themselves the same way, like they expected everyone to sit up and listen when they talked. Douglas wasn't sure whether that expectation annoyed him or not. Part of him respected it. Still, he wished he knew more about the man. Brannoc wasn't keen on answering any of his questions, and for obvious reasons Douglas was hesitant about throwing him in a cage.

He stared back at Brannoc, ignoring the random chatter of the others as they waited for Pello, who was late. Again. He was all for starting without him—Pello was next to useless—but the others might snatch at any excuse to call foul. Ariana especially seemed to be watching Douglas for false moves. The fury was a new member and didn't seem to trust him. But unless she found something beyond rumor that proved Douglas had done wrong, she was powerless. Until then she would just keep watching him. She was doing it now, one hand pulling on the tip of the braid at the small of her back as she talked to Kell. Douglas bet she had a weapon in there somewhere, patted down or not. Not that a fury needed one, but she probably carried one out of principle.

Ione, on the other hand, talked to no one, though she did peek out from behind her thick black hair to smile a little at something Aengus had said to her. Douglas looked away. Ione didn't strike him as being powerful enough to be on the Council. He suspected that the only reason she had a chair was that no one wanted to take her spot. That suited him just fine. Given the choices, he'd take a meek witch any day.

Kell was the one other member who consciously chose his seat, though he made the decision seem arbitrary. Douglas noticed that he always picked a chair far from him. Most of them kept their distance, but Kell more so than the rest. It was only natural. If Douglas pushed his will on Kell, it would impact him heavily, strong willed or not. Vampires were more Douglas's domain than humans were, since they too were connected to death and, despite popular mythology, had souls. The idea that they didn't was ridiculous. Vampires were a lot of things, but truly dead wasn't one of them. They also weren't truly human, either. The idea intrigued him, but he'd yet to find a vampire willing to let him experiment. Perhaps after he was finished with Bridin, Douglas would alter his cage design for new quarry.

Pello finally showed up with a jolly wave and an apologetic glance at Douglas. He shook his glamour off as soon as he passed through the doorway. The glamour was either a gift or purchased from someone, as Pello didn't really have one of his own but needed it to get to the meeting from wherever he was nesting these days. With it, Pello looked like just another dirty hippie. His hair hung in long dreads and his stained Hawaiian shirt was unbuttoned, framing his slight paunch for everyone who did, or did not, want to see it. Without the glamour, Pello looked the same, but instead of the illusion of jean shorts and flip-flops, Douglas could now see Pello's goat legs and hips jutting out under his shirt.

"Ugh," Ariana said, looking away and blocking the sight of Pello with an outstretched hand. "Filthy satyrs. Can't you wear pants?"

Pello winked at her. "I am as nature made me." He held his arms out. "Why, baby, you like what you see?"

"No," Ariana and several others said. "And I don't like what I smell, either," she added. "What will it take to get you covered and clean before a meeting?"

"You're too removed from your heritage if nudity bothers you, sister," Pello said, taking the empty seat at the table.

"It's not nudity in general that bothers me, but yours specifically." She grimaced. "I don't want to sit where your dirty ass has been."

"Pants are too constrictive," Pello mumbled.

Ariana's grimace softened to a look of impatience. "What if I get you a kilt or something? You'd only have to wear it to meetings."

"Deal," Pello said. He sneaked a look at her. "Can I model it for you?"

Ariana sighed and tugged on her braid. "Satyrs."

Aengus and Kell laughed, and Ione gave another rare smile.

"Enough time wasted," Douglas said, and the laughter died, everyone in the room going still.

Except Brannoc, who took a single long sip of his beer. He set the pint glass down gently onto a coaster. "Let's get the meeting going, shall we?"

Douglas stared lazily at the petitioning were. The girl was thin, willowy, and didn't have an ounce of Alpha in her. She stood before the Council practically shaking.

"So," Douglas said, "you want us to approve your brother's transfer in from New Jersey?"

The girl nodded. "He"—she had to stop and start again, her eyes never leaving Douglas as she stuttered—"he wants to help me with the rent. I'm—I'm trying to go back to school." Douglas stared back at her, keeping their eyes locked, watching her sweat. He grinned. That made the trembling much worse.

"What are you going to school for?" Brannoc asked. The girl turned to him, visibly relieved. Her shaking slowed a little.

"I want to be an art teacher."

"What age range?" Brannoc gave her a reassuring smile and rested his chin in his hand. He glanced at Douglas and his smile grew slightly larger.

The girl eased some more, obviously more comfortable with this subject.

"Young," she said. "Pre-K to second or third grade if I can."

"That's a good age," Brannoc said.

Douglas cleared his throat, attempting to bring the attention back to himself. He wasn't going to let Brannoc take over the meeting. Yes, Brannoc would have to deal with her more than Douglas would. Yes, she was weak and so Douglas had no real worry about whether or not her family moved into the city. But he refused to give Brannoc any opening. He did a quick scan around the room. He could tell by their faces how they all were going to vote, and could see no gain in exercising his dominance in this particular case. But if he made it seem like accepting the girl's petition was his idea, well, that he might be able to use. Especially since another weak wolf in the area would stretch Brannoc's resources even more. And Douglas wanted Brannoc to be spread as thin as possible, spending most of his time rebuilding the pack. What did he care if some were from Jersey moved into a loft in Belltown?

Douglas pursed his lips and pretended to be thinking about it. "Well," he said slowly, "I don't know how the rest of the Council feels, but I see no reason why we wouldn't approve your petition."

The girl blinked at him with surprise. She turned toward the rest of the Council, who nodded at her. Brannoc stood up and grinned, extending his hand. The girl let out a short sob before falling to her knees in front of Brannoc and grabbing his fist in both of her hands. She bowed and placed her forehead against his knuckles. He pulled her up and whispered something to her. Then he handed her off to Aengus, who escorted her to the door.

"Have Zeke get you something from behind the bar, miss," Aengus said as he slipped an arm around the girl. "You must be wanting to celebrate. And to calm your nerves, of course." He turned the grateful-looking girl over to the bodyguard.

The meeting went normally after that. A few skirmishes to settle, and a petition or two to move into the territory that Douglas vetoed unless the applicant was weak. He couldn't do much about the few strong ones who were here already, but he could keep any more from coming. No one argued against him much, beyond Brannoc. That was normal as well. As it was, today Douglas only half argued, concerned more about watching Brannoc for effects of Bridin's disappearance than anything else.

He couldn't find any clue that told him something was wrong. Brannoc must know by now. At the break—Pello had to "drain the lizard"—Douglas couldn't help approaching Brannoc. He needed to know how much the pack suspected. Were they missing her yet? "When are you going to bring in that successor of yours?" Douglas asked, sidling up to Brannoc at the bar.

Brannoc accepted a beer from Aengus and took a drink before he answered. "I can't see how that's any of your business, Douglas."

"I assume she will take your place on the Council someday. Isn't it natural for me to be curious?"

"Nothing about you is natural." The man returned to his beer, the conversation clearly over in his opinion.

He couldn't help himself. "Surely you won't keep that lovely girl secreted away forever?" Brannoc stared at him, his fingers tapping slowly on the pint glass, but Douglas pretended not to notice as he paid Aengus for a bottle of water.

"I didn't realize you were so interested in my daughter," Brannoc said slowly.

"Like I said, the path of the Council and this territory concerns me deeply."

"I see. Well, then, you should know that my Council seat will be in very capable hands, because my daughter is a lot like me." Brannoc's eyes followed a drop of condensation as it slid down the glass. "Except less warm and fuzzy."

Aengus laughed at that.

"Takes after her mother, too," Brannoc said, finally glancing at Douglas. He slapped a few bucks on the bar. "Her ma would tear out your jugular as soon as look at you." He seemed wistful for a moment. "Unless you were on her good side, of course. Then no worries." He smiled before heading for the back. "But, then, there weren't a lot of people on her good side. And there aren't a lot on my daughter's, either."

Even to Douglas, the pride in Brannoc's voice was unmistakable.

8

HOLD ME CLOSER, NECROMANCER

J parked my car near the west entrance of Woodland Park Zoo thirty minutes before I had to be there. The promising weather from this morning had made a bipolar shift to gray and cloudy on my drive, so I dug around the back seat for my blue zip-up hooded sweatshirt. If you've lived in Seattle for any length of time, you carry a jacket with you anywhere, especially in spring. You get used to the moody weather and give up on umbrellas. Umbrellas are for tourists. Natives know that the rain doesn't come straight down here like other places. Seattle's rain slips in, tricky, like a ninja, and attacks from all sides. I pulled on my sweatshirt and dug out my wallet so I could pay for a day pass.

I loved the zoo. I hated seeing animals in cages, but I still loved to walk around listening to the grunts of sea lions and the bloodcurdling shrieks of peacocks, getting closer to a polar bear than I ever would on the outside. My mother used to take me and Haley all the time. The way the zoo used to be, before massive remodeling, many of the animals were in cramped cages smaller than my bedroom.

When I was a little kid, I asked my mom if the zookeeper ever let any of the animals out to run. My mom, tired from walking and carrying her pregnant stomach around, leaned into the railing in front of the tiger cage for support. She looked at my dad instead of answering me, a pleading expression on her face. Haden had only been my dad for a few years, but he was the only real dad I'd known. Before he married my mom, he told me I could call him Haden if that made me more comfortable. Adults don't usually make those kinds of offers to kids. When they'd married, I'd asked if I could have his last name too. I didn't want to be the only Hatfield in the house, a hazy connection to the past. LaCroix was my solid present. I had wanted to be a LaCroix so badly I would have asked Santa for it at Christmas.

My dad handed her a soda and fielded my question, giving her a much-needed breather.

"No, Sam," he said, "they don't let any of the animals out. Why, you afraid the tiger's going to get out and eat you?"

"No, it's just . . ." I dug around for words. "The tiger is so big, and the cage is so small. Doesn't he get bored?"

My dad eased his giant frame down to my level so I didn't have to crick my neck up at him. I loved it when he did that. It made me feel special.

He looked at the tiger pacing around and then back at me. The truth never seemed to be what I wanted when my parents had to think before answering me. It meant they were trying to figure out a nice way to explain something terrible.

"He probably does get bored, Sam. Real bored." He

scratched his beard. "Sometimes, we don't treat other creatures like we should." Dad pointed to the donation box by the cage. "That's why the zoo has to go begging."

The answer was ugly, which meant it was probably true. I was glad he didn't lie.

"Can I give my money to the tiger?" I'd gotten five dollars for helping my dad stack wood.

"I thought you were going to get ice cream."

"I was, but . . ." I twisted the bottom of my shirt. I wasn't sure how to explain myself. Ice cream was good, but tigers were better. I looked at the ground. "I want to give it to the tiger."

Dad nodded and stood up, pulling out his wallet. He handed me my five and a twenty. "Why don't you put that in there, too."

I shoved the bills into the box, and I felt better about the tiger. Surely he'd have a bigger room soon. Twenty-five dollars was a lot of money.

My dad still bought me ice cream.

The animals now had plenty of room. You didn't see them pinned in by bars. Instead, they'd designed the cages to look like the animals lived together, all in harmony. The tiger looked less bored sunning in a field. It was a pleasant lie. He was still in a cage, but I could live with the compromise. At least the tiger wasn't being killed by poachers. Or Mercedes-driving freaks. I'd put Brooke's head on the couch before I'd left so she could watch TV. She'd asked me to put a pencil in her mouth so she could change channels on the remote after I left. The thought made my stomach twist.

My hand went automatically to my medicine bag—I tended to use it as a touchstone when I was nervous—only to realize I'd forgotten to put it back on after I'd showered that morning. Not that I believed it held some mystic power or anything, you know, besides the power to make me feel better, but I still wished I had it. I shoved my hands deeper into my hoodie. I'd just gotten here and already things were not going my way. Super.

I wasn't sure exactly where the guy wanted to meet me. The Asia exhibit was huge. Was he being difficult by not specifying? Testing me? Amused at watching me try to figure it out? Part of me was too pissed off to care. Another part of me decided I should be too scared to be angry. This guy had killed my friend just to send me a message. What would he do if I missed a meeting?

I decided to pick a spot in the exhibit and stay there. When you're a kid, they tell you that sticking to one spot is the quickest way to be found by someone looking for you. I bought a criminally overpriced cotton candy and parked my ass by the sign for the Asia exhibit. I'd almost bought the popcorn. You can look tough eating popcorn. I bet even bikers eat popcorn, though they probably put lots of butter on it. Bikers don't care about cholesterol. But something about a pink fluffy ball screams pansy to most people. I decided that pansy was probably a better look. That way there was no possible chance this guy could take me for a threat.

He showed up, bang on time, like he'd been watching me. I'd never found punctuality to be particularly creepy until now, but the way Douglas appeared made me think he'd been following me around, which gave me a serious case of the willies. I'd never been afraid of a man wearing jeans and a polo shirt before, either. I think he could wear anything and still maintain an air of menace. He could probably pull off the cotton candy thing, too.

"You're early," he said. He noticed me staring at his clothes. I hadn't figured him for a jeans person. Of course, even his jeans were clean and pressed. They had creases. I'd always imagined evil in impeccable Italian suits and hand-made leather shoes. Sort of demonic CEO chic. He seemed to follow my thinking. One hand plucked at the stitching on the leg. "Suits," he said, "stand out here. I prefer to blend."

I nodded, looking him in the eyes. Brown eyes rarely look cold, but his were flat and icy. They held no warmth at all. But I stayed locked on them because it seemed like a good idea to keep watch on the danger. I kept my mouth shut because I didn't want to piss him off. Maybe if my answers were short and sweet, my own head would stay attached to my shoulders. Maybe. At that thought I felt my anger rise up and take a seat next to my fear. This was the man who killed Brooke. My mouth started before my brain could catch up to it.

"If I was late, would you have cut off my head, too?" I stared out at the passersby as I said this.

"Perhaps. Punctuality is important." He said it like my question was one he heard every day. I wondered if it was.

"Sam, is it?"

I nodded again.

"Do you have a last name, Sam?"

"Yes, I do." I tried to push my anger away for now. It wouldn't do Brooke any good if I got killed provoking this guy just to make myself feel better.

He let out a barking laugh that made me want to cover my ears. Like his eyes, the sound was cold, joyless, as if he'd heard someone else make the noise and was trying to mimic it.

"Cautious," he said, "that's a good trait, too. Perhaps you aren't a complete waste of my time after all." He motioned toward the exhibit with his head and started walking. "All right, Sam, this way. I have something to show you."

I fell in line behind him but not too close. Something told me that, as much as I didn't want him angry with me, I didn't want him interested in me, either. Oh, good, subtlety—one of my strong points. Might as well dig my grave now.

"What do you want me to call you?" I asked. I was pretty sure I had his name right, but you never know. Maybe he liked to go by Monty.

"I prefer Douglas."

Am I the only one who thinks that psychopathic killer types should have imposing names like Vlad the Impaler, Genghis Khan, or Vigo the Carpathian? As a name, Douglas was a letdown.

Douglas looked straight ahead as he walked, hands in pockets, relaxed and calm, like he was on a Sunday stroll. "You were expecting something more sinister, perhaps?"

"Yeah, I guess I was." I didn't think letting him know that he intimidated me was a bad thing.

No barking laughter this time. "Would it make you feel better to know that Douglas means 'dark river' or 'river of blood'?"

"Not really, no."

We walked in silence for a few minutes, winding our way through small groups of children and animal displays. Douglas finally stopped in front of the panda exhibit, which maintained a decent crowd, even on an overcast day like this. Woodland Park Zoo normally didn't have pandas, but a zoo in China had loaned them in some sort of exchange program. The pandas had been at the zoo for a week. I had an affinity for pandas. Something about clumsy vegetarians struck a chord with me.

Douglas stayed back from the crowd, sitting on an empty park bench. I joined him, happy that I could still see the pandas from my spot.

"Why are you here, Sam?" He didn't look at me but kept his eyes on the crowd.

"You invited me, Douglas." I wasn't trying to be a smart-ass, but sometimes the truth comes out that way.

"I meant in Seattle, idiot, not the zoo." He frowned, apparently exasperated already. I think I'd lost whatever points I'd gained in his mind. I tried to keep my eye on the big picture—that this guy was dangerous—but I was also getting tired of all the cloak-and-dagger crap.

"Hey, watch the name calling," I said. "And what do you mean? I live here."

"Yes, so you've said, but you should have appealed to the Council when you moved into the area."

"I didn't move into the area. I told you, I live here. I have always lived here." I took a deep breath. "And what Council?"

"Your guide should have told you all of this."

"All of what? What the hell are you talking about?" Anger leaked into my voice. I couldn't help it.

"Drop the act, Sam. It won't do you any good."

My desire to yell nearly overwhelmed me. Deep breath, count to ten. Then, through gritted teeth, "There is no act. I have no guide, and I don't know what you're talking about. What don't you understand about that?"

Douglas turned and really looked at me then. His face remained flat, but I saw a little twitch of surprise around his eyes.

"You really have no idea what I'm talking about."

"No," I said, "I don't."

"But surely . . . who taught you to control—" He paused and regrouped. "What did you do, then, when you got your powers?"

"What powers?"

"This denial is bordering on ridiculous."

I rubbed my temples with the tips of my fingers. "What powers?" I managed not to yell, but barely.

Douglas swore and closed his eyes. "I saw my first spirit when I was a child, Sam. You can't tell me that you haven't had some sort of experience. Your aura isn't that weak. Even if you can't accomplish a full raising, you must have seen something by now."

"Full raising?"

"Of the dead, Sam. Necromancy. You're a necromancer, like me."

I laughed, saw he wasn't joking about the necromancy thing, then stopped. "I'm nothing like you," I said. I guess my keep-my-mouth-shut policy had gone out the window. "Necromancy." I laughed again. "You could have at least worked up to that one. You know, started with 'Luke, you have the power' or something like that." I snorted. "Come over to the dark side."

Douglas sighed. "Yes. Yes, you are like me." He scanned the crowd, which was thinning out a little as the weather continued to lean toward the worse. "Look at me, Sam."

"I am looking at you."

"Not with your eyes." He turned to me and grabbed my chin. His hands were cold and dry, and I didn't like them on my skin one bit. "Now, close your eyes."

I closed my eyes. I didn't want to, but I didn't have another option.

"Now *look*." He let go of my chin.

Douglas's order didn't make any sense at all. And yet, my mind automatically obeyed. Something in my head opened up and spilled out, which sounds gross, but it wasn't. Whatever had just happened felt good, like my mind was a man stretching after a long plane ride cramped in a seat where a kid was kicking him from behind. My sight poured out and spread. I could see, really *see*, like echolocation but with a boost. I cast around with it. I saw a kid walk past me with a balloon; the balloon was a bare outline, but the kid was a walking kaleidoscope of colors. His father held his hand, and I could see him too, but his colors didn't shift as much as the child's did. The father's color bled slowly from one to the next and with less diversity. I wondered what that meant.

My eyes still closed, I turned my head to the right. The flowers and bushes burned green tinged with orange, and the pandas shifted colors like the kid with the balloon. Wait. Not all the pandas.

"There's something wrong with one of the pandas," I said, eyes still closed. I watched, but the panda didn't shift colors at all. He was cast entirely in shadow except for one small spark of incandescent blue in the upper left of his chest. There's no way that could be a good thing. Next to the flowers, the bushes, the passing people, the panda looked . . . wrong. Like a tear, an empty hole into space.

"Yes," Douglas said. "I know."

My head turned toward Douglas, like in a horror movie. You shout at the screen, "Don't look! Run!" but no one ever listens. Douglas didn't look like the panda, but I could tell they were linked to each other. Douglas glowed that same icy blue, but instead of all that empty dark space, his blue was broken up with shifting, swirling lines of blacks, grays, silvers. What the hell?

I felt like I might throw up if I kept looking, so I tore my vision away and put my head in my hands to reorient and slow things down—to regain myself. Big freaking mistake. My hands, my arms, my legs, were all coated in that blue, like a layer of radioactive dust. My gut tightened and my jaw clenched. Why wasn't I like all the other freaky tie-dye people who kept walking past? Where were my other colors? Once past that initial layer of blue, there was nothing. Not even the darkness. Just a hazy blur that blocked out the colors of the bench and the flowers around me. Like the panda, it felt wrong. Not the same kind of wrong, but wrong nonetheless.

I opened my eyes. Light, colors, sound, all came back in a blaring wave. My head hurt from the sudden onslaught, and I felt dizzy. I never wanted to close my eyes again.

"What just happened?" I kept my gaze directed toward the ground while I tried to regain myself.

"You looked into the heart of things, into the pulse of the world."

I bit back a retort. Telling Douglas that he sounded like the deep-voiced announcer from a daytime soap opera wouldn't help anyone.

"Why don't I look like everyone else?" I asked.

"Because you're not like everyone else, Sam. Necromancers are linked to death. The underworld, the spirit world, which-ever particular appellation you choose to give it, you are one of the ties that binds this world to that."

"But I don't look like you, either."

Douglas didn't answer. The silence stretched out, and I fig-ured he wasn't going to answer that. Okay. Try again. Douglas got up and walked over to the enclosure. I followed until I leaned up against the railing. The area had cleared even more so that only a few stragglers were looking at the pandas.

There were three pandas in the enclosure. Two of them ambled about, stopping to gnaw on the occasional clump of bamboo. But the third sat on his own in the far corner, and I couldn't help but notice that the other two wouldn't go near him. And that he wasn't eating bamboo. He held some in his paw, and he stared at it, but he didn't eat any. "What's wrong with him?"

"He's dead."

A kid had wandered up behind Douglas and, after over-hearing him, started to cry. The kid ran to his mother, grasping onto her slim waist. She glared at us and walked away. Douglas didn't seem to notice.

"What was that?" I asked.

"The big male, Ling Tsu, died his first night here. The zoo panicked. They had promoted the exhibit for weeks, and Ling Tsu didn't even belong to them. Someone I do considerable business with gave them my number as a . . . temporary solution until they can sort things out." Douglas stared evenly at the pandas. They could have been furniture for all the reaction he had to them. "The zoo was in a tight spot, things being what they are with China and all."

"What's wrong with China?"

Douglas turned his stare on me, but this time it was tinged with derision. "Trade imbalance, human rights violations, contaminated medicines?"

I shook my head. I tried not to watch the news. Too depressing. They just don't make very good episodes of it any-more.

Douglas sighed again. "Lead-based paint on toys?"

"Oh, right. They made a reference to that on *Law & Order*, I think."

I watched as one of the pandas did the slow panda version of a frolic. "So, you're telling me the zoo commissioned you to make a zombie panda in order to avoid a potential international incident," I said.

"In a nutshell, yes."

"And I'm supposed to believe this because . . . ?"

"Because you've seen it, Sam."

He said my name like I was a disobedient child. I got the feeling that Douglas wasn't used to people doubting his word.

"Sorry, but this thing sounds a little far-fetched for me. And why on earth are you showing me this anyway? Here, kid, an undead panda. Enjoy?" I shook my head. "Screw you, Douglas."

"You insolent—" Douglas cut himself off and took a deep breath. He turned those cold eyes on me, and I stepped back, just a fraction, but enough for him to see how much he scared me. Fine, let him see.

"I brought you here to make a deal, Sam. The panda is just an example of a larger idea. People die inconveniently all the time, too. Senators, heads of state, CEOs, dictators. Sometimes other people need to keep them around just a little longer. That's what I do. The right people with the right money have my name. They could have yours, too."

"I don't follow." Why would I want politicians to have my name? Politics gave me a rash.

"Power, Sam. I'm offering you power and wealth. I could teach you, if you want. Your power isn't great, but I could bring it out, show you how to make the most of it. I've kept governments from collapsing. And it's not just politics. Do you think the Stones would still be on tour without my help?"

I mulled that one over. Really, it could be any of the Stones. They'd been living the rock 'n' roll life for quite a long time now. And while it was easy to picture Mick as the undead, it had to be—"Keith," I said, pleased with my quick turnaround. Douglas didn't look too impressed with my answer, and I guess it was kind of obvious. Ramon had been operating for years under the assumption that Keith was a cyborg, and being undead wasn't far off from that. Same general idea, just different method.

I began to wonder what he meant by politics. Zombies in the Senate and as heads of state actually cleared a lot of things up for me. In fact, if you told most people that the White House was being run by the legions of the undead, they'd probably just say, "Figures." Who else was Douglas keeping alive? An image of Jimmy Carter flashed in my mind. Would he start campaigning for the rights of the reanimated if he passed from the mortal sphere? "Is it Jimmy Carter? The queen? She's been around a long time."

"I'm not about to hand over my entire client list to you, Sam."

"That wasn't a no."

"Drop it."

I shook my head. "You don't have Hitler in your basement or anything, do you? Tabloids are always claiming he's still alive. Him and Elvis. Because I can't condone that sort of thing. The Hitler thing, not Elvis. I've got nothing against the King."

Douglas slammed a fist against the wooden barrier keeping us from panda country. His nostrils flared slightly before he regained his composure. "This isn't a joke."

Sadly, I didn't think it was, either.

"Despite your behavior," he said, "the offer still stands."

Before the zoo, I thought Douglas was a run-of-the-mill psychotic. I was wrong. The guy must have been completely bat-shit nuts. The bad thing was, I believed him. And the even worse thing was, I was beginning to believe what he'd said about me.

"You." I stopped and licked my lips, trying to get a handle on my anger. Count to ten. Screw it. "You killed my friend, and now you want me to work with you?" My words came out in a whisper.

"I had to get your attention," he said.

"You want my attention, hire a skywriter. Send a candy-gram. Don't decapitate people."

Douglas shrugged, like all of my options were the same.

"Think of her as your first lesson," he said.

"Her name is Brooke."

Not even a shrug this time. "I will keep this simple for you, Sam. Join me and live. Defy me, and I will take you, your friends, and your family down one by one. I will twist and mold the facts until the Council turns against you. I will slaughter you, exterminate everyone you love, and get the Council to sanction the whole thing. No recourse, just death."

"What Council?" I asked, exasperation leaking into my voice.

"You have a week. Use it wisely." And he left. The psycho just walked off.

A week to figure everything out. That didn't seem like a lot of time. Especially if the week was anything like the last twenty-four hours. My system couldn't keep taking shocks like that.

I leaned down and folded my arms on the wooden rails, resting my chin on top of them. I watched the pandas and tried to see them as I did before, like I hadn't looked at them in my head, but it didn't work. My eyes kept being drawn to that third panda in the corner. Ling Tsu now had two handfuls of bamboo, one in each paw. His eyes moved back and forth between them before he threw them down in what I imagined was the panda equivalent of disgust. When your whole life was eating bamboo and suddenly that was taken away from you, what did you have? Ling Tsu couldn't eat, and his fellow pandas wouldn't go near him. He was alone, and I couldn't help but think that he would have preferred to go back to that great bamboo forest in the sky. I didn't care how much money whoever had thrown at Douglas, this felt wrong. Unlike Ling Tsu, Brooke understood what had happened. I didn't know if that made her existence better or worse.

I threw away my cotton candy and headed out before I broke down and started crying in front of the panda exhibit. I could at least wait until I got to the car.

9

THE FUTURE'S SO BRIGHT, I GOTTA WEAR SHADES

$\mathbb{I}$ got back to my apartment in time to see Mrs. Winalski fishing around for her keys.

"Looks like I'm not the only one out on the prowl," she said. She waggled her eyebrows at me suggestively.

"I just got back from the zoo."

"You disappoint me, Sam."

I did my best to look apologetic as I opened my door. I like Mrs. W, I really do, but I didn't feel like talking. All I wanted was to go into my quiet apartment, sit down, and try to sort everything out.

Mrs. W gave me a parting wave, and I slunk into my dim living room. Brooke looked asleep. Did she still need to sleep? Frank had positioned her as best he could in the chair, wrapping a T-shirt around her neck for added balance. I tried not to imagine her stump of a neck or that clean, sharp cut that looked like it'd been made with a hot knife. Too late. Already the vision of it surfaced in my mind.

I didn't bother to turn on any lights. Instead, I eased down onto my couch, careful of my back, and closed my eyes. Blessed silence, blessed darkness.

"How was the zoo?"

I didn't have time to measure, but I think I jumped about twelve feet. I twisted in pain from the sudden jerking movement, my eyes rolling over to Brooke. She stared at me from her perch on my easy chair. Either she was a light sleeper or she hadn't been napping at all.

"Sorry," she said. "Forgot you were sliced and diced."

I sucked in a breath and settled slowly back onto the couch. As uncomfortable as I felt, Brooke had to feel way worse. "No, my fault," I said. "I guess I'm a little wound up." I looked at her more closely. "Is that my Alkaline Trio T-shirt?"

"Yup."

"Man, I just got that."

Brooke tried to look down at the shirt, but failed. "You took me to see that show, Sam, and I listened to those CDs you let me borrow. Something tells me they'd be strangely okay with their T-shirt's new use."

I couldn't really argue with that.

"It was the guy with the potato, wasn't it?"

"I thought you didn't remember your—you know." I pantomimed slitting my throat, a slightly misguided attempt at levity. But I couldn't say "death" to her. I just couldn't.

"I don't, not really. But I've been seeing pieces, mostly from when I was in the box. Voices talking—one sounded familiar."

"His name is Douglas."

We sat for a minute in an uncomfortable silence.

"He's scary, isn't he?" Brooke's voice was quiet, serious. I had never heard her sound like that.

"Yeah. Yeah, he is." It was scary when someone threatened everyone that you loved. If I didn't do what he wanted, what would happen? An accident for my neighbors? My sister's head in my freezer? My stomach dropped thinking about it. There was no way to know where he'd strike, and no way to guess what I could do to keep everyone safe. And no point dwelling on what might be—I'd go crazy if I kept that up. I shifted a little in my seat. "Can I ask you a question?"

"Shoot."

"What's it like? You know . . ." I trailed off, waving vaguely at her head.

"Being a head? What do you think it's like?" Her voice took on an edge.

I imagined it would be horrible, but I waited for Brooke to continue. I needed to hear it from her, and I thought she needed to vent.

"I've been stuck in your apartment all day watching the news to see if they've discovered my body yet. It's weird, Sam, really freaking weird. I'm dead, but I'm not. When I see a commercial for restless legs syndrome, I start to cry, and I can't tell if it's because the commercials are so annoying or if it's because I'm jealous of their legs, restless or otherwise." She paused to blow a hair out of her face. "And I just blew a hair out of my face. Something totally normal, but now I have to wonder, How did I do that? All of the simple things are suddenly complicated." She frowned, but it quickly morphed into

Brooke's beatific smile. "On the upside, I no longer have to work at Plumpy's."

I looked away, staring at the blank TV. Even in her position, Brooke was trying to stay positive. I wanted to be positive for her too, but I felt sick inside. Out of the corner of my eye, I could see Brooke—Brooke's head—staring at me. I wanted to reassure her, but I didn't think I could be very convincing. I wanted to crumple in on myself.

"Sam, this isn't your fault."

I lay back against the couch, not really seeing anything. I closed my eyes. "In what way is this not my fault?" I asked. "He killed you as a message to me. Without me, you would still be alive. If I'd had a better slap shot, I wouldn't have broken that taillight and none of this would have happened."

"A lot of things in life would improve if you'd work on your aim. But you didn't kill me," she said, eyes intent. "He did. You can't take the blame for every psycho in Seattle."

"But I can try."

Brooke laughed, and I felt a little better.

I heard the rattle of keys and the lock tumbling over. Ramon entered, keys in one hand, a pile of books in the other, and a paper bag in his mouth. The keys went into his pocket, and he tossed the bag at me. It felt hot, and I could hear the crackle of foil inside. A familiar, and delicious, smell floated up from it.

"For you," he said. "My mom's afraid you might starve. Something about vegetarians—she always thinks you guys never get enough to eat."

Despite all the turmoil, I dug into the bag. Ramon's mom was an awesome cook, and my stomach practically cheered at the sight of one of her meals. Rice, beans, oh, dear God, she'd sent some of her homemade tortillas. My day was looking up.

Ramon tossed his books onto the coffee table and flopped down next to me. "I checked out a few books that I thought might help you."

I nodded at him, focused on my food. A fork, I needed a fork. I got up and grabbed one from the kitchen, then returned to my rice and beans. I scanned titles as I ate. He'd picked up some books on voodoo, death, and the spirit world. If he'd waited until after my meeting, I might have been able to narrow down his choices. He just had to borrow books on necromancers. I swallowed thickly. We weren't only researching Douglas anymore. We were researching me. I could now be lumped into the same category as him. The scoop of rice that had been on my fork fell off. I swore and scooped it up again, though my enthusiasm had waned some.

Ramon sat forward. "I wasn't sure if you'd want any, Brooke."

"Thanks, Ramon, but I'm on a diet," she said, her face completely serious.

"Yeah, you could stand to lose a few more ounces, *chica*." He nodded toward the TV. "They find you yet? I was in class, so I couldn't hear anything."

"No, not yet. But my parents aren't due back until this afternoon."

Brooke tried to be brave, but I could see her eyes well up. I put down my food and grabbed a paper towel. I couldn't just sit there and let her cry.

"Hey," Ramon said, "don't cry, okay? We'll get him, won't we, Sam?" He looked at me, face grim, and even if I hadn't meant to already, I knew we were going to do something about Douglas. I hoped Ramon had a plan, because I could certainly use one.

Brooke stopped crying and hiccuped a little. "The cops won't be able to do anything about it, will they?"

They both looked at me. I guess I was the expert. I thought for a minute before answering. "No, I don't think they will."

"But they're probably going to question us, huh?" Ramon asked.

"Yeah, we were the last to see Brooke, um, intact. But I don't think we should tell them anything beyond what they can discover from the surveillance videos."

"Why not?" Ramon asked. "We know the bastard who did this. Why shouldn't we sic the cops on him?" He sat hunched forward, his ears getting red.

I crumpled the paper towel in my hand. I thought about the things Douglas had said at the zoo. Powerful friends. "I doubt the cops could touch him. We'd just be putting more people in danger. If we were lucky, he might be slightly annoyed by it."

"Sam's right," Brooke said. "All you'd be doing is pissing off psycho man. And then he'd kill one of you. I want him stopped, but not at the expense of you guys."

I pushed back the errant strand of her hair so she wouldn't have to blow at it anymore. "We'll get him, Brooke. Promise."

"I know you will," she said.

I rocked back on my heels and sat on the floor. "I just wish I knew how to get some more information."

"Yeah, I had an idea about that," Ramon said. He pulled a slip of paper out of his back pocket and handed it to me. I opened the paper, which turned out to be a long list of fortune tellers, palm readers, occult shops—whatever Seattle had to offer in the area of the supernatural. The world I was now a part of. Ramon nodded at the paper. "I figure, if one phenomenon—you know, Brooke—is real, then maybe some of this other stuff is, too. And maybe if we go and talk to some people, we can find someone who can actually help us." He reached over and stole one of my tortillas. "I mean, there have to be others, right?"

"Ramon," I said, "if it wouldn't confirm Mrs. W's suspicions, I would kiss you right now."

"Lay off. My mug is only for the ladies."

Frank knocked and walked in, already in his Plumpy's uniform and carrying a large paper bag.

"Hey, guys, Brooke," he said, shutting the door and coming over. He set down the sack and opened it. "I was getting ready for work and remembered my dad had this!" He pulled out what appeared to be a—

"Is that a bowling bag?" Ramon asked.

Frank nodded enthusiastically. From his excitement and our lack thereof, I figured we were missing something. "You want us to forget our troubles with a rousing bowling tournament?"

"What? No," Frank said, shaking his head. "It's for Brooke."

"Frank," Brooke said, "I lack a few of the basic components. Like bowling shoes. And arms."

"And the desire to waste a perfectly good evening rolling a borrowed ball and drinking overpriced soda," Ramon added.

"You're just mad because you have to use the bumpers," I told him.

"Lies."

Frank shook his head again and opened the bag. "No, look, see this?" He pointed at a metal doohickey in the bottom of the carrier. "This is meant to hold the ball in place, and your shoes of course, on your way to the bowling alley. But I figured it would be good for holding Brooke's head, too. See how the part for the ball is circular? We could put her neck there—with padding of course—and then we could take her out with us and no one would know."

"Because walking around with a bowling bag is perfectly normal," Ramon said.

Like Ramon and I had ever been normal. I'd always been relegated to the misfit fringe, as if the other kids could sense something innately off about me. Turns out they were right. I was different. I didn't really mind being on the outskirts of popularity, but I'd never quite figured out why Ramon had ended up there. The only thing strange about him was his association with me. I shrugged. "A lot more normal than walking around with a severed head."

"Yeah, but we'll be doing both."

I waved him off. "It's Seattle. We got a whole lot of weird going on. No one will notice."

Frank crumpled a little. "It's a bad idea, isn't it?"

"No, Frank, it's actually a very good idea," Brooke said.

He perked back up. "Really?"

"She's just saying that because she won't have to carry it," Ramon mumbled to me.

"It won't be so bad," Frank said. "See?" He closed the bag again and showed us the outside. The bag was designed like the old-school ones, but it was black and it had a large white skull with crossed bowling pins underneath it.

"What does it say on the back?" Brooke asked. Frank flipped it around. It said *knock 'em dead*. Frank clutched the bag and waited for us to decide if we wanted to use it or not. Honestly, even if it didn't work, I couldn't have told Frank no right then. It seemed to mean so much to him that he'd helped in some way.

"Good thinking, Frank," I said.

"Really? You'll use it?" He looked hastily to Brooke. "I mean, if you want, Brooke."

Brooke beamed at him, tears back in her eyes. "That would be fantastic."

Frank blushed.

"So, how did your meeting go?" Ramon asked, changing the subject.

While Frank went about setting Brooke up in her new handy-dandy carrying case, I filled them all in about Douglas, tie-dyed kids, and a panda named Ling Tsu. They didn't scream, and no one ran from me shouting "pariah." All in all, they took my newfound freakishness quite well. Better than I was taking it. I felt like screaming and running, but as the school counselor had always told us, you can't run from yourself. That didn't stop me from getting the heebie-jeebies every time I thought about it.

Still, I had some pretty good friends. I couldn't be too terrible if they were sticking around.

𝔄 few hours later, Ramon, Brooke, and I were back at my apartment. After Frank had gone to work, we'd spent some time going through the people on Ramon's list, but the whole thing had been a bust. I think most of the people we'd visited were fakes. A few denied that they knew what we were talking about but had shooed us out of their shops pretty quick. One palm reader even pretended she didn't know English anymore. I'd left my number with a few of them but didn't expect calls anytime soon. So now we all sat, quiet and dejected, in my apartment. Though I'm not really sure what Brooke did could be called sitting.

Brooke cleared her throat, which I don't even want to get into because it was still freaking me out a little. "Hey, guys, it was a good idea. Really. It just didn't work, that's all." She smiled at both of us. "But we'll figure it out."

The phone rang, and Ramon answered when I made no movement to get it. Self-pity and guilt had shut me down, and I was too busy thinking about how nice it would be to crawl into my closet for a week and hide until Douglas came to kill me. Sadly, that thought was almost comforting compared with the idea of him tracking down everyone I cared about one by one. I heard Ramon hang up. "Telemarketer?" I asked. "Someone else threatening my life?"

"Nope. An appointment with Maya LaRouche. She got our number from somebody, thinks she might be able to help." He smiled and picked up Brooke's case. "So get your coat. We're going to Ballard."

Ballard is one of those little areas in Seattle that I don't go to unless I have a reason, and once I'm there I always wish I went more often. There are a lot of good restaurants, bars, and clubs that I don't visit simply because Ballard's a pain in the ass to get to, no matter where you're coming from.

Ramon directed me to a small residential street and a little yellow two-story with a garden. We parked and walked up, looking around for any sign that this was the right house. I wasn't really sure what we were looking for. Did we think there would be a giant crystal ball in the front yard with a flashing arrow? I checked to make sure my medicine bag was hidden under my shirt. I needed all the comfort I could get. Pouch in place, I caught up to Ramon, who was already at the door.

The door opened on the second knock, and any greeting I had mustered died unsaid. My mouth stalled at the sight of the girl holding the door, and my brain lumbered to get it running again. Gorgeous with a capital G. She looked like an Egyptian queen—all high cheekbones and golden brown skin. But the intelligence in the brown eyes that stared back at me told me she didn't skate on her looks. She held her hand out. "Dessa LaRouche."

She shook my hand firmly, confident enough that she didn't try to break any bones, but no dead fish, either. "Sam LaCroix, right? What happened to your face?" Before I had a chance to explain away the bruises, she'd angled slightly toward Ramon. "And you . . . I know you."

My head snapped over to Ramon, who had gone uncharacteristically silent. He knew pretty girls? Ramon had been holding out.

"You were in my biology class," Dessa said. "Ramon something."

"Hernandez," Ramon said.

I vaguely remember Ramon mentioning a Dessa, though he'd mostly referred to her as "girl of the goddess body." If Dessa kept Ramon this quiet, I might need to hang around with her more often.

Dessa paused, frowned at the bowling bag in Ramon's hands, then waved us in and closed the door.

Ramon glanced around, trying to take in as much of her house as he could. All the walls I could see were done in earth tones—warm browns and greens—interspersed with photos and paintings. The house looked nice, not in an overly stylized way, but in a lived-in fashion. Dessa lived in a home, not a house. There's a difference.

We walked through a set of French doors to a small room that looked nothing like an office to me, except for the two heavily laden bookshelves. Lace curtains billowed from an open window, and the walls were what my mom would call a pale, soothing lavender. I didn't see a desk or a computer, just a small glass coffee table, a teapot, and a few overstuffed chairs arranged around it. In one of the chairs sat a woman calmly drinking tea from an old china cup. Her smile hovered just over the rim of the cup, and she gestured for us to sit. Maya LaRouche looked like a leaner, slightly older version of her daughter, with one exception. She had eyes like new copper pennies. Those eyes shifted her from beautiful to striking and surreal.

She put down her tea and poured some for Ramon and me without asking as we sat down. "I'll need my daughter to remove your friend before we start."

I looked at Ramon. "Why can't he stay?"

"Not that friend." She pointed at the bag. "That one." Maya smiled at the look of panic on my face. "It's okay," she said, "I know what she is. I'd welcome her, but she'll muddy my reading."

Dessa picked up the bag.

Maya motioned at her to unzip it. "You understand, dear?"

"Yes, ma'am," Brooke said.

Maya nodded kindly, and Dessa took Brooke out of the room. Any doubt that I'd had about Maya LaRouche being the real deal completely disintegrated.

Once she came back into the office, Dessa didn't sit down until her mother nodded at her. More out of respect, I think, than subservience.

"Dessa tells me that you may have a problem that I can help

with," Maya said. Her voice rolled with a hint of an accent that I couldn't place.

I looked at Ramon. I didn't know what he'd told Dessa over the phone, or how much I should tell them now. He shrugged at me. I guess he didn't know how to handle this, either.

Maya followed our back-and-forth with those new-penny eyes, assessing us. "I see," she said. "Why don't I do what I do while you boys think it over a little?" She leaned in to refill her tea. "But first, boy, you're going to have to take off your juju bag. That thing is messing me up as bad as your friend was."

I blinked at her.

"Your medicine bag. Take it off."

I reached for it, but hesitated. "How did you know?"

"I'm a seer, boy, not some third-rate carnival psychic, and right now I can't see anything with your juju blocking me."

"You can't?" I pulled my pouch off and set it on the table. "I'm sorry, I've had it forever." I frowned at the bag, suddenly uncomfortable with it. "I didn't realize that it actually did anything."

"Makes you invisible to me is what it does, and probably other things." She closed her eyes and sat back. I didn't know what to do, so I took a sip of my tea, which turned out to be chamomile. It's a little unnerving, being focused on like that. Which made me think that the oh-so-soothing lavender walls, lace curtains, and chamomile tea were strategic. No one likes being dissected.

A few minutes stretched out, filled with the tiny sounds people make when they're trying to be quiet. I kept my eyes on Maya, examining her face for any hint of what she was thinking. Her brow creased a little and then went flat.

"There you are," she whispered, mostly to herself, I think. Her eyes opened, and she tilted her head toward me.

"Who bound you, boy?" she asked.

"Huh?" I felt like I'd been saying that a lot recently. My mind seethed with unanswered questions. I hadn't gotten used to one thing, and now Maya was telling me there was something else? "Does that have anything to do with the dead thing, because—"

"I know you're a necromancer, Sam," she said. "That's not what's troubling me."

"It seems to trouble everyone else," Ramon said.

"Look, Mrs. LaRouche—"

"Maya."

"Maya, this week's been full of people who seem to know a lot more about what's going on than me, and it's getting old," I said. "So, if you could just pretend that I have no idea as to what you're talking about and start over, I would really appreciate it."

She patted my leg sympathetically and took a sip of her tea. She cradled the cup in her hands, resting them in her lap.

"I know what you are, Sam, because I can see signs of it all around you, and because I've seen them before. What I do find strange is that only the outline of your aura is visible. That's not normal. It's as if someone has bound you, and all I'm seeing is what's leaking out." I opened my mouth, but she stopped me. "It's exactly what it sounds like, dear. Someone has tied up your magic. A binding is usually done to keep a person from, or from causing, harm." She frowned at the teacup in her hands. "I've never seen it used to harness like this. It's as if part of you has been locked away."

Her words echoed in my head. Someone had locked part of me up, and the idea that they might have done it because they thought I was dangerous made the tea heavy in my stomach. You don't hobble nice beings. I'd always considered myself to be a good person. Was I wrong?

Ramon cleared his throat, drawing Maya's attention. "Could that be why he didn't know until now?"

Maya nodded at him. "Yes, it very well could be."

"Can you tell who did it?" I asked.

Her brow creased again. "No. It's messy, trying to keep something still that doesn't want to be. Like trying to wrap ribbon around a river. You understand?" I nodded. She closed her eyes again and concentrated. "When I look, it blurs— almost looks like two different bindings. But I can't imagine that." Her face relaxed and smoothed. "Then it clears and I see a necromancer, like you." She sighed. "I wish I could tell you more, but the binding . . ." She shrugged.

I stared into my chamomile. "So someone like me did this?"

"I'm afraid so."

Well, that narrowed my suspect pool to zero. I only knew one other necromancer, and that was Douglas. No way he did it. If he'd gotten hold of me as a kid, he probably would have cooked and eaten me then and there.

"Sam," Ramon said, "I think you should tell her." His face seemed very serious. So unlike Ramon.

"All of it?" I asked. He nodded.

"All of what?" Dessa asked.

"I think we're going to need more tea," I said.

Ramon filled everyone's cups as I told the two women about the last forty-eight hours. Telling them seemed risky, but like Ramon, I trusted them, and we needed help from someone. Since they hadn't yet tried to kill anyone I knew, they were at the top of my list. Halfway through, Dessa got up and pulled a bottle of whisky out of a drawer. She poured a little into all of our glasses, giving her mother a bit extra after she saw Maya blanch at the mention of Douglas's name. The two didn't strike me as heavy drinkers, so I took some pride in the fact that my story had driven someone else to drink, too.

"You're screwed," Maya said when I stopped.

Not something you want to hear from a seer.

"Yeah," Ramon said, "we know."

Dessa reached over and grabbed her mother's hand as Maya said, "As bad as it may seem, Ramon, I don't think either of you understands exactly how bad your situation is." Her strong voice sounded tired. She stood up and leaned on her daughter. "Let me think this over, Sam, and I'll see what I can come up with. In the meantime, I'll make some calls. There is someone who I think can help you."

I thanked her and made sure Dessa had my number as they escorted us down the hall. At the doorway, Dessa handed Brooke's bag to Ramon before giving me back my medicine bag. I didn't want it around my neck until I knew what was going on, so I shoved the small pouch into my pocket. Yeah, it made me sort of invisible, but what if it did something else I didn't know about yet?

Maya touched my face with her hand. "I wish I could be of more immediate help."

"That's okay," I said.

"In the meantime, take care. And, Sam?"

"Yeah?"

"I'd go talk to whoever made that pouch for you."

"Why is that?" I asked.

"Because whoever it is, they know what you are, too."

I must have looked surprised, because Maya added gently, "That pouch is built to hide what you are—exactly what you are. It does nothing else as far as I can tell."

I thanked her again.

We said our good-byes and more thank-yous. I studied the darkening sky as we walked to my Subaru, both of us now silent. Ramon didn't speak until after we had both buckled our seat belts.

"Are we going where I think we are?" he asked.

"Hell, yeah," I told him, turning the key in the ignition. I steered the car toward the highway that would take us to my mother's house. "And I hope she's got a few good answers."

"I hope," Ramon said, "that she's made cookies."

I glared at him.

"Don't look at me like that. If we were going to interrogate my poor mother for whatever, you'd be secretly hoping she'd made you tamales. I'm just honest enough to admit it."

I didn't bother to respond. He was right. Ramon's mother was a top-notch tamale maker, and out of pity she'd come up with a vegetarian recipe so I could enjoy her handiwork. They were amazing. But cookies or no, Tia LaCroix, my mother, and maker of medicine pouches, had a lot of explaining to do.

10

WAITING, FOR A GIRL LIKE YOU

Brid knew she'd been out of the cage. They'd cleaned her up, but she could smell blood on her skin. Her blood. And when she was napping she had hazy aconite-fuzzy flashes of things. A steady pull on her shoulders. Sharp pains. The cool feel of concrete on her cheek. Since there wasn't any in the cage, she could only assume she'd been out. And she'd healed, which wouldn't have happened in here. Or at least she'd healed on the outside. The uncomfortable feeling on the inside hadn't gone away. She didn't like not knowing what they'd done. Or losing time. She wasn't even sure what day it was now.

Her nostrils flared as she breathed in. She closed her eyes. Meditation had never been easy for Brid. It was hard for someone like her, sitting so still for so long. Which of course was exactly the reason her father had trained them all to do it. Being able to sit still, to control yourself, he said, was just as important as being able to run. Brid didn't like it, but she could see his point.

She sat cross-legged, hands resting palms down on her thighs. She never felt comfortable doing that weird finger-circle meditation thing.

She slowed her breathing, willing her heart rate to follow suit. Her pulse wasn't complying. It kept chug-chug-chugging along. She wasn't sure how long she'd been in the cage, but she could feel the restlessness growing. Her jog had been cut short by the abduction, and the cage just wasn't big enough for any real exercise. Sit-ups weren't cutting it, and there wasn't enough room to sprint.

And she couldn't change.

The only thing she could do was bully her pulse into slowing down, force her body to give her more time. She couldn't do it forever. But she didn't need forever. She just needed until she got out or was rescued. And if neither of those things happened, then her captors would probably solve her restlessness permanently.

Brid ignored that possibility and concentrated on her heart. Breathing through her nose, she pictured it slowing, moving to a lazy beat. After an unknown amount of time, her mind emptied, and all she knew was that measured rhythm.

Then footsteps.

She kept her eyes closed and listened.

"Success?" That was Douglas.

"There wasn't much I could do, but I think I bought us some time." Brid frowned, not recognizing the other voice.

"If it keeps Brannoc off my doorstep, I'm grateful."

The other person scoffed. "If you'd let me handle it in the first place, instead of involving that idiot—"

"James." Douglas's voice held a hint of warning.

The person called James sighed. "I know."

"Which form did you use?"

"Dragon. They shouldn't be able to pick up that scent, and if they do, I doubt they'll recognize it."

"And you made it look like she went away?"

Brid shifted uneasily. She didn't like where the conversation was going.

"Yes."

"Where did you leave her things?"

There was a pause. "The less you know, I think, the better."

"You're probably right."

"Is there anything else you need?"

"No," Douglas said. "I will see what I can do to strengthen the trail, make them think she went off somewhere on her own."

Another pause. Brid leaned back on her hands.

"Do you think it will work?"

Brid almost didn't hear it, James asked so softly.

"We'll have to wait and see."

She heard some clanging noises, which made her think that Douglas and his accomplice were in the kitchen. Until now, it had just been Douglas and Michael. With the new voice, the tally was up to three. She didn't have any use for the information right now, but she made note of it.

Brid uncrossed her legs and stretched them straight in front of her. She leaned down and grabbed her toes, resting her forehead against her knees. Stretching felt good.

She usually checked in with her family before she went anywhere. Usually. But if they didn't know when she'd disappeared, they might think she'd just stayed the night at a friend's. Although it was normal for pack members to go days without seeing one another, they generally checked in with the Alpha, especially if they were deviating from any regular schedule. Unless you were rogue, you checked in. Brid especially, but her father would cut her some slack, shrugging the lack of communication off on her busy class schedule. The plan had simplicity on its side. It might buy Douglas enough time to finish whatever it was he was trying to do. Brid didn't like that at all.

The clanging stopped and she heard more footsteps. She stilled midstretch.

"Your concern is noted, James."

"Then why not get rid of her?"

"I can't pass up the opportunity." Douglas's voice held a strange mixture of excitement and worry.

"You've studied weres before. Find another shifter to guinea pig."

"Weres, yes, but hybrids? No. Even if the packs didn't normally keep to themselves, the fey sure as hell do. I've never seen anything like her and her brothers."

"Then take one of the brothers, or one of the other hybrid offspring. Not the *tánaiste*."

"What do you think I wanted to do? Even with our precautions, they'll figure out she's missing soon. Their guard will be up, their security doubled. It was a fluke Michael got her in the first place, even I can admit that. No, we'll have to do our best to make lemonade out of Michael's idiocy."

"I just hope the gains will be half as great as your risk."

They walked away before Brid could catch Douglas's response. She turned her head and rested her cheek against her leg. She desperately needed something to tip the scales in her favor. In the meantime, she'd have to be patient. Look for an opening. And hope she got to take another bite out of Michael.

11

SHE LOVES ME LIKE A ROCK

My mother is not a big fan of the straight path. She says you don't learn anything by toeing the line. "Do you think," she says, "Little Red Riding Hood would have learned a damn thing if she hadn't wandered off to pick some flowers?" Very popular at PTA meetings, my mother. Good thing they gave her the willies.

You don't have to really speak to her to discover her preference for the curvy trail. You just have to walk from her gate to the front door. My mom's cottage sits back from her fence, nestled in the shade of several large pine trees. Between the slatted wooden gate and her welcome mat lies a lot of space that most people would make into a pleasant green lawn. Not Tia LaCroix. She has no use for lawns—she calls them "bland ornaments." You can bet you won't find a single eggshell-white wall in her house either. In lieu of a lawn, she planted a garden. But the word *garden* doesn't really paint the whole picture. You can't fully grasp it until you open the gate and walk on the cobblestone path through what one mailman described as the "forests of LaCroix." The mailman would've probably disliked her because of the extra walk, but she always made him cookies on the holidays, or when she decided it was a holiday, and very few people can resist that kind of bribery.

Simple, her garden is not. But beautiful, well, that goes without saying. Mom has a green thumb and perhaps a few other people's as well. It's worked well for her. She has that little herbal shop in Fremont, and her online business is thriving.

There seems to be no design to the forests of LaCroix. At least, I've never been able to figure one out. When I tried to tell that to my sister, Haley, she looked at me like I'd lost all my brains. "Of course there's a design, stupid." I'd watched my mother wander around, seeming to plant at random, stopping here and there to touch the soil and adjust vegetation. Maybe Haley is able to see things that I can't.

I think Mom built the path for more reasons than to teach life lessons. Walking the path gives you time to calm down, marshal your thoughts, and center yourself.

Currently, I decided that "pissed" would be my center. I marched up the path, ignoring the fleeting smells of basil, lilac, pine, rosemary, and a thousand others that met us in the night air. Pretty smells weren't going to distract me from my anger. Not tonight. Ramon carried Brooke's bag and kept his mouth shut. For the most part anyway. "Just don't go in all yelling," he said.

"I'm not stupid." Only stupid people yell at my mother. Or Ramon's, for that matter. They were very different, but they were both the kind of woman you said "yes ma'am" to and meant it.

Ramon glanced at me. "I'm just saying, you know, watch

it." We stepped onto the porch, and Ramon stopped to adjust his clothes.

I was about to knock, but the door swung open before I had the chance.

"Oh, it's you," Haley said, tilting her head a little to the side. "Who kicked your ass?" She reached out to touch the bruise on my cheek, but I batted her hand away.

Haley had gotten all the looks in the family and seemingly all the talent, too. She was one of those people who excelled at everything she attempted without actually trying to. Since she was my little sister, that made me proud. A little envious too, but mostly proud. I wished I had half her drive. I couldn't imagine Haley in my stead; a college dropout with no real plan or goal. She would have a list of options or a five-point plan the minute she left school. Some people are just annoying that way.

Her looks plain made me nervous. I trusted my sister to be smart, and she could definitely take care of herself, but I didn't trust fifteen-year-old guys. I'd been one.

She glanced down at the bag Ramon was holding, her long black ponytail shifting with the movement. "Did you bring me a present?" She reached for it, but Ramon moved his hand out of her grasp.

"Sorry to disappoint," I told her. My sister didn't really mince words. It'd gotten her into a lot of scuffles growing up. Then she developed a mean sucker punch, and the fights stopped. "Feel like letting us in anyway?" I asked.

Haley gave me a lopsided grin and stepped back, managing a mocking half bow at the same time. I ignored her and walked in.

My mom was fixing a cup of tea when I entered the kitchen. I've always been amazed at how my mom and sister could seem so alike at times and yet be so different. They were about the same height, and they shared the same freckles, but that's where the similarity ended. My mom was calm, slender, and blue-eyed with strawberry-blond hair that she usually pulled back in a braid. My sister was slender but curvy, with black hair, steely eyes, and no compunction about getting in your face. And yet, looking at them, there was no doubt they were mother and daughter. Both were confident and smart, and both fiercely loyal, but my mom will get you to do what she wants and make you think it was your idea. Not in a mean way, but very crafty.

"Hey, honey, cuppa?" she asked. My mother had never once been surprised to see me show up. I didn't know how she did it. I'd always thought it was some sort of mom superpower, or that she'd LoJacked my car. Now I wondered if there was more to it. "What happened?" She hesitated, then reached for my cheek.

I shook my head. "A fight, but that's not what I want to talk about. I'm not really here for a pleasant social call."

She turned away from me and grabbed up an extra mug anyway. "Then you must be here on an angry social call. I'll make us some hot chocolate." My mom believed in the universal healing powers of hot chocolate, especially if the wound was an emotional one.

I opened my mouth to protest, but my mom talked over me. "You want any, Ramon? I have real whipped cream." She poured the milk into a pan—enough for Ramon, I could tell. Mom knew he would say yes. After she put the milk away, she got out her ingredients, one of which was a hint of cayenne. It sounds weird, I know, but it's good.

"Yes, please," Ramon said, coming in the doorway. He kissed her on the cheek and set Brooke's bag on the table.

I scowled at him, trying to remind him that we were angry. Ramon ignored me.

"How's your mother?" My mom set up a couple of mismatched mugs with one hand while stirring the milk with the other.

"She's doing great," he said. "She wanted me to thank you for that ointment you gave her. She said it's working real well."

My mom smiled and nodded, adding the chocolate to the milk.

"Mom, c'mon, we need to talk."

She frowned at me. "What is so important that we can't be civilized?"

I crossed my arms and leaned against the pantry door with my shoulder, trying to avoid putting pressure on my back. All the riding in the car had irritated it. I nodded at Ramon. "Just open the bag."

Ramon reached for it, but when Haley entered, he hesitated. He glanced from her to me, questioning.

Part of me thought I should keep Haley out of it. She was still young, and this whole thing was dangerous. Yet keeping secrets hadn't really helped me so far, and something told me that the more Haley knew, the safer she might be. She'd probably figure it out anyway.

"Go ahead," I said. "No more family secrets."

From the corner of my eye, I could see my mom glance sharply at me, but I didn't look over. I kept my eye on the bag. Ramon reached over and flicked open the clasp.

"Oh, thank God," Brooke said. "It was starting to smell like hot yak feet in here."

I watched my mom and Haley very carefully. Haley looked startled for a second, but quickly recovered. Neither seemed as shocked or as freaked out as I had anticipated.

Haley crouched a little and looked in the bag. She smiled brightly. "Oh, hey, Brooke. Sorry about, well, you know." She drew her finger swiftly across her throat.

"Thanks." Brooke smiled at my sister. "How's school?"

"It's okay. You know, the usual. Hey, so what's it like?"

I kept an eye on my mom and watched as she paled a little. "Haley, why don't you take Ramon and Brooke into the living room? Your brother and I need to talk." Despite her obvious stress, my mom still managed to pour the hot chocolate into mugs, cover them with fresh whipped cream and a pinch of cayenne, and add a cinnamon stick to them. She was like the Jedi master of hot chocolate.

Haley shrugged and Ramon grabbed Brooke's bag. As my sister followed Ramon into the living room, a mug in each hand, she shot me a look that clearly said that I'd better fill her in later.

My mom sat down at the table and sipped her hot chocolate, leaving a full mug for me on the counter. I stayed standing. She closed her eyes. "Oh, Sam, how could you?" she whispered.

Out of all the things I thought she might say, that was not on the list. "What do you mean, how could I?" I said, voice rising. "You think I did this?"

She blinked at me. "You brought me your friend's head in a bowling bag, honey. What did you expect me to think?"

"I expect you to know I'm not a killer," I said through gritted teeth. See? I wasn't yelling.

"I didn't think that." She shifted a little in her seat. "Not really. Unless it was an accident?" She raised her eyes to mine.

"Yeah, I was slicing tomatoes and accidentally sliced off my friend's head. Mom, please. I didn't kill Brooke," I said firmly.

"Okay," she said, "but you still need to explain why you brought her back. Brooke's head is evidence. Not to mention the trauma the poor girl has gone through." She shook her head. "It would've been kinder if you'd left her . . . in peace." My mom looked very uncomfortable with the whole topic.

I closed my eyes and leaned against the pantry door. "I didn't bring her back. Somebody else did. I had nothing to do with Brooke." I turned away so all I could see was the stove. Looking at my mom was making me angry, and I needed to get past that. Douglas's time limit was *tick tick ticking* in my mind, and I didn't have time to yell and scream. If I survived, I could be angry then. I softened my voice. "But you might want to explain why you immediately assumed I had something to do with Brooke's mini resurrection." I tossed my protection bag onto the table. "And you can start by explaining what's in that bag and who bound me."

My mom's shoulders slumped like I'd taken all the air out of her. Part of me delighted in the sight, happy that I'd gotten a little revenge. A larger part of me felt like crap. No son likes to see that look on his mom's face and know he caused it. I joined her at the table, grabbing my hot chocolate on the way. "I'm sorry."

The smile my mother gave me was a little watery. "No, you're not."

"Okay, no I'm not, but . . ." I rubbed my hand over my face and tried not to shower my mother with profanity. The situation called for it, and old habits die hard. "Shit, Mom, you've certainly sunk me in some deep—"

She glared sternly at me. Her old habits died hard too, apparently.

"Um, well, let's just say you've sunk me in pretty deep." My initial anger was dampening down. I'm just not an angry person. That's not to say I wasn't still pissed on some level, or that I'd instantly forgiven my mom, but I could probably avoid any further lashing out. For now. You know, *tick tick tick*.

She took a shuddering breath. "You shouldn't apologize anyway. I've earned it." She paused, then patted my sleeve. "I've earned it and more." She stared at her hands. "I'm not sure where to begin."

"Begin at the beginning," I said, "and go on till you come to the end. Then stop."

She let out a shaky laugh. "You and the Mad Hatter."

"Actually, the king said it. And it's your fault. Shouldn't have gotten me a library card."

She ignored me. "Your father was late to the hospital."

12

SWEET CHILD O' MINE

"I was very upset, you know. Your father was the one who insisted on hospitals and ob-gyns, and then he wasn't even there. If I'd had it my way—at home, with a midwife—I wouldn't have been so infuriated by his absence." She picked at the handle of her cup.

I'd always been surprised my mom had me in a hospital. She had Haley at home and was a midwife herself on occasion. Especially if one of the girls in what Haley jokingly called Mom's coven got pregnant . . . wait a minute. I looked up at the ceiling for a minute and cursed my thick-headedness.

"You're not Wiccan, are you?"

"No, of course not." She sounded slightly surprised, like I'd accused her of being Baptist or the pope. "Whatever gave you that idea?"

I looked around our kitchen, at the dried herbs hanging from the ceiling and at the seasonal calendar on the wall. I thought of my name, and her workshop with its potions, ointments, and mortar and pestle. I rested my chin in my hand, matching the way she sat. "You know, I have no idea." The sarcasm was pretty obvious.

"Wicca is a religion, Sam."

"And you're just a witch, is that right?"

"Of course."

I rubbed my face with both hands and tried to not howl in frustration. "When you keep little supernatural details a secret and you tell your kid that you're a witch, you shouldn't be surprised when—you know what? Never mind. I don't have time for this right now. We'll get back to it at another time."

She sat up primly and nodded, like everything I said was everyday conversation. Maybe for her it was. I was realizing that there was a lot I didn't know about my mother.

"I hated hospitals, but Kevin insisted. No child of his would be born using what he called 'hippie methods.'" He reduced thousands of years of my family's traditions to a two-word phrase."

If my mom hadn't told me, then she probably hadn't told Kevin. "He didn't know what you were, did he?"

She shook her head, and I saw her tear up, even after all these years. "I hate secrets more than hospitals." She got up. "Wait here." My mom left the table before I could reply. When she came back, she held a dusty shoe box. Her hand trembled slightly as she opened it, but it was steady when it pulled out a folded piece of beige cloth, tied up with ribbon. She untied the ribbon and unfolded the cloth. She sniffed. "I made this for Kevin as a present."

My mother had cross-stitched a family tree. At the crown of the tree were my maternal grandparents. I used my finger to trace down to my mom, then me. I was a root. There were other roots left blank, which told me me that at one point my mother had been optimistic about her life with Kevin. The Hatfield side was noticeably sparse.

"Why isn't his side filled in?"

She'd been keeping it a surprise, she said, digging through Kevin's papers and making phone calls, trying to fill in the gaps. Kevin didn't talk much about his family. Even so, she was surprised when she found out he had a brother. How could Kevin not tell her? Was his brother a drug dealer? Was he dead? Curious as she was, she knew better than to ask Kevin. He'd accuse her of snooping, no matter how good her intentions. No, best to continue on her own.

She hadn't been sure the spell would work. She'd never tried it using a sibling's hair. Tia dropped a few strands of Kevin's hair into the boiling water, added the pungent herbs, and closed her eyes, breathing in the rough scent of the tracking potion. She bit her lip and concentrated, focusing on the name she'd unearthed—Nick. To her surprise, the liquid changed hue like it was supposed to, meaning it was viable. She made up a sick friend to visit, told Kevin she'd be back in a few days, then packed her bags. Tia felt a twinge of guilt at the added subterfuge but knew that, in the end, it would be worth it.

Tia had always liked Oregon. It was hard not to like someplace so green. And the land Nick lived on nestled right up against the coastline. She could smell the salt tang of the water as she walked up the drive from her car. Everything was so clean, fresh, and new, she couldn't help but smile. If only Nick had been in the same condition when he'd answered the door. He was taller than his brother and not as classically handsome. Leaner, his hair a rich dark brown to Kevin's dirty blond. His eyes were brown and weighted, like he'd already seen a lot for someone so young. He looked like a stray that had been abused and starved, and Tia immediately wanted to bundle him up and make him soup. He seemed surprised to see her, as if he hadn't seen anyone in quite a while.

"It would appear that Kevin has been keeping secrets," she said. She held out her hand. The man stared at it suspiciously until she took it back. "Tia Hatfield," she said.

Nick nodded with a small smile, like he'd expected the answer but had still hoped it would be something different. "Nick Hatfield," he said, "but I suspect you knew that." He moved back from the door, sweeping a thin, pale arm out in welcome. "*Mi casa es su casa*. Not," he said with a grimace, "that you'd want it."

Tia stepped in and could see why. The wood floor, what parts were visible through the heaps of dirty laundry, needed a good cleaning, as did the rest of the one-room cabin. The kitchen counters and table were covered in dirty dishes and empty tin cans. The stairs leading up to the loft were cluttered with discarded books, papers, and what looked like pieces of chalk. She didn't see a bathroom, so she assumed there was an outhouse somewhere on the property.

"It's, um, lovely," she said, settling into an old floral-print recliner.

Nick's laugh sounded rusty. "It's a hole," he said, "but it's free." He slumped onto a worn love seat. "The old Hatfield cabin." He looked aimlessly about the place as if he hadn't seen it in a long time. "Luckily, Kevin has about as much interest in it as he does me, so I got it without much of a fuss." His glazed eyes settled onto the dish pile. "I'd offer you something, but, again, I don't think you'd want it."

Tia pursed her lips in frustration. The situation was intolerable. She wanted to get Nick to talk, but she couldn't sit idly by and pretend the man wasn't living in filth. "Right," she said, slapping her hands on her knees and getting up. "I'm going to get some food." She looked at the cans. "Real food. While I'm gone, you're going to clean yourself up." Then she left before he could argue.

Two hours later, she had the kitchen area sorted, though not entirely clean, and a passable stew going on the small wood-burning stove. Nick perched hollow-eyed in the chair, watching her movements with fascination. She ignored him, finishing her cooking and cleaning in silence.

Nick sat in front of the Mason jar full of wildflowers Tia had placed on the table, staring at them and his meal with equal parts of wonderment and confusion. Then he dove into the stew, barely pausing to grab the spoon. He didn't speak until the bowl was empty. "You," he said, staring forlornly at the bottom of his bowl, "are wasted on my brother."

She refilled his bowl and got herself a small helping. She ripped a biscuit in half slowly before dipping it in the stew. "You don't know that," she said.

Nick shrugged and looked away. "I know my brother."

Tia instinctively reached out to touch his hand, to comfort

him. The minute she did, his head snapped up, and he looked at her. His eyes lost their focus—just for a second—before he cursed under his breath.

"Does he know that you're a witch?" he asked. His voice was kind, with no hint of reproach.

She felt her breath catch. She shook her head. "I'm going to tell him. I—"

"Don't."

"Excuse me?" Tia might have gone behind Kevin's back, but she didn't want to lie to her husband forever.

Nick grabbed both her hands in his, squeezing them gently. "Listen to me carefully . . ."

"Tia," she offered.

"Tia." He gave her hands another squeeze. "This is going to sound harsh, but you have two choices. If you want to stay with him, you're going to have to hide what you are."

Tia pulled her hands away and sank back into the chair. "I can't." She smoothed her skirt over her knees. "I don't want to live that way."

Nick leaned back into his own chair. "I don't blame you. The other option is to leave. Take that baby and go your separate ways."

Tia felt the blood leave her face. Then panic fluttered in her chest, her fear of losing Kevin tangible.

"I'm sorry. You come in here, make me dinner, and I scare you." Nick studied the stew in front of him, poking it absently with his spoon.

She straightened up, pulling herself together. "Apology accepted." They both went back to their food for a moment,

Tia turning things over in her head. She hadn't told him she was pregnant. She'd begun to show, but only a little. Most strangers didn't realize when they saw her. "How did you know?" she asked.

He blushed and looked away. "When I accidentally read you, I could tell."

She folded her hands in her lap. "I hate to be so abrupt, but it seems to be that kind of day. May I ask?"

He nodded slightly but didn't make eye contact. "I'm a necromancer."

Tia became still.

Nick turned toward her. "That scares you?"

It did scare her. Not a lot, but enough to send a small shiver up her spine. She knew necromancers were just a different kind of creature, much like herself. That it was a power given by the goddess. But somehow she could only see its attachment to the darker side of things.

"No," she said, "it doesn't scare me."

Nick laughed, surprising her. "So sweet of you to lie," he said when he recovered.

She sighed. "Fine, a little."

"Most people are scared."

"Some of you have given us a reason to be."

His eyes narrowed. "There are bad apples in every bushel."

She felt herself flush. "You're right. I'm sorry." Tia smoothed her skirt again, even though it didn't need it. A frightening thought came to her. "Nick." She felt her mouth go dry. She started again. "Nick, is it dominant? I mean, does Kevin . . ."

"You're worried about the baby?"

She didn't trust herself to speak. She nodded.

"Kevin never manifested," he said. "It's not like lycanthropy, where every kid gets it. But that doesn't mean he's not a carrier."

"So there's a chance?"

"Yes." His eyes flicked back and forth, searching her face. "Don't take it like that. Who knows? Maybe witch trumps necromancer."

She tried to smile and failed.

"If not, Tia, you might need to move."

"Will Kevin take it that poorly?"

"No. Kevin is . . . angry. If he finds out, he will most likely cut the baby out of his life and move on, but he's not dangerous. Douglas Montgomery is."

"From the Council?"

"Yes. Look, Douglas is territorial, paranoid, and strong. And his vote goes a long way." Nick's gaze landed briefly on her stomach before it returned to her eyes. "If your baby manifests . . ." Nick sighed and rubbed the crease where his shoulder met his neck. "Let's just say you don't want Douglas paying attention to him."

"Why not?"

"Best-case scenario? You leave, like me. Douglas doesn't like to share space. My talent isn't worth the effort to hunt me down, but if I'd stayed, I would have been considered an annoyance. Enough to be a decent scuffle should he take me on, but not so much that I keep him up nights. And I didn't want to hang out until I became a temptation."

"Worst-case scenario?"

"There are rumors as to how he got his power. Like I said, you don't want Douglas Montgomery taking an interest in your child's talent."

Tia raised her eyebrows. "You're suggesting that a member of the Council can steal talent?" She frowned. "Even if that is possible, the karmic debt alone . . . it's unthinkable. The Council is supposed to protect us."

"Yes, it is. But I suspect Douglas has begun to dominate the other members. Pushing them toward his desired direction."

"Unthinkable," she said again, softer.

"I know. Normal people complain about their corrupt legal system, but even the most crooked cop can't take your soul." Nick scratched his chin. "Look, I didn't mean to scare you. Like I said, worst-case scenario."

They sat silently for a minute.

"I should go," she said, standing. "Do you want me to let Kevin know where you are? Maybe he's gotten past whatever happened between you?"

"I was born," he said with resignation. He stood and stretched. "And Kevin's never gotten over it. It's best if you just let it go. Thank you for all of this." He gestured around the cabin and smiled, but it was weak, sad. She was pretty sure that smile was the one Nick used the most. "I haven't seen . . . people in a while. It was nice."

He pulled a notebook and pen from one of the piles and scribbled something. "My number," he said. "Just in case."

"You have a phone?"

"I know," he said, "it doesn't look like it. But there's one in here somewhere. If it hasn't been shut off."

She folded up the piece of paper and stuck it into her pocket.

He turned to the door.

She reached out her hand and then pulled it back. "Would you like a blessing?"

He turned back to her and blinked. Without a word he dropped to his knees and bowed his head.

She whispered the spell under her breath and lifted his chin with her hands. She kissed both of his eyelids before drawing a symbol of good fortune on his forehead.

He stood up and gave her a gentle hug. "Thank you."

"It's weak," she said. "I haven't been practicing."

"It's still more than I had before." He let go of her. She opened the door. "Nick, why don't you challenge Douglas if he's so bad?"

Nick examined the sky as if he'd find his answers there. "Because I wouldn't survive it."

She let the screen door swing shut behind her and made her way back to her car. Though she didn't look back, she knew that Nick watched her the whole time.

𝕴 stirred what was left of my hot chocolate with my cinnamon stick. Some of the melted whipped cream clung to the stick, following in its wake. I wasn't really sure how to take everything my mom was telling me. She'd known I was a necromancer and hadn't told me, which stung. She'd also never mentioned she was a witch, but I was more amazed that I hadn't figured that out than I was hurt by it. Or maybe all my other anger and frustration was eclipsing that little nugget of information. And lastly, I had an uncle who was just like me. I wasn't sure how to feel about that, either. We didn't have much in the way of extended family, so a hidden uncle was a bit of a blow. That he was another necromancer just made the secret worse. I felt like the part of me that had been cut away had just grown back. And now a madman in pressed jeans was hunting that small cluster of relatives and friends. I let go of my cinnamon stick.

"So you guys always knew that I'd be"—I stopped, searching for a word that sounded better than what I was— "different?"

My mom refilled her mug. "No. Well, yes. The odds of you being straight human were small." She smiled. "I was hoping you would take after me. But I guess most parents wish that."

I struggled with my thoughts. Would I want to be different? "How?" I shook my head. "When did you know?"

She held her mug up, breathing in the scent of the chocolate. "Right after you were born, I gave you a test."

"Like a blood test?"

She shook her head as she took a sip.

Tia brought everything she needed with her to the hospital. After giving her baby a kiss, she grabbed her overnight bag and felt inside the small inner pocket for the bag of dried herbs that she had prepared at home. Mumbling the words of the spell, she sprinkled them on her tongue. The taste was pleasant, a sweet, green flavor. She placed a few on her son's tongue. He grimaced. She smiled and took a steadying breath. Then she placed her lips against his forehead and closed her eyes.

At first she saw nothing. Perhaps she'd done the spell wrong? But then she felt it, that whisper of arctic chill. The cold died for a second, replaced by the green smells of early spring, the taste of sunshine and growing things. But the cold came back a second later.

He would take after his uncle.

Tia pulled away and opened her eyes. With a finger, she wiped the herbs out of her baby's mouth. She curled up on the small bed, her son held close in her arms, and cried. The chemical smell of the pillowcase and sheets overwhelmed her, and she cried harder, wishing for the familiar smells of home.

The nurse came in a little later and handed a clipboard to Tia. Then she took the baby. "I'll bring him right back," she said. She nodded at the clipboard. "You want to wait a bit to fill those out? See if your husband gets here?"

Tia shook her head. For all his talk about wanting a family, Kevin had been surprisingly detached from her pregnancy. It was like he was waiting to find out what the baby would be before he decided to love it, the way some dads hold a baseball mitt all through the delivery, only to throw it away when they discover their bouncing baby boy is really only the first two *B*s. He didn't say any of this to her. As far as she could tell, he had no idea that she knew. But it had hurt to watch him going through the motions.

The nurse left with the baby, and Tia started writing. An

uncharacteristic flare of anger burned through her. If he couldn't get here in time, then he'd just have to deal with the consequences. She filled out the first and last blanks easily: Samhain Hatfield. But what about the middle name? Tia had brought a list of possibilities, feeling that she really couldn't choose until after she'd met her baby. Names were important, and nothing on the list fit.

Tia took a sip of her water and turned to gaze out the window, thinking. An enormous crow sat on the window ledge and stared back at her. Crows were ambiguous creatures. Many saw them as ill omens, some as omens of change. Others thought them messengers to the gods or guides to the other world. Everyone seemed to agree that they are sacred in some way. Tia wasn't sure how to interpret the birds but felt in her heart of hearts that the goddess left evil out of most creatures. Humans being the exception, of course.

This particular crow, however, gave her a bit of the willies. It was so big, and it just kept staring. Tia focused on her paper again, but out of the corner of her eye she could see the black blob of crow waiting patiently.

The nurse brought Samhain back in, cooing at him and making faces.

"He sure is a cute one."

Tia smiled at her in thanks and took the baby back. The nurse glanced at the clipboard. "Need a few more minutes?" she asked.

"If you don't mind."

The nurse seemed to support Tia's indecision. "Name's an important thing," she said. "Nothing more disturbing than people just filling out these forms without hesitation. Child's going to carry this for the rest of his life. Some thought should go into that." She reached over and gave Samhain's nose a little tug. "You take all the time you need." She said good-bye and shut the door behind her.

Tia set the clipboard aside and held Samhain instead. A blur of black caught her eye and she looked back at the window. The crow had brought friends. Many, many friends. The ledge was cluttered with them, and they were all staring at Samhain. The birds were an omen; whether good or ill, she couldn't know. Either way, she wouldn't ignore them. Samhain was already starting out at a disadvantage, and he certainly didn't need angry omens on top of that.

She settled the baby into the crook of her left arm and completed the form. When she was finished, she read it over. It felt right. She rang for the nurse and handed the clipboard to her. If the nurse found the name strange, she didn't say anything. Either she'd gotten used to oddly named babies or she'd developed the manners to hide her dislike.

After the nurse left, Tia clambered out of the bed and headed toward the window. She held the baby up so the crows could see him. She felt a little silly standing there, pre-senting her child. But she'd rather feel silly than not show them enough respect. She straightened her spine. The crows continued to stare, unmoving. Tia stared back. "I'd like you to meet my new son, Samhain Corvus Hatfield." She said the words softly, but she knew the birds heard her because once she was done, they took flight. All except that first crow.

He let loose a loud caw, then settled down to watch over the baby well after Tia had climbed back into bed.

I looked at the family tree, very detailed except for the blanks. All those empty roots stared back at me.

"You never gave it to him?"

She traced a whorl in the grain of the table with her finger. "I took Nick's advice. I never told Kevin about what we were, but it was like he knew somehow anyway. The marriage crumbled after that."

"Because of me."

She looked up sharply and gave me a stern look. "Absolutely not. Don't ever think that, Sam. The marriage failed because there were too many secrets, too much keeping us apart."

Even though I believed her, my heart still hurt as I pushed the family tree away. I felt like I'd been scooped clean and had my insides replaced with brambles. Every time I twisted around to think, a new thorn would bite into me. So many fresh pains, and I hadn't even sorted out my old ones yet. So far being a necromancer sucked. Or maybe it was just being me.

The silence stretched between us. Questions bubbled in my head, but none I felt like asking yet. I cleared my throat. "You told me Corvus was a family name."

"It is. Family Corvidae." She tilted her head at me. "You never looked it up?"

I'd never felt the need to. I had been operating under the assumption that I was named after some long-dead great-uncle or whatever. Laziness had gotten the best of me. Laziness, and my belief that I could trust my mother. If only I'd Googled my name, I would have found picture after picture of the big, black bird. Still, there are worse things to be named after. I grimaced. "Good thing the hospital didn't have a pigeon problem."

She gave me a tiny smile and raised her mug to her lips. "If you'd seen the size of that crow," she murmured, "you'd have done the same thing."

13

I PUT A SPELL ON YOU, BECAUSE YOU'RE MINE

"So how did the whole binding thing happen?" I asked. She got up and poured what was left of the hot chocolate into my mug, whether I wanted it or not. She seemed calm, but I could tell that this was hard for her.

I wrapped my hand around the newly warmed cup and thanked her.

"You don't have to tell me this all now if you don't want to." I knew it would be better if she did. Right now, any clue as to what was going on would help. But I couldn't force any more out of her. Even though I was angry, I didn't want to hurt my mother.

"No, it's best to get it all out now."

It was late at night when Tia woke. She threw back the sheet and slid out of bed. The floor felt cold on her feet. She slid into some slippers and pulled her robe tighter around herself.

The hallway was quiet except for a few rustling noises from the nurses' station. Tia avoided the station and went straight to the nursery. She should have been surprised to see

Nick there, but she wasn't. He looked a little healthier. He'd gotten some sun, though he was still too pale, and he'd put on a few pounds.

"How'd you get in here so late?" She smiled to soften the question. "Visiting hours are long over."

He turned toward her, shoulders relaxing when he saw who it was. "You'd be surprised what talking can accomplish. One quick story about driving all the way from Portland to see my only nephew, and I'm right in." He ran a hand through his short brown hair. "I guess I'm just not very threatening."

"I'm sure it helps that the story is true."

He nodded. "That it does." He looked her over quickly. "How are you holding up?"

She walked up to the glass and looked in at little Samhain, who was sleeping, one fist shoved into his mouth.

"I'm fine," she said.

"Now, why don't I believe that?" He shoved his hands into his pockets and rocked back on his heels. "He takes after me, doesn't he?"

Tia didn't trust herself to speak. Her eyes filled, and she let the tears come. They answered for her. Nick pulled her into his arms, squeezing her against him. She should have protested. After all, she didn't know him well, but she was tired of facing this alone, and she needed that small gesture. She listened to his strong heartbeat and thought only of the rhythm of it, the warmth of another person, and closed her eyes. He smelled like trees, cloves, and sweat. It wasn't unpleasant.

Nick loosened his arms and stepped back but kept his

hands on her shoulders. He leaned down to look her in the eye. "Hey, it's not so bad."

She couldn't help it; she laughed. "Not so bad? You can't even live in the city because of what you are, and your brother has disowned you. He will do the same to his baby if he knows." Panic suddenly gripped her. "And what about Douglas? We have to do something."

He gave her shoulders a squeeze. "Calm down."

"I can't! He's in danger. What if I can't protect him?" She eyed Nick's face, searching for any solace. She found none.

"Tia, he's going to be in danger his whole life. Even if he was normal, you'd feel this way, I'm sure. Your baby's just going to have . . . more specific problems, that's all."

She pulled away from him. "How can you be so cavalier?"

He went back to looking through the window. "What do you want me to say? That your baby is doomed to live a life of fear and isolation? That there's nothing you can do?"

"Isn't that what you've done to yourself?"

Nick shrugged. "So? Doesn't mean I can't have hope for someone else." He placed a hand against the glass and smiled at her son. "I want to believe that change is still possible." He waved at Samhain with his index finger. "You know what the great thing about babies is? They are like little bundles of hope. Like the future in a blanket." He stopped waving and shoved his hands into his pockets again. "Maybe your kid will turn things around."

She made a decision. It coalesced in her chest and hardened there like an unpleasant pearl. Nick was right. Babies were hope, a blank slate for the future to write on. But he had to make it there first.

"We need to hide him," she said softly.

"How do you mean?"

"You said you could recognize me by my aura?"

"Yeah . . ."

Tia could tell he didn't like where this was going, but it was the only chance she had. "Well, if we bind his powers, his aura might be too weak to be noticed, right?"

"Tia, that's dangerous. Dangerous and hurtful. You might as well remove one of his limbs."

"But will it work?"

He crossed his arms, frowning at her. "Theoretically."

She touched his elbow. "We can undo it later, I promise. When he's old enough to protect himself."

Nick's eyes on her grew heavy. "I can't help with this, Tia. I understand your reasoning, but I can't in good conscience be part of a binding like this."

"I understand," she said stiffly. She wrapped her arms around herself and tried not to notice how lonely it made her feel. "Would you like to hold him before you go back?"

Nick straightened up. "Do you—I mean, is that okay?"

She nodded and gestured toward her room. He went in to wait for her while she fetched her baby.

Nick sat on the edge of the hospital bed awkwardly. "Are you sure I'm holding him right?" He had Samhain cradled in his arms. He'd taken off his jean jacket and pushed up the long sleeves of his shirt. Tia tried her best not to notice the fact that Kevin hadn't looked this excited holding his own son.

"For the third time, you're doing fine." She took the chair by the bed, adjusting her robe to get comfortable.

Nick gave her a schoolboy grin. "He's beautiful."

"Thank you."

He turned back toward the baby, hiding his face from her. "What did Kevin say?"

"That I gave him a hippie name. And I'm not sure if he knows," she said, answering the unasked question.

Nick sighed. "Did he even hold him?"

Tia picked at the tie of her robe. "Briefly."

Nick tugged off the small blue knit hat and smoothed Samhain's thin hair back with his hand before cradling the baby's head in his palm.

Then Nick's lips parted slightly. "Oh, wow."

"What?" Nothing seemed wrong. The baby stared myopically at his uncle, but that was normal.

Nick put the hat back on the baby's head, making sure his ears were covered. "Sorry, little guy."

"What?" she said again. "Is there something wrong?"

The baby grabbed his index finger, and the sad smile returned to Nick's face. "No, nothing's wrong. But I changed my mind. I'll help you bind him."

"Not that I'm ungrateful, but why the sudden change of heart?"

Nick waggled his finger, but Samhain held on. "I thought maybe if he was like me, he'd be okay." He pinched the end of Samhain's nose. "Why couldn't you have been like me, little guy, huh?"

Tia bit her lip. "I don't understand. I thought he was like you. Unless I did the test wrong?"

"No, you did it right. I was just hoping he'd be, you know, weak. Not worth the hassle."

"What do you mean?" She asked the question, even though she feared she knew exactly what he meant.

"I was hoping his power would feel like a trickle. But it feels like a river. A big, icy river, and he's just a baby." He kissed Samhain's knuckles. "No, you're right. He needs to be hidden, and now."

She felt the fear grip her heart, making it trip in her rib cage. "What if I moved? Took the baby with me?"

Nick shook his head. "Wouldn't do any good. Maybe you'd move into a district with a nicer Council, maybe not. Either way, Douglas Montgomery would hear. No, we bind him. We bind him now and hide him right under Douglas's nose."

He looked sadly down at the baby. "I'm sorry, little guy. I truly am."

The first pass didn't work. Tia was still tired from the birth and the stress, and it had been hard to gather what she needed while at the hospital.

"What do we do now?" she asked.

Nick pulled a safety pin out of his jeans and pricked his finger. He used the blood to draw a small symbol on the baby's forehead and another over his heart. "We try again," he whispered, and closed his eyes. Minutes passed. The temperature in the room dropped, but Nick's eyes stayed closed. When the cold snap ended, his eyes opened. He sagged forward and kissed his nephew on the head. Tia couldn't see Nick's face, but she could hear thick sadness in his voice as he whispered to the baby. She had to lean close to hear that he was begging Samhain for forgiveness over and over.

THE DEVIL INSIDE

$\mathbb{J}$ stared at the swirling wood grain of the table while my mom cleared away the mugs.

"So Uncle Nick bound me, and that was it?"

She ran water for the dishes. I got up and grabbed the dishcloth so I could dry. "His seemed to work where mine failed," she said. "But even that one wasn't perfect." She washed the inside of her mug and set it in the sink.

"What do you mean?"

"You kept . . . leaking," she said.

"Leaking? I'm not a container, Mom."

She added a dish to the mug. "In some ways, all humans are. We contain organs, blood, emotions, power. In your case, even with the extra barriers, a little kept slipping out." She washed another dish and handed it to me. "Do you remember when I made you that pouch?"

"Vaguely. I'd been having nightmares."

"No, honey, you were seeing spirits. Even with the binding in place, the ghosts were finding you, seeking you out. You were terrified. Your uncle wasn't around, so I did the only thing I could."

I dried the dish and placed it on its shelf.

"I made your medicine bag. Most medicine bags protect. Yours was more like a shield. As long as it was on, you wouldn't show up on the spectral radar, so to speak." She handed me a dripping cereal bowl.

I dried for a moment, letting everything soak in. I could see why my mom had done what she'd done, that it all stemmed from good intentions and a need to protect me. That didn't stop me from being angry. She had just postponed the inevitable. I still had to deal with Douglas, only now I had zero knowledge and even less training.

I put away the cereal bowl. "Why didn't you tell me all of this? Especially after Kevin left. Unless Dad made you hide, too?"

Glancing over, I could see her mouth crook up a little. "Haden never made me feel ashamed of anything. He found out what I was and didn't care. In fact, he seemed delighted." She handed me the last dish and pulled the plug out of the sink. The water gurgled out noisily. "We argued about telling you. He said you needed to know. But I was still so afraid. I think part of me hoped you would never have to find out. I felt guilty about what I'd done, how weak I'd been." She turned on the faucet, rinsing the last bubbles from her hands. "Sam, what's going on? I mean, why is this coming up now?"

"Let's just say some things have surfaced." I didn't think I was keeping secrets as payback, but with so much to sort through, I had no desire to get into the whole mess with her. Besides, she'd worry.

"Sam." She stopped when she saw the expression on my face. "Fine. I guess you don't owe me an explanation."

"Later."

"Fair enough." She flicked the excess water from her fingers. "Promise you'll take care of Brooke?"

"Already planning on it." I handed her my towel so she could dry her hands. In the switch-off, my fingers met hers, and I felt my vision open up like it had in the park. Now that Douglas had shown me how to do it, I couldn't help myself. It was automatic. The difference was that in the park I'd had to close my eyes and work at it. But this time it was much easier. Maybe because I was touching her, or maybe because her emotions were running high. Either way, it felt like a wildly spinning Rolodex in my head. It whirled madly before clicking abruptly to a spot. I could see a lot on that page. I knew that my mom was a witch, and I could really understand what that meant. By the greens and browns, my guess was that her specialty was earth magic. I could feel emotions spilling over me: relief that she was telling, worry about my reaction, love for me and Haley, sadness.

Most surprising was her fear. I blinked at her and pulled back my hand. "You're afraid of me."

"Sam—"

"No, don't. I saw it. You're afraid of what I am, what I can do." The idea that my mother, the one person who was supposed to love me without reservation, could fear me made my stomach clench up. I stepped away. "Please," I said. "Please don't argue."

She dried her hands and hung the towel on the stove. "A

powerful necromancer can raise the dead. He can read the soul, like you just did. I've heard some of them can even push on a person's spirit and influence the people around them to do things. If that isn't a power to be feared, Samhain, I'm not sure what is."

I shook my head. What she said sounded scary, but I couldn't agree with her completely. "I was born with it. You always said nothing is born bad. How can the gift be given to me by nature and be inherently evil? Seeing the dead is freaky, but—"

"I didn't mean just the dead. I said soul." I saw her eyes fill with pity as she looked at me. "Some races are more secretive than others. Whether they do this out of fear of persecution or the desire to keep family knowledge, I don't know. We all have our secrets, I suppose. A few are unknown because of their general rarity." She sighed. "Necromancers manage to fall into all of those categories at once: secretive, afraid of persecution, and rare. From what I saw Nick do, and from what I've seen you do, my guess is that necromancers have more than a connection with the dead. You have some connection to the human spirit as well. Otherwise how could Nick read me when he met me? How could you read me just now?" She reached out, paused, then straightened my hair like she used to do when I was little. "I'm not afraid of you, Sam. But the power inside of you, I believe, is worthy of my fear."

Her cold dread washed over me and I understood. She feared the power would corrupt me, that it would get out of hand. Perhaps someone else would use me for evil. For the first time, I was afraid of the thing inside me.

I stared at the floor, feeling the lead weight of everything settle in my chest. "Do you know you hesitate before you touch me?" She started to say something, but I cut her off. "Since I was a kid. I thought it was the way you were, but then you had Haley." My throat felt thick, but I kept going. "There was never any hesitation with Haley. I always thought it was because I reminded you of Kevin. That I took after the Hatfield side of things too much." I laughed, and it soundly sickly, hurt. "I've never been so wrong about something and so right at the same time."

"Sam."

"No," I said. I kept my gaze on the floor. My insides twisted, and my eyes burned. I didn't want to hear anything else right then, even if it was an apology.

My mom tried to hug me, and I wanted to let her. I wanted to put my arms around her and hug her until my arms ached. Mom and Haley were the only family I had, and when you have so little, you want to hold on tight. I hated fighting with either of them. But the minute Mom touched me, I felt her fear and anxiety roll over me again. It was like a sucker punch to the gut. I jerked back, choking on the nausea and pain. Mom reached for me again. "No," I managed. "Don't. Oh, God, don't." I slid to the floor and tried to contain myself. I wanted to curl into a ball. I managed, at least, to stay sitting.

My mom stood anxiously above me, unsure what to do. "I can't help being afraid of it," she said.

"Just go away," I whispered. "Leave me alone." I'd never wanted so badly to be by myself. There were lots of times growing up when I felt isolated. Being the lone boy in a family can do that. Your biological dad showing no interest in you only shores up the feelings that are already there. So I'd felt alone a lot. But this was the first time I really wanted it.

"I'm sorry," she said.

"I know." I'd felt that too. I swallowed hard. My body shook. I curled up and rested my head on my knees.

She pulled back from me. "Are you still angry with me?"

"Just go!" I screamed it, but even that felt like restraint. I wanted to howl until I was nothing but sound.

She hovered over me for a moment. When she left, I heard her whisper, "I didn't mean it to go this way." Then I heard the kitchen door shut.

I stayed shaking, tucked in a ball, until Ramon came in and told me it was time to go. He pulled me up off the floor, and I made him wait outside while I splashed cold water on my face. I caught my reflection in the darkened window as I dried off. It didn't look like me. But then again, I wasn't really sure who I was anymore, was I? I rested my head against the cool glass and tried to get back to normal. I wanted to laugh. How the hell could I even come close to normal now?

I threw the towel on the counter and left.

Ramon said my good-byes for me. He came out of the house, his arms half full of snacks, some new jeans my mom had picked up for me, and a container full of herbal teas and things to help me sleep. Guilt was riding high. I told Ramon that I didn't think I had much time to sleep, but he pointed out that

I'd be next to useless if I didn't rest. The body is much like a battery, he said, and if I didn't recharge it, I might as well just hand myself over to Douglas now.

I took the tea.

Haley walked us out to my station wagon. "So, you see the dead and stuff, huh? How very *Sixth Sense* of you."

I snorted at her. "Thanks. At least you're not running screaming into the hills."

She shrugged. "I think it's pretty cool."

I unloaded all my stuff into the back of the car. "Yeah, I guess. Surprised?"

Haley made a scoffing noise. "That you'd get the super-weird gift and be a freak even among freaks? Not really. I've always known you were a weirdo."

"Again, thanks," I said. I shut the back of the car and walked up to the front.

"No problem."

"I suppose you want me to stand out here on the street and tell you all about me and Mom's conversation?"

"Psh, no," she said. "I listened at the door."

"That's my girl."

Ramon waved good-bye to Haley and got in the car, placing Brooke's head gingerly into the seat next to him.

Haley leaned against the side of my Subaru and crossed her arms, giving me a look I knew all too well. I was about to get a mini lecture. "You have to forgive her."

"You don't know what you're talking about, so shove it." I zipped up my sweatshirt. "I've sort of had a lot thrown at me lately."

"So?" she said. "That doesn't give you an excuse to forget everything else she's done for us." Haley got up in my face and stared me right in the eye. I'm always surprised by the amount of force and confidence there is in her eyes. I shouldn't be. It's been there since she was a baby.

"You don't understand."

"She screwed up," Haley said, jabbing me in the chest. "Deal with it. If anyone should get a free pass, it's Mom."

"This isn't like forgetting to sign me up for Little League or not letting me go to the school dance, Haley. We're in the real world now, and whether she meant it or not, Mom's mistake is probably going to get me killed. I'm sure you want me to be all forgiveness and light, but I can't."

She glared at me.

I wanted to hug my sister and try to get rid of that glare, but after the incident with Mom, I was afraid to touch her. What would I find? "Look, Haley, I know you're smart. You'd probably whup my ass on *Jeopardy!*, but this particular situation is new to all of us, so shut it."

Haley leaned back against the car and recrossed her arms. I mimicked her stance until she caved. She threw her arms around me and hugged me tight. Gingerly I hugged her back, resting my cheek against her forehead. I almost cried when I didn't find any fear in Haley. She might be worried about me and Mom making up, but she wasn't going to run away from me screaming.

"Just don't take too long," she mumbled into my sweatshirt. "Things start to fester when you do that."

"I'll do what I can." I squeezed her once and let her go.

Haley wiped her tears away with the heel of her hand. "See you later, jerk."

"Okay, snot-face."

She smiled a little and walked back toward the house.

"Hey, Haley?"

She stopped and half turned.

"Wanna go visit Dad next week?" I never said his grave. I didn't need to. "I have a few days off," I said softly. I knew Haley would rather go with me. Mom's grief seemed different from ours somehow. Probably due to being a wife instead of a child.

Haley nodded but kept her eyes on the ground. "I'll get some flowers out of Mom's greenhouse."

"Thanks."

"Welcome." She sniffed. When she looked up, her eyes were sad. She shooed me with her hand. "Now get."

"I love you, too."

She waved without looking back and went inside.

15

I HEAR YOU KNOCKIN',
BUT YOU CAN'T COME IN

By the time we got back to my apartment, I was ready for bed. I was emotionally wiped out, confused, and still angry, and my back felt like fresh hell. I probably should have shown it to my mom, but she would have freaked, and I'd had enough for the evening. That didn't change the fact that I needed a new dressing.

I pulled the first aid kit out of the drawer slowly, hissing as the muscles in my back burned from the twisting motion.

"Should have had your mom look at that," Ramon clucked at me sarcastically.

"Thank you. Help me, okay?"

He didn't press the issue but tore off the old bandage with little in the way of care.

"You hate me, don't you?"

Ramon didn't answer. He prodded a few sore areas, ignoring my complaints.

"It doesn't look infected," he said. "Not yet. And it does seem to be healing." Ramon picked up the antiseptic and poured some onto a gauze pad. He wiped the long scratches carefully with the gauze before smoothing on the ointment. "If it starts to get nasty, I'm calling your mom."

"Duly noted," I said through clenched teeth. I'm not a super-wuss, but my whole back felt like one solid bruise, and though the ointment soothed the scratches, it still hurt.

Ramon finished with the salve and taped on some new padding. "We're going to need to get some more supplies soon, too."

I grunted in reply and grabbed a mug out of my cabinet. I heated water in a pan on my stove. I popped some ibuprofen and stared at the water while it heated up. I know, watched pot, blah-blah-blah, but staring at the water was soothing. I'd learned a lot since yesterday, but I felt no closer to under-standing what I needed to do. I'd run out of ideas. I couldn't join up with Douglas. Besides being morally sketchy, it was suicide. Running wasn't much of an option. He'd either find me and kill me, kill someone else if he couldn't find me, or do some as yet undiscovered, horrible third option. And even though I knew now why my powers were bound, that didn't change the fact that they were bound.

When the water finally boiled, I made some of my mom's sleep-aid tea. I handed Ramon his mug and sat carefully in the chair, leaning into the armrest to try and stay off my back. Ramon had turned on the news for Brooke. Sandwiched between a story on the Seahawks and the weather was a thirty-second blurb on Brooke.

"Hey, that's my house!" she chirped.

The newscaster didn't reveal her name or picture, stating only that a young girl had been found murdered early that day. Thankfully, they didn't have any shots of Brooke's family, and they hadn't managed to interview them, either. I hoped her parents were getting a little time to mourn.

After it was over, we flipped to the other stations to see what they had to say. Nobody else had information, either. It appeared as though the cops were managing to keep a tight lid on it. The newscasters must have been foaming at the mouth. Seattle wasn't a mecca for violent crime, and once they saw a prom photo of Brooke, all the TV producers in the state would be kicking up their heels in evil glee.

Ramon and I sat in awkward silence as the news cycled into a story on the salmon population. I think he wanted to comfort Brooke, too, but wasn't any more sure of what to say than I was.

"I'm sorry, Brooke," I said. It was lame, but I needed to break the silence.

"I know," she said with a sniff. "Do you think we can change it now?"

The newscaster was babbling about some missing businessman with the unfortunate name Dave Davidson when Ramon changed it to the cooking channel.

Once my tea was done, I said good night to both of them and went to my room. In my drained state, I wouldn't be much help to Brooke, so I left her to Ramon. He had better people skills anyway. I pulled my medicine bag out of my pocket and put it back on. It seemed kind of futile now, but it made me feel better.

Even though I was tired, I couldn't fall asleep right away. I felt like I'd gone through half of my vinyl already, but the music wasn't helping. My brain wouldn't turn off, and I kept wondering how Brooke's family was doing, when the cops were going to question us, and if anyone at the zoo had noticed that one of the pandas wasn't eating his bamboo. It also took a while to find a comfortable spot where my back wasn't bugging me. Later, I had a nightmare. I was trying to get to the ferry docks downtown while being chased by man-eating pandas. Some dreams don't need Freud to figure them out. My next step was going to involve a ferryboat and something I dreaded worse than a panda with a thirst for blood.

$\mathfrak{F}$or the second day in a row, I was startled out of a deep sleep by knocking. I jerked, rolled, and fell out of bed, trying not to scream while I considered how long it was going to take my back to heal if I kept waking up this way.

Ramon came running into my room. "Sammy, get off the floor. Now."

"Can you just tell them we don't need Jesus, Girl Scout cookies, or whatever the Mormons worship, and let me lie here in peace?"

"It's the cops."

An image of Brooke's head on my armchair flashed in my mind. "Don't just stand there, help me up," I said, holding a hand out to him. With Ramon's help, I quickly pulled on a sweatshirt. "Ramon, Brooke's head—closet."

Ramon went running out of the room. He came back in, whispering explanations into Brooke's bowling bag as he hid her in my closet.

I thought that might be the first place they would look,

but for all I knew, the number one place for finding severed heads was under the kitchen sink. I was kind of new at this. Either way, we had no time for anything else.

Detective Dunaway was polite, asking if now was an okay time to talk. He looked large in my doorway, but as I ushered him in, I was surprised to see that he was about average size.

"Can I get you something?" I asked as I waved him to the easy chair.

"If you have coffee made," he said, "I wouldn't say no."

Ramon went to fetch some while I sat across from the detective. He looked to be entering his forties in better shape than I ever hoped to be in. His brown hair was short and his jawline clean; he didn't have to rely on a mustache to intimidate like some cops did. He wasn't big, and he wasn't showy, but I wouldn't want to get in a fight with him. I sat on the couch facing him, hoping my hands weren't shaking, as Ramon handed me a cup of coffee. The detective took a cup as well and was he-man enough to drink it black. I can do without sugar, but I need cream at least, damn it.

The detective took a sip and thanked Ramon.

"You boys know why I'm here?" Dunaway, apparently, was not a word waster. He set down his cup without taking his eyes off of us.

Out of habit, my eyes flicked over toward my skateboard, the usual reason for me to talk to the cops. He followed my gaze, and the hard look on his face lessened.

"Nope," he said. Then he sighed and leaned back into the recliner, facing both Ramon and me on the couch. "Either of you call in to work today? Stop by? Talk to a coworker?"

Ramon shook his head.

"No," I said. "We don't really go by work unless we have to, and the only people we ever really see outside of work are Frank and Brooke. Not that we saw them this morning," I added hastily.

"When's the last time you saw Brooke?"

A few minutes ago, in my closet, but of course I couldn't say that. I pretended to think on it, but I already knew the last time I could say I saw Brooke. "Tuesday night at work," I said, rubbing the back of my neck with my hand. "We saw her to her car, then took off. Not really a place I like to hang around."

He pulled his notebook out and started writing in it.

"Why?" Ramon asked. "Is she in trouble?"

"You could say that," Dunaway said, eyes still on his notebook. "What happened after she left?"

"We went home," I said.

Dunaway flipped through a few of his pages. "Does it usually take you half an hour to get home? I talked with a"—he stopped and checked his notebook—"Mrs. Winalski, who says you came home thirty or so minutes after the time I have you clocking out." He let go of the paper and stared at us. I felt my hands go cold against the coffee mug. "She also said you looked a little roughed up." His eyes went to my face.

Of course she did. Mrs. W would want to protect me, so she'd tell the nice policemen all about how beat-up young Sam looked. It alibied me, sure, but I don't think she realized that telling them I look roughed up didn't really help. For all they knew, Brooke could have done this.

"You don't live that far," the detective prompted.

"We had a little problem after work," I said.

"A problem with Brooke?"

"No," I said, "with some cracked-out dude. He thought I was someone else, and when I tried to correct him, he got a little rough. Brooke was already gone."

Dunaway tapped his pen against his pad. "He do that to your face?"

The bruises on my face had yellowed a bit, and the scratches were healing. Luckily, they were more like abrasions than anything else, otherwise Dunaway might mistake them for defensive wounds. Brooke had strong nails.

"Yeah," I said.

"That all he did?"

I hesitated but figured, what the hell? For all I knew, they'd picked up the fight on a mall surveillance camera or something. No, better to be honest now than to be caught in a lie right out of the gate. Especially since I was already hiding something. I showed Dunaway my back.

He didn't comment or ask if I was okay. I guess as a cop he'd seen worse. "You pick a fight with Freddy Krueger?"

I shook my head and pulled my shirt back down. "I don't know what he used."

Dunaway leaned forward in his chair, squinting. "You mind if I take some pictures before I leave?"

"Suit yourself."

"Can I ask why you didn't come to us?"

I shrugged, a movement I instantly regretted as the pain

shot up my back. "With what?" I said. "Some crazy guy jumped us? We didn't see much," I lied. "And, no offense, but most of our exposure to cops involves problems with us and our skateboards." I kept myself from shrugging again. "We just wanted to go home and lock the door, you know?"

To my surprise, it looked as if he did. "Have you seen this guy since then?"

"No."

"Why?" Ramon asked. "This guy hurt Brooke or something?"

Dunaway suddenly let out a breath that made him look five years older. "Your friend Brooke was murdered sometime late Tuesday night." He looked at both of us. "We haven't released her name or anything to the press yet, for the family's sake among other things, so I want you boys to keep this to yourselves, okay?"

I closed my eyes and leaned into the couch, ignoring my back. Of course, Brooke's death wasn't a shock—her head was in my closet—but now that I no longer had to pretend I didn't know about the murder, it felt like a release of sorts. My muscles let the secret go, and in its place I found a bone-aching sadness. Brooke was gone. Not completely, sure, but a talking head couldn't fill the girl-sized hole in my life. I would never see her at work. I would never see her change and grow into the devastating woman we all knew she'd be. Ramon and I had both held a secret pride knowing that someday Brooke would be unleashed on the bar scene and that she'd take no prisoners. Our own little heartbreaker. And now that would never happen. Anger burned away the sadness.

"I'm sorry," Dunaway said, and I could tell from his tone that he meant it.

I nodded with my eyes closed. Weren't we all?

Dunaway took a few snapshots of my face and back before he left. He also took what was left of Ramon's skateboard. He told us he'd probably talk to us again. Ramon, Frank, and I held the dubious honor of being the last people to see Brooke intact. They had a few shots of her on a camera at a self-checkout line in a grocery store after that, but that was it. Luckily, Mrs. W could vouch for us coming home. Though we could have followed her home, I think Dunaway suspected that the killer had been waiting for Brooke at her house. I suspected he was right.

Ramon went to class, promising Brooke he'd be back with Frank to keep her company. I called work. Going into Plumpy's was the last thing I wanted to do right now. Brooke's death made a pretty good excuse. I didn't have time to waste at work anyway. Douglas's deadline ticked away in my brain, and I was nowhere near a solution. But I did have a destination.

16

PAPA WAS A ROLLING STONE

J had to drive onto the ferry because I didn't want to muck about with the bus system, if there was one, on Bainbridge Island. Bainbridge is a fancy place, chock-full of natural beauty and the kind of people who can afford natural beauty. The kind of people who don't really need bus systems. Besides, I wanted to get in and out and on the next ferry as soon as possible.

I hadn't talked to my biological father since the divorce, which was fine by me. He got a new wife, and I assumed new kids, and started over without so much as a backward wave in my direction. My mom doesn't bad-mouth him; she thought I should form my own ideas about people, so she'd stuck to the old "if you don't have anything nice to say, don't say anything at all" routine. The fact that she never had anything to say about him told me that Kevin Hatfield was not a nice man.

I was angry at the abandonment, but it was an old anger—the calcified pain from when my life was broken. An emotional bone spur. I tried not to think about it. The fact was, all I had were hazy memories of him. I was young when they split up. All I really remembered was that Mom cried a lot. Then we got an apartment, just the two of us, which she hated because she hated all apartments. But in the apartment she cried less. Then she met Haden, and she was happy. I was one of the few kids I knew growing up who didn't want their biological parents to get back together. My childhood could run up a lot of psychologist bills. The whole no-daddy thing is supposed to be a big deal, I guess. I didn't see it that way. Haden was around to teach me to play catch, to ride a bike, all that Norman Rockwell kind of crap. As far as I was concerned, Haden was my father. Kevin Hatfield could take a long walk off a short pier, preferably into a teeming mass of hungry, rabid sharks, if sharks can get rabies.

In my entire life, I hadn't once entertained the thought of going out to visit Kevin Hatfield. I hadn't needed to. Today, I needed to. I had to find my uncle Nick, and my biological father's house was the way to start. No one knew where he was. My mom didn't have his address or his phone number anymore, and she couldn't remember where the cabin was. She'd only been there once, and that was around twenty years ago. He might not even live there now. But I had to track him down. It was the only way I could think of to get my binding removed.

The ferry ride to Bainbridge is a short one, only about thirty minutes. I spent the time above deck watching the ferry cut through the water. People milled about, and every once in a while, the door would swing open and I'd hear the guy with the acoustic guitar playing for change. Then the door would swing closed again and all I'd hear was the waves as the ferry cut through the water.

I've lived here my whole life, and I've never gotten sick of looking at Puget Sound or the Cascades. The day so far was clear and chilly as I leaned against the metal railings. It probably wouldn't stay clear for long. Washington weather is fickle, spring weather doubly so. By the time the captain gave the five-minute docking warning, I was frosty on the outside and leaden on the inside. I really, really did not want to get off the ferry.

Arriving on Bainbridge Island is the opposite of arriving in Seattle. When you got in your car and waited to unload off the ferry in Seattle, you saw the Space Needle, cars, and a mound of urban construction. Once you exit the ferry terminal on Bainbridge, however, it's mostly trees. Pine as far as the eye can see. Well, pines, firework and coffee stands, and eventually a casino. You drive through the Port Madison Indian Reservation when you leave the island. I couldn't help but smile as I went past the casino. I didn't really get gambling, since I'd never had money to throw away, but as I passed through all the beautiful countryside that I'm sure once belonged to the tribe, I sort of hoped they would rob the white man blind. Perhaps not politically correct, but the feeling was there all the same.

I found the Hatfield residence fairly easily. Online directories are wonderful things. Kevin's house was huge. The stained wood seemed to grow right out of the forest around it. Whatever he did for a living, it paid well.

I knocked before I could talk myself out of it. The woman who greeted me must have been his wife, though she was younger than I expected. Elaine Hatfield couldn't have been a day over thirty. Hell, I could date her. And if the thought of dating my theoretical stepmother hadn't made me want to vomit in the bushes, I'd do it, too, just out of spite. Elaine was hot in a soccer-mom kind of way: curly blond hair, body-hugging sweater, and a smile so white it could only have come from the dentist. Mrs. W was right. I needed to get out more if I was finding Kevin's wife attractive. I usually don't have a thing for trophy wives.

"Can I help you?"

I had to clear my throat to get the reply out. "Is Mr. Hatfield home?"

"Not at the moment," she said. She left it sounding like he'd be back in five. Probably in case I was a psycho.

"Actually, you would probably be the one to talk to," I said, like the idea had just occurred to me. Elaine had been the one I wanted to see. I thought it might be easier to talk my way in if she was the one who answered the door.

She arched a shaped brow at me.

"I'm looking for Nick Hatfield," I said. "His brother."

Her blue eyes widened, and she invited me in.

The inside of the house was like the outside: tasteful, natural, expensive. Elaine offered me coffee, but I politely declined. I hoped I wouldn't be there that long. The homemade cookies were harder to say no to. I'm not made of stone. I nibbled on a chocolate chip cookie while I sat across from her in what she called the breakfast nook and what I would have called a dining room. This house could have eaten my apartment and still been hungry.

"Have you ever met him?" I asked. This would be a lot easier if she knew Kevin had a brother.

"I've only seen him once," she said, "a little after my first daughter was born." She smiled briefly. "My husband doesn't talk about his family much. I probably wouldn't have even known if he hadn't shown up." She absently rearranged the cookies. "Haven't seen him since."

The conversation was making her uncomfortable. Or maybe she had a thing about rearranging cookies. "Something about him bothered you?"

"No." She said it quickly.

I put my hand on hers. "You can tell me," I said. "It's okay." I meant to reassure her. Instead I felt a small part of myself give her a little nudge. I don't know how else to explain it. I didn't mean to do it. Didn't even know that I could. Her eyes softened slightly, and her body posture eased.

"Nick didn't bother me. He seemed sweet. Sad, but sweet. He just wanted to hold Lilly. But then Kevin came back. Said he forgot his keys. Kevin saw Nick and just . . . freaked."

I squeezed her hand in encouragement. "Then what happened?"

"They got into it. Kevin yelled something about Nick not touching her. Not"—she frowned, struggling for the word—"ruining her. Nick said she might need help."

"Help?"

"A guide. She might be dangerous, he said."

"And that upset you."

"She was so little. How could she be dangerous?" She shook her head. "Kevin swung at him and Nick left. Haven't seen him since." Light came in from the window, making her blond hair glow. "I asked Kevin what he meant, but he told me to ignore it. Said Nick was . . . had issues."

"I see." She had wanted to say *crazy* but was too polite. That would be an easy answer for Kevin. Don't listen to my brother, he's crazy. It would explain the distance between them and his attitude. Very neat and tidy. "You weren't worried? About your daughter?"

"I was at first." She glanced at the cookies, silently offering me another. I took it. So sue me, they were good. She smiled as I bit into it, happy that I was enjoying something she made. That one look did it. I genuinely liked Elaine. Which made me feel terrible about questioning her, but she was all I had.

"But Kevin told me not to worry. Said my great genes would win." She looked sheepish as she said it. "Corny, I know, but it made me feel better."

I smiled in agreement, but the inside of me felt sick. Kevin hadn't left this family. Elaine was normal. Plain ol' vanilla human. On some level, he must have known Mom was different and he blamed her. And he thought this time, without my mom to screw up the mix, he would dodge the hereditary bullet. As I watched Elaine light up while talking about her family, I realized I was rooting for her. Kevin could suck it.

"Kevin doesn't like to talk about the past," she said. "I probably wouldn't have even known he was married before if I hadn't stumbled across the divorce paperwork."

"And that didn't bother you?"

"We all have our secrets," she said. She seemed to snap back into herself. She smiled again, this time pulling out all the watts. "Like you came for any of this. I swear, staying home with the kids is great, but sometimes you get so starved for adult conversation you'll talk telemarketers to death." She picked up a cookie, breaking it into pieces but not actually eating any of it. "Is Nick your father?"

The question startled me, and it must have showed.

"You look like him here." She ran a finger along her jaw. "And around the eyes." She took my silence as a yes and kept going. "That's why I let you in. You look like them, and I thought it might be nice to actually meet some of Kevin's family." She crumbled another chunk of cookie. "When I asked my husband about his first marriage, he said they didn't fit." She pulled out a single chocolate chip and stared at it. "Irreconcilable differences," she said. "A nice phrase with so many meanings. From the way he acted, it sounded like, well—" She blushed. "I'm sorry, I didn't mean any offense."

"None taken." Things began to click in my head. Little puzzle pieces slipping neatly into place. I'd had conversations like this before, where halfway through you realize that you're each talking about different things. As we continued talking, an unsavory idea formed: Kevin had led her to believe that Nick was my father. Elaine thought I was the irreconcilable difference. After all, there are few things more irreconcilable than your wife having your brother's baby. And since my mom never sought child support, that must have just strengthened the lie. It would probably never occur to Elaine that my mom wouldn't want to take Kevin's money. Somewhere deep down, Kevin Hatfield had known that I was marked, so he pawned me off on his brother. For a life of sought-after normalcy, it was a small price, I guess. Not one most of us would pay, but whatever.

I would just as happily tell everyone that Nick was my dad, but I didn't like how the lie made my mom look. Mom takes oaths very seriously, and that's all marriage really is, a promise. Elaine probably wouldn't have believed me, though. Why would she? I was a stranger. I chewed on the last bit of cookie mechanically, not really tasting it.

"May I use your bathroom?"

The information I'd gotten was useful and all, but not the real reason I'd come here. I shut the bathroom door carefully and began quickly—and quietly—to search for anything that might have some hair of Kevin's on it. It appeared to be a guest bathroom, though, and showed little signs of actual usage. I flushed the toilet and ran some water before I left, disappointed. Now what? I didn't think I could do the nudge thing again, not on purpose, and I couldn't actually ask for a lock of Kevin's hair. And without it, my mom wouldn't have any way of tracking Nick. My hair was too far down the genetic line to be useful.

I thanked Elaine for the cookies and made parting small talk as I started to make my exit.

"I'm sorry that I couldn't be of more help," she said. "I can't believe he just abandoned you. It's unforgivable. He seemed so nice when I met him."

"I'm sure he had his reasons," I said. Sometimes it's easier to just let people think what they want to. I shook her hand and let her escort me to the door. "Thank you for talking with me."

Elaine straightened a family photo in the entryway. "You're welcome. It was nice." She smiled a little. "I've never really gotten to talk to anyone related to my husband before. I guess I didn't realize how much I'd wanted to until you showed up."

As we walked toward the foyer, the weight on my shoulders lifted and I relaxed, knowing that I'd soon be back on the ferry and that I wouldn't have to come back here again.

If only I'd left thirty seconds earlier.

A small girl, probably around five years old, padded down a set of stairs and into the entryway. Her brown hair was braided, as sober as her expression.

"Quiet time isn't over yet," Elaine said.

"I know," the little girl said. "Sara wet her bed."

"Oh." Elaine turned to me. "Excuse me." She ran up the stairs, leaving me with the kid.

The girl was small, with dainty features like Elaine. Unlike her mother, she gave off a natural strength and authority. The look on her face right now reminded me a lot of Haley, when Haley was in a rare completely serious mood.

She stuck out her tiny hand. "I'm Lilly," she said.

"Sam." I took her hand to shake it and stopped. Her palm felt cold in my hand, icy, just like Douglas's had felt. Probably just like mine felt to her. Lilly's eyes popped wide like saucers.

"You're like me," she said.

I could've lied, told her I didn't know what she was talking about, but it seemed both distasteful and useless. Kevin Hatfield was creating his own little version of hell by having children and surrounding himself with the exact kind of people he despised. And though part of me howled with laughter, the rest of me was kicking it and telling it to shut up. Poor Lilly was as screwed by heredity as I was. Would Kevin continue to ignore it? Or would he get her the training she needed?

"Yes," I said, "I am like you."

She frowned at me, an adult expression of concern that seemed at home on her face. "Something's wrong with your inside, did you know that?"

"Yeah."

"You should get that fixed," she said.

"I'm working on it."

"That's good," she said. "Would you like to meet them?" She continued to hold my hand in a cold death grip, completely unconcerned about the whole thing.

"Meet who?"

Lilly pulled me into another room, some sort of play area covered in pastels.

Yanking me over to a small easel, Lilly began to flip pages and tell me about her friends. She introduced me to them like they were important, like she didn't get to talk about them much. I took a good look at Lilly's friends. Something seemed off. When Haley was little, she'd drawn our pets, our family, and her friends, which were usually kids we knew or stuffed animals. Lilly's friends all looked like adults.

I tapped the paper on one in particular. "Lilly, who is this?"

"I don't know his name," she said. "I can't understand him. He talks different."

She flipped the page and showed me another picture. "He's nice, though. He talks to me with his hands. I think he used to live here, but his house was like this." She pointed to a sketch on her paper. Lilly had drawn a pretty decent rendition of a longhouse.

I didn't know what kind of curriculum kindergartners got, but I was pretty sure most of them didn't know what a longhouse was. Lilly must have known what it looked like because her friend was a long-dead Native American, which would explain why she couldn't understand him.

"Lilly, can your mom see your friends?"

"No," she said, "and she doesn't like to talk about them. It makes her uncomfortable. She calls them imaginary." Lilly looked me in the eye, her expression pleading. "The Shadow People aren't imaginary, are they?"

I could tell her they were. Maybe then she'd live a normal life. A normal life where she constantly questioned herself and thought she was crazy. A life where she not only had to hide from everyone around her but also from her own mind, her own senses. Then I thought about what Nick had said to Kevin, about how Lilly needed a guide, how it might be dangerous. Teaching her to hide from what she was wouldn't keep her out of danger. I was proof of that.

"No, they aren't imaginary."

She grinned. Something told me Lilly didn't do that very often.

"Lilly, this may sound weird, but do you think you could get something for me?" She nodded. "I need some of your daddy's hair, like from one of his hairbrushes or something. Do you think you could do that?"

"Why?"

"I can't tell you that right now."

"Will it hurt Daddy?"

"No," I said, "it won't."

She pouted, thinking. "Promise?"

"I promise," I said, making a little X over my heart. "But we need to keep this between us, okay?"

Elaine came back down with another little girl a few minutes later. She thanked me for staying and entertaining Lilly. I told her Lilly was a great kid, the expected response, but that didn't make it not true.

Elaine introduced me to Sara, who was only three. Her hair was a pale blond, pulled up in pigtails, one of which was pressed into her mother's chest as Sara rested her head there. Although shy, Sara's expression was more open than Lilly's. I wondered how long it would stay that way. I didn't shake Sara's hand. I didn't need to. From the way Lilly hovered over her baby sister, I knew I'd get the same response, and I didn't want to scare Sara by touching her. Instead, I said good-bye and thanked Elaine for her time. Before I left, though, I wrote down my number on a scrap of paper and handed it to her.

"Just in case," I said, looking at Lilly as I handed the paper to Elaine.

Elaine was too polite to ask "in case of what?" to my face, but I could tell she was thinking it. She looked worried, and I wondered if on some level she knew her daughter needed help that she couldn't give. Even if she never needed it, or if her mother threw that scrap of paper away, I hoped it would help for Lilly to know that I was there. That someone believed her, and would listen to her, even if he hadn't been dead for a hundred years. It was all I could do.

I patted the small travel hairbrush in my pocket and headed for my car.

17

STRANGERS IN THE NIGHT

"That," Ramon said, "might be about the funniest thing I've ever heard." He shoved a spoonful of Chunky Monkey ice cream into his mouth, chewing as he talked. He offered the next bite to Brooke, who was positioned on the edge of the kitchen table so Frank could brush out her hair.

"Which part of the story amuses you?" I asked. "The bastard-child-of-my-uncle part, or the two-new-half-sisters part?"

"Usually, I'd say both," he said, "but I don't like anything that besmirches Tia's honor."

"Big word," I said.

"I know," he said, digging his spoon around the bottom of the container. "I've been reading. You should try it."

Frank paused, midbrush. "You don't think your uncle is really your—"

"No," we all said in unison.

Frank huffed and went back to brushing. "Okay, just asking. How am I supposed to know if I don't ask?"

"It's okay," I said.

"I mean, your mom didn't tell you about the whole

necromancy thing, and that makes your uncle being your dad seem kind of small. You know, in comparison." He stopped brushing and contemplated Brooke's long blond hair. "What do you want me to do with this, Brooke?"

"Can you braid it?" she asked.

"I could try," Frank said, "but I can't make any guarantees. So it might be messy."

"Here," Ramon said, handing him the ice cream and taking the brush. "French sound good?"

"You can French braid?" Brooke blinked in surprise.

"*Chica*, I got three little sisters that I used to help get ready for school. Three *picky* little sisters. I could do this in my sleep." He stuck the end of the brush in his mouth and started to separate her hair into manageable pieces. "Any real man can French braid a girl's hair," he said around the handle.

Brooke closed her eyes in contentment. I hadn't really thought of it, but this was probably the first prolonged contact she'd had since she'd died. People, even reanimated ones, need to be touched.

Frank finished the last bite of the ice cream and threw the carton away.

"You owe me a thing of Chunky Monkey," Ramon said.

"But I only had, like, two bites."

"You know the rules."

"C'mon." Frank looked at me in appeal.

"Them's the breaks, Frank."

"You guys are assholes," he said, digging into his pockets and pulling out a wad of dollar bills. He threw them onto the table. "There's your blood money. Happy?"

"Very," Ramon said.

Brooke sniggered. "It's blood monkey money."

I relaxed into my chair and sang softly, "Blood monkey, that funky monkey."

Even Frank laughed at that. We all did, maybe more than we normally would have. We needed a little tension breaker. For me, anything that distracted me from the tiny countdown clock in my head was a good thing.

My phone rang, so I quietly excused myself. I didn't want to interrupt their good time. It was nice to hear Brooke laugh.

Once I'd shut my bedroom door, I answered it.

"Hi," the woman said. "I'm looking for Sam LaCroix?"

"May I ask who's speaking?"

"No, but you can tell him I was given his name by Maya LaRouche."

I guess I wasn't the only one playing the cautious game. "This is Sam," I said.

I could hear a little laughter in her voice when she said, "And this is June Walker. My sister, Maya, tells me you've been having a bit of trouble up there."

"You could say that."

"Want to tell me what's going on, exactly?" Her voice was soothing, but I felt like I couldn't give in to it just yet.

"What do you know about Douglas?" I asked.

"I assume you mean Douglas Montgomery." She paused. "I know enough to have moved away from my sister and my only niece. That me leaving them on their own was better than me being up there."

I mulled this over for a second. I didn't know this woman, and I didn't know her sister much, either, but Maya LaRouche had been the only person so far who'd really helped me. I needed someone in my corner.

"Are you . . ." I pulled at a loose thread on my blanket. "I mean, do you know anything about necromancy?"

June laughed. Not really the reaction I'd been expecting. She had a nice laugh, big and full, like she wasn't afraid of anything.

"Honey, down here they'd call me a voodoo queen. I can raise the dead so fast, your head might spin clean off."

I relaxed. She hadn't called me crazy and hung up, and for some reason I believed her when she said she was like me.

"You better start at the beginning," she said, "because if I have to keep asking questions and dragging answers out of you, we'll be here all night."

I held the phone in one hand, lying flat on my stomach to take some of the pressure off my injured back. Then I told her everything. It came in a torrent, leaving me empty and shaken at the end. June had to ask me to slow down a couple of times, and she asked me a few questions along the way, but mostly she listened and let me get it all out.

The line went quiet when I was done. I heard a click and an intake of breath, the sound of a cigarette catching flame. "Sounds like you have a bit of a knack for trouble, Sam."

"Not usually," I said.

No booming laugh this time, just a dry chuckle. "I believe in this, like in many things, you're just a late bloomer."

"So, can you help me?"

"I think you know that's not an easy answer," she said. I heard resignation in her voice. She'd given up fighting when she'd moved, and she knew it. That didn't mean she liked her choice.

"I'm hobbled here," I said. "Basically, I am the proverbial lamb to the slaughter. What I need is a little help."

"What you need is a teacher, and I can't see a way to do that. I can't come up there. You can't come down here."

"Why not?"

"Because," she said, "you're in another territory. I'd have to petition your Council if I was doing anything besides passing through. Which would alert Douglas and get us both in trouble. Same thing for down here. Besides, this area isn't good for new necromancers right now." She paused. "Too much new death. Katrina caused a lot of anguish, you know? You come down here right now, you don't know how to shield?" She snorted. "I'd have to carry you around on a stretcher, probably. Too much for you. Shut you down." June sighed. "And no one there will risk helping you."

"That keeps coming up," I said.

"And a necromancer without guidance is dangerous."

"Dangerous?"

"Depending on the level of power, yes."

"Please," I begged, "I just need a little help. Anything."

The line was silent for a long time.

"I'll see what I can do, Sam. In the meantime, I'll send what I can your way."

She hung up without a good-bye. I placed the phone on my nightstand then let my body go limp, enjoying the comfort of my bed. What did she mean, she'd send what she could my way? A week ago, I'd have assumed she meant good wishes, but now I wasn't so sure.

Ramon and Brooke were watching the news when I came out. Frank sat at my kitchen table hunched over his laptop. I peeked over his shoulder. He was Googling "necromancy."

I clapped him on the shoulder. "Thanks, Frank."

He flushed. "I'm not really doing anything," he said.

"You're trying." I grabbed my hoodie and slipped into it, zipping it up and stuffing my black knit watch cap in my back pocket. Best to be prepared for any weather.

"Where you going?" Ramon asked.

"I need to get out for a bit," I said. "Clear my head."

Frank looked up nervously from his laptop. "Are you sure you should go out by yourself?"

Ramon nodded. "Want company?"

"No," I said. "You guys hold down the fort. If they really want me, they can just as easily kill me in this apartment as they can out there." I pointed at the screen, which was showing more news reports on Brooke's death. "Let me know what they've found, okay?"

"You got it, Sammy."

I grabbed my skateboard and left.

I bumped into Mrs. W on my way out.

"Face is healing nicely, my boy." She opened her purse and pawed around for her keys. "What's on the schedule for tonight? A little skullduggery, I hope."

I pushed the elevator button and laughed.

"I don't even know what that means, Mrs. W."

She tsked as she pulled out her keys. "What are they teaching the youth these days?"

"Not enough, I guess." The door dinged and opened. "Catch you later."

"Do me a favor, will you?"

I put my board in front of the door, keeping the elevator open. "Sure."

"Meet a nice girl and do some not-so-nice things, okay?"

I let the door go. "Sure thing, Mrs. W."

"Make me proud, son. That's all I ask."

The streets were bone-dry, which made me happy. Too much water and all you have is a warped board and wet feet. I can't skate like Ramon can. I can't do any fancy tricks, but getting from point A to point B was enough tonight. There was nowhere I needed to be, not right then. Things I needed to do, sure, but what? In so many ways I literally had no direction. But with my board, I didn't need one. The only goal was to clear my head. I walked out of the parking lot, let go of my board, and chose the hill to my left, more for its smoothness than the direction. I pushed off with my foot and headed down.

I passed a few house parties as I went. Some were the mixed-CD type; a few were the band-in-the-basement type. I favored the latter. Music is a big thing in Seattle. We don't get heavy rain, but we get it frequently, and there are some springs when you don't see dry skies for weeks. You add the wet to the chill in the air, and it can get kind of unpleasant. So we have lots of indoor activities like watching a local band in somebody's basement. Between the hot press of bodies and a couple of smuggled beers, it's easy to forget about the weather. Tonight I wasn't very tempted to crash, so I skated past even the promising-looking shindigs.

Though spring had arrived on the calendar, the air still held a little of winter's bite. I felt the cold nip at my face, and I focused on it. I heard the sound of cars and people. I watched as neon and lights slid by. I kept my focus on the city at night and let everything else go. I didn't want to think about anything. I just wanted to feel.

The last thing I felt was someone grabbing me as I slowed down at a crosswalk.

18

DON'T ROCK THE BOAT, BABY

The van door hissed as it slid open. Douglas watched, keeping his face a bland mask as Michael tossed Sam unceremoniously into the back seat. Michael jumped in and shut the door behind himself, plunging the interior into darkness. Douglas shifted the van into gear and pulled away from the curb.

"Please remember to buckle him in. It wouldn't do to kidnap him only to let him die in a random mishap," he said. He heard a grunt from Michael and a thump as Michael pushed the boy's inert body to the floor. "Or," Douglas said, his voice flat, "I guess you could just do that."

"I've done this before, you know."

Douglas glanced into the rearview mirror, catching Michael's unpleasant grin in the flash of the passing lights.

"You really don't like him, do you?"

Michael frowned. "Do you?"

Douglas changed lanes, keeping a wide berth between the van and the car in front of them. "My personal feelings toward people are not a component that I consider." His gaze returned to the rearview mirror again. "It's one of the many reasons I'm able to stomach you as an employee."

Douglas winced inwardly at the bark of laughter from the back seat. He supposed it was a good thing that Michael assumed he'd been making a joke. Douglas didn't doubt his superiority over Michael even for a second; still, a fight with him would be inconvenient. Douglas found werewolves to be a mercurial bunch on the whole, as close to their beastly sides as they were. These days they either developed an iron control early or learned to enjoy rural life. Having Michael in Seattle was a bit like letting a cat loose in an aviary. It wasn't so much a question of if he was going to cause trouble, but when. He was collateral damage waiting to happen.

Still, he was a tool Douglas could use. Douglas wouldn't have gotten this far if he'd been afraid of risk or potentially dangerous allies. In fact, one could say he'd become quite adept at using both.

Back at the house, Douglas peeked under Sam's eyelids, checking the pupils for reaction to light. Sam would be in pain, but Douglas didn't see any permanent damage. He supervised as Michael put Sam into the cage with the girl, making sure to keep an eye on Bridin. She had a knack for pushing all of Michael's buttons, and Douglas had an interest in keeping everyone intact. For now, at least.

Michael tossed Sam at Bridin's feet. The boy only warranted a cursory glance from her.

"What's this?" she asked.

"Lunch," Michael said.

Bridin made a face that was only slightly more mature than sticking out her tongue. Michael gave her the finger.

"Children, please," Douglas chided.

The girl looked away. "I'm just saying, you guys keep up at this rate, I'm going to run out of sitting room." She gazed sideways at Sam. "Who is he, anyway?"

"Nobody," Michael said. "That's who."

Douglas thought she'd have to be dead to not catch the tone that plainly said Michael didn't care for Sam. Which, of course, would make the boy irresistible to Bridin. He'd just made her acquaintance, but Douglas felt he understood her much more than his lackey did. He watched as she eased over to Sam and smoothed his sandy hair.

"I don't know," she said as she pushed back a tuft of hair, revealing a little of Sam's face. "He's kind of cute." She gently touched a few of the healing scuffs on Sam's cheek.

Michael made a sound of revulsion. "You wouldn't." He looked Bridin up and down, his lip curling in disgust. "Then again, maybe you would. What's a half-breed care, huh? Blood's already watered down, why not thin it again?"

Bridin continued to run her hand through Sam's hair in speculation. "You know, Michael, it's that kind of thinking that's made your family so inbred."

Douglas reached out and put a hand on Michael's chest, stopping him before he moved forward. Michael didn't advance, but he continued to glare at Bridin. "My family," he spat, "is not inbred."

Bridin ran a finger down Sam's jawline, stopping at the point of his chin. "Oh, really?" she said. "Because before my father took over, there weren't that many wolves in your pack. And you didn't keep the best of records. You'd probably rut your own sister if she were in heat."

Douglas grabbed the back of Michael's neck, exerting his will, letting it flow over Michael's anger. He felt the rage getting ready to push the were closer to a change. Douglas smoothed it down, relaxing Michael as best he could.

"That is quite enough," Douglas said. Bridin had a good mask. She didn't let much emotion get through that she didn't choose to show. Still, Douglas could tell that she'd noticed his control over Michael. A control he shouldn't have. Only a pack leader should've been able to do what he'd just done, necromancer or not. He left before she could ask any more questions, but he could feel her eyes on him as he walked up the stairs. He watched her out of the corner of his eye as he pushed Michael through the door. Douglas could almost hear the whirring of her thoughts as she dealt with all the information she'd just gathered. He'd underestimated her and would have to be a little more careful in her presence. Finally, a bit of a challenge. The door clicked as he secured the locks.

Douglas opened the window in his study so he could feel the breeze coming off Lake Washington. The gentle *pat pat* of James's feet heralded his entrance. Douglas was wise enough to know that he only heard the sound because James wanted him to.

"How is it coming with the girl?"

"Slowly," Douglas answered, "but I feel like I'm getting some good data." He rested his hands on the windowpane and let his shoulders relax. James was the only one he could relax in front of. The only one he trusted. It was a rare feeling and he valued it.

"And the boy?"

"In the cage. Easier to keep an eye on him that way." Douglas leaned back from the window. "The lazy part of me's hoping she'll eat him. Save me the hassle of training him."

"I'm sure Michael would volunteer."

"Yes, I'm sure he would." They both stared out the window, James examining the grounds, Douglas looking at the stars. Not many were visible.

"Perhaps," James said, "it is time for a trip to one of your vacation homes. The San Juans, I think. Maybe take a sail around a few of the harbors."

Douglas grew still. "What makes you suggest the island house?"

"You seem unsettled."

"I feel unsettled."

James leapt up onto the windowsill, his tail flicking back and forth in a lazy fashion. "But why? Little hiccups have happened, but nothing you can't handle. Everything seems to be flowing in your direction." ·

Douglas made a noncommittal sound in his throat. "Does it?"

James's tail flicked again, this time more sharply. "The police have found the body of the girl, but they have nothing in the way of evidence."

Douglas scoffed. "The police." He had never found them to be particularly threatening, and he currently saw no reason to believe otherwise. "What could the police possibly do?"

James ignored his question and continued. "You have the boy. You have the *tánaiste*. And with your experiments, well."

He turned his head from the view of the water to Douglas, his eyes like liquid mercury in the moonlight. "Your power base grows every minute."

"You think I'm being foolish."

"It isn't my place."

"When has that ever made you hold your tongue?"

James arched his back and resettled. The twitching of his tail would have told Douglas how agitated he was if his tone hadn't already told him the same thing.

"You're worried?" Douglas said.

"Yes."

"You never worry," Douglas said, amused despite himself.

James kept his face pointed toward the lake. "You're a powerful man, Douglas. But I'm afraid."

"That I'll lose?" Douglas smiled. "Don't fret, my friend; I've made arrangements for your upkeep."

"I don't think you'll lose."

"That I'll win, then?"

"I don't think you've thought the repercussions through. Right now, the other Councils are happy to let you puppet-master your people. But if you topple them completely, if you establish rule, they cannot let that go. It will be war, Douglas." He paused, his tail flicking. "And if they find the cage, or your notebooks"—he turned and blinked those mercury eyes at him—"war will be the least of your worries."

Those precious little notebooks, all lined up neatly on their shelves, would hang him. They both knew that. What he'd done to get the information would be deemed criminal. But the information itself? That carefully hidden knowledge plied from the flesh? Well, they'd find ways to destroy him several times over. Most creatures didn't like their sense of safety violated, their weak spots known outside their own tribe. And Douglas was coming damned close to knowing it all.

"Yes, I know." Douglas breathed in the scent of lake and pine all around him. A boat cut through the water, causing a wake that broke upon the shore. "If I stopped every time I did something risky, I wouldn't have gotten this far."

"If you're so sure," James asked, "then why do you feel unsettled?"

Douglas tapped the windowpane with his thumb. "Maybe I'm beginning to feel my age. Or perhaps I'm in need of a change of scenery."

"Perhaps." James jumped down from the windowsill. His tail swished as he sauntered toward the door. "I'm going to make a sweep of the perimeter," he said from the hallway. "There's a strange smell on the breeze."

Douglas listened to him leave. The water swirled around the rocks until the wake died down. He settled into an old overstuffed chair in the corner of his study. Hands on the rich fabric, head back, eyes closed, Douglas listened to the night around him. All he needed was a little rest.

19

KICK-START MY HEART

$\mathbb{J}$ didn't want to open my eyes. My week so far had consisted of some pretty nasty awakenings. Between the cold floor against my cheek and the pain in my head, I didn't think this one was going to go any better.

I opened my eyes only to shut them immediately when it felt like the light was slicing into the back of my skull. This awakening sucked already.

I hate it when I'm right.

"Try putting your shirt over your head, and then open your eyes," a female voice said. It was a nice voice, young and light. I held on to the slim chance that I might have been captured by friendly but possessive nymphets. I needed something to hope for, and that scenario seemed as likely as anything else pleasant.

I moved to pull my T-shirt over my head.

"Slowly," she warned.

Slowing down helped, and soon the shirt blocked some of the light. I enjoyed the relative darkness, trying to ignore that the inside of my mouth felt thick and cottony. If it's not one thing, it's another.

"Now open," she said. "Once your eyes have adjusted to that, you can start to remove the shirt."

"Thanks," I said.

I lay there quietly for a moment and tried not to think how stupid I probably looked with my Batman T-shirt cocooning my head. I needed to figure out where I was and what was going on.

"You smell odd."

"Again, thanks," I said. "I'll change deodorants."

"No," she said, "the deodorant is fine. It's something else." I could hear the soft whoosh of breath as she breathed in and out. "Spices," she said. I could hear the amusement in her voice. "Did they season you for me, or do you work in a kitchen?"

I didn't want to think about the fact that she could smell me, or that she'd just joked about eating me. At least I hoped she meant it as a joke. Maybe she was some new beastie that ate human flesh. The way things had been going, I really couldn't be sure, so I just answered her question and saved my thoughts for later. "Both are fairly possible, but it's probably the ointment on my back. Where am I?"

"A basement."

"I don't suppose it's the kind of basement with a freezer full of Popsicles and an old Nintendo or something?"

"No such luck. There's a freezer, but knowing the owner, it's probably not full of Popsicles," she said. "How are you feeling?"

"Horrible. But compared to a few minutes ago, better."

"Try lifting up the shirt."

I tugged the shirt off. Too fast. The light stabbed, and I rolled to the side out of instinct, which was a mistake. I passed out before I could throw up. Lucky me.

𝕿his time, when I woke up, my head was on something soft. Which was good because someone was smacking me.

"Sorry," she said, "but I think you have a concussion. You need to stay conscious."

I grunted and looked toward the voice. I saw a single dusky thigh, the color some fair-skinned people turn when they get sun. The lucky few who don't burn. I came from fair stock, so I was well versed in sunburns. I tilted my head and looked up. Slim shoulders and a pointed chin.

And naked. No way. I had to still be unconscious.

"This is my favorite dream."

She laughed one of those laughs that made you feel lighter inside, like you had to join in. Infectious.

I felt my face burn. "I'm not asleep, am I?"

She shook her head, still laughing. Her auburn hair swayed with the movement. She'd cut it short in the back, letting it hang down to her chin in the front. Strips of green and purple intertwined with the red, a curtain she hid behind when she stopped shaking her head. But I didn't get the idea that she was shy or nervous. It made me think of a lion or some other predator peeking out through the bushes. Looking at her hazel eyes made me feel like a bunny.

I needed to say something cool. If I could be smooth now, then the stupid thing I'd just said might be forgotten. "Come here often?" Ouch. Maybe I could blame that on the head injury?

"Every third Wednesday. How do you feel?" Her mouth still twitched from laughing.

"Like an idiot."

"I meant physically."

"Like an abused idiot. My head hurts, and I think the cuts on my back reopened." I pushed my tongue out of my mouth a few times. "And my mouth tastes like a grease trap."

Her brow knitted into a tiny V. The effect was devastating. "Grease trap?"

"It's the thing that catches the fat, grease, and whatever's left over on a grill. I always thought it smelled like someone puked in a bag full of pennies. All rotting fat and blood."

She nodded slightly, thankfully not grossed out at all by what I'd just said. "I see." She leaned back, palms on the floor, ankles crossed, completely unconcerned with her nakedness. She caught me staring, and I quickly looked away. And smacked my forehead right into a metal bar.

She laughed again. "I'm glad you're here. You're very entertaining."

"Thanks," I said, rubbing my forehead. "I aim to please."

"Sorry," she said. "It's not nice to laugh at a stranger's pain."

"So, if they're not strangers, they're fair game in your eyes?"

"Of course. What good are friends if you can't be honest with them? Pain can be funny. Those home video shows on TV make millions off it." She leaned forward and dusted off her hands. "Sit up. I'll look at your back."

I sat up and ignored my head. I held my back straight and waited. Her fingers were soft as they traced the long lines of scab from my shoulder down. She poked when she needed to without apologizing. When she paused, I thought she was done examining, but then she slid her fingers down the marks again, each tip caressing a separate wound at the same time.

"Who did this?" she asked.

"I don't know."

"I'm sorry." Her voice held true regret. I'd just met her, but she was taking responsibility for my injury. Strange.

"You didn't do it." I stared at my socks, wondering why they'd taken my shoes. Were shoes somehow dangerous?

"No, but I know what did." She moved in front of me, pulling my chin up with her hand. I noticed how tiny her hands were, and how her lips, when closed, made a firm little bow. "What's your name?" she asked.

"Sam," I whispered. Between my dry mouth and her soft hands, that was the best I could do.

"Brid," she said, and she smiled. It sounded like "Bridge" when she said it.

"Is that short for Bridget?" My brain clacked like a broken hamster wheel, and my breaths were too short and shallow.

"Bridin," she said, "*tánaiste* of the Blackthorn pack."

"I wish I knew what that meant." Then I let my eyes relax so I could take in the real Bridin. She glowed like copper wire wrapped around an emerald core. It was like her soul was on *fire*.

I swallowed, hard.

"It means that I am next in line to rule my pack," she said, very matter-of-fact.

"Pack of what?" Few good things come in packs, except inanimate objects, like a pack of cards or a six-pack. Brid was far from inanimate.

"Wolves and hounds, mostly," she said with a shrug, like it was no big deal. She could just as easily have been talking about the weather.

I stared, and I breathed, and it was all too much. "Look, Bridin, you're probably the prettiest girl I've ever seen, and between that and what you've just said, I think I've blown a circuit."

She arched an eyebrow.

"On top of all that, you're naked. And while I'm going to hate myself for this later, could you put on some clothes? At least just for a little while, so I can think. Then you can go right back to being naked. All the time. With my full blessing."

She gestured around with her free hand. "And what, exactly, would you like me to wear?"

I looked around. Bookshelves crammed with old books, walls of solid concrete, a single expensive-looking wooden chair in the middle of the floor, torture devices, beakers, and a table with restraints that I didn't like the look of. The floor itself held an unpleasant stain that I didn't care to think about. The whole thing had the effect of a tidy little dungeon. And the cage we were in was totally empty. "Ah, hell."

Bridin ended up in my T-shirt and boxers. It seemed only fair since she couldn't get into my pants. I mean, fit into my pants. Whatever. When I'd taken off my shirt, I noticed something else was missing. I checked my pockets just in case, but there was no sign of my pouch. I hoped they hadn't thrown it away.

"So," she said, pushing her bangs behind her ear, "I've shown you mine, now you show me yours."

"If you wanted to see that, you should have peeked when I was undressing, like any normal person."

"Of course I peeked. That's not what I meant."

"You lost me, then."

She placed her hand over her heart. "Were-hound." She gestured toward me.

I almost said "human." But then I realized that wasn't the right answer. Not anymore. My hand felt cold as I mimicked her movement and placed it over my heart. "Necromancer. Or at least that's what people keep telling me. I don't seem very good at it." I stretched and looked around the room, pretending I wasn't trying to get a better look at her legs. She had cute knees. Can people have cute knees? "I feel kind of stupid saying necromancer."

"Why is that?"

"I don't know. I can't tell if I'm just not used to it, or if the term seems too Dungeons & Dragons." I slid my hands along the bars. I don't know what I was looking for. I'm not MacGyver. I can't break out of a steel cage using bubblegum and a shoelace. Not that I had any bubblegum in the first place. Or a shoelace. A cold spot under my palm made me jerk my hand back. It felt like dry ice.

Brid sprawled on the floor. "And what else would you call yourself? Ghost master? Dead-wrangler? Mayor of Zombieville?"

"You might have a point. Dead-wrangler isn't half bad, though, and I've always wanted to be the mayor of something. Or maybe el Presidente for life." I held my hand over the cold spot and closed my eyes. I saw a symbol traced on the back of my eyelids, like when I used to draw something with a sparkler over and over and then shut my eyes. I didn't recognize the symbols. I hadn't expected to. "Do you know what these symbols mean?" I asked.

"No, but I get their intention."

I opened my eyes; nothing could be gained by keeping them shut. I pulled my hand back into the cage and rubbed it on my jeans. When Brid didn't follow up, I asked her what she meant.

"This cage is built out of iron. Cold iron inhibits any fey, and I'm half fey." At my blank look, Brid grimaced. "Fairy," she explained.

"Then why not just say, 'I'm half fairy'?"

"Because," Brid said dryly, "most Americans picture Tinker Bell when they hear fairy. I am not Tinker Bell." She leveled a glare at me until I held up my hands in surrender. Once I had gotten her point, she continued.

"The cold iron wouldn't be a problem, but the runes are done in silver. Weres have an allergy to silver."

I thought back to what all those werewolf movies I'd seen said about silver bullets. "So this cage is killing you?"

One of Brid's eyebrows quirked up in an amused fashion. "Do I look like I'm dying?"

"Touché."

"The iron means no magic, and it gives me a bit of a rash. The silver runes keep me from bending the iron." She made a face. "And healing."

I tapped my finger between two bars, back and forth. "So they've been planning on getting you for some time." At least long enough to build a cage. I had no idea how long that took. "I'm probably just here as an afterthought."

"I don't know about that. Your back doesn't look like an afterthought."

"I don't follow."

"Some kind of were did your back. I can't tell you which one exactly, though I can make an educated guess. I do know it wasn't one of my pack."

"You're sure?"

"Positive. And there aren't a lot of rogues in this area. Besides, you must be worth something; otherwise, they'd have killed you already."

"Anyone ever told you that you're a very reassuring and positive person?" I asked.

"Nope."

"I can see why." I paced along the corner of the cage. "Earlier you said 'were-hound.' What does that mean exactly?" I paused midstep. "If you don't mind. I have no idea if that's a rude thing to ask, but I'm tired of not knowing anything."

"That's okay," she said. "I'm a directness kind of gal. It means that I'm a hybrid."

Since we had nothing but time, Brid filled me in. Her mother was a werewolf, her father some sort of fey hound. I still wasn't sure exactly what that meant, but I didn't want to interrupt her story with a ton of questions. I guess her pack had been falling apart. The marriage between her parents had been somewhat politically motivated. Her father had the numbers to strengthen the pack. Most had been grateful. Others, Brid informed me, were less than thrilled about the idea of blending the two different races.

"Racist werewolves. Great."

"They saw it as a weakening of the species," she said.

"But, biologically speaking, the more varied a gene pool, the stronger the species. Hybrids are usually genetically superior."

"I knew I'd like you."

I quit my pacing and sat down across from her. "So, what happened?"

She hugged her legs to her chest, resting her chin on her knees. "Eventually the pack came around." She grinned. "Babies tend to have that effect, and my mom had plenty of babies."

"How many?"

"I have four older brothers."

"Wow. And you're next in line?"

"Turns out I'm the most qualified candidate," she said. "Not that I mind, but it's a lot, you know?" Brid sighed. "Anyway, once the pack saw that the children were healthy, more of the wolves married hounds. Especially when they saw the benefits as the children grew older."

I raised an eyebrow at her and waited.

"When a werewolf changes, it takes some time. How much depends on the wolf. It also hurts. A lot. For fey hounds, however, the change is instantaneous; it's also painless. There's other stuff too. I have a partial immunity to silver, for example. But, of course, there are drawbacks." She patted the floor with one hand. "I can't change in here. A wolf would be able to, no problem. It was those kinds of things that the remaining hold-outs latched on to." She tightened her grip on her knees. As I watched, her hazel eyes became dim and shadowed. "My grandfather's brother, the one who wanted to be next in line, was one of them."

I didn't like to see that shadow. If I'd known her longer, I'd have put my arm around her or something. Brid continued to give me a brief sketch of what had happened, mostly involving her great-uncle's failed coup.

"It cost us," she said. "A few died, including my mother."

"I'm sorry."

Brid hid behind her bangs. "It's okay."

"What happened to the rebels?"

"Their leader was executed. The rest . . ." She pushed her bangs back, tired of hiding. "My father took pity. I think he'd decided enough wolves had died. He shipped them off to other packs if he thought they were able to be rehabilitated. Some of the children were allowed to stay if they chose."

"You look like you don't agree."

When Brid looked at me, the shadow had passed from her eyes. A small fire burned there instead. "I understand his choice. Some of it I even agree with. But since one of them now has us in a cage, I can't say I'd do it again."

"What, you'd kill 'em all?" I phrased it like a joke, but Brid didn't answer it as one.

"I would do what it took to keep my pack safe. If that meant killing, then yes, I would."

Brid went quiet. I guessed she was all talked out. Which was okay. I'd already heard enough to know that, while I was probably safe right now, I didn't want to endanger Brid's people. She'd meant it when she said she'd kill them all. Duty wasn't a word I heard much, but I could tell that was the way Brid looked at it. And with a bit of a shock, I realized that I understood how she felt. Douglas had come into my world, endangered my family and my friends, and taken someone close to me. Would I be able to kill him if it meant ensuring the safety of my people? The answer came a little too quickly. Yes. Absolutely. The fact that I didn't have to even think about it scared me. Maybe my mom was right. Maybe something truly dark and scary lived inside me.

I glanced at Brid. I tried to imagine her turning into something large and bloodthirsty. Did she morph into the Hollywood wolfman or something else? I tried to picture her out of control, killing everyone in her way. If I didn't look at her eyes, it was hard. She appeared so tiny, so gentle. But when she looked at me, I could see the monster surface. I could see steel and determination. Did I look the same way—a wrapping of scrawny muscle and innocence covering an inner core of evil and violence? I didn't want to think about it anymore. Unfortunately, I was in the wrong venue for that. Stuck in this cage, all I could do was think.

I nudged Brid with my toe. "Maybe you should go back to being naked."

𝕭rid did not go back to being naked, not because of modesty, but because the temperature in the basement plummeted. God, if there was one, hated me.

No one came down to give us blankets. As it got colder, I pulled Brid into my arms without asking. Her body went stiff at first. When I didn't try anything, she relaxed into me. I don't know how long she'd been stuck in the cage, but from the way she nestled into my chest, I think it had been a few days. Despite our talk earlier, I still didn't know that much about her kind. If they were anything like real wolves, though, she had to feel starved for affection. Wolves are pack animals, and Brid was probably missing her companions. I put my chin on her head and rubbed her back absently with one hand. She shook a little, like she was either trying not to cry or trying to keep me from noticing. I ignored it. Brid just needed to let go for a moment. I'd had a bad couple of days. I could feel everything roiling inside of me, and I'd have given a lot to have someone tell me it was okay and to just let it all out. Brid's week had probably been worse. She got to fall apart first.

We must have fallen asleep like that, despite the dim basement light. All I know is that I woke up when locks clicked open on the basement door. Brid woke up too and pulled back from me enough so that she could look up.

Douglas walked down the wooden steps, heels making hollow sounds on the boards.

"Sam," he said, "how pleasant to see you again." He got a curious look on his face as he took in Brid and me. "And I see you've met Ms. Blackthorn."

"I thought you were going to give me a week."

"Yes, well, I didn't like the look of things. You did not, to paraphrase Dylan Thomas, seem like you were going to go gentle into that good night."

I stared at him blankly.

He sighed theatrically as he rolled up his shirtsleeves, slowly and methodically, keeping an even cuff. "Let me see if I can find terminology more suited to your understanding. I didn't think you were going to come over to the dark side. And don't insult me by lying that you were."

"You've been keeping an eye on me."

"Of course not. I'm much too busy for that. I've had others keeping an eye on you for me." His expression became rueful. "You are not the axis around which my world turns, Sam."

"You sure know how to make a guy feel important."

"I try." He eyed me quizzically. "You didn't think I'd let you go with no leash at all?" He pulled the chair near the cage back against the wall, baring the stained floor.

"I guess I did."

Douglas got out a few odds and ends from a box I hadn't seen on the bookshelf. He selected a large piece of chalk and stood before me like a professor. Just another day in the office for Douglas.

"I'll give you a choice," he said. "Become my apprentice."

"Or?"

He shrugged. "Or I can kill you now."

I mulled over that little offer of joy. "What if it doesn't work? What if you try to teach me and I fail?"

"I can just as easily kill you then. I believe in motivating my pupils."

"Right. Apprenticing sounds fantastic."

Douglas walked forward, muttering, reaching for the cage door. He gave Brid a meaningful stare. "No funny business now."

Brid held up her hands. I got up and walked toward the door. Douglas mumbled something else, and I felt the power of the cage shut off. It was sort of like the low-level whine of a stereo when it isn't playing—you never realize until you shut it off that it'd been emitting a small amount of noise the whole time.

Douglas handed me the chalk. "Draw a circle."

I looked around for a second before Douglas pointed downward.

Ah.

While I did my best to go back to my kindergarten days and produce a decent circle, Douglas lectured.

"There are many levels of necromancy, ranging from weak to strong. At the weak end, the end you are probably at, you are more of an antenna. You draw whatever spirit or ghost is around toward you, but you have no real control. The next level up has that as well as the ability to broadcast. Essentially, you can communicate with various smaller entities as well as summon. After that, things become interesting."

He reached into a box and threw a rag at me. "Not big enough," he said. "Do it again."

I wiped away most of the circle and started over. Brid came to the edge of the cage to watch.

"A necromancer with sufficient power and proper training can act as an ambassador between this world and the next. He can summon larger creatures, read living human souls, and potentially influence them. He can raise the dead." Douglas examined my circle and nodded grudgingly. "Passable."

"You mean like that panda?" I stood up and stretched. I stepped outside my circle and examined it. Not bad. My kindergarten teacher would have been so proud.

"Yes," he said, "like the panda. However, depending on your needs, you can bring it to varying stages of reanimation."

"Like the difference between the zombies in the *Thriller* video and the ones in *Resident Evil*?"

Douglas considered this. "Yes and no. The *Thriller* example isn't bad, given your limited realm of experience, but the other end of the spectrum is much more lifelike. Ling Tsu looked like the rest of the pandas, did he not?"

"I guess."

"What are the differences, then, between Ling Tsu and the creatures in *Resident Evil*?"

"He didn't look like he was covered in barbecue sauce?"

Douglas casually backhanded me. He hadn't even looked in my direction. The effect on my bruised face was phenomenal.

I cradled my jaw with one hand and tried again. "Differences, right. Well, he wasn't trying to escape the enclosure and eat everyone; I guess that is a difference. And I didn't see any hanging flesh or blood. You know, evidence of his undead state. Of course, that might have to do with the way he died."

Douglas nodded as if he hadn't reached out and back-handed me a second ago. "Better. Yes. Although Ling Tsu has the ability to function and make decisions on his own, I control his primary will. That is one of the main skills you need to cultivate as a necromancer. Each time you raise or summon something, you are betting that your will is stronger than its own. If yours isn't, at best it will go back from whence it came; at worst, it will tear you into bite-sized pieces. Depending on the creature, naturally."

He took a small case out of the box and opened it slowly. "Incidentally, even if Ling Tsu had suffered from external wounds, I could have smoothed them out." He pulled what appeared to be a small silver dagger out of the case. "That's what one is able to do with both talent and education." He put a small stress on the last word, somehow making it threatening.

It was everything I could do to not take a few steps back. I wondered if I could run past Douglas, dodge his knife, and make it to the top of the stairs. But that would leave Brid in a cage she couldn't get out of. Plus, Douglas wasn't stupid. Something would be at the top of the stairs to greet me, even if I could get that far. The situation was definitely not in my favor.

Douglas swept his arm out, slicing the air with the knife. "Another basic skill is the protective circle." He gestured toward the floor with the blade. "You can draw it out of anything: chalk, salt, blood. In the dirt, if need be. The choice depends on what you are summoning, the materials at hand, and the urgency of the situation." He looked at me. "Bottom line is, the stronger the circle, the better. Especially if you are trying to raise one of those nasty things that might eat you, like I mentioned earlier."

"Bite-sized pieces?"

"Exactly. The circle can be modified for the practitioner to include important symbols or what have you. A simple one like this is fine, as long as you activate it correctly." He made a small slice in his arm and stepped into the circle. The blood dropped, hitting the concrete. The air rippled out until it hit the edges of the chalk, and then the circle lit up in a blue flash. Douglas pulled a piece of gauze out of his pocket and tied it around the cut in his arm without setting down the dagger. He'd had some practice.

"Does it always flash like that?" This time I did take a small step back.

"Yes, though this circle was a trifle enthusiastic. A lot of old blood can do that sometimes. That's why most practitioners have a permanent circle. Enough power in one place can leave a memory." He straightened his shoulders. "Now that I'm in the circle, and it's been invoked with blood and my will, I'm protected." Douglas closed his eyes, mumbling softly to himself.

The temperature in the room dropped some more, and I

had to wrap my arms around myself. I couldn't help but wonder, if he was protected inside the circle, shouldn't I be in it, too? Would it actually be safer to be closer to Douglas? I moved toward it, but Douglas waved me off without even opening his eyes. I frowned. My understanding had been that the inside of the circle was good and the outside bad. I kept thinking of the phrase "bite-sized" and hoping that Douglas was summoning something that wouldn't want to eat my face.

Douglas stopped mumbling, and his eyes snapped back open. They had become a solid icy blue. He looked creepy as hell. He shouted a final word. I tried to hear what it was, but I couldn't make it out.

Ghostly forms began to crawl out of the floor and float through the walls. I could see faces, clothes. People of various ages, various shapes. The single unifier seemed to be a violent death. Their throats were slashed, or they were sliced open like gutted fish. Some of them had what appeared to be burn marks; others had cuts all over their bodies. Most of the wounds could have been made with Douglas's knife.

I counted ten people in all. And they were headed my way, all of them moving to avoid the circle. I couldn't tell if they were afraid of it or of Douglas. I backed up until I smacked into the cage and couldn't go any farther. Douglas watched, eyes still that eerie blue, his face otherwise expressionless. He made no move to help me. I felt a small hand touch mine. I grabbed on to Brid's hand without looking back at her. It made me feel a little bit better.

The spirits converged, then crowded onto me in one solid mass. Some people say that ghosts aren't real, that they can't hurt you. Those people are wrong.

The spirits poured into me, hands grabbing, slicing, hurting. The pain drove me screaming to my knees. I dropped Brid's hand on the way down. I shut my eyes and tried to curl up into a ball. I don't know how long I screamed or huddled there on the floor. All I know is that when Douglas finally called them off and the pain stopped, I couldn't get up. I could only lie there, gasping, my face wet with sweat and tears, my whole body a constant tremor. I watched helplessly as Douglas walked through the circle, breaking it. He took his time getting over to me. His black dress shoes held a beatific shine, even after all he'd just done. I could see a small spot of blood on them.

"You have blood on your shoe," I said through chattering teeth.

Douglas absently wiped his shoe on my jeans. He leaned down so I could see his face. His eyes were back to a chilly brown. "I think you've learned enough for tonight."

I didn't say anything.

He straightened. "Get up."

At that moment, I would have loved nothing more than to stay curled up on that floor forever. Instead, I pulled myself up slowly and got back into the cage. Odd how earlier all I wanted was to get out of that cage, and now I couldn't wait to climb back in. Any Douglas-free place looked good to me. I crawled to the other side of it and collapsed. Brid came over and put my head in her lap.

Douglas left without a word.

"Why didn't they come after me?" she asked. She sounded mildly curious, but the tightness in her muscles told me she was angry.

"Because it was my lesson," I said with a chatter. "He had complete control, and he sent them after me."

Brid ran a hand absently through my hair. "No," she said, "the lesson was for both of us. And I think we learned it well."

"My mom will be so happy to see my report card."

Brid laughed softly, relaxing, and I felt better. If we could both laugh at it, then maybe we'd be okay after all.

"Maybe June will send me that help soon."

Brid slid another hand through my hair. "June?"

"She's another dead-wrangler."

"I think we have enough of those, don't you?"

A minute later, a big guy brought down a blanket. I couldn't see who it was, but I felt Brid stiffen at the sight of him. When he left, Brid tucked the blanket in around me and curled against my back, protective. I stayed in a ball. The blanket smelled of lavender, something I wouldn't have expected of Douglas's linens. I didn't find it particularly relaxing. It made me homesick. My mom used lavender laundry detergent. Was she okay? Was she worried? Did my family even know I'd been taken? My need to be rescued was outweighed by my desire to keep them safe, though. If they came after me, they might get hurt. I wanted out of here, but not at the expense of my loved ones.

Brid shifted, moving the blanket up right under my eyes. She slipped an arm around me. Then, over the lavender smell, I could smell the outdoors—sun on the earth, wind through the trees, green things growing, the smell of life. Brid. I relaxed and let sleep take me.

20

C'MON, BABY, DON'T FEAR THE REAPER

We were woken up a few hours later. A big lug of a guy escorted us up to a bathroom. My whole body ached, I was groggy, and it hurt my eyes when I stumbled into the light. It took me a minute to register that the brightness was because we were in sunlight. Morning, then.

We were led down several hallways, and cut through the kitchen on the way to the bathroom. The kitchen was bright, airy, and extremely spartan, much like the rest of the rooms I walked by. Douglas, apparently, didn't care for clutter. The cheeriness of the kitchen surprised me, though. Bright yellow walls and white curtains. Strange.

The guy let Brid go first. I leaned against a wall and stared out the window while I waited. Apparently, Douglas didn't carry the spartan look over into his landscaping. Statues dotted the lawn, a random assortment representing different bits of Greek mythology. I looked over at the hedges and smiled. Douglas had lawn gnomes. I didn't figure him for that kind of guy. I frowned. One of the lawn gnomes was flipping me off. I closed my eyes and opened them again. The gnome stood normally, holding a tiny shovel over his

shoulder, no middle finger in sight. Maybe they were drugging me when I wasn't looking.

I glanced over at the guy watching me. He looked familiar.
After a full minute of peeking, I realized I'd seen him before.
Tuesday night, he'd wiped the floor with me. "Oh, goody," I
said. "It's you."

The guy actually grinned at me, baring a lot of very large,
very white teeth. "How's the back?"

"Fantastic," I said. "Much better than the rest of me."

His grin faltered. The guy looked surprised. He shouldn't
have been. Sure, he could kill me, but it would be fast: a
quick snap of the neck, a blow to the head. Douglas would
kill me slowly, one excruciating slice at a time. If this guy
hadn't picked that up by now, he had a head full of sawdust.
He needed a reminder, if only on the chance that it might
drive a wedge between Douglas and his lackey.

I crossed my arms over my chest. "I hate to break it to you,
but you're not the king of the wild things around here."

He came at me then, only to halt in his tracks when a cat
sauntered into the hallway. The cat was mostly white, with
big black spots on his head, chest, and tail. He had huge
silver eyes that he trained on the man. The cat parked itself in
the middle of the hall, tail flicking. The man relaxed and
resumed his original position, leaning on the wall across from
me. Weird.

I slid down the wall and reached out to pet the feline. Both
the cat and the man seemed startled by this. When the cat
didn't bolt, I scratched his ears. He took it with quiet dignity,

like a king letting his subject kiss his hand. Cats always look like that to me. After everything else, I expected something strange. I'm not sure what: a man-eating cat, a cat that shoots lava from its eyes, something. It was nice to encounter something normal. I scratched under his chin.

After Brid came out, I took my turn in the bathroom. Surprisingly, the guy let Brid come in after a few minutes to help me wash up. She ran a small washcloth under warm water before using it to wipe all the dried blood off me from yesterday's new cuts. "You're starting to look a bit battered," she said.

I looked past her into the mirror. The bruises on my face had yellowed, and the scabs on my scratches were coming off. I had a few small fresh cuts on my forehead, arms, and chest. I couldn't see my back, but I'm sure it was yellow and scabby too. The man let Brid put a little Neosporin she found in the medicine cabinet onto the claw marks and some of the bigger scratches. I guess they were happy to kick the crap out of me, but they were worried I'd get infected.

After that, we were escorted back into the cage. The big guy brought me a paper plate with a few slices of cheese, some brown bread, and a chunk of ham. Brid got a hot bowl of what looked like stew. It was a pretty big bowl. We each got a plastic cup filled with water. Glass, apparently, was too dangerous.

After he left, I started to eat, putting the cheese on the bread and ignoring the ham. "I'm kind of surprised they aren't starving us."

Brid swallowed a large spoonful of the stew. I don't think she even chewed.

"They want you healthy enough to endure Douglas's lessons, or to at least not die until he wants you to. And I guess they don't want me to eat you."

I looked at her.

"I'm kidding," she said. "Well, kind of. I don't normally eat people."

I ate slowly, watching Brid devour her stew. "Not that I want your food, but what gives?" My plate was tiny compared with what they gave Brid.

"Faster metabolism," she said. "I need more food and much higher levels of protein. Besides, it's easier to hide drugs in stew."

I paused midchew. "You know they're drugging you, and you're still going to eat it?"

Brid shrugged. "They aren't trying to kill me. It's a sedative. Keeps me docile. And I don't have much of a choice. If I don't eat, I grow weak and then I die. I'd rather be drugged and strong."

I tossed my ham onto her stew.

"Are you sure?"

"I don't eat meat," I said.

She snatched the ham and gobbled it up in three bites. The girl was a machine. "I can't believe it," she said. "They locked me in here with a vegetarian."

"I know," I said, finishing off my cheese. "A lamb among wolves."

Brid snorted and kept eating.

After a while, the big guy came and took our plates, surprisingly without incident. I waited until he left to talk.

"What's the deal with Happy, there?"

"Happy's name is Michael Jacobs," she said.

"And I take it Mr. Jacobs has nothing to do with your pack."

"He is dead to us." Her tone was flat. No love lost there.

"Charming," I said. "And what, exactly, does that mean?"

"It means that he is rogue. We no longer acknowledge him as one of our own. If he needs help or protection, we don't give it. If he asks to join another pack, we don't recommend him. In our eyes, he is dead."

"His choice or yours?"

"Both."

"He was the one who did my back."

She grunted. "Figures." Brid glanced up at the top of the stairs. "Remember the coup I told you about?" I nodded. "Michael was in on it." She looked like she might say something else, but then she decided against it.

Brid didn't seem too keen on talking about it, so I let it be. I still felt tired, so I grabbed the blanket and leaned against the bars to rest. After a few minutes, I felt the blanket lift and Brid slide in next to me. Without opening my eyes, I held my arm up so she could get comfortable, and then crooked it around her shoulders. She felt hot against my side. It was nice, like having a heater under the blanket with me. For the first time since I got there, I actually felt warm. I hadn't slept next to a girl in a while. I'd missed it. But as good as it felt, I didn't push it. I wouldn't, however tempting it was, take advantage of my situation. After we got out, if we got out, she'd better at least give me her number.

Some time after another bathroom break and what might have been lunch, my lessons continued. If yesterday had taught me anything, it was to keep the lip to a minimum and to pay attention. Oh, and if he made me draw a circle, to get into it as soon as possible.

Douglas let me in the circle, but I think that was only because he wasn't summoning anything. At least, I didn't think he was going to. But the knife never left his grip, and he made me draw the circle, of course. Several times. Then I spent the next hour learning how to close a circle.

The blood part was easy. Douglas cut my arm. I bled. Easy. The will part, well, I had will in spades. But the rest of it? Not so good. I couldn't get my power to cooperate. I assumed this was because of the bindings. I didn't tell Douglas that. If he couldn't figure it out, I wasn't going to enlighten him. The downside was that he thought I was being stubborn. After a couple more stinging slaps to the mouth, I got my power chugging enough to close the circle. I'd never consciously used my gift before. It felt like that first big breath after being underwater for a long time. When I shut my eyes, I could see the circle in my head. If I stretched out my fingers, I thought I would have been able to touch it. Elation surged through me at my success.

Douglas was less impressed. As soon as he decreed it good enough, he made me release it. After that, I went back to the spectator role. As long as I got to stay in the freaking circle, I didn't care.

Michael came down into the basement, his hands full of

something covered in a sheet. He handed the thing off to Douglas and then went quickly back upstairs. I guess he'd seen the show before.

Douglas pulled back the sheet, revealing a gray dove in a cage. There were a lot of scenarios of what could happen to that dove, and none of them were pleasant. As far as I could tell, Douglas only took things out of cages for a reason.

He closed the circle after telling me, "I don't trust yours yet." He handed me the bird.

"What do you want me to do with this?"

"I want you to hold it so I can slit its throat," he said. "I can do it myself, but it's easier if someone else holds it."

I hesitated. I don't like to kill things, one of the many reasons I'm not a carnivore, but as much as I didn't want to be instrumental in the bird's death, I didn't think Douglas would give me another option.

Grabbing a fistful of hair, he yanked my head back. "Problem?"

I tried for honesty. "I don't want to sit here and watch you kill a dove. I don't like killing things."

He gritted his teeth. "You kill every time you eat."

"Yeah, plants. Not animals."

"You're vegetarian?"

"Yeah."

He laughed.

"I fail to see why that's so funny."

He backhanded me then, which made me release the bird. I might have let it go on purpose. Douglas retaliated by hitting me in the face so hard that I fell to my knees. Usually, when someone goes to hit you, you can catch some indication of their intent in their eyes. Not Douglas. His eyes stayed the same flat brown the whole time.

Michael trooped back into the basement and caught the bird with a net. It took him all of two minutes. I stayed on my knees. It seemed like the best place to be.

Douglas once again shoved the dove into my hands. He placed the tip of his dagger under my chin, raising my head up to look in his eyes.

"Listen carefully. When we summon, when we raise, we are trespassing in death's domain. For that passage, we must pay." He enunciated each word, speaking slowly and clearly, like I was a child. "When we pay, we must use death's coin. Flesh, blood, sacrifice, these are tender that death understands." He pressed the knife into my flesh, enough so that I felt it, but not enough to cut. "I can take that payment from either the bird or you. Choose."

The bird struggled in my hands. I tightened my grip around it.

"Just be quick," I said. I held out the bird.

A silver slash, and the dove was dead. Blood spilled directly onto the ground. With each drop, I could feel Douglas's power rise. I really didn't want to see what he needed that build up of power for.

In the movies, zombies just seem to appear. They shamble in from offscreen and try to eat your brains. Or they are the newly dead that sit up and try to eat your brains. They never seem to show what happens if a zombie is buried safe and snug in the ground.

Since we were on solid concrete, it took a minute. The floor made a cracking noise as it split open, revealing a few inches of dark topsoil beneath. Bones inched up out of the dirt, each sliding right back into place as if they'd never left. The small bones of the hand came together, joining with wrist, arm, elbow. Muscles and tendons attached, twisted and inched their way back onto the bones. Flesh reassembled, shaping the body into something recognizable. Hair sprouted and grew. The eyes went from dried-out husks to liquid-filled orbs. A rumpled suit came last, sliding onto the flesh of the man. I wondered if the clothing was Douglas's choice or the zombie's. It was like watching time-lapse photography of a body decomposing, but backward. I couldn't take my eyes off the spectacle.

The finished body was a man, maybe midforties, with a receding hairline. His suit looked a little dirt-stained, but all in all he looked like your average American businessman. Except he was dead. And not just soul-dead like most cubicle workers, but actually dead.

"Go ahead," Douglas said. "Ask him a question."

"Why is a raven like a writing desk?" The zombie stared back at me blankly.

Douglas glared at me. I heard Brid stifle a giggle from inside the cage. Good to know I wasn't the only one who'd read *Alice's Adventures in Wonderland*. How come I couldn't meet a nice, naked, well-read girl until I was kidnapped and thrown into a cage?

"Sorry, it was all I could think of," I said. I tried to sound apologetic.

"You have to ask it something that it knew when it was alive. People don't become omniscient just because they have keeled over."

"Um, sir?" The man stared at his hands, confused. I snapped my fingers and he looked up. "Yeah, hey, how's it going?" The zombie blinked. "Hey, can you tell me your name?"

"David Andrew Davidson."

The name rang a bell. They'd had a small blip on the news about his disappearance when we were watching for information on Brooke. He'd vanished a month ago. I swallowed. Looked like he hadn't skipped town, after all. "How old are you, David?"

"I am forty-three years, eight months, and sixteen days."

"Are they always this literal?" I asked Douglas.

"Not usually. They can't lie, of course, but some force of personality remains. I'd wager that Mr. Davidson here was fairly literal and exacting before he met his unfortunate end."

David stood roughly at attention. Whenever he wasn't talking to me, his focus seemed to slip back to Douglas. "What's the last thing you remember, David?"

The man fiddled with his tie, straightening it. "I got off the bus at the Park and Ride. I was walking to my car and then . . ." His hand moved slowly from the tie to the back of his head. "Pain," he said.

"Is that it?" I asked softly.

David frowned. "Yes." His eyes swiveled toward the large wooden restraint table that was set off to the side. "No."

He was becoming agitated, and I didn't want to put him

through any memories of torture or his own death. I guess when Douglas had listed sacrifice as one of death's coins he hadn't meant emotional and personal sacrifice, but the pagan god ritualistic kind. I couldn't imagine wanting anything so bad I'd kill someone for it. I wondered what Douglas had needed all of David's blood for. "It's okay, David. You don't have to remember." He eased and his attention went back to Douglas.

"Is there something specific I need to ask him, or can we put him back to sleep now?"

Of course, Douglas wasn't content sending David the Zombie back. First, he had to order him around. Douglas made him scrub the floor of the basement while he watched over his shoulder the whole time, pointing out each missed spot or blemish. David was forced to strip down and do calisthenics, far more than I think he had done in real life. While the zombie was thin, his body had little in the way of muscle definition. Then Douglas made him reenact his own death. I heard every scream, every plea, every pain David Andrew Davidson had been put through. And all because I'd shied away from asking about it. I couldn't be certain that was why, but from the look in Douglas's eyes while we watched, I felt pretty confident that was the reasoning. I watched until David eased and grew silent again. I was afraid of what would happen if I looked away.

Poor Mr. Davidson got put through the wringer just so I could learn a few things about zombies, like how strong they were, how easily controlled, and that they looked just as silly as live people when they did jumping jacks. Maybe I needed the lesson, but I think it could have been carried out in a more dignified way. David used to be a living being, after all. Again I felt like Douglas was giving me a dual lesson. Sure, he was showing me how to raise a zombie, but he was also showing me exactly what he was capable of. I could just as easily become the one doing the jumping jacks.

Finally satisfied, Douglas put David Andrew Davidson to rest. He ordered him back into the ground by his full name and waited until the floor completely resealed itself before he broke the circle.

"How come you needed his name to put him down, but not to raise him?" I asked.

"I used his name to call him; I simply didn't shout it the first time. The name is unnecessary, though it makes things infinitely easier." Douglas opened the cage and gestured me back in. I went quietly. "If you know the name, it's easier to locate the soul. Without the soul," he said, "we are nothing." He locked the cage, acknowledging Brid with a nod, and then left without another word.

Brid lay on the floor, stomach down, slowly kicking her heels and looking the picture of the 1950s teenage girl. Except Brid was in a cage instead of sprawled on a fluffy, heart-shaped rug and talking into a princess phone. And, hopefully, she wasn't adolescent either.

"How old are you?"

"How old do you want me to be?" she asked, batting her eyelashes.

"Stop that."

"Fine. I just turned nineteen." She took her chin out of her hands, using her arms to brace herself up instead. "And what have we learned today?"

"Zombies are strong, they don't feel pain." I paused. "Physical pain anyway." David had certainly been able to feel remembered pain. You don't scream like that unless you feel something. "They also don't tire, and Douglas is an asshole."

"We already knew the last one," she said.

"Yeah, but I felt like we needed to go over it again." I sprawled on the floor next to her. "Oh, and if I control the zombie completely, I can order it around."

"And?"

I scratched my head. Man, I could have really used a shower. "And what?"

Brid nodded down at the floor. "Where's the blood?"

The floor, though still stained, appeared to be empty of even the slightest drop of blood. Interesting.

"Either it came off when David the Zombie scrubbed or it drained when the floor cracked, right?"

"No," she said. "I watched. The blood sort of . . . oozed into the floor before that. Kind of creepy, really." She ran her fingers through her bangs, hand-combing them. "What was it like?"

"Awesome," I said. "Terrifying. Nauseating."

She eyed me from beneath her hair. "So you aren't going to go out and start your own undead slave business?"

"No." The answer came without hesitation.

"Not even tempted a little? Raise a math whiz and get him to do your homework for you? Have a zombie architect design your house?"

"No way," I said. I thought of Brooke, sitting at home in a bowling bag. "No one deserves to be treated that way."

"I knew you were a nice boy," she said, leaning over and nudging me with her shoulder.

"Hm, yes. All us nice boys hang out in cages learning how to raise the dead. Torturing little birds . . ." I looked at my hands. I couldn't see any blood on them, but I wiped them on my jeans anyway.

Brid kissed me softly on the cheek. I forgot about my hands.

"You're still nice," she said softly.

I nodded, clenching my jaw to keep my eyes from tearing up. Brid's faith was reassuring, but I was wondering how nice I'd be after a few more days of Douglas's training.

Dinner was a repetition of the last meal, except they added an orange. Either Douglas had forgotten I don't eat ham, or he left it in an attempt to teach me yet another lesson. Of course, Michael could have prepared the meal and done it trying to piss me off. I had a lot of time on my hands to think about these things.

I gave the ham to Brid and went about peeling my orange.

"At least now I won't get scurvy," I said.

Brid finished the ham, licking the juice off her fingers. "I'm glad you're looking on the bright side of things."

"Of course, with no sun, I'll eventually get rickets."

"No, you won't," Brid said.

"But I'm not getting enough vitamin D."

"I know, but in adults they don't call it rickets. It's called osteomalacia." Brid swallowed another mouthful of her stew, smiling at my surprise. "I take a lot of biology classes and study under the pack doctor." She took another bite. "We do have some medical personnel scattered about the pack, but I want to be able to do basic stuff."

"Surely you don't have to worry about osteo-whatever," I said, popping a piece of orange into my mouth.

"You never know when knowledge might come in handy, so I try not to limit myself. Besides, I liked the word. Rickets," she spoke it clearly and slowly, biting off each syllable.

I pushed my legs out, stretching them. "Do you guys heal fast? Or is that just a movie thing?"

"We do, but it still does take some time. If you bleed out too fast, all the healing in the world won't do you any good. And if you're choking, you still need the Heimlich. We need air just like anything else."

I folded my cheese into my bread. "Don't need a silver bullet to do you in, huh?"

"No, but it certainly helps."

I choked a little on my makeshift sandwich.

Brid gave me a wicked grin as she licked her spoon.

I drank some water to stop my coughing fit. I didn't want an overenthusiastic Heimlich from Brid. I didn't know what was fact or fiction yet about werewolves, but I didn't want to find out about superstrength the hard way.

After a final bathroom trip, we were escorted back to the cage for the night. Michael flipped the switch, and we were thrown into darkness. Brid, used to far more physical exertion than me, began to pace back and forth. There wasn't enough space to do sprints. Even walking, she pinged back and forth like an angry bee.

"You okay?"

"This cage is driving me crazy," she said, continuing to pace.

"You claustrophobic?"

"No, but I can't change and I can't run."

I listened to her feet as they padded back and forth. They reminded me of the tiger at the zoo pacing his cage.

"We need to change frequently, Sam. I can put it off by burning excess energy, but if I wait too long, I'll start to go a little wiggy."

"Wiggy is bad."

"And I don't know if they did this on purpose, but I can't change in here!" She shouted the last part, and I heard her fists bang into the bars. Brid continued to scream, loud and angry, beating her fists in counterpoint.

I scrambled to my feet and went to her. I didn't want to get between her fists and the cage, but I didn't want her to hurt herself either. I made soothing sounds and touched her shoulders, giving her a second to acknowledge my presence. You never want to spook an already freaked-out animal. The same goes for people. I slid my hands down Brid's arms until I got her wrists. Taking hold of them, I pulled her arms in toward her chest, hugging her. I let her scream until she got it all out, keeping the comforting sounds going until she finished. Her body quaked and shook.

"We'll think of something," I whispered into her ear. "Don't worry. I'll help. I promise."

"Something," Brid mumbled. "Thanks." Her voice sounded slightly hoarse.

I placed my chin on the top of her head. I rocked her slightly, trying to think of something, anything, more useful.

"Something," she repeated. Her shaking slowed. "Thought of something."

I didn't even get out a full *what* before Brid spun around and grabbed my chin, pulling my head down and gluing my lips to hers. Despite the force, her lips were somehow gentle, and she tasted a little of beef stew, something I hadn't found to be particularly erotic until just now. One of her hands slid back into my hair while the other sneaked around my waist, pulling me closer to her. Her hands were soft and hot. I grabbed her waist, the tips of my fingers sliding under the T-shirt, finding the smooth skin at the small of her back.

"Wait." I pushed back, reaching for air.

"What?" I could hear the tinge of exasperation in her voice.

"Are you—" I stopped. "Is this—" Taking a deep breath and mentally kicking myself, I continued. "I don't want this to be something you feel pressured into, something you'll regret later."

"You said you'd help me. You promised."

"I know."

What felt like my T-shirt hit me in the face.

"Good," she said. "Now take off your pants and shut up."

I only have so much restraint. I didn't get undressed as fast as Brid, but I was close.

Brid lay on top of me, naked and sweaty, her head tucked under my chin.

"Thanks," she said. "I feel much better."

"Any time. When you feel restless, hungry, bored, a little sleepy. Literally, any time."

She laughed softly. "I take it you enjoyed yourself, then?"

"Hell yeah. In fact, I plan on recommending werewolf sex to all my friends."

"So that's it, huh? You're going to pawn me off on your pals?"

"No, they'll have to find their own." I gave her a squeeze. "Except for the girls. My mom always told me to share and play nice with girls."

"Ew," she said, sliding off me but cuddling up to my side. "I can't believe you just mentioned your mom."

"You started it."

I heard a thumping noise, like somebody had just run into something, and then a mumbled curse came from somewhere outside the cage. I froze, and Brid went rigid beside me.

A young girl's voice piped out of the darkness. "Son of a bitch! Honestly, who the hell puts furniture in the middle of a room?" Her voice crackled with indignation. "And in a room with no windows. This is turning out to be such a huge pain in my ass—"

She stopped midtirade, and I heard a small clicking noise. A bright ball of light suddenly burst into existence above the head of a young girl. She blinked at the light, apparently satisfied, and then turned her eyes on us. Tiny ebony eyebrows shot up, and her mouth quirked into a wicked little smirk. Gray eyes flicked to the cage and back to us.

"You guys have quite an interesting alternative lifestyle here." The girl's manner of speech and facial expressions made her seem older, but she looked ten and innocent, with two soot-black pigtails, freckles, and a black-and-red Catholic schoolgirl uniform. She even wore kneesocks and saddle shoes.

I grabbed my jeans and turned away, trying to pull them on.

"Please," she said, "like I haven't already had the full tour." She whistled when she noticed my back. I assume because of my injuries. I mean, my ass just isn't that spectacular. "Who's been kicking the crap out of you?"

"Everyone." I zipped up my pants. I threw my Batman T-shirt at Brid along with my boxers when she made no move on her own to get them. She gave me an amused smile before slipping them on.

"Right," the girl said, "business." She whipped out a BlackBerry and began hitting buttons. "Please tell me one of you is Sam LaCroix."

I raised my hand. "Present."

"Finally." She walked up to the bars, pointing an accusing finger in my face. "You are a rather troublesome young man to find." She hit a few more buttons on the BlackBerry. "I freaking hate nicknames. I tell people, give me the whole name, it's easier. But nooo." Her brow furrowed, and she focused her attention back on me. "Usually Sam is easy though. Samuel, Samwise, there are only so many things a shortened Sam could be. So why were you so difficult?"

I poked my chest. "Samhain."

The girl snorted. "I should have known. New-age Celtic-loving hippies, making my life hell." She continued to type, her face brightening. "Right, there you are. Samhain LaCroix." She looked back up at me. "You think you can get yourself out of that kinky love cage you're in and talk to me? I'm on a tight schedule."

I crossed my arms over my chest. "Little girl, do you think we *want* to be in here?"

"You seemed happy to be there when I showed up."

"Touché," Brid murmured.

I glared at her. "Hey, how 'bout you stop with the smart-ass remarks, and maybe we can get out of here?"

The girl studied the cage door, her gray eyes tight with concentration. "No can do," she said.

"Of course not," I said, resting my forehead against the cold bars. The symbols buzzed in my head, sharper and more in focus than they had been before. Nothing else had been easy lately, so why should this be?

"Why not?" said Brid.

The little girl pointed at the symbols. "These wards have been drawn by a necromancer," she said.

"And?" Brid and I said in unison.

The girl rolled her eyes. "Duh, a necromancer's power kind of handles all the death stuff, right? You know, power over souls and all that business."

I rolled my hand, motioning her to continue.

"Well, I'm a Harbinger. You can't get more death and soul than me." She flicked the bars with her finger. "So I can't open this."

"Death and soul?" Brid asked.

The girl tapped her foot, impatient. She pointed to herself. "Dead. As in a doornail. I took a dirt nap, pushed up some daisies, reached room temperature, pined for the fjords—"

"Pined for the fjords?" Brid said.

"Monty Python," the girl and I both said at the same time.

"Oh." Brid gave her a sympathetic look. "Sorry."

She hit some more buttons on her BlackBerry. "Yeah, well, cancer's a bitch."

"Well said," Brid responded solemnly.

The girl smiled. "Sorry if that came off snarky, but when you've been dead awhile, the self-pity thing gets old quick, the horror wears off, and you sort of get over yourself. At least, I did anyway."

I banged my head once into the bars. "I have to ask. I don't want to ask, but I have to. What's a Harbinger?"

"I guide souls from this plane to, well, I can't tell you where."

"You're Death," I said, giving her the once-over. "In saddle shoes." I don't know why I was so surprised. It wasn't any weirder than anything else I'd been dealing with.

"Kinda," she said. She looked at Brid. "I like your shirt. Batman is my favorite."

"Thank you."

"Not to be rude," I interrupted, "but can you maybe tell me why you're here, since you can't get us out of the cage?"

"June called in a favor. Wait, I better do this right." She straightened her skirt and adjusted her blazer. Then she pulled herself up to her full height. "Hi, my name is Ashley, and I'll be your Harbinger today. I will be acting as an interim instructor for all your necromancy needs." She flashed her best stewardess smile and gave a little Vanna wave.

"Ashley, as delighted as I am to meet you, don't you think it might be hard to teach me? I'm in a cage that you can't get into. Oh, and—" I grabbed the bars with both hands, "I'm a little distracted right now by the fact that *I'm being held by a psychotic killer.*"

Ashley cocked a single eyebrow, a look of mild amusement on her face. "Geez," she said, looking at Brid. "Is he always this big of a drama queen?"

Brid grinned at her but didn't answer.

21

MAKE A LITTLE BIRDHOUSE IN MY SOUL

Ashley hovered cross-legged in front of me, ignoring the empty air beneath her, rapt as I caught her up on the last few days. I had just finished with the bit about going to my mom's and learning about being bound.

"Man, I really wish I had some popcorn for this." She made a face. "That sounded a little insensitive, didn't it? I just meant, you know, you've had a lot going on."

Brid lolled on the floor next to me. "That's okay," she said, her chin in one hand. "He doesn't mind."

I looked at her.

Brid snorted. "If I don't offend you, then I know she never will."

"You're not offensive."

"I'm blunt, which bothers some people, and I slapped you in the face."

I thought about that, but not for very long. "Personally, I've found your approach rather refreshing after the past few days."

Ashley rolled her eyes. "Okay, moving on."

I shrugged. "Anyway, then I talked to June—"

"Who then talked to me," Ashley added.

"And then I got jumped." I leaned back on my elbows.

Ashley chewed on her lip. "You said you got it from your father's side?"

"Yeah, turns out my dad's side is just lousy with it. I've got two half sisters who have it too." I needed to concentrate on getting out of there, but I couldn't pass up a chance to help out Lilly and Sara. If I didn't do something, Lilly's big, serious eyes would haunt me like those creepy kids you sometimes see in velvet paintings. "Ashley, do you think you could check in on them? Make sure they don't . . ."

"End up like you?" she offered sympathetically.

"Yeah," I said. "I would just feel better knowing someone was looking out for them."

"No worries," she said. "It's part of my job." She flipped open her BlackBerry and made a few notes. "Anything else? You didn't get attacked by headhunters or fight a sea monster or anything, did you?" Her little glowing orb swam lazy circles around her head.

"Nope."

"Good," she said, "because you're screwed enough as it is."

"Thanks," I said, "and I wish everyone would stop reminding me." I sat cross-legged on the floor. "Let me ask you a question. Do I always have to kill things to use my gift? I mean, assuming I ever get to use it?"

"No," she said. "Every necromancer has his own slant on things. Some parts of the ritual can't, or shouldn't, be skipped, though. For safety reasons, you should always do the circle. It doesn't have to be invoked with your blood, but that does make for a very strong circle. Your will should be enough."

She scowled at the light ball, which had begun to do figure eights in the air. Chastened, the ball resumed its original circle.

I turned my head, trying to hide my smile.

Ashley cleared her throat. "Even spit works to strengthen a circle, just not as much as blood. To call spirits, again, sometimes a symbolic offering speeds things up. As for raising the dead, yeah, that kind of takes a big payment." She scratched her nose. "But that depends on the necromancer. A strong one can get by with very little blood. He won't need as much of a power boost, but the offering should be there. The amount of blood also depends on the quality."

I felt relieved that I wouldn't have to start slaughtering bunnies to get things done, but the last thing she said worried me. "The quality?"

"It's not just how powerful the necromancer is, but also how powerful the blood is. You'd get more, you know, oomph out of a goat than a chicken. It's simply a bigger payment. That being said, a more powerful necromancer could do more with a smaller sacrifice than a less powerful one could. They run more efficiently," she said. "Here, think of it this way: Douglas is a hybrid car, and you're a clunky old truck."

"Thank you for that."

Ashley glared at me until I pantomimed shutting my mouth and throwing away the key.

"You both need gas to run, but the hybrid wouldn't need as much because it can draw from its internal power source, the electric battery. It uses a small amount of fuel more efficiently. The truck lacks that internal power source. It can get to the same place the hybrid car can, but it takes tons more gas to do so."

"I should trade you in," Brid said.

"Don't make me sic Ling Tsu on you," I told her.

Ashley gave us the same look she had given the ball. Brid giggled, but I managed a straight face. Ashley ignored us. "The truck," she said loudly, "has to rely completely on whatever kind of fuel it has. Some need premium, some can take regular, et cetera." She gave me a graceful shrug. "Not a perfect analogy, but . . ."

I nodded. A thought came to me. "Is there a way for me to get past the binding, you know, besides finding my uncle?" Finding Nick, even with Ashley's help, might take too long. Kevin's hairbrush was at home on my dresser, so a tracking spell was out. We'd need a witch for that anyway. I could try giving Ashley his name, but I didn't know the whole thing. She'd gotten lost finding me because she'd only had Sam LaCroix to go on. I only had Nick Hatfield. I didn't even know what Nick was short for. Nicholas? Nikolai? There were probably a lot of Nick Hatfields on this earth. We didn't have time to sort through every one.

"Besides a bigger, badder necromancer?"

"Yeah. I'm a little short on those, and the one I do know . . ." The one I knew would probably love to eat my liver with a nice Chianti. "I don't think I should ask him."

Ashley squinted in thought. "I'm not really sure. I've never run into this." She tapped her BlackBerry with her thumb. "It wouldn't hurt to look." She closed her eyes. "Now, open up and say 'ah.'"

I did it, even though I thought she was joking, which made her smile. The smile quickly dissolved into a frown.

"Sam, did you say your mom tried to bind you first?"

"Yeah, but it didn't work."

"Why?" Brid asked.

"It's hard to tell, and I've never really seen it before, but if I had to hazard a guess, I'd say that both bindings worked." She opened her eyes.

Brid and I sat in stunned silence, hers more stunned than mine, I think. Maya had said there was something hinky about the binding. Even with that knowledge, I felt the impact of Ashley's confirmation. "Come again?" Brid asked.

Ashley gave me a sympathetic look. "Both worked, Sam. Your uncle's heavier binding almost blocks it, but I can see the trace of your mom's there." She shook her head in amazement. "Unbelievable. I've never seen someone whose power was bound, let alone more than once. It's like they cut a piece of you off."

No wonder I'd always felt lost. I actually was. The knowledge felt terrible, but in a strange way, it also felt good. Now I knew why I'd never connected to anything. Why I felt like I was outside the world around me, moving at a different speed from everyone else. That amputated piece of me explained everything, even why I'd failed at college. But that kind of blanket excuse can be dangerous. Crutches usually are.

"Once is practically unheard of, and you've had it done twice," Brid murmured. "Unreal."

Even among the anomalies, I was an anomaly. I took some

pride in that. Or I would have, if my source of pride hadn't also been my death sentence.

Ashley stood up and dusted herself off.

"You're going?" A surge of panic shot through me. Even if Ashley hadn't been able to get me out of the cage, she had at least been able to answer some of my questions. How could I possibly figure out how to beat Douglas if I didn't learn?

"I'll come back," she said. "I'm sorry, but it took some time to find you, and I do have a day job. I'm ten minutes late for Mrs. Jenkins as it is."

"Wait," I said. "I know you can't get me out, but can you do something for me?"

Ashley raised an eyebrow, her small face lighting up. Looked like little Ashley loved a negotiation.

"Can you let someone know where we are?"

"Depends," she said.

"On what?"

"On who the person is."

I tried to think. Even if we could find him, Nick might not be willing to help because he was afraid of Douglas. My mom? The last thing I wanted was to have to buy a bowling bag for my mom's head. Or Haley's. Ramon? He knew what was going on, but I didn't know who he could tell. He couldn't just attack Douglas's house with a skateboard. I yanked my thumb at Brid. "What about her pack?"

"Not unless they have a necromancer on staff."

Brid shook her head.

"Why does that matter?" And why was everything so complicated lately?

Ashley pinched the bridge of her nose. "Let me see if I can explain this simply. I'm dead—do we all get that?"

We nodded.

"And we all understand that not everyone can see dead people?"

I said yes while Brid said, "But I can see you."

Ashley sighed. "That's because you're with Sam." She looked at us, but we returned blank stares, obviously not getting it. "As a Harbinger, I'm only visible if I am collecting, or if I am summoned into the presence of certain professionals." She pointed at me with her whole hand. "Necromancer?"

I nodded, getting it. Brid could see Ashley because of me. Interesting. I stuck my thumb at my chest and looked at Brid. "Mayor of Zombieville." I pointed at Ashley. "Citizen of Zombieville."

"Ah," Brid said. "You know, it's not nice to point."

"So my mother tells me." I chewed on my lip. "What about June? She's a necromancer. Can you get a message to her?" I asked. "Please let her know what's going on. She doesn't have to come herself, but I need you to ask her to contact Brid's family or someone who is willing to help us."

Brid grabbed my shoulder. "And Sam's mom."

I frowned at her. "I don't want my mom getting hurt."

"Of course not," she said impatiently. "What I meant was to have Ashley talk to June and see if she can ask your mom to release her part of the binding from afar."

I turned my head and blinked at her in surprise.

She gave my shoulder another squeeze. "You have two, Sam. Your mom did one binding ritual on you, then your uncle Nick finished you off with a second one. Some of your power is better than none, right?" Brid nudged my chin up with her finger until all I could see were her hazel eyes. "Worth a shot," she said.

I pulled my gaze back to Ashley. "Is that possible? Can you ask June to contact my mom and Brid's pack? Tell June I know she can't act herself. And tell her thank you."

"No problem," Ashley said. "Now we just need to talk about price."

"I don't have anything right now," I said, "and I can't pay you if I don't get out of here. Besides, I thought you said it was your job."

Ashley waved my logic away with one tiny hand. "Guiding lost souls and keeping an eye on little baby necromancer sisters, that's my job. Running messages? Not my job."

I chewed my lip. "Well, what did June offer you?"

"All transactions are confidential."

"What would you like?" Brid asked, head tilted to the side.

"Waffles," Ashley said promptly.

"What?" Whatever I'd been expecting, it hadn't been that.

"And not the frozen kind, either. The good kind. With fresh strawberries, whipped cream, and real maple syrup. None of that compote garbage."

"You want waffles?" I tried to keep the skepticism from my voice. "No firstborn or a pot of gold?"

"I'm not a leprechaun, Sam. And what would I do with a baby?" Her eyebrow shot back up, and she crossed her arms. "I want waffles. Take it or leave it."

I glanced at Brid, who was staring at Ashley shrewdly.

"Let's talk numbers," she said. "Are we talking, like, twenty waffles all at once? Or a waffle a week for six months? What?"

"Every day for two years," Ashley said.

"That's outrageous," Brid sputtered.

"I don't care what we pay if it gets us out," I said.

Brid glared at me. Clearly I was weakening her bargaining position. I thought she was forgetting the big picture, but I caved under her glare and held up my hands in surrender.

"Every week," Brid countered.

Ashley's eyes narrowed. "Every day, one year."

"Six months," Brid said.

Ashley pursed her mouth. Finally, she nodded.

"Done," I said.

Ashley reached out her hand. I shook it. A grin split her face.

"Great," she said. She whipped out her BlackBerry and hit a button. A small swirling vortex opened up above her. What looked like a stream of sparrows came out and grabbed onto her clothes. Ashley waved.

"You guys take care, okay?" The birds flew back into the vortex, pulling Ashley with them and plunging us into darkness once again.

"I guess that explains how she got in here," Brid said.

"Just when I think things can't get any weirder." I wrapped an arm around Brid. "Now what?"

"I'm going back to bed." She slipped away from me. I heard the blanket slide across the metal as she settled in. I wanted to join her, but waiting and doing nothing was driving me crazy.

I gripped the bars, feeling the cold on my hands and letting the symbols crystallize in my head. I knew I wouldn't be able to break whatever Douglas had done, but I could at least try and muddle my way through it. Learn the symbols, something.

There was no way for me to keep track of time, so I don't know how long I sat there holding the bars. My hands felt frozen stiff when I pried them off, and my shoulders hurt. I guess I'd been tensing them the whole time. I hadn't learned much, but I had found what seemed like a weakness around the door. If I had infinite time or a gigantic boost of power, I might be able to spring the door open.

Since I didn't have either, I crawled back under the blanket with Brid. It felt like hours before my hands warmed up enough for me to fall asleep.

22

EASY LIKE SUNDAY MORNING

Ramon scooted into one of Plumpy's plastic booths across from Detective Dunaway. He took a sip from his soda.

"I appreciate you meeting with me," Dunaway said. "I'm sorry to take you away from your work."

"I only work here because of Brooke and Sammy." Ramon picked at the edges of a rogue ketchup packet. "Now . . ." He didn't know how to finish that sentence. Sam was gone, and Brooke wouldn't be back at work ever. He wouldn't have been here, either, except he thought his absence would look suspicious. Besides, what would he do if he wasn't here? Sit around the apartment going crazy? He shoved the ketchup packet away in frustration.

Ramon had caught a bus out to Sam's mom's house earlier and dropped Brooke off. Haley had graciously agreed to head-sit. Ramon could have left Brooke at the apartment, but he'd been afraid that the cops might want to look through it while he was at work. Brooke wanted to go, anyway. She thought she'd make a good distraction for Sam's family. Ramon had agreed, especially after he'd seen Mrs. L's face. Normally, she glowed with a gentle inner light. But when he'd dropped Brooke off that morning, her radiance was all but gone. Mrs. LaCroix was taking Sam's absence pretty hard. Not that Ramon could see any other way to take it.

"You still haven't heard from him?" Dunaway pulled out his notebook.

Ramon shook his head. "Negative." He hadn't wanted to call in the cops before, but when Sam didn't come back, he couldn't see an alternative. In the wake of Brooke's murder, Sam's disappearance would be noticed. If Ramon or Frank didn't call Dunaway, they'd look really fishy, so Ramon decided to head it off at the pass. Besides, some cops were tools, but Dunaway seemed okay, like he would listen, even though Ramon hadn't been able to tell him much.

"Do you mind if we go over it again?"

"Sammy came home from visiting scenic Kitsap County Friday afternoon."

"Who did he go there to see?"

"His douche-bag father."

Detective Dunaway looked up from his notebook.

"I'm sorry—his estranged father," Ramon said, "who is a douche bag."

Dunaway laughed, turning it into a discreet cough at the end. He flipped back to another page in the notebook.

"You said he went out there trying to locate his uncle?"

"Yeah."

"Any particular reason?"

"Sammy's gotten really into his roots lately." Not exactly a lie. Mama didn't have any patience for liars, but Ramon felt comfortable dealing the occasional half truth.

"Then what?"

"Not much. We hung out with Frank and Brooke." He stopped himself and stared at the floor, trying to look sad. "Sorry, I guess I'm not used to it. I meant we hung out and talked about Brooke."

Dunaway nodded sympathetically. He waited patiently for Ramon to continue. Ramon felt sure that Dunaway could wait for a very long time.

"After that, he took his board and left."

"Did he mention where he was going?" Dunaway tapped his pen against the pad. "Maybe when he'd be back?"

"Nope." Ramon got up and refilled his soda from the fountain machine. Technically, employees only got one meal per eight-hour shift. Not that he'd ever paid attention to the rules. One of the kids behind the counter opened his mouth to say something. Ramon stared at him until he shut his mouth and looked away. Plumpy's owed him many things. Free soda was *numero uno* on that list.

Ramon tapped the cup and waited for the foam to settle. "I offered to go with him." He finished filling it and popped the top back on. "Said he wanted some alone time." Ramon slid back into the booth. "I should have gone with him."

Dunaway rubbed absently at his neck. He looked tired. "You don't know if that would have helped. That might have made you a missing person, too."

Ramon shrugged. Maybe. Then again, maybe not.

"Anything else?"

"He talked on the phone for a bit before he left," Ramon said, "but I don't know who with."

Dunaway asked him more questions, none of which he could answer. After a while, the detective closed his notebook and looked out the window. He tapped his pen against the cover slowly, and Ramon could almost see the thoughts circling above his head. Finally, the pen stopped.

"You know, we found some video of the attack on Sam."

Ramon stared at his soda.

"From the night Brooke was killed."

His eyebrows shot up, and he pushed away his drink. "Yeah?"

Dunaway stared him right in the eye. "I've looked at those tapes over and over." He paused to see if Ramon would respond. When he didn't, the detective continued. "Some weird things on those tapes. Weird things all over this case."

Ramon looked down at his hands. "Tapes?"

"A few of the local shops had surveillance cameras set up. Some of the footage is grainy, but most isn't too bad. Good enough for me to see a guy stopping a car with his fist." As if to illustrate this, Dunaway held up his own fist, staring at the knuckles.

Ramon felt his mouth go dry. "Drugs?"

"Drugs don't help you stop cars," the detective said softly, almost to himself. He put his fist down. "Then there's Sam's injury. I've slowed the tape, zoomed in, run it through filters. Never see a weapon. Just the guy's hand."

"Huh."

"Strange things are piling up: the murder, the attack, and now Sam's disappearance. And you know what?"

Ramon shook his head. He didn't want to know what.

"All those strange things keep coming back to you three."

When Ramon didn't respond, the detective got up to leave, leaning over the plastic table and offering his hand. Ramon hesitated out of surprise. No cop had ever offered him a handshake. He took the officer's hand and shook it.

"I don't know what trouble you boys are in or what's going on yet, but I'm going to find out. Just be careful, all right?"

Ramon nodded.

Dunaway released his hand. "I'll try to keep you in the loop if I can."

Ramon nodded again, grateful.

Dunaway slipped his notebook into his pocket and headed for the parking lot.

Dread settled in Ramon's stomach as he watched the detective drive away. For the hundredth time, he wished he knew what to do. He squeezed his eyes shut and thought. He didn't know what had happened to Sam, but he didn't think he was dead. No, Douglas seemed like the kind of guy to leave the body as a message. But Ramon couldn't hang around anymore, waiting for things to work out. He had to find a way to do something. He drank his soda, ignored the ending of his break time, and furiously sifted for ideas. He needed a plan. A fragment of his conversation with Dunaway floated to the top. Sam had talked on the phone.

Bingo.

Ramon threw away his cup and went into the back. He pulled on his zip-up hoodie and reached for his spare board, since his usual ride was sitting in an evidence locker somewhere, after its debut as a weapon. He missed that board. If anything, he had to find Sammy so he could buy Ramon a new ride.

"Where are you going?" A touch of panic lit Frank's face.

Ramon grabbed Frank's shoulders. "I gotta go."

"But it's the middle of your shift," he said. "You have seniority. You can't just *go*." Frank began to look a little wild around the eyes.

Ramon picked up his spatula and handed it over to Frank. "It's time, man."

Frank stared at the shiny metal spatula in his hand. "I haven't been trained."

"Frank, a drunk monkey could do this job." He clapped him on the arm. "You're ready."

"No! I can't!"

Someday, when Ramon had the time, he was going to find out where Frank got his lack of confidence from, if only so he could help raise the boy right. For now, all he could do was make sure his faith in Frank's ability to manage this dumb-ass job showed in his eyes.

Frank calmed and gathered himself, standing up straight and tall, shoulders squared. "I won't let you down."

"That's my boy." He saluted Frank and snagged his board.

"What do I do if the manager shows up?"

"Tell him I had a family emergency."

Frank nodded, and Ramon shot out the door. Wheels hit pavement with a soft whir as he steered his board away from Plumpy's. The weight in his stomach lightened. It felt good to be taking action. And he hadn't even had to make Frank lie for him. If Sammy wasn't a family emergency, he didn't know what was.

Ramon tossed his board against the wall of the apartment. He went to Sam's phone and started scrolling through the caller ID for names he didn't recognize. June Walker. Had to be. Out of the few he didn't know, she was the only one who'd called even close to the right time. He dialed, his heart skipping in anticipation. A woman answered. Her voice reminded him of Dessa's: intelligent, warm, with a hint of sarcasm. Dessa's usually had more than a hint.

"June Walker?"

"Depends on who's asking." She sounded amused.

"Do you know a Sam LaCroix?"

"Who is this?" All amusement evaporated.

"This is his friend Ramon." He paced, too jittery to sit down. "I know you called him. What did you talk about?"

"Why don't you ask him?"

"Because I haven't seen him since Friday." The line got quiet. He could hear a few birds and June's breath, but nothing else. Then he heard some mumbled curses and the clattering of what sounded like a bowl.

"Ramon, right?"

He nodded, realized she couldn't see him, and then told her yes.

"Let me call you back, Ramon." She hung up before he could respond.

Twenty minutes and half a bag of Cheetos later, June called back.

"Sorry," she said, "but Sam's messenger got lost." June's voice quieted like she was talking away from the mouthpiece. "Yes, I know you have other things to do, but really—would you get away from my waffle maker?"

"Excuse me?"

"Sorry," she said, "I didn't mean you. Look, Ramon, do you know Sam's mom?"

"Since sixth grade."

"Good. Get ahold of her. Tell her she needs to try and break her binding on Sam."

"I thought we needed Sam's uncle for that."

"For one of them. It's a long story."

"You think she'll be able to do it?" He wiped some leftover powdered cheese on Sam's couch. Sam could yell at him when he got back. He had decided that if he did enough stuff to piss Sam off, then Sam would have to stay alive if only so he could yell at Ramon. So far he had messed up Sam's CD collection and eaten his junk food. It was a good start.

"To be honest, I'm not sure. But she needs to try. Douglas has him."

Ramon heard the click of a lighter as June lit a cigarette. He assumed it was a cigarette. If it was a bong, they were doomed.

"And Ramon?"

"Yeah?"

"I need you to do one more thing."

Ramon used his own cell phone to call the other number, just like June had instructed. At first, no one answered. After a few rings, a very chipper male voice came on.

"Hey, you've reached the den, home of many. Leave a message, and we might get back to you. Don't hang up, don't talk too long, and don't expect us to remember your number." There was a smacking sound in the background and a pause in the message. "Ow! You want to do this? Didn't think so. Right. Leave it at the beep, people."

Ramon felt like smiling, despite the situation. The guy's cheerfulness was infectious, even over the phone. The machine beeped.

"Hey," he said, "my name is Ramon. You don't know me, but my buddy is stuck somewhere with . . . I don't know. Her name is Brid, that's all I know." Ramon couldn't think of what else to say, so he just left his number and hung up.

He didn't know how he was going to get to Sam's mom's, but he didn't feel like riding the bus again. This time of day it would take too long, and he already felt antsy. Frank was at work. He could take Sam's car, but he didn't have a license. A cab would be too expensive. He picked up his spare board and locked the front door.

Maybe he could call Sam's mom? No, he didn't want to ask for another favor, not after having her Brooke-sit. Besides, he didn't think she'd like what he had to say to begin with.

Ramon walked over to the door next to Sam's and knocked. Mrs. Winalski answered immediately. The bright pink of her sweats almost blinded him. "Sorry, Mrs. W. Bad time?"

"No," she said, slightly winded, "just doing my yoga. At my age, you have to work to stay flexible, if you know what I mean."

Ramon tried his best to not know what she meant.

"Any news from Sam?"

Ramon thrust his hands into his pockets. Mrs. W always made him feel like he was under inspection. "Sort of," he said. "That's why I knocked."

"Stop fidgeting," she said. "I won't bite. Now, out with it."

He straightened up. "Do you think you could give me a ride out to Sam's mom's house?"

She nodded and held up a hand, telling him to wait, before he could explain or even offer her gas money. Two minutes later, she popped out in jeans and a bright purple V-neck sweater.

"Wow. You're fast."

"Time waits for no one, Ramon, not even me. C'mon."

Ramon hugged his skateboard to his chest with one arm and half jogged to catch up with her.

Mrs. Winalski owned a candy-apple-red 1965 Mustang GT convertible, and she drove it like she could die at any minute and needed to get five things done before that happened. With an immaculate interior and a wax job that would do any car wash proud, the car was clearly Mrs. W's baby. That didn't bring him any comfort as he shut his eyes, gripped the door, and tried to remember the names of all the saints.

He didn't crack his lids until he felt the car slow to a stop. He was surprised that Mrs. W hadn't needed directions. Not that he'd been in a state to give them.

"We're here," she said, climbing out of the car.

"Did you go up on two wheels there for a while?"

She laughed. "I could grow to like you, Ramon."

Ramon didn't respond to that. He concentrated on getting his legs to stop shaking instead. Then he followed her up the walkway.

"Sammy bring you here before?"

Mrs. Winalski shook her head. She jabbed the doorbell with her finger. Haley opened it and immediately burst into a grin.

"Hey, Mom, Mrs. W's here!"

Sam's mom peered around Haley before welcoming them in. Tia hugged them both, a strained smile on her face.

"You said you'd never been here." Ramon gave Mrs. W his best accusing stare while he placed his skateboard carefully next to the door.

"No," she said, following Haley into the kitchen. "You asked if Sam had ever brought me here."

Tia shut the door behind them and ushered Ramon into the kitchen.

"Libby is an old friend," she said. "I asked her to keep an eye on Sam for me."

"Is she—" He made wavy gestures with his hands, though he wasn't sure what that might indicate.

"She's a witch, Ramon, like me."

"Okay, then." He took a seat at the table and tried to remember a time in his life when Tia's statement would have sounded odd.

While Tia assembled a platter of sandwich stuff, Ramon

filled them in on what he knew. Once he'd finished, he gave Sam's mom a moment to digest it all. He piled cheese onto some bread, hoping to eat in the meantime.

Mrs. W, however, did not screw around. "You've got to remove the binding now, Tia."

Tia clasped her hands and stared at her white knuckles. "I don't know if I can. He's so far away." Her voice cracked, and she trailed off. Haley reached over and covered her mother's hands with hers.

"You did what you thought was best, Mom," Haley said. "Not perfect, no. But it helped. You did good."

Tia looked up, grateful.

"But now we need to try something else," Haley said. "If Sam doesn't have his powers, he won't stand a chance against Douglas."

Ramon wasn't sure if Sam stood a chance even with the binding removed, but he didn't want to say that. Saying it might make it true.

Libby agreed with Haley, and they both kept on her until Tia finally said, "Okay."

Ramon held on to Brooke's bag and sat back, watching. He didn't know what to expect, exactly. So far they'd brewed some kind of green liquid with a lot of plants he couldn't identify and mumbled a lot of things he couldn't understand. There'd been some candle lighting and the general kinds of things one would expect from witches. He was glad that they didn't kill anything, that he hadn't seen any eye of newt or tongue of whatever, and that they hadn't danced naked around the room. Ramon didn't really need that kind of thing right now.

"It looks like they're cooking," he whispered to Brooke.

"Shh," she said. "I think it's a spell. Can you push the sides of my bag down a little bit more? I can't see that well." Ramon shoved down the sides. "Thanks," she said. "Man, this is so cool. It's like *Practical Magic* meets Rachel Ray or something." Brooke glanced over at Mrs. W. "Or maybe Julia Child."

Ramon shrugged. "Just looks like fancy cooking to me." Brooke ignored him and kept watching, her eyes alight with curiosity.

Fascinating as it was, he still felt antsy. When his phone went off, he set Brooke's bag on a corner table so she could see. Then he excused himself and went out back.

"Hello?"

"Tell me what you know." The voice had a low growl in it and didn't sound anything like the person Ramon had heard on the message. This voice wanted to bite his head off. The hair on the back of his neck began to rise. He pushed it down with the palm of his hand.

"Douglas has her, but I don't know where."

The man grunted. "That's okay. I think we do." He sounded like he was about to hang up.

"Wait," Ramon said. "Tell me where. He has my friend, too."

The line went quiet.

"Please," he said.

"Fine, but don't get in our way. And if my daughter gets harmed because of your bumbling, your blood is mine."

"Understandable." Ramon said it like people threatened his blood all the time. He ran in and got a pen so he could write down the address.

Once he had the information, he couldn't stand still. Sitting back down with Brooke and the girls was unbearable. Sam needed his help. Ramon was useless here. He had to go as soon as he could. His heart thudded away at the decision. He was used to being the one that got them in trouble. It was usually his fault they got chased by security guards for skateboarding in the wrong places; it was his fault they'd gotten detention over and over in high school. His fault they got thrown out of the Sadie Hawkins dance. All worth it, of course, but his fault. But he'd never before had to seriously worry about his safety or Sam's. Except for the Sadie Hawkins incident. He'd almost lost a finger that time.

Things had definitely changed. If they screwed up now, they wouldn't be getting off with a ticket or a slap on the wrist. He only had to look at Brooke to remember how bad it could go. But what was he supposed to do? It was Sammy.

He snuck past the room where the girls were, through the kitchen, and out the front door, quietly grabbing the keys to Tia's car on his way out.

23

SCHOOL'S OUT FOREVER

The whip-crack of pain across my already injured back made my whole body seize up. It didn't bring me to my knees. I'd already been on those. Now I was on my hands and knees trying to breathe past the pain. Either Douglas was tired of the visceral thrill involved in beating me bare-handed or his hands were getting sore from smacking me around. Whatever the reason, the end result was the riding crop in his right fist. I'd have told him he looked silly walking around a basement waving a riding crop, but I liked myself enough not to.

Douglas grabbed a fistful of my hair and jerked my head back. He leaned down, getting close enough that I could smell the musk of his aftershave. "I can't tell," he said through gritted teeth, "if you are intentionally screwing up or if you're really this useless."

I licked at a crack on my lip from an earlier blow and wondered why I couldn't be both.

"I'm trying," I said, putting as much calm in my voice as I could manage, "as best I can." He had been running out of patience with me, and I didn't want that. Normal Douglas freaked me out. Angry, out-of-control Douglas? No, thank you.

Under Douglas's tutelage, I'd been trying to summon a spirit for what felt like forever. I'd managed the circle after a few tries, but not much else. I wanted to point out that at least I'd gotten better at that. Shouldn't I get a gold star for effort?

When I hadn't been able to manage a general summoning of even the most basic spirit, Douglas gave me a list of names. Apparently that old adage is true—names have power. Even with the list, I'd struck out. The spark of ignition was there, but I'd run clean out of gas. Great, now I was comparing myself to cars. If I ever saw Ashley again, I'd kick her.

"I suggest you try again," Douglas said. His tone had cooled. Not reassuring. No, a definite threat lived in that tone. He held the crop loosely in his grip. If I screwed up again, ol' Douglas might take a few steps up on the violence ladder. I licked my lips and tried again.

I eased my body into a cross-legged position. It hurt my back more than staying on my hands and knees, but my arms would get too tired the other way. My eyes closed as I took a deep breath.

The basement looked much different when I shut my eyes. When I relaxed and really looked, things floated up from the darkness. Brid shone to my right—twisting copper and emerald. The cage around her held the colors of Douglas. The wards on the bars burned beaconlike at the top. Douglas, with his nauseating swirls of grays, silvers, blacks, and ice blues, stood to my left.

But that wasn't all. The room itself seemed filled with a shifting haze. I didn't know what that was. I'd never seen it before. Was it supposed to look like that?

I concentrated on my hazy circle. My blue was a richer color than Douglas's was. He'd drawn his own circle earlier after telling me that he still didn't trust mine. I compared the two. Both blue, mine a dimmer electric, Douglas's a vibrant ice color. The circles didn't sit still completely. They held to the lines we'd drawn, anchored to the floor, but in the air they shifted and moved, just like our auras did. Mine looked weak. Douglas was right. His circle was better.

Okay, no more screwing around. I called up one of the names Douglas had given me into my mind. Not as easy as it sounds. I was tired from the earlier effort. And the bleeding. I could feel the tickle of southbound blood on my lower back. Ashley had said that I didn't need blood to summon lesser spirits, but at this point I figured every little bit helped. Keeping my eyes closed, I reached around and swiped what I could off my back. Then I handprinted the floor in front of me with it. Kind of like finger painting in kindergarten, only gross.

I just hoped Ashley was right. With that thought sitting in my mind, a strange thing happened. It felt like something thin inside me snapped, bursting into a million pieces at once. I sucked in a breath, my spine going rigid with the force of it. This was what closing my first circle had felt like. Times a thousand. Every cell in my body took a shuddering gasp. The dam inside me had broken and all my power came rushing out. Years of unused, untouched potential, all at once. I'm not sure where it came from or why it had happened all of a sudden, but I had to let it go. I felt like I'd explode if I didn't.

Brid gasped, and I heard a sudden commotion in front of me. My eyes popped open.

A giant hole gaped in midair, like someone had cut out a piece of the basement with a pair of scissors.

Ashley, still in Catholic-girl chic, stood in the portal, talking to one of the freakiest things I'd ever seen. And I'd seen a talking severed head and a zombie panda. He—I assume it was a he—stood a good three feet over Ashley, putting him somewhere in the seven-foot zone. He wore a simple linen skirt around his waist, and golden cuffs encircled two of the biggest biceps I'd seen outside of professional wrestling. Though heavily muscled, he wasn't hulking. In fact, he looked more like a swimmer who lifted weights. A lot of weights. But his head was what gave me pause. He had the head of a jackal. From watching endless hours of *Animal Planet* with Frank, I'd learned that jackals come in many colors, from brown to black to gold, usually. I'd never seen this particular kind of coloring. His muzzle appeared to be a dark gray, shifting into various silvers all the way down to where the fur of the neck met the human part of the body. Frightening, yes. But he held a kind of terrible beauty as well. As I stared at him, my mouth hanging in slack-jaw style, I could think of only one word—awe.

"I'm just saying these new codes are ridiculous." Ashley's arms flailed about as she spoke, her face vehement. "What do they care if—"

The creature cleared its throat loudly and tipped its head slightly toward us. She stopped, hands fluttering down to her hips. She looked around.

"Geez, Sam, talk about a learning curve." She whistled and examined the open portal around her. I couldn't make out anything behind her except a houseplant in a very ornate golden pot.

"Seriously," she said, "this is pretty good. You even brought Ed here. Not many people can summon Ed." She jerked her thumb toward the jackal-headed man.

Nice to meet you. The voice boomed inside my head.

"Nice to meet you too . . . Ed." I gave him a little nod before I turned a slightly panicked look toward Ashley. "What are you doing here?"

Her eyebrows shot up. "You must have summoned me. I was just talking to Ed about some new legislation that came down from on high. Or up from down low, depending on how you look at it." She scanned the room, eyes in judgment mode. "This place looks different in the light. Not better, mind you, just different."

Ashley's face stilled. Since she was very expressive, I couldn't imagine what had caused her to go all poker-faced on me. I followed her gaze. Oh, right. Douglas. He had that effect on people.

Ashley jabbed Ed in the stomach lightly with her finger, indicating that he needed to look.

Ed twisted his head and smiled. *Douglas Montgomery,* he said, tongue lolling out in a laugh. *Is it finally time?*

Douglas looked to be the picture of calm, but I could see his knuckles whitening as he held on to the crop. "It will never be time," he answered.

You know what people say about the word never. Ed's tongue curled up over his nose before slipping into his mouth. *And Ammut is always hungry.*

Douglas gave a tight-lipped smile, then his power flowed over mine. Not a pleasant sensation. It felt like I'd been plastered in gritty mud and stinging nettles. I tried to push back, but I was already drained to pretty much empty. He overpowered me, and the portal snapped shut.

The room got very quiet. I tried to stand up, but exhaustion coupled with the sudden flow and stop of power was too much for my body to take. I wasn't done healing. Crap, I think I was still bleeding. I'd finally hit the point of *enough.* I needed sleep and food. I didn't care which came first.

Douglas's shoes made crisp sounds on the concrete as he walked over. He cuffed me with the back of his hand. Then he drew back and did it again. And again.

His eyes were fevered, and spittle flew from his lips. Douglas had hit the point of enough as well. He picked me up by my neck and threw me into the concrete wall. The roughness of the wall bit into my back and my scabs and made me scream. My teeth clicked shut as I bit off the sound.

He pushed his face close to mine.

"Do you have any idea what you've done?" He shouted the words at me. "Do you?" He hit me again instead of waiting for the answer. Full fist this time. I heard Brid growling in the background, but it was smothered by Douglas's semicoherent accusations.

I couldn't answer him. Even if I had the will and energy to open my mouth, I truly had no idea what I'd done.

He picked me back up by the throat. I realized that I'd been picked up by my throat a lot lately.

Douglas held me there, pinned against the wall. My world began to fade around the edges. His face came in close to mine, and I watched as the anger drained away from him. He'd come to a decision of some sort, but he wasn't sharing. Instead, his breathing steady, his face calm, he held me against the wall as my vision folded in. Panic gripped me, but I was too far gone to care. I slipped into nothingness.

24

COME TOGETHER, RIGHT NOW, OVER ME

Ramon parked Tia's car on a side street. The afternoon had morphed from blustery to a more cheerful, partially sunny day as he'd headed north. He estimated that he had fifteen more minutes before the weather did its bipolar thing, probably shifting into a misty rain. He grabbed his skateboard and got out of the car. The skateboard was the closest thing he had to a weapon.

He checked the address he'd jotted down. The mailbox in front of him told him he had the right place, but that was all he had to go on. Douglas's house seemed to be set back on a big piece of land. Ramon steered clear of the long gravel driveway, choosing to stick to the cover of the trees instead.

The brush was thick, making progress slow. Once the house came into view, Ramon crouched down, trying to get the lay of the land. Not for the first time, he questioned the decisions that had led him away from a life of crime and evil. Casa Douglas was *huge*. The great expanse of manicured yard should have dwarfed the house, but the flat plains of grass added to the scale of everything. A sea of grass between him and the house. Trees and shrubbery on all sides, blocking any view of neighbors. Huge detailed sculptures dotted the lawn at odd intervals. A few lions and some Greek statues were all he could make out. The house even had some crazy marble columns and a pediment at the top. He couldn't quite figure out the design, but it looked like gladiators or something. The effect was a bit much for the house, but then again, people did all kinds of crazy things when they had money.

This much land, this big house on the water . . . Douglas must have deep pockets. That usually meant a lot of security, but Ramon couldn't see any. Not that he knew what to look for, but the lack of a fence definitely troubled him. If he'd spent more time developing a life of crime, he was sure he'd have been able to spot all kinds of helpful things. He had a large exposed area to cross. All Douglas had to do was peek out the window and Ramon would be history. Still, he needed to try. He took a half step forward.

An arm wrapped around him from behind and yanked him off his feet, making him drop his skateboard. Another hand went over his mouth. The hand smelled like dirt.

"Are you Ramon? Nod if you are."

Ramon nodded slowly.

"By all that's holy, would you chill out, Bran? Who else would he be?"

He recognized the other speaker from the answering machine message. The grip on him loosened. Ramon put his hands out, showing he was unarmed, and turned around slowly.

A handful of people stood around him. The group included

a couple of the biggest freaking wolves he'd ever seen, and they weren't leashed. No way those were dogs. At best, they might be wolf hybrids, if that could be considered an at best. Ramon tried to appear calm, knowing that animals sense fear. He didn't want to do anything to give those wolves an excuse to gnaw on one of his legs.

The man who'd grabbed him was tall, maybe six feet, with a grim set to his face. His brown hair was cut in a short, plain style, like he didn't give a damn what it looked like as long as it stayed out of his face. He wore jeans and a tank top, despite the rainy weather.

The guy next to him was smaller, but still a bit taller than Ramon. He had auburn hair and a prominent nose. Ramon could see some resemblance to the other guy around the jawline, but where the tall one seemed all business, this one smiled and practically bounced on his feet.

The smaller man held out his hand. The guy had a good, firm handshake and his skin felt hot to the touch. "Sean," he said. "And this is the rest of the Merry Men." He jerked to the group behind them.

"So you guys are here to get . . . ?" Ramon couldn't remember the name. Bridget?

"Our sister," Bran said. "It would be safer if you'd wait here. We'll do our best to get your friend out if he's still alive."

Ramon squared his shoulders and was getting ready to tell off General Jackass when Sean stepped between them. "You'll have to excuse Sunshine here; we're all a bit worried about Brid." He spread his hands in a "you understand" gesture.

"What he means is, our pack leader gave you permission to join us, but we're worried about your safety. If you choose to come with us, please do what we say."

Ramon let his shoulders slump. "I understand. I've got baby sisters." He tried to make eye contact with all of them. "But Sammy is family, too. I don't know what's up with you guys or your giant, mutant dogs, but I'm willing to swallow some ego if it gets my friend out in one piece."

Sean rolled his neck from side to side and started shaking out his muscles. He looked like a boxer right before he goes into the ring. "Now that we're all playing nice, shall we get on with it?"

Bran might have been tough looking, but it was Sean who sent a shiver up Ramon's spine. He looked way too happy about the prospect of violence.

25

I'M GOING TO BREAK MY
RUSTY CAGE AND RUN

When I woke, I couldn't move. The first thing I saw was concrete. I was still in the basement, though I couldn't tell if I was relieved by that or not. I doubted that Douglas would move me if he wanted to do something nefarious, but there was some comfort to be found in the familiar surroundings. At least I wasn't in some shiny new hell.

My arms were bound in worn leather straps that appeared to be stained with things I didn't want to think about. My legs were bound in the same way. The wooden restraint table I'd been admiring had been pulled away from the wall, and I'd been strapped to it. Not very encouraging. I tugged at the straps, bucking my body as best I could, looking for any kind of give. None. I swore, if I survived this, I'd never sleep again. Each time I'd woken up lately, things had gone from bad to exponentially worse.

"Sam?"

I turned my head, but between the restraints and the table I didn't have much wiggle room. If I angled it up a little, I could just see Brid standing in the cage. At least she looked all right.

"Are you okay?" she asked.

"I'm tied to a table."

She gave me a stare that could liquefy stone.

"Sorry," I said. "I guess life-threatening situations bring out my inner smart-ass. If you don't count the table, I'm no worse than I was before." Except my throat felt sore, but I didn't tell her that. I didn't want to add to her worries. And the very fact that I thought telling her that would make things worse for her almost made me laugh out loud. She was in a cage, and I was strapped down to a freaking table. Seriously, how much worse could this get?

"Bad, Sam, this is bad." Brid chewed on her lip. "Whatever you did scared him. Douglas is unbalanced on a good day." She shook her head. "He smelled like fear, and I don't think he likes to be afraid."

"That does sound bad." I tugged again on my arm restraints. Solid. "What do you think the chances are that this contraption is a temporary punishment?"

"Zero," she said. "It reeks of blood and terror. This whole damn room stinks of it, and I'm tired of being in here."

"I know." I stopped pulling and relaxed. No sense wasting what little energy I had.

"What the hell happened to you?" she asked.

"I don't know." What the hell *had* happened to me? "It was like I went from zero to sixty in a second." I had to stop making car analogies. If I survived this, I'd tack it onto my list of resolutions.

"We need to get out of here." Brid grabbed onto the bars. "You have to try and call Ashley."

"I don't have a circle. Besides, I don't know if I can again. I think last time might have been a fluke."

"Douglas said the circle was for protection. Ashley isn't malevolent as far as I can tell. Just picture her in your mind and call her by name."

I was skeptical, but I closed my eyes and gave it a shot anyway. We could only gain from trying. I conjured her up in my mind, saddle shoes and all. I took my power and aimed it at that image. When I felt it was strong enough, I whispered her name.

She popped into the room almost immediately.

"Great Caesar's ghost!" Ashley looked quickly about the room before she ran over to me. Despite her experience, I think my ability to get into new and life-threatening situations shocked her. Personally, I was hoping it was a phase that I would grow out of. At least, I hoped I had a chance to grow out of it.

She reached for my wrist, only to jerk her hand back the second she touched the leather. She shook her hand like she'd been burned. "You know, I like this guy less every second."

"You can't get me out of here, can you?" All hope seeped out of me.

She shook her head mournfully. "I'm sorry, Sam. Those damn things are practically soaked in *power de Douglas*, if you get my drift. If he does much more necromancy in here, I won't be able to walk around."

"It's okay, Ashley," I said, even though we all knew the situation was far from good.

"I don't understand," Brid said. "I thought he wanted to train Sam up? It just doesn't make sense that the first time Sam's successful, he does this."

Ashley sighed. "I'm afraid, from what Ed was telling me, it does make sense." She began to examine the table I was on. "I think he was okay with having you around as long as you weren't a threat." She climbed under the table. "But once you raised Ed—" There was a muffled thump. "I don't think you understand what you did with that."

"No, I don't."

"Ed's an upper-level entity, Sam. Most necromancers wouldn't even try. But you did it without any training or effort." She climbed out from under the table.

"But I was summoning you. We probably just got Ed as a bonus."

Ashley dusted off her hands. "No, you didn't. You should have just gotten a portal showing me. Geez, Sam, you shouldn't have even gotten a portal. I should have just heard you calling."

"So once I did that?"

Brid slumped in the cage. "You officially became too dangerous."

Ashley patted my cheek. "Exactly. Look at it from his point of view."

"I don't ever want to do that."

She half smiled. "I know. But in one day you went from not being able to close a circle to summoning Ed."

"So, I finally succeed at something, and now I'm going to be killed for it."

"Your mom must have snapped her binding," Brid said.

"Great, even when she's trying to help me, it almost kills me."

Ashley stamped her foot. "Damn it, this is frustrating. Why won't anyone let me do my freaking job?" She nibbled at a thumbnail. "There must be something," she mumbled.

"Hey," Brid said, "can you tell Sam how to open these bars? You know, now that he's outside? If he can get me out, I can undo those straps."

Ashley lit up and gave a little skip of joy. She placed her small hands on my temples. "Close your eyes."

I obediently shut them. One of her hands moved away from my temple and there was a sudden burning on my side. I looked down toward the pain. Little girl had cut me.

"Hey, whose side are you on?" Why did everything involve my blood lately? I wasn't a friggin' pincushion.

"Sorry," she said, though she didn't sound the least bit apologetic. "This is one of those things we need blood for. Or at least, it will be faster with blood." She reached up on her tiptoes and smeared my blood on the symbols etched into the bars on the cage. "This cage, these symbols—all done with necromancy. So to be undone, they need a necromancer. And that's you, my friend. Now concentrate, Sam. I want you to picture the cage, the magic inside it."

I squeezed my eyes shut. "Okay, now what?"

"What we're looking for is a weakness. A small flaw we can exploit. Few spells are perfect, and it will be a lot easier to deal with that than anything else."

"I already know where the weak spot is."

"You do?" She sounded surprised.

"I found a flaw earlier when I was studying the cage." I could still picture it in my mind. "I just didn't know what to do about it, or if it was even helpful." I frowned. "At least, I think it was a flaw—"

"Don't go doubting yourself now. It's all we've got," she said. "Now, what I want you to do is concentrate all your power on that spot. Shove everything you've got into it."

"What will that do?"

"It should overload it. Like when too much electricity flips a breaker."

I found the weak spot in the spell and did what Ashley said. It didn't smash like I'd hoped. More like a slow chipping away. Sweat beaded on my forehead. We didn't have time for chipping. I clenched my jaw, dug deep, and pushed all I had into that one spot.

The breaker tripped, and the glow of the spell on the cage vanished. "Done," I said.

"Great," Ashley said, "now we just need to pick the lo—"

I heard a dull snap.

"Never mind," Ashley said.

Two seconds later, Brid's face hovered over mine. She smiled, and it went all the way to her eyes. A quick kiss on my mouth, and then she started undoing the leather cuff that held my right hand. The clasp was rusty, but she got it undone fairly quickly. One arm freed, I motioned Brid toward my feet while I worked on the other arm.

The sound of the lock in the basement door being drawn

made us both stop. Brid wouldn't have time to free me completely. I mouthed the word *hide* at her and Ashley. Since I didn't know who was coming downstairs, I didn't want to say it out loud. I didn't know what was fact or fiction yet about werewolves, but I didn't want to risk Michael hearing us if the superhearing bit ended up being true. Added to my list of resolutions, right after never going to sleep again, I resolved to learn everything I could about everything.

Ashley disappeared in a blink. Brid crept under the stairs. She wouldn't go back in that cage, not if she could help it. Which was smart. If she hid in there and ended up getting locked in again, then we were both up the stream sans paddle.

I slipped my right hand back into the restraint, doing my best to look tied up. The door banged open. I arched up and saw Michael coming down the steps, his arms full. I could see a big bowl and a few other things. He saw me and smiled.

"Good to see you awake," he said, the shit-eating grin on his face getting bigger.

"And why is that?"

"I was afraid you might sleep through all the fun." He set down his armload on the floor.

"You really don't like me, do you?"

"No, I don't."

"Why?" I asked. "What did I ever do to you?"

Michael crossed his arms and leaned against the wall. "Can't a guy just hate someone on sight anymore?"

"I guess if you're a jackass, sure."

Michael didn't rise to the bait. He just grunted. He hadn't once backed down from an insult so far. Michael was the kind of guy they invented the phrase "hair-trigger temper" for. I was curious. And afraid.

"How come you're so chipper?"

"Because," he said, "I finally get to help kill you." He seemed really pleased about the prospect too.

My pulse sped up, but I tried to keep the smile on my face. It's one thing to know there's a chance people might kill you, or that it's probable that they will kill you. But when they confirm it, with a smile, it's a whole other thing altogether.

Douglas came down the steps, his sleeves rolled up and ready. His face serene, he walked slowly toward me.

"I thought you said you'd only kill me if I didn't learn."

Douglas took his knife down off the bookshelf and studied it.

"I finally did something you told me to do, and I get trussed up for my effort. What gives?"

"You are too vexing to live."

I waited for him to go on. Nothing. He just checked the edge of his knife.

"That's it? C'mon, in the movies you can't get a Bond villain to shut up. You're not even going to outline your evil plan for me? Maybe if you pick up your cat and pet it while sitting in an oversized chair, something will come to you." Was that Bond or Austin Powers? Or Inspector Gadget? It was amazing how easy it was to get those things confused. I didn't actually want to hear what he had planned, or why I vexed him. My only thought at this point was buying Brid some time. I couldn't look over at her. I just stalled and hoped.

"I'm not a Bond villain, just as you are no Sean Connery."

Douglas put the knife back on the shelf and went for a piece of chalk. "But out of pity, I will, as they say, throw you a bone." He selected a large chunk of chalk that would have been more at home on a sidewalk hopscotch diagram. "I don't know how you hid from me. I don't know how you veiled your gift once you were here. What you did actually managed to surprise me, and that hasn't happened in quite some time." He leaned down and began the circle. "Too many unknowns with you. And since your gift came out to play, I no longer need to train you to draw it out."

"So you were planning on killing me the whole time?"

Douglas blew away some of the loose chalk. "Yes." He filled in a thin spot in the line. "Unless you proved useful. But most likely, yes."

He had to draw a big circle to get the table and himself inside, so he stood up and moved to another chunk of the floor. Unfortunately that took him right in view of the cage.

The room exploded into motion. Douglas shouted at Michael, who leapt toward the bars. Brid dove out of hiding. She let out a warrior scream midleap and changed. I'm not sure what I expected. Some amount of twisting limbs, maybe some mucus. I guess when she told me that the process was fast, I didn't really get what she meant. One minute, Brid was howling in midair, her arms extended, wearing my Batman shirt and my boxers, the next minute she was vapor. It was like Brid exploded into a million pieces, and when those pieces came back together, she was a white blur of fur and teeth. My shirt and boxers drifted to the floor.

Michael turned so fast I didn't see him move, but it wasn't

fast enough. Brid caught his arm in her teeth. Her momentum too great to hold on, she continued forward, slicing his arm in the process. Brid hit the ground, sliding on her paws. In her new form, she was pure white, except for the inside of her ears, which were pink like the inner recesses of seashells. Even in her animal form, she was breathtaking. Watching her move was like stumbling onto a hidden glade in the forest and finding a startled deer. Perfection of form and movement in nature—you can't help but be awed by it.

I caught a spot of crimson on her tail and the back of one of her ears. She'd only looked pure white at first. I'd never seen markings that color before. Her eyes were a blazing red. As she glared at Michael, the blaze grew until it looked like she had balls of flame for eyes.

A popping sound later and Brid was back, only naked now.

"I'd fight you wolf to wolf, but the change would take you way too long. I might grow old waiting." She went into a fighting stance, her face hard.

Michael flicked his arms out and opened his palms. "I can change what I need to." His voice lowered into an eager growl. As I watched, his hands thickened, claws growing from the pads of his fingers.

"C'mon," he said, "where's your dainty claws?" His voice took on a taunting lilt. "Oh, right," he said, "you can't do a partial change, can you, half-breed?"

"I guess I'm just not as perfect as you," she said, sweetly. She flicked her arms out in a similar motion. Instead of claws, each of her hands held a short sword. Each blade flared out from its pommel, a little over two feet in length. Brid eased back into her fighting stance and smiled. As she did, the blades burst into the same flames I'd seen in her eyes earlier. She lunged at Michael, who dodged her thrust. He rolled to the side and slashed out with his hand. When they pulled away from each other, Brid was bleeding from her rib cage. The wound looked shallow, and she ignored it. They started circling each other.

A small black-and-silver blur zoomed past my head, hovering next to Douglas. The blur slowed and landed on the top of the bookshelf, morphing into the shape of Douglas's cat. It flicked its tail and settled.

"We have a problem." The cat's voice sounded grim. Despite everything, I was surprised when it spoke. I'd never seen a cat talk outside of a Disney movie. No wonder everyone had looked at me funny when I petted it. You don't pet things that talk.

"Now what?" Douglas asked.

"Intruders," the cat said.

Douglas cursed under his breath. "What kind?"

"Wolves, front and back of the house, and what appears to be a kid with a skateboard." The cat's tail snapped back and forth. "I recommend postponing the ritual and doing some damage control."

"I can't help you much without blood, and there will be plenty of that with the ritual. Two birds, one stone, James. The defenses will hold until then."

Brid threw Michael into the wall to the side of us. He bounced back from it and hurled himself at her like nothing had happened.

"Take care of it," Douglas said to the cat.

"But—"

Douglas made a slashing motion with his free hand. "Take care of it!"

The cat gave a final flick of its tail before jumping off the bookcase and morphing back into the black-and-silver blur. It shot up the stairs.

Douglas twirled the knife in his hand. "We'd better get started."

26

EVERYBODY WAS KUNG FU FIGHTING

A howl issued from the other side of the house. The hair on the back of Ramon's neck stood up in reaction. The group around him tensed. "What does that mean?" he whispered.

"It means," Sean said, dropping into a runner's crouch, "get ready."

Ramon clutched his board. He put one hand on the ground and leaned forward, matching Sean, who gave him a wink and a grin before turning his head back toward the house. Bran didn't smile but held himself in a similar position.

A sharp yip echoed, and the group was off. Ramon ran after them, feet slipping in loose leaf cover and dirt. Though he had never tried out for track, he knew he was pretty fast. You don't spend years skateboarding and not learn how to run from cops. But this group outstripped him easily. Two dozen or so wolves pulled to the front, their people following in their tracks. He wondered if they had the same number of people flanking the other side of the house. Sean and the rest seemed to trust the wolves, letting them run without orders or direction, the whole group moving in unison. The image made him think of a flock of birds flying in formation.

Ramon quickly fell to the back. As he watched them leap over bushes and fly across the grass, he wondered if they were cyborgs. Humans just couldn't do that stuff. He made the sound effect from *The Six Million Dollar Man* under his breath as he kept on after them.

A gout of flame came out of nowhere and burned the grass in a swath next to him. Ramon twisted away from it but managed to stay his feet. When he looked up he saw a shiny black blur tearing about like a hummingbird. The blur banked and unleashed another line of fire at the approaching group. As it slowed, he could actually make out what the blob was—a dragon. Only about the size of a housecat, the dragon produced a stream of flame ten times its size. The group scattered but kept moving forward.

A shattering crunch of a noise split across the lawn as the statues cracked open. Very living cargo spilled out from under the leftover pebbles and dust. The lions leapt onto a few of the wolves, rolling them away from the group. The fights continued to the sides, blood and dust flying.

The Greek statues were even more terrifying. Ramon watched as the minotaur lifted up a wolf and hurled it. Seconds later, three other wolves pulled it down. It stood back up and shook them off like they were puppies. Ramon wasn't sure what the nymphs were doing, and he didn't want to know. The gladiators from the bas-relief he'd seen earlier began to shimmy down the columns. So Douglas hadn't just been eccentric with his décor. "Heads up!" Ramon shouted. A few of the men looked up and saw the gladiators. They howled and took off, dodging swords and slamming into shields. The effect was chaotic but, at the same time, handled with a practiced precision. Sean and his group were well trained, that was obvious.

Ramon saw one of the wolves get pulled into a hedgerow when it got too close. He heard it howl, but he couldn't see what happened to it. One of the men ran over and pulled it out. The wolf was bloodied but still alive.

The tiny dragon continued to swoop down, swiping at their eyes with one of its four taloned feet. Ramon heard a few yelps of pain, but not many. One huge, gray wolf leapt at the dragon, snapping at it with its jaws. The wolf missed, but the move forced the dragon to fly higher. This happened a few more times, and while the dragon was getting some good hits in, Ramon was relieved to notice that the group had gained on the house. The dragon was outnumbered, even with its strange backup crew. The creature ignored the odds against it, spitting fire, clawing, and giving the fight its best shot. Even though it was keeping him from Sam, he had to give the little guy some respect. To take on a group like this, even a dragon must have *cojones* the size of watermelons.

After another swoop and yelp, Ramon pulled back his arm and hurled his skateboard, giving it all he had. Distracted by the seemingly bigger threat of the wolf's jaws, the dragon never saw the spinning board coming. Fire-breathing mythical creature or not, an airborne skateboard hurtling upward at that speed hurt like hell, Ramon was sure. He'd been hit by a few boards, and they'd hurt him like hell, too. Dragon and skateboard collided in midair, the metal of the trucks making a large thwacking sound against the creature's skull before the whole mess came crashing down.

He paused to snag his board, ignoring the stunned creature a few feet from it. Then he ran. He broke the board a second later as he swung at what appeared to be a pack of vicious lawn gnomes. The little creatures were crawling all over Sean, their red hats bobbing and weaving as they poked him with tiny shovels. One clobbered Sean's knee with a miniature wheelbarrow. Ramon chucked the broken ends of the board at the one with the wheelbarrow and kicked another. Once Sean had a handle on the gnomes—he started winging them at the minotaur—Ramon continued to run toward the house.

Bran leapt over the steps leading to the front porch, slamming into the door as he went. The big guy never even hesitated. Surprise rippled through Ramon as he watched the door give way. Everyone else poured through the gap after him. A split second later, Ramon heard a similar creak and snap as another door split on the other side of the house.

Ramon ran up the stained wooden steps. He jumped through the hole that Bran had made, hoping Sammy was still okay somewhere. And that he wasn't too late.

27

UNCHAIN MY HEART;
OH, PLEASE, PLEASE, SET ME FREE

The fighting continued around the cage, but I ignored it. From the yips, groans, and thuds coming from Michael, it was clear Brid could take care of herself. I was more concerned with Douglas. He walked toward me, eyeing me like he was trying to decide where my light meat and my dark meat were. I kept myself from grabbing at him with my free arm. It wouldn't do any good. He stood out of reach, so all I'd accomplish was revealing the only trick I had.

He came at me with the knife, slicing into the still-bound arm. I gritted my teeth, but the scream came anyway. A long thin line of red erupted along my arm, right above the blue of my vein. He caught my blood in a bowl that was way too big for my liking. Big bowls mean more blood, and Douglas was the greedy type.

He jumped back as a snarling ball of Brid and Michael slammed into the bookcase, but didn't lose any blood from the bowl. He waited until Brid kicked Michael in the stomach and bobbed to his other side, leading Michael off in the other direction. I watched, breath caught, blood dripping from my arm onto the ground.

I felt the first drop hit.

As it splashed back up, a sensation tore through my body, like sticking a fork in a light socket. With that one drop I knew something very important.

Douglas had killed a lot of people in this room. And a lot of other things.

And they were pissed.

More of my blood fell to the floor. My eyes went wide, and my breath came in short gasps. My whole body went rigid.

Anytime I'd tried to do something involving necromancy, I'd floundered. I'd stumbled along blindly, trying to figure out how things worked. I didn't have to do that this time.

When I'd looked at the room earlier, I'd seen a haze and wondered if it was normal. I knew the answer. The air looked hazy because it held an amalgam of different specters. They were all angry, and they were all howling for Douglas's blood. I doubted there were many places on earth that looked like that. I wanted to cover my ears, drown out the sound of it. I wondered how Douglas could even walk into the basement, how he could concentrate over the din. Or were they simply calling out for help from the first necromancer that came around besides their killer?

Another drop hit. I was damn near choking on power. My muscles were so rigid I couldn't draw a full breath. I knew I could tell the spirits to be quiet. I knew they'd have to do what I said. But I forced myself to listen, to hear all their pain. To pull it all inside me until my chest ached with it.

Because I listened, they told me what to do. I didn't see any other option. I had to hope they wouldn't hurt Brid. I accepted their offer, and my power blew outward, throwing the room into chaos.

The floor split, and creatures came up from the ground, forming as they climbed, just like the first zombie I'd seen. I heard a loud crash as the fridge under the stairs upended, glass vials spilling all over the floor. One broke open, and the energy inside me expanded. Blood. Douglas had been keeping vials full of blood in his fridge. The spirits didn't like it as much as mine. It wasn't fresh. But they used it all the same.

The creatures that materialized this time were under my control, and I sent them at Douglas. They flew at him, their hands out, aiming for his throat, his clothes, anything. He held up his arms, throwing out his own power and keeping them at bay.

I felt him try to activate his circle. Too late, he realized he'd never finished it. He'd been in too much of a rush after Brid's attack.

Another drop bled into the floor, and I egged the spirits on.

Suddenly people were pouring into the room, people I didn't recognize. No, not people. In the throes of magic, I could see twists of color, some like Brid, and some like nothing I'd ever seen. Wolves came at their heels. The giant beasts hurled themselves at Douglas. I felt that nettle-and-mud feeling as he used his will to turn some of the weaker spirits away from him and onto the wolves. I watched as a confused zombie turned from Douglas and leapt onto a tall, short-haired man in a tank top. I did my best to keep them pointed away from the strangers and toward the real enemy, but Douglas had more training than me. His tactic worked, keeping a mass of undead bodies and spirits between him and the intruders.

The room was turning into one solid brawl.

Douglas went back to his spell, words streaming from his lips. He used the blood from the bowl to draw symbols on my legs and over my heart.

The world tunneled in and became only two things: the spirits and Douglas. Between the anger and the built-up power, the spirits were in a frenzy. They attacked anyone or anything they came into contact with. I couldn't send them back. The best I could do was try for damage control and hope that everyone would be okay.

I heard a shout, and my vision tunneled out again: Ramon at the top of the stairs, Ramon barreling toward me, an antique lamp in his hand, swinging at anything in his way. Douglas didn't even look. He just made a negligent pushing motion with his hand, and a zombie attacked Ramon. The ragged creature picked him up and threw him under the stairs. The crowd shifted and blocked my view.

28

BEEP BEEP'M, BEEP BEEP, YEAH

Mrs. W drove right up the damn driveway like an old bat out of hell. Tia crouched down in her seat, but Haley leaned forward, anxious to get there.

"Are we not even going to try for stealth?" Tia asked, grabbing onto the door as they hit a pothole in the road.

Mrs. W snorted. "Ramon's already here, and from the looks of it, a lot of other people are, too. Stealth is a long-gone concept."

Haley had to agree. As they approached the yard, she could see scorched earth and broken doors. She tried to make sense of it. Had there been a flamethrower fight? A minotaur lay bleeding next to what appeared to be a shredded lion. Tiny red hats were everywhere. A few men were lounging around a pretty Greek lady, and one guy was fighting the shrubbery. "Where do you think Sam is?" she asked. She squashed the tremor of fear in her voice. Fear wouldn't do her or Sam any good. This was a rescue mission. She had to concentrate on that.

Tia unfurled from her crouch, her desire to examine the yard apparently more powerful than her fear of Mrs. W's driving. Or, Haley thought, it might just be because the car was finally going under eighty miles an hour.

Tia squinted, looking for a sign. She pointed toward the back of the house. "There," she said.

"You sure?" Mrs. W asked, even though she'd already started driving over grass to get there.

"Yes," Tia said, eyes going toward the eaves of the house. For the first time, Haley noticed the biggest freaking crow she'd ever seen. How had she missed that?

"What the hell is that?" she said. Her mom mumbled in response. She wasn't sure if she heard correctly, but it sounded like Tia said, "Sam's crow."

"Hold on." Mrs. W downshifted and hit the gas, tearing huge chunks out of the yard, her face filled with devilish glee. "I hope ol' Dougie has a good gardener on staff."

Haley hunkered down in her seat and braced herself for the end of the ride. There was a small thump and a cry as the car hit something. Mrs. W slammed on the brakes, and they all piled out.

Whatever they'd hit had been thrown a few yards and wasn't moving. Haley immediately ran toward it, ignoring her mother's protests. The curled-up form of a black-and-white cat was embedded in the ground. Despite the hole it had caused, the actual body of the cat seemed fine. Haley picked it up gently, running her hands over it while looking for any wounds. Nothing.

"Haley." Her mother came to a stop behind her. "You shouldn't do that. You don't know what it is."

"It's a cat."

"You don't know that for sure."

"What does it matter?" Haley asked. "What do we need to know besides the fact that it could be hurt?"

"It must be nice to be young," Mrs. W said wistfully.

"Haley, put it down." Tia's voice was firm.

"No." She brushed some dirt off the cat's face and it opened its eyes. Haley had never seen a cat with silver eyes before. "It's beautiful."

The cat stared at her for a minute before leaping out of her arms. In midair, the cat morphed into a tiny dragon and flew in a wobbly path toward the woods, hiccuping fire the whole time. Haley stood dumbfounded.

"What on earth?" Tia stared off after the creature.

"Well, thank heavens for that," Mrs. W said. She looked around, taking in the yard. She frowned at the men lounging close to the pretty lady and the guy fighting a berserk hedge. Mrs. W grabbed Haley by the shoulder. "You and your mom go get the boy, okay? I'm going to stay out here and deal with this lot."

Haley nodded. Tia was already sprinting toward the house, yelling at Haley to stay there.

She stayed put for all of two seconds. Haley couldn't just sit there and let them have all the fun. She looked back to where the cat had disappeared. "Ingrate," she mumbled, and snuck off toward the house.

29

BALLROOM BLITZ

Sweat beaded on my lip as I tried to maintain some measure of control over the situation. But with my blood flowing onto the floor and my energy waning under the strain, I didn't think I had much more in me.

Douglas continued to mumble and throw my blood around. I couldn't see everything he was doing, but I didn't really want to. I didn't need to see him to know that his spell was coming together. I could feel the power of it pressing on the backs of my eyelids. I shuddered as the spell crawled along my skin. It felt oily and unclean.

The power of the incantation jackknifed up, and I knew Douglas was almost done. If I had any tricks, the time to use them had come.

As he reached across me to draw a symbol on my head, I jerked my right hand out of the cuff and slammed my fist into his eye. My knuckles connected with his cheek and brow, and I felt his surprise. He stumbled back, and I grabbed for the knife. My palm wrapped around the top of the blade, which cut into the soft flesh of my hand. I managed to get a finger or two around the hilt. Jaw clenched, I yanked the knife away from Douglas, the pressure causing the blade to cut deeper into my palm.

Douglas lunged, his mouth carved into a snarl. As he did, I reversed the knife and threw my arm forward, putting as much force as I could into the stab.

The world slowed down as the knife blade bit into his throat. The sounds of fighting around me dimmed. In the new quiet, I could hear the wet pop as the blade slid home. The hilt protruded from his neck, my hand keeping it in place. I wanted to keep it there forever, like my hand on that knife was all that was keeping him pinned still. Douglas's eyes went panic-wide. Anger changed to surprise and fear, the emotions boiling over onto my skin. He hadn't thought me capable of this. He'd underestimated me greatly, and I felt that thought register. I could literally feel his pain. How had he been able to kill so many times if it felt like this?

We stayed frozen like that, both of us overwhelmed. The image of Douglas bleeding, dying, my hand on the hilt of the blade, burned itself into my brain. It would probably stay with me until the day I died.

He jerked away from me, pulling the knife free from his neck. Blood fountained, spraying me in the face. I must have hit an artery. His blood struck my tongue—a viscous, heavy saltiness. My heart shuddered. No, not my heart. Douglas's heart.

We'd completed the spell.

Power ran through me, stronger than before. My body convulsed with it, but I didn't drop the knife. Douglas fell to his knees, and another wave took me. Something old and brittle shattered in my chest. My heart fluttered for a split second, tied to Douglas's floundering beat. I felt the rhythm stumble and slow.

I felt him die.

At the same moment, I felt another death, like a flickering motion on the edge of my field of vision. My eyes stayed stuck on Douglas, but in my mind I could see Brid. Her face and hands bloody, her pale form standing over the crumpled heap of Michael. She'd gotten her revenge, though she didn't look happy about it. She didn't cry, but she looked sad that it'd had to come to this, that she had had to kill one of her own.

Brid was the only point of stillness in a sea of motion. Everyone else around her was still battling the dead. But Brid made no move to help them. Instead, she stared as Michael's blood leaked out from the tear in his throat.

I watched with her. I felt it as the red pool spread at her feet.

And it was too much.

I screamed then, an unending peal of torment. The pain was excruciating. The pain felt glorious. I could feel every nerve in my hand, every cut in my back, every sensation magnified until the line between good and bad blurred into something so awesome, so awful, that I had to open my mouth and let it out.

I felt the room still, the fighting pause, everyone and everything hanging on to that scream. I couldn't get a handle on it. In my mind I grabbed at it, tried to find an edge, but there was none. Power clawed at my insides, trying to get out.

My gift was tearing me apart.

I continued to scream, though my voice was becoming hoarse. I'd never known how much damage a sound could do to my throat. And I didn't care. I kept screaming because it was all I could do.

It was Brid who grabbed my face. She looked tired and drawn. I didn't realize how hot my cheeks were until her cool hands burned into them. I dimly remembered that Brid's hands usually felt hot to me. Was that bad?

I looked for the horror in her eyes. Horror for what had happened, for what I'd done, for what I'd become. I couldn't find it. Brid looked at me like she needed me to focus on what she was saying.

I stopped screaming. I grabbed her wrist with my free hand and held on.

"Put them back," she whispered.

Was she whispering, or was I having a hard time hearing? I could see the creases in her lips as they moved. She wanted me to put something back. Wait . . . someone. She wanted someone put back. But I couldn't remember who or what.

Brid must have seen my confusion. "The dead. Put them back." She enunciated each word. Her hair shone in the light, the colored streaks weaving through the rest of it. She shook my face, trying to get my attention. "Put the dead back in the ground, Sam, now!"

Of course. The dead were scattered like toys that I needed to put away. Biting, undead toys. I shivered against the chill of her palms and nodded. I didn't even have to try to find them. The spirits were all there at my fingertips. Go to sleep, I told them. It's done. It's all over.

One by one, I felt them return to the earth. The power poured away with them as they went, but it didn't leave entirely. I could feel it curled up in my chest like a sleeping cat. The table shuddered as the floor shifted back into its original shape. I didn't see it. I stared into Brid's eyes until she told me I was done.

I don't remember anything after that.

30

BACK IN BLACK

$\mathfrak{F}$or the first time in a week, I woke up somewhere pleasant. Okay, a hospital bed isn't usually described as *pleasant*, but no one was whupping my ass or throwing me into a cage, so on the whole, everything seemed fantastic to me. The room was light and airy, and the blankets were soft. The comfortable bed made me feel better about the fact that my entire body ached. But, to be honest, I was kind of surprised to be alive, so complaining about the pain wasn't too high on my list.

The room was empty—empty except for someone I'd never seen before. He sprawled in an easy chair next to the bed, idly flipping through the comics section of a newspaper. He wore jeans and a T-shirt that read CONTROL THE POPULA-TION: SUPPORT CANNIBALISM! in big block letters. Between his reddish hair and easy manner, I figured him to be a relation of Brid's.

"You made me miss Sunday," he said, not looking up from the paper.

"Excuse me?" I coughed. He handed me a plastic mug of water with a bendy straw, still not looking up.

"Sunday's comics," he said. "So now I have to catch up." He tossed the paper onto the floor. "I miss *Calvin and Hobbes*."

"Don't we all."

We stared at each other for what felt like five extremely long seconds. The window was open, and a soft spring breeze drifted in. "So you're the guy who did the no-no cha-cha with my baby sister."

My stomach twisted. Was he pretending to be nice to cover the fact that he wanted to eat my face? If I ever ran into a guy who'd even touched Haley, I knew I'd want to smack him around. I closed my eyes, ready to accept whatever action this guy felt he had to dish out. "I'm in hell, aren't I? You're the devil, and I died in Douglas's basement."

He cocked his head. "You always this high-strung?"

"No. I mean, I don't think so," I grunted as I tried to sit up, which turned out to be much harder than I thought. The guy hopped out of his chair to help me. With a little finagling, we managed a position that didn't make me want to vomit from the pain. He even slipped another pillow behind my back so I could rest comfortably. "Sorry," I mumbled. "Bad week."

"So we've been told." He eased back down in the chair.

"Is that how you knew? You know, that Brid, um . . ." I'd never had to talk to someone about sleeping with his sister. The experience was just as awkward as I would have imagined. The guy jumped in, saving me from my embarrassment.

"Calm down, captain. Brid and I are close, but we don't talk about everything." He scratched his chin. "At least, I don't think we do. Either way, she didn't say anything to me.

But let me tell ya," he said, tapping his nose, "this thing isn't just for ornament."

"I don't even want to think about what you're implying. Can we change the subject, please?"

He crossed his feet and rested them on the edge of my bed. "Humans, always so uptight. Fine. You hungry?"

My stomach practically sat up and begged.

"I know that look," he said with a laugh. "What do you want?"

"Anything?"

He nodded. "You've reached semihero status right now," he said, standing up and stretching. "I'd take advantage of it."

I'd hit that level of hungry where anything sounded good. I'd chew on a block of wood if they brought it to me right now. But as I thought, a promise came to mind.

"Do you have waffles?"

His mouth twitched after I'd said it.

I felt a stab of annoyance. What was wrong with waffles? I never thought I'd have to get defensive over a breakfast food but— "What's so funny?" I asked.

"You almost died, and you want waffles." He slapped my shoulder, which hurt. "I think we'll get along just fine."

He ambled toward the door. "Anything else?"

"If it's not too much to ask, could I have fresh strawberries and whipped cream, too? No compote. I'm, uh, allergic. And two plates, please."

If he thought the request odd, he didn't say so. "Right," he said, ticking the list off on his fingers. "Waffles, strawberries, whipped cream, two plates, no compote."

"And maple syrup."

"Got it."

"Thanks." I realized I didn't actually know his name so I tacked on a lame "you."

"You're welcome," he shouted from the hallway, "and it's Sean."

"Oh," Ashley groaned, eyes rolling dramatically. "This is awesome." She dug into her second helping with as much gusto as the first. Once Sean had seen Ashley eat, he'd quickly called down to the kitchens for more waffles. Then he crouched in the easy chair, chin in hands, taking in the spectacle.

"She's like a machine," he said, voice awed. "You sure you're not a werewolf?"

Ashley shook her head while she scooped up a blob of whipped cream with her fork. "Why?" she asked. "Do you eat a lot of waffles?"

"We eat a lot of everything," he said.

"Why is that?" she asked. I stabbed a strawberry with my fork.

"Higher metabolism." His eyes stayed riveted on Ashley. "Dude, your stomach is like one of those giant sinkholes in Venezuela."

Ashley examined her now-empty plate with a look of regret on her face.

"Don't lick the plate," I said.

"I wasn't going to."

"Yes, you were." I handed her the rest of my waffle and turned to Sean. "So you're like Brid, a hybrid?"

"Yeah," he said, sneaking a strawberry from Ashley's plate. She reached out to smack his hand but stopped when I looked at her. Sean popped the strawberry into his mouth, unconcerned.

He stopped chewing when an older man entered the room. Sinewy and lean as the older man was, I'd seen a lot bigger than him lately. But appearances, I'd learned, were deceiving. He held himself with authority, and from the way Sean suddenly grew quiet, I was willing to bet the man had power coming out the wazoo.

He sat down on the edge of my bed. "My name," he said, "is Brannoc Blackthorn. I'm Bridin's father." The subtext being that he was also the head of Brid's pack, which meant, as all things werewolf went, Brannoc was the toughest badass in the city. Just telling me he was Brid's father was enough to get my adrenaline going. I hated meeting parents.

"Sam," I said, shaking his hand. "Thank you for the cavalry."

He squinted, just a slight tension around the eyes, and I felt like he was sizing me up. I didn't know what he was comparing me to. Other boys Brid had brought home? Other necromancers? I hoped I passed inspection. Brannoc was the kind of guy I wanted in my corner, not against me.

"You're welcome, though you understand we were mostly there for my daughter."

"Of course." I wished he'd get on with it. I didn't think he was going to hurt me, but he was still an imposing man, and I would feel better if he was elsewhere.

"I wanted to thank you, Sam, for helping her stay safe."

"You're welcome."

He had stubble on his chin, and he looked tired. From the lines around his eyes and mouth, it looked like he spent a lot of his time smiling. He didn't smile now. I wasn't the only one who'd had a hard week.

"Where exactly am I?" I asked. "I need to call my family, let them know I'm okay."

"Your mom knows where you are. We sent her and your sister home for a shower and some sleep." His mouth twitched, and I could tell he was trying not to smile. In that moment, I could see hints of Sean in his face. I bet on a normal day, a day when he wasn't totally bogged down with worry, Brannoc would be a lot of fun. "It took some convincing," he said. "I don't think your mom trusts us entirely." He waved me off before I could say anything. "Which is exactly what I would be thinking in her place. They'll be back in a bit."

He got up from the bed. "This is our own private clinic, Sam. You can stay here until our doctor says you're okay to go."

"I don't have insurance."

"I'm your insurance," he said. He turned to Sean. "When he's well enough, he can visit his friend." Then he left before I could ask what that meant. When I bugged Sean, all he would tell me was that Ramon had a room down the hall and that he was fine. Then he quickly changed the subject.

My mom kept squeezing me until Sean told her she might pop my stitches. She hadn't hesitated at all when she did it. Besides the finally healing wounds on my back, I had some nice patchwork on my arm. I'd barely even have a scar. Well, on my arm. My back was going to look pretty freaky once it healed. Ashley reminded me that chicks dig scars, and at least I wasn't dead. Not much for sympathy, our Ashley.

Haley came with my mom and Mrs. W. My mom looked worried and kept adjusting my blanket and my pillow, like she couldn't figure out what to do with her hands. Haley looked excited to see me, and Mrs. W looked like she always did. I guess it takes a lot to impress Mrs. W.

My mom explained, somewhat sheepishly, that she'd arranged for Mrs. W to get an apartment next to mine in order to keep an eye on me. I'd like to say I was surprised, but I think I'd run all out of that. Mom waited for me to get angry, but I told her I understood. It'd been a good choice, really. In all the time that she'd lived next door to me, she hadn't missed a thing. Mrs. W handed me a package of those deli-made chocolate chip and M&M cookies.

"So is your name even Mrs. W, or should I call you Special Agent something or other?"

"I'm not a secret agent, Sam. I never lied to you about anything, I just didn't *tell* you everything. Big difference."

"I see."

"Don't take it too hard," Mrs. W said. "It turns out I liked you anyway." She opened the package and took a bite out of one of the cookies. "Besides," she said, wiggling her hips, "there was a dance studio right down the street. Because of you, I learned how to salsa." I tried not to picture Mrs. W doing any of the forbidden dances.

Once Haley got Mom to settle down, mostly by grabbing

Mom's hands and telling her to cut it out, she went through her part of the story. Apparently, I had passed out again. Haley had unhooked me from the table and dragged all 150 pounds of me the whole way to the car. And I could tell by the look on her face, she'd be cashing in on that for a long time.

Halfway through Mrs. W's reenactment of her speeding car chase, complete with *vroom* noises, a man knocked on the door frame.

"Excuse me," he said, entering the room without waiting for a response. He held a briefcase almost as shiny as his shoes, and he opened it on the table.

The way everyone stopped and stared, I could tell they didn't know him. I didn't recognize him either. He had close-cropped dark hair and a nice suit, nice enough that I knew he'd probably had it tailored.

He handed me a very large stack of papers.

"What's this?"

He glanced up from another file that he'd pulled out of his briefcase. "You're one Samhain Corvus LaCroix, are you not?"

"I am."

"Then I need you to sign all the orange-highlighted spots, as well as to initial all the pink-highlighted areas."

I'm not sure what I expected him to do, but asking me to sign on the highlights wasn't it. I leaned into my pillow and stared at him, trying to read the guy. Nothing but a stern, yet somehow blank, face.

"And why would I do that?" I asked carefully.

The man put down the file. "So I can do my job and transfer the estate to you."

"The what?"

The man sighed. "Did you or did you not kill one Douglas Montgomery?"

"I'm not answering that without a lawyer." It seemed like the right thing to say. That's what they always said on TV, anyway.

"I am your lawyer." The man looked at me dryly and handed me a business card that informed me that he was Mr. Paul Mankin, Esq.

"I'm pretty sure I'd remember hiring a lawyer." From the firm set of his jaw, I think he wanted to kill me. That seemed to be a fairly popular choice lately.

He pointed at the stack in my hand. "Those papers state that you, Samhain LaCroix, did kill one Douglas Montgomery in what the Council deems a sanctioned fight to the death. When such an event occurs, the Council appoints an attorney"—he jabbed his finger into his own chest—"me, to represent you and take care of all the details. You survived. Douglas didn't. Therefore, in accordance with Council law, you inherit his position on the Council, at least temporarily, as well as all his worldly goods and possessions."

I stared at him, stunned. Did he just say what I thought he said?

"I get all his stuff?" I said slowly. "Including his house?" The house I'd been trapped in for days. A chill went down my spine as I thought about it. I had no desire to set foot in it ever again.

"Yes." The lawyer handed me a pen. "And a temporary Council seat until you can be voted in properly or until we find a more suitable candidate."

I took it, but I didn't sign. I looked at the group around me, none of them giving me any hint as to what to do. "Is this standard?" I asked.

A lot of shrugs and a few blank looks. Ashley was the only one who nodded.

"The Council frowns on dueling, but according to the witnesses, Douglas didn't give you much choice, so you should be free and clear." Mankin stared at me patiently, waiting for me to get on with it. He must have gotten paid by the hour.

"So it's all legit?"

He nodded.

I started skimming the pages. I knew I was supposed to read them, but I really didn't care at that moment. "Why not just sell the house? Or give it to one of his descendants?"

"Douglas had no descendants," the lawyer said, "and we can't just sell the house. The Council has deemed it too . . . dangerous to hand off to ordinary humans."

"Great, so I won the creepy death house."

"Yes," the lawyer said, either missing the joke or not thinking it was funny. I was betting on the latter. As much as I hated the idea of owning my prison, he had a point. Not that it would be much better in my ignorant hands. Still, I'd rather risk myself than some innocent newlyweds or something. Maybe I could bulldoze the house and burn the rubble. Then I could bury the ashes and start over.

I finished flipping through the pages and began to sign on the highlighted marks. I barely even read parts of it. One chunk did catch my eye.

"It says I have to take care of the funeral arrangements according to the deceased's wishes."

The lawyer nodded. "Again, standard. It's to keep the victor from desecrating the corpse. Dignity is very important to the Council. In this particular case, though, it will be unnecessary."

"Why?" Sean asked. "Didn't Douglas have dignity?"

"No corpse," the lawyer answered.

I froze. No corpse? Not good. No corpse meant he could still be around. Anyone who has ever watched a soap opera or a slasher flick knows that.

"What—" I had to lick my lips and start again. "What do you mean, no corpse?"

For the first time, the lawyer seemed to look at me as a real person. He fidgeted with his tie and then awkwardly patted me on the hand. "I don't think you have anything to worry about. From what I've heard, the boost in your power base alone is proof that he is truly dead. The spell he used would only have transferred his powers to you if he died."

"He's right," Ashley chimed in. She gave me a reassuring smile.

"Besides," the lawyer continued, "from Douglas's paperwork, it is my understanding that he had a rare *pukis*." At our collectively puzzled looks he said, "It's a creature that originates from the area around the Baltic states—a house spirit, if you will."

An image of Douglas's talking cat came to mind. The lawyer kept speaking as I wondered if the pet store carried *pukis* food. Did they eat Friskies? Was that beneath them? I was quickly getting out of my depth.

"It wouldn't have been out of character for it to steal the body and hide it away," the lawyer explained. "Either for burial or . . . hoarding purposes."

"This just keeps getting better," I said, going back to the form. "My killer death house might also have a rotting body hoarded in it and something called a *pukis*. Just great." I wondered how much renting a bulldozer cost. And would I have to get a license in order to drive it myself? It was worth looking into.

After the lawyer left, happily clutching his paperwork, Ashley shooed everyone out except for my mother and Sean. He'd pulled guard duty, I guess. He didn't tell me why I needed a guard, only that it might look bad if I died in their care. I hoped he was joking. My mom sat quietly in the corner, staring at her hands as if willing them to stay still.

"Since you've leapt from Plumpy's employee of the month to fancy necromancer—" Ashley said.

"Hey!" I pointed an indignant finger at her. "I was never employee of the month."

Ashley flashed her dimples at my outburst. It worked, too. I instantly forgave her.

"You warrant a few personal spirits." She checked her appearance in a mirror on the wall. She frowned, apparently not liking what she saw. She scrunched up her nose, and her outfit changed into a different blouse and skirt. She nodded at that, satisfied.

"Show-off."

Ashley smoothed her skirt, making a point of ignoring me. "These will act as guides, go-betweens to the land of the dead. I've decided to be one of yours."

I grunted, twisting a little to adjust my pillow. "What, did I lose a coin toss?"

"A Harbinger as a guide is nothing to scoff at," she said, scolding. Her tone would have sounded ridiculous on any other young girl, but Ashley managed it well. "You should be grateful."

"Thank you."

She ignored any sarcasm in my voice and told me that I was quite welcome. After pointedly looking at me and my mom, she left. I got the feeling that Ashley would not be a quiet guide.

Sean got the idea, too, but he only went as far as the outside of the door, which he explained merely gave the illusion of privacy.

He pointed to his ears. "These aren't for ornament, either."

My mom and I sat in silence for a time. She pulled the chair up next to my bed and held my hand. Her skin looked pale, her eyes bloodshot.

"Tired?" I asked her.

She squeezed my hand. "I'm supposed to be worrying about you," she said.

"I think you've met the quota on that this week." We fell silent again. I let the minutes stretch as I happily sat there with my mom. There'd been a time when I'd thought I might not see her again.

"Sam—" Her tone was soft, like she was about to launch into another round of apologies. She started crying again. Though we had a lot to work through, I didn't want to deal with it then. Even if I wanted to, I couldn't stand the tight look of worry on my mom's face, or to see any more crying.

"No, Mom, it's okay." I gave her a faint smile and grabbed a tissue from the bedside table and handed it to her. "We're going to start over. What's done is done." I stared at the bruised area around the stitching on my arm. "And we're both going to have to live with that."

She leaned her head onto my hospital bed and started to cry even harder. I rested my arm on her back and let her get it all out. After this past week I really understood how good that felt.

Once she was done, she scooted me over and joined me on the hospital bed, hugging me roughly to her. We sat like that and listened to the quiet sounds of the hospital.

"When you're better, we'll go find your uncle. Get that last binding removed," she said.

"No rush," I said. "I should probably get used to what I have first."

She smoothed my hair back with her hand. "Deal," she said. She looked like she wanted to cry some more, but she didn't. My mom always tried to be strong for us, whether we needed it or not. I guess it runs in the family, because now I was trying to do the exact same thing for her.

They made me sleep after that. When I woke up, the sun had gone down and the room was dark. The darkness felt comfortable, like a warm bed on a rainy night. I could hear the quiet beep of a monitor down the hall. Curled up next to me, and no longer wearing my clothes, was Brid. She slept, her eyes dancing under the lids, her hand cradled to her chest.

My heart did a small painful skip. She looked exhausted. I brushed a lock of hair behind her ear. Brid's eyes popped open. Then she kissed me firmly on the lips, a kiss I returned with little hesitation.

"It's good to see you too," I said.

"I wanted to check on you sooner, but Daddy ordered me to rest."

"Sounds like a good order."

"Yeah." She leaned on my chest, staring into my eyes. It was unsettling, like she was examining me for something.

"You're kind of creeping me out," I said.

She poked my rib cage. "You feel like taking a little walk?"

The clinic differed from regular hospitals in several ways. One, I didn't have to wear paper peek-a-boo pajamas. Someone with a sense of humor had stocked the place with flannel wolfman pajamas, the images resembling the monster movies from the '40s. Very flattering. No slippers, though. Brid told me that most of the pack avoided shoes when they could, so they didn't bother. So I got to walk around the hospital in nothing but some socks they'd dug up for me.

Another difference was that the building itself resembled a big house more than anything institutional, at least in layout. The medicinal smell remained, and most of the surfaces were easy to wash. There were a lot of fresh flowers about, and plenty of skylights. I didn't see much staff either.

And if the waffles were anything to go by, the food tasted about eight thousand times better.

The other differences ran toward the odd side of things. Some of the rooms were glorified cages. The outer rooms, like the hallways and lounge areas, had no windows. When I pointed that out, Brid said it was in case someone escaped before their release time. I wasn't sure I wanted to know what that meant.

A few of the beds had metal restraints, which Brid told me were made out of silver.

"I thought silver was bad," I said, looking into one of the rooms.

"They're padded so the silver doesn't scar the wrist."

"Why use it at all, then?"

"Weres can't break silver." Brid shrugged, slipping an arm around me. "When werewolves grow up in this city, they have their pack to guide them through the change. It's natural, a part of life. But not everyone has the benefits of a pack," she said, "and some are outsiders. Everything about the process is new to them. Adult shape-shifters are strong." She frowned, and I could tell she didn't like what she had to say. "Occasionally, we have to restrain them for their own safety, until they learn."

Brid tightened her arm around me as we came to a door. I could feel the worry pouring off her. Now that I'd noticed it, I couldn't believe I hadn't felt it earlier. A thought seeped into my brain. It had been a tumultuous day, and I had believed that if anything was seriously wrong, someone would have told me.

"What's wrong with Ramon?" I asked. Fear clenched my gut.

In answer, Brid opened the door.

I had to force my feet to take me into the room. Brid wouldn't be this anxious if Ramon were okay. She also would've answered me. The flip side was that someone would have told me immediately if he'd died. I pushed myself past the doorway. Whatever had happened, Ramon had survived. We could get past anything else.

Ramon lay on the bed, arms and legs chained, an IV tube jutting out of his forearm. His skin looked red, flushed. Sweat drenched his sheets. He wore no shirt, so I could see the flesh roiling beneath his skin. Bran stood at his side, watching him, concern clear on his face.

"What happened?" I said. "Did he get—" I cleared my throat. "The only thing I saw was him hitting the floor."

"He landed square on a broken glass vial," Brid whispered. Her voice sounded hoarse and sad. "No one knew Douglas had been collecting blood samples. Or what he had planned for them." She hugged herself. "Rare ones, too. We don't know where he found it."

I rubbed my sweaty palms on my pants. "What did he get exposed to?"

"Bear," Bran said. He stood back, giving the bed a wide berth.

Brid stood back, too. They were treating him as if he were dangerous. Ramon would have gotten a kick out of that.

I pointed to one of the chains. "Are these really necessary?"

Bran's look was sympathetic. "We don't ever chain unless

it's necessary. Bear is a volatile strain, and Ramon's body is fighting it." A thread of respect entered his voice. "He's holding his own, though."

I stood over him, wishing I could do something. I'd been so happy to be free that I hadn't even begun to tally up my debts. I owed Ramon a lot.

They let me hang around for a bit, giving me time to talk to my friend, even though I wasn't sure if he could hear me. When they decided that I needed more rest, they steered me back to my room.

"We'll take good care of him, Sam," Brid said.

"Like he was family?" I choked over the question, my throat constricting as I tried to hold everything in.

Bran helped me into my bed.

"He is family now," he said softly.

31

LIVE AND LET DIE

𝕴 got released from the clinic before Ramon. They gave me a pill bottle full of sedatives so I could sleep and sent me on my way.

Brid assured me that Ramon had made some improvement, but I couldn't see it. He'd have to stay at the clinic for a few more weeks at least. Brannoc promised me he'd watch over him as if he were his own. He seemed like the kind of guy who took his word very seriously. When I expressed my fears to Ashley, she told me that she'd heard that fey couldn't lie. I hoped she was right.

Until then, I had to play the waiting game. Not my favorite pastime, especially with this sick, unsure feeling in my stomach.

Sean offered me a ride, but I needed a touch of the familiar to settle myself. I'd handled a lot of upheaval in the last week.

I called Plumpy's. Frank got really excited when he heard my voice, but the boss wouldn't let him come get me. As stoked as Frank was to see me, he had bills to pay. Bills, however, were no longer a problem.

"You pick me up, Frank, and I'll hire you as an assistant."

He sounded intrigued but wary. We had trained him well.

"Honest, Frank. I've got more money than I know what to do with." Something good should come out of Douglas's filthy blood money. And I counted freedom from fast food as something good.

"Yeah—wait. How much you paying?"

I felt a flutter of pride. Our little Frank was growing up. Ramon would be proud. The flutter died, and I was back with that sick feeling. "Salary, man. Full benefits. Three weeks' paid vacation. Health insurance. Whatever you want."

"I'll be there in ten minutes."

𝕴 made Frank take me back to my apartment, stopping only to grab Brooke from my mom's house. He babbled at me the whole time. I only half listened, letting his voice roll over me, happy to see him again. Happy that at least Frank had made it through this whole mess unscathed.

As good as it was to see him, his puppy-dog enthusiasm was exhausting me. I sent him to the store when we got back. I hadn't had much food in my apartment to begin with, and now I had even less.

"He's just excited to see you," Brooke said. Before he left, Frank had positioned her bag on the table so she could see me. I'd embedded myself in the couch and refused to move.

"I know," I said, rubbing my temples. A headache was brewing. Maybe I needed to bust into those sedatives now.

"You ready to talk," she said, "or would you rather continue your pity party?"

"That's not fair," I said.

"News flash, Sam." She eyed me steadily until I realized how ridiculous my last statement had been. I was telling a girl who'd recently lost damned near everything that things weren't fair. If they ever gave rank for stating the obvious, I would have made captain just now. Brooke was right. Of course things weren't fair. And yes, my life wasn't what I wanted it to be, but sitting here and wallowing wasn't going to change anything.

"Sorry," I said.

"I know," she said, her cheeks becoming flushed, "but you don't have anything to be sorry about. Yeah, I'm sort of dead, Ramon is sick, and you got the shit beat out of you. You also met a girl, got strange mutant powers, and kicked some ass."

"You're oversimplifying," I said.

"And you're overcomplicating," she said, her tone firm. "Let it go."

"I killed a man."

"A bad man, Sam. A very bad man." A strand of hair fell in front of her eyes, and she blew at it, but it kept coming back down. I slowly pulled myself off the couch and tucked it behind her ear.

"I still didn't want to kill him," I said, looking at the floor. I waited for some feeling to emerge. Remorse, maybe. But nothing came. I felt hollow as I stared at my dirty carpet.

"I know," Brooke said, her voice soft.

Another chunk of hair worked its way free from her ponytail holder and drifted in front of her face. She let out a frustrated grunt and blew it out of her way. When it drifted in front of her eyes again, I tucked it back with the other one.

"I can't live like this," she said.

I gave her chin a tweak. "You won't have to."

"Thanks," she said. "For everything."

My chest ached, but not from an injury. I took one of my sedatives, anyway. I turned the TV on for Brooke and crashed out in my room. It felt like heaven.

When I got up, I couldn't get settled. Even with Frank and Brooke there, the apartment felt empty. I missed Ramon.

The sudden inactivity after weeks of tension and adrenaline was driving me crazy. I needed to find something to do. Luckily, after checking my messages, I realized I had plenty. The first thing I did was get hold of my lawyer. Detective Dunaway had called several times; while I couldn't put off the interview forever, I needed to buy myself some time. I asked Mankin to take care of it. It was nice to hand a problem off to someone else. I should have gotten a lawyer years ago.

"Are you ready?" I asked. We were losing light, and I didn't want to trip over any gravestones. The wind blew cool against my cheek as I waited for Frank. I could smell freshly cut grass and a mixture of flowers.

He nodded, his brown eyes open too wide, like he was trying not to cry. He wiped his nose on his sleeve. "Do we really have to do this? I mean, she's not dead, just sort of in limbo, right?"

I could understand his resistance. Who wouldn't want his loved ones back, even if it was just a piece of them? And the part of me that hurt, the part that was still raw over Brooke, started to bargain with the rest of me. Why not keep her around? I had the ability, so why not use it? But looking down at Brooke, at the state she was stuck in, I understood how selfish that feeling was. So I told the raw part of me to shut up and deal with it. "She's a head, Frank. That's pretty close to dead, or at least pretty far from life. She deserves more than some crappy half life."

"But—"

"It's okay," Brooke said. "It's time. Being a head blows." She flashed him a smile. "Besides, I'll always be with you in your heart."

Despite the situation, we all started to snigger. "Thanks," I said. "I needed that." My heart felt lighter than it had in weeks. We stood in silence, staring out at the cemetery. Even before I knew about the whole necromancer thing, I'd always liked cemeteries. They were peaceful, like libraries and churches. The trees around the perimeter blocked out any ambient noise, so all I heard were birds. All I smelled was grass and flowers. It was a good place to be.

"C'mon," Brooke said. "Let's blow this crap-shack."

Frank carried Brooke's bag to her grave site. I grabbed one of the green plastic vases the cemetery staff had left by the trash cans and stuck it into the ground. I put the bouquet of gladiolas that I'd brought with me into it. Brooke had been fascinated by the fact that she could pick out her own flowers. There were several other bouquets already surrounding the temporary marker. They hadn't had time to put up a permanent tombstone yet.

Frank opened up Brooke's bag. "Nice," she said with a sniff as she looked around. "I'd like to know who brought those carnations, though. Yuck. I hate carnations."

Frank patted her hair awkwardly. Brooke smiled at him, taking the gesture as the act of comfort it was meant to be.

I heard a car door slam. Dunaway walked across the grassy slope toward us, his long stride purposeful.

Frank frowned. "I thought your lawyer took care of him?"

"So did I."

Dunaway didn't want to wait, apparently. From our brief meeting, I wasn't too surprised by that. Had he been following me or just scoping out the cemetery? In a classic Frank move, I watched as he tried to hide Brooke behind his back. Yeah, because that didn't look suspicious.

"You okay, Sam?" Dunaway's concern sounded genuine. "You look terrible."

"I feel terrible, Detective." I looked up at him, trying to keep my face open and honest looking. It's harder than it sounds. "I thought we were meeting tomorrow?"

"We are."

"Then why are you here?"

"Public place," he said. "Why are you here?"

I nodded toward the flowers. "Paying my respects."

He scratched his chin, examining Frank, then me, then Frank. "Every time I think I get a handle on this case, it changes."

"I'm sorry."

Dunaway leaned down and wiped some dirt off of Brooke's temporary marker. "And the things I've seen. The security tapes. The car. The fight." He straightened her marker, even though it didn't look crooked. "Her death." He stood back up. "Anyone feel like telling me what is going on around here?"

I looked at Dunaway, really looked. And I felt bad for him. He was a good, solid man stuck in a crap situation. And he wasn't going to give up anytime soon.

"Frank," I said, "would you show the nice detective the bag, please?"

"You sure?"

I nodded, never taking my eyes off Dunaway. I could tell the precise moment when he saw Brooke. All the blood left his face and his hands twitched down by his sides. The silence dragged on, and then the blood rushed back into his face. "What kind of shit—"

"I can explain everything," Brooke said.

He stepped back. The violent eruption of red in his face went back to white. I think if he weren't so well trained, he would have done more. Instead he just stood there. Finally, he whispered, "Did she . . . ?"

"I sure did," Brooke said, "and I wish, just once, someone would have a better reaction to me. A 'good to see you, Brooke' would do nicely."

"Good to see you, Brooke," Frank replied immediately. I guess Ramon and I weren't the only ones who'd been training Frank.

I pushed up the sleeves of my jacket. I'd had Ashley talk me through the ceremony earlier. I just hoped I got it right. At least I didn't have to worry about running out of power now.

"This wasn't the way I planned it, but I can tell you're not going to give up. And frankly, we could use some help, ah, smoothing some of this over."

Dunaway looked sharply at me. "I'm not letting anyone get away with murder."

"I don't expect you to. But," I said, waving at Brooke, "this is an odd situation. I'm not asking you to go against your morals, just listen to her. After that, we'll see." I pulled out a container of salt and started to draw a big circle around the grave. The groundskeeper was going to be pissed. "I'd like to take care of this soon, so you better get crackin'."

I ignored Dunaway and set up the spell. I waited in the grass while he questioned Brooke. It felt good to sit here. I felt welcome, like all the dead around me recognized me as an old friend. It should have felt creepy, but it didn't. I didn't want to analyze it. There had been so much bad lately, it was nice to take some good at face value.

Once Brooke had answered everything to the best of her ability, I invoked the circle. I didn't even have to try. The circle bloomed to life, solid electric blue. Dunaway and Frank stood back from the grave, watching me as I worked. I had Brooke's head inside the circle. I'd set up the barrier to keep everything contained. I wasn't afraid of Brooke.

"You ready?" I asked.

"I really am, Sam." Her answer was gentle. "Are you?"

"I don't know."

"Do your best, I guess. That's all anyone can ask." Her eyes welled up around the corners. "Now get off your candy ass, LaCroix, and do your job."

Ashley had told me that every necromancer does things a little differently. It has something to do with the way we think, how we envision things in our mind. I didn't want to just throw Brooke's head into her coffin like it was no big deal. She wasn't a misplaced Lego to be tossed back into the box. She was a person.

I cut my arm down by my elbow. That way I could hide the cut while it healed and it wouldn't interfere with anything. It's funny, in movies, when people need blood, they always slice their hands. That's never made sense to me. You use your hands a lot, and they're hard to heal. I let the blood drip into the grass and called Brooke's body out of the ground. The earth split easily and let her up, I think because she was newly dead. Or maybe it was because she wanted this as much as I needed to do it. Once her body was completely out, I gave her back her head, knitting the flesh together at the neck. She stood in front of me, smiling, hugging herself with her arms.

"Feel better?" I could barely choke out the words. I couldn't tell if it was the joy of seeing her whole again or the pain of letting her go.

Brooke threw her arms around me and kissed me on the forehead. I hugged her back, holding her as tight as I could.

"Thank you." She leaned down and pulled a strip of cloth out of her bowling bag. Frank had put it there to cushion her neck. I guess we didn't need it anymore. She wrapped the strip around the new cut on my elbow, tying it into a neat bandage. Then she reached up and wiped my cheeks. I hadn't realized that I was crying.

Brooke looked out of the circle and smiled. She nodded at

the detective and waved at Frank, her grin growing bigger. He used the sleeve of his hoodie to wipe his eyes. Brooke's smile turned a little sad as she watched Frank break down.

"You sure?" His voice broke on the words.

She nodded. "I can't stay this way, Frank." He returned her nod, his shoulders slumping in acceptance. "Hey," she said. He looked back up at her and she blew him a kiss.

Frank reached out and caught it.

I put Brooke back in the ground, everything going off without a hitch. A thoughtful—and shaken—Dunaway said good-bye with promises that we'd talk about all of this tomorrow. I shook his hand and walked back to the car, a dejected Frank in my wake.

I took a few of the sedatives once I got home. I needed rest, and I didn't think there was any other way I was going to get it. I felt drained down to nothing.

Frank slept on the floor. He didn't feel right about taking Ramon's spot, even after I told him Ramon would tell him to get his ass on the couch.

I slept like a sedated baby. When I woke up, I felt refreshed and fairly happy. My blankets were warm, my pillow soft, and I didn't want to get up. It was *my* pillow. It had been an uphill battle to get back to it.

"You're going to get bedsores if you don't get up soon."

I twisted and fell off my bed with a shout. I peeked past the edge of my bed. Brooke, the whole Brooke, peered back at me. Her hands curled over the mattress, her back arched like a cat ready to pounce.

"What the hell?" I yelled.

Frank ran in. His face broke into a smile.

"What?" Brooke said, resting her ghostly hands on her hips. "You didn't think I'd leave you losers on your own, did you?"

"Yeah," I said, grinning. "I kind of thought you would."

"Psh, whatever." Brooke pulled a ghostly pen and clipboard out of thin air. "Ashley said you needed another adviser, so we worked something out." She tapped her pen against her lips. "Now, what should we do first?"

Detective Dunaway called me later that day. We'd been playing Mario Party, Frank and I hitting buttons, Brooke ordering us around. She'd made us choose Princess Daisy and Princess Peach for the computer players so she could yell derogatory names at them while we played. I felt better than I had in a long time.

"I'm not sure what to do with the info you've given me," he said, "but I'll figure out something. Something to give the family closure at least."

"You're not going to drag us into the station?"

"And tell them what? I'd be in a shrink's office before I finished my first sentence."

"Thanks," I said. "I hope it doesn't get you in trouble."

"I'll be okay," he said. "I've still got a lot of questions for you, though."

"I know," I said. "I'll give you what I got."

"And, Sam?"

"Yeah?"

"If it ever turns out that you had something to do with this, I'll hang you out to dry, shrink's office or no."

"I would expect nothing less."

I hung up and went back to the game.

After a few days of rest and contemplation, and Brooke's constant hounding, I had Frank start setting things up for our move. My apartment was too small for three people and a spirit, so we might as well make good use of Douglas's house. I needed to get over what had happened there. It was also the only way to get Brooke to leave me alone. She could be very insistent when she wanted to be.

In the meantime, I'd clean the house of anything unsavory or dangerous. That way if I hated the place, I could sell it. Or bulldoze it. I hadn't totally given up on that plan yet.

Besides, I would need the extra room when Ramon got better. I was sure he'd get out of the clinic. He had to. So we needed the house because when he got released he couldn't exactly stay at his mom's to deal with his new, um, "lifestyle changes." A were-bear in my apartment building would be just as disastrous.

I needed to take the house on, if only to prove to myself that I was right—that this power could be used for good. I needed to accept what I was. What I am.

My name is Samhain Corvus LaCroix. I am a necromancer.

Now, if only I could say that with a straight face.

Local citizens were shocked today when Woodland Park Zoo announced that the panda, Ling Tsu, died late last night. Zoo officials are "stunned by the unexpected death." They haven't released a cause of death at this time, telling members of the press only that there were several unexplained findings in Ling Tsu's necropsy. Zoo officials wish to publicly apologize to the Chinese zoo. "With the current political climate being what it is, we hope to make reparations as quickly as possible in order to continue the trading program that we currently have with China," one inside source informed the *Seattle Times*. "Thanks to an anonymous benefactor, that might be possible. Because of the generous donation, we are already beginning talks with Chinese officials about setting up a panda preserve in Ling Tsu's memory."

Until then, the police will continue their investigation to answer the baffling questions that have surfaced in this case. When questioned, a representative from the police department said, "I just wish we knew why there was so much salt."

Acknowledgments

Novels don't happen by themselves. Here are some of the people who helped me, so now you know exactly who to blame:

Adam and Gryphon, you're amazing, thank you. My mother, of course; my brothers, Darin, Jeremy, and Alex, and their families, for all their support and general greatness. Grams, Dad, Michele, Ann, Brian—I am lucky that there are too many of you to list. Thank you, my family, for your support, even if half of you have no idea what, exactly, it is that I do.

Devon "Porkchop" Fiene, Abby Murray, Tiny and Erica Crane, Jose Perez III, J'romy Armstrong, Ben "Man of" Steele, and Rachel Trujillo, for baby wrangling and first reads (I owe you); Jen Violi, for guidance—both spiritual and line-by-line; Parker, for thumbs-ups and general shenanigans; Casey "Fox Bandit" Lefante, for encouragement and orphans; Dense, Blake, Jason Buch, and Brent McKnight, for bad movies and reminding me what readers want; Barb Johnson, Trisha Rezende, Jeni Stewart, and the rest of Team Parkview: Where would I be without you all?

Sharon Cumberland, for getting me into graduate school in the first place; Joanna Leake, for reading stories about unicorn death matches and not instantly throwing me out on my ass; Joseph Boyden, for playing the good cop and for always making me stay for another round; Amanda Boyden, for making me throw away the first chapter and for telling me what I needed to hear. Thanks to Ed Dieranger, former NOPD, for all my police-related info. If I got any of it wrong, I swear it's not your fault. To my agent, Jason Anthony, for being simply amazing, and his team at Lippincott Massie McQuilkin for the same. Many thanks to my film agent, Sylvie Rabineau. And of course, to my editor, Reka Simonsen, at Holt, for making this a wonderful process.

You are all, fully and completely, chock-full of awesome.

GO FISH

LISH MCBRIDE

© Adam Aman

What did you want to be when you grew up?
A writer. Yes, I was that kind of nerdy kid. Then I wanted to be a veterinarian and a writer. Then I realized that vets have to poke animals with needles, so it went back to wanting to just be a writer. I did work in a veterinarian clinic for three or so years, though.

When did you realize you wanted to be a writer?
I was pretty little. Basically, as far back as my memory goes. It seems like I've always wanted to be one. My friend Abby used to want to be a cloud. I think that would have been a much cooler response.

What's your most embarrassing childhood memory?
I did a lot of ridiculous things as a child. But my brothers have made so much fun of me for those moments, I think the shame is gone.

What's your favorite childhood memory?
Wow, that's a big question. I feel lucky that I have so many to choose from. My mom (and also my stepmom) used to read

to me every night. I have fond memories of curling up with my mom and hearing *The Lion, the Witch and the Wardrobe* for the umpteenth time—or *Bunnicula* with my stepmom. I remember making bike tracks with my brothers in our yard, and catching Dungeness crabs on the beach. I grew up in the woods, so we did a lot of outdoorsy stuff. We also would have movie nights at my Mom's house where we'd watch a themed marathon (like the Indiana Jones movies or *Star Wars*) and we'd make mini pizzas. Little stuff like that have stuck with me.

As a young person, who did you look up to most?
I always wanted to be more like my mom—still do. She's so patient and she's always good for advice and we like to do a lot of the same things. As I've gotten older, I think I appreciate her even more. She really stepped back and let us develop who we were. I think I'm part of a small percentage who actually wish they could be more like their mother. I also remember thinking my brothers were pretty amazing. My oldest brother, Darin, is six years older than me, so he always seemed like this smart, mysterious figure. He would bring me books and make author recommendations. He was the person who had me read the Earthsea books and introduced me to *The Stranger* (Seattle's alternative newspaper).

My brother Jeremy was amazing because he was so good about teaching me to do stuff that he wasn't even interested in. Again, I remember him being so patient with me. He helped teach me how to read, even though he has never been a reader. He has no interest in books whatsoever (but reads to his daughters all the time), and yet fostered my love for them. He helped me to ride my bike, tie my shoes, all that stuff. I remember one year for Christmas, he walked me into a bookstore and said, "Pick a book. Whatever one you want, that's what I'll get you." I picked, *The Thief of Always* by Clive Barker. He then wrapped it and put it under the tree and wouldn't let me open it until Christmas morning. I had to wait weeks knowing *exactly* what it was. Torture.

My younger brother didn't come along until I was eleven, but even so he's always been this great, easygoing kid. I'm sure he doesn't feel like it, but I wish I had been half as together and relaxed about things as he's been.

What was your favorite thing about school?
They had books there and I was asked to read them. I honestly remember critiquing my first-grade reader. I started reading early, so apparently I felt it was a waste of my time.

What was your least favorite thing about school?
I didn't understand the social aspect very well. I think I was pretty naïve in that respect. In general, I liked school until junior high. That's when school and I stopped getting along.

What were your hobbies as a kid? What are your hobbies now?
Again, I lived in the woods, so hobbies were things on the ground. Most of my spare time as a kid involved reading. At least until my brother Jeremy harassed me into going outside. Then we rode bikes and climbed trees and such. I don't know if I really had hobbies. I played soccer. Does that count?

As for now . . . I still read a lot. Have themed movie nights . . . huh. I really haven't evolved much.

What was your first job, and what was your "worst" job?
My first job was filing in my Dad's office during the summers. My worst job would probably be my short stint as a fast-food

worker. (Where I did catch the grill on fire more than once.) It was pretty awful. I feel like working fast food is a good motivational tool to go back to college.

How did you celebrate publishing your first book?
I think I just ran around going, "Eeeee!" and then called every family member, friend, passing acquaintance. . . .

I couldn't really afford to do much else. We'd just moved cross-country and I had only finished graduate school a few months before. Probably someone bought me a drink, perhaps even dinner. My friends are pretty awesome and they take me to dinner for things.

Where do you write your books?
Anywhere I can. I used to write in an office when I lived in New Orleans. It was awesome . . . at first. Then I started to go stir crazy. That's too much time in one room. So now I write nomad-style: at people's houses, coffee shops, bars, my couch, anywhere that's handy. Some of *Necromancing the Stone* (book two) was written in Mexico, New Orleans, Mississippi, Seattle, and I edited parts of it in Edinburgh and in my friend Brenda's kitchen. Nomad seems to be working for me, though sometimes I miss that office.

What sparked your imagination for *Hold Me Closer, Necromancer*?
It started as a short story. Sam came first—I wrote a terrible short story while I was bored in alternative school (a brief stint—maybe a few months?) about a fast-food worker who kept getting attacked by vampires and werewolves and whatever. I put the story away and mostly forgot about it. Then in college, I needed something to write about and I dug up Sam and wrote another terrible short story. That's where

Ramon first appeared, as well as very flat versions of Brooke and Frank. I think it ended with Plumpy exploding and Brooke being eaten by zombies. I kept thinking on the characters and the story line and just slowly built it up from there. By the time I needed material for a novel for my thesis to graduate, it was closer to a recognizable version *HMC,N*. Still pretty rough around the edges, though.

Sam raising the dead kind of came out of me thinking about how hard it would be for me to be a necromancer since I'm vegetarian. In a lot of the books I was reading, you have to have a blood sacrifice to bring back the dead . . . and I can't even kill things to eat them.

What challenges do you face in the writing process, and how do you overcome them?
The biggest challenge is the one most beginning writers don't really notice—getting your butt in the chair. In order for books to happen you have to *sit down and write them.* It seems like common sense stuff, but you hear it all the time—people trying to "find time" to write. You have to make it yourself, and that's a hard juggling act for fledgling writers. I schedule meet-up times with friends and we get together to write. We show up unless we're sick. It helps.

I get frustrated while editing, too. Editing is very, very necessary, but to me, it feels like running in loose sand—like no actual movement is happening. For this, I've realized that I need to balance my editing with actual writing, even if it means I need to take a break from something due to work on something that's not. I'm still learning to iron this one out. Juggling your writing life with everything else can be kind of difficult at first.

Which of your characters is most like you?
I'm sure they all have their little bits of me, but none of them are actually *me*. Sam is nicer than I am. Brid is much cooler than I am. Ramon is more suave than me, but I like how good he is at being a friend to Sam. His friendship with Sam is similar to the one I have with one of my besties (I call her Porkchop). My level of snark is close to Ashley's. I'm pretty awkward like Frank, and like Brooke and Brid, I grew up with tons of brothers. So a little bit of me here and there. Apparently, I like to spread it out between characters.

What makes you laugh out loud?
I grew up in a pretty funny family. Comedy was kind of always around—in books, movies, TV, etc. *Monty Python*, *The Kids in the Hall*, *The State*, *SCTV*, and *Saturday Night Live*—I can still remember parts of the spiel from the Dan Ackroyd skit "Bass-o-Matic." My dad and I both read Dave Barry in the paper, and I used Garfield to help me learn how to read. (I'd read the words I could and guess the rest of them from the pictures.) So it's really not that hard to make me laugh. I think good comedy is really hard to create. I lucked out and got some pretty funny friends, too. It's nice that I have a job that lets me put all that silly into action.

What do you do on a rainy day?
Um . . . I live in Seattle. So I do everything on a rainy day. You can't avoid it. Ideally, I prefer to be on a couch, reading, drinking tea . . . maybe with a fire . . . but generally, I have to just put on a jacket and get about my business.

What's your idea of fun?
I like doing new things. My friend Porkchop is great at finding new things for us to do. Like buying me tickets to go see *Evil*

Dead: The Musical (it was amazing) and finding obscure festivals. She went to Lumberjack Days last year. I want to go next year. Lumberjacks doing . . . things! And, I don't know, probably some funnel cake. What's not to like?

I love going to the movies, plays when I can swing them, and when I can't, sometimes I like to watch cartoons. I started hanging out with my boyfriend because I found out he had cable and that the cartoon *Freakazoid* was playing at two AM. So I came over and made him watch it.

Basically, if you see an activity and think, "What kind of geek enjoys that?" you're probably referring to me.

What's your favorite TV show or movie?
Okay, seriously, these questions paralyze me. I have these things broken down into genre, time period, what mood I'm in, and even then it's a list. I love *The Princess Bride*, and *Better Off Dead*, and *Hot Fuzz*, and *Black Sheep* (the mutant sheep one, not the Chris Farley one), and *Black Books* and *Futurama*, and *Home Movies*, and *Pushing Daisies* and . . . and . . . *collapses onto floor*

If you were stranded on a desert island, who would you want for company?
Someone who could build transport to get me off said desert island.

If you could travel anywhere in the world, where would you go and what would you do?
Right now? Hm. Mostly, I'd like to go visit family and friends (as I am writing this, it is close to the holiday season) so we're talking California, Maine, Mississippi, New Orleans, Tennessee, Ashville, Edinburgh, Ireland . . . SOMEONE BUY ME A PLANE.

If you could travel in time, where would you go and what would you do?

It's funny how many times I get this question and how my answer is always the same: I want to go back in time and tame a dinosaur so I can ride it. Then I want to visit Shakespeare to see if he had help writing all those plays or what the deal was. Then I want to visit Charles Dickens so I can punch him in the jaw, as I do not enjoy Dickens. (Yes, I understand he was instrumental in blah, blah, blah. That doesn't mean I can't give him just one good right hook, just to get it out of my system.) And I want to do all these things while riding my dinosaur.

What's the best advice you have ever received about writing?

I got a lot of good advice over the years—especially from the group I went to graduate school with. I guess the basics are the best—write what you're passionate about. Trust your characters and by extension, yourself. Don't be afraid to slash and burn and edit away all your cleverness. It will probably be a better book in the end. Keep on keepin' on—there's lot of times when you look at your project and it just seems so big, and so overwhelming—and the odds of it getting picked up and published are equally daunting. But the odds are worse if you quit.

What advice do you wish someone had given you when you were younger?

Youth is very short-lived, despite the fact that, at the time, it feels like the whole world. High school ends and then you can move. Try to enjoy this age as much as you can—it won't look so bad later. And yes, college will be much better than high school.

I was given all of this advice, but didn't quite believe it at the time.

Do you ever get writer's block? What do you do to get back on track?
Not really. I get frustrated with certain plot points sometimes, but I either power through them knowing I can fix it later in editing if it sucks, or work on something else for a day or two. I had a difficult time writing after the whole Hurricane Katrina business, but since I was still in school, I had to keep writing, which I'm grateful for. I produced some awful things during that time, but at least I was still writing.

What do you want readers to remember about your books?
I hope they make them laugh. I hope they have fun. Anything else is purely a bonus.

What would you do if you ever stopped writing?
I'd probably go crazy, or at the very least I'd become incredibly grouchy. Writing helps even me out. I don't think many writers ever stop or retire. Most of us just die. I can't tell if that's creepy or reassuring.

What should people know about you?
I mean well.

What do you like best about yourself?
My ability to avoid giving a straight answer to a serious question.

Do you have any strange or funny habits? Did you when you were a kid?

I'm sure I do. I have to take off my glasses to eat. That's kind of weird, right?

I'll have to ask Man-Friend.

Well, first he said, "Me." And then he said, "You fall asleep to stories of murder and death." This is true. I'm an insomniac, so sometimes when I can't sleep, I watch murder mysteries (like *Poirot*, or *Inspector Lewis* or *Midsomer Murders*) or for a while, I watched those documentary forensics shows. They are quiet (in tone and volume) and not bright and flashy. I keep telling Man-Friend that, but he still insists that it's weird.

And I'm positive that most of the things I did as a kid were strange. When I asked my mom, she said she always thought it was weird how, when I went to sleep every night, I'd pile up my stuffed toys around me so that you could only see my face. She said it reminded her of that scene in *E.T.* I did this because I thought that if someone tried to come get me while I was sleeping, I'd be harder to find. The stuffed toys would protect me, or at the very least hide me for a little while. I'd practice not breathing to see how long I could hold my breath, just in case I had to hide. Apparently, I was a paranoid child. I didn't sleep well then, either. I remember sometimes if the whole stuffed toy thing wasn't working, I'd drag my blanket into my brother's room and sleep under his bed. I guess it made me feel safe. (If a psychologist ever reads this, I'm sure they are going to have a field day.)

What do you consider to be your greatest accomplishment?

It's a toss-up between "That Time I Wrote a Book," "That Time I Rebuilt After a Hurricane," and the "That Time I Moved

Cross-Country to Go to School." All were scary for different reasons. All of them changed my life significantly.

I know a lot of people say their children, but I feel like any accomplishment my kiddo manages will be his own. I'll just sit there and be proud. Or horrified. You know, whichever is more appropriate at the time.

What do you wish you could do better?
Most things. I wish I were better with languages. I'm positive my agent and editor wished I were better with grammar. I wish I could build things and fix things. I would say I wish I could write better or be a better person, but I'm hoping those things just come with time. The other stuff might come with more classes. Except for grammar. I've given up on that.

What would your readers be most surprised to learn about you?
I'm always surprised at what surprises them. I was talking to someone on Twitter the other day about how jealous I was of their tickets to go see the *Mary Poppins* musical. She said that she found that to be surprising. I said, "Why? You've never met me, know very little about me, so how can you be surprised?" She pointed out that my tag name on there is @TeamDamnation and that I write about zombies and horror. She kind of had me there, except I reminded her that one of my characters (Ramon) likes show tunes. When I told this story to my mom, she said, "You like musicals? But you always made fun of them when I watched them." And I said, "Well, yeah, but I make fun of most things." She honestly didn't know I liked them. Weird.

So I don't know what they would be surprised at. Maybe they would be more surprised if this was the first question and not the last, because I feel like they got a lot of info out of me at this point.

With the defeat of Douglas, Sam is trying to get used to his new life as necromancer extraordinaire. However, things are not going so well. His best friend is a werebear, his sister is being threatened, and Sam's pretty sure his new house hates him. But one question still remains. Is Douglas *really* dead?

Find out in

NECROMANCING THE STONE

WELCOME TO MY WORLD

$\mathbb{I}$ tasted blood as I went down. I lay there for a moment, crumpled at the base of an old pine tree, and relearned how to breathe. I wondered when I had gotten used to falling on my ass. Or more specifically, being thrown on it. A squirrel flitted onto a tree branch, stopping to throw me a look that said, "Oh, it's just you again."

"Everyone's a critic," I mumbled.

Sean's head bobbed into my vision, blocking my view of the squirrel. "You're talking to yourself," he said. "Did you hit your head too hard? I'm trying to be gentle, but you humans are so damn fragile." He scratched his nose. "Amazing that any of you survive, actually."

"I was talking to a squirrel," I said.

"Oh, well, that's okay then."

Not much fazed Sean. He offered me a hand and pulled me slowly to my feet. His brother Bran came up from behind him and grabbed my chin, checking my pupils, my ribs, and any other spot he thought I might have injured. I was getting used to this, too.

Because Brannoc wanted to *keep* me alive, I was getting self-defense lessons from Brid's siblings. She has four brothers, though I didn't meet Sayer and Roarke until a few weeks after my abduction and escape. They were currently off running errands, so Sean and Bran were picking on me today—under the watchful eye of Brannoc, of course. Usually the whole clan of brothers joined in the fun. I believe this was to remind me what would happen if I wasn't nice to their baby sister. If I ever displeased her, these boys would be the ones shredding my remains.

Because after Brid got done with me, remains were all I would be.

My self-defense lessons wouldn't actually help me if I came up against anyone in the pack. Brid and her brothers are hybrids—part werewolf (on their mother's side) and part fey hound (on their father's). The rest of the pack was either straight werewolf or fey hound, either of which was enough to take one scrawny necromancer. I glanced over at Brannoc, who was sitting under a tree, keeping an eye on things. Even though he was relaxed, his back against the bark, a piece of grass between his teeth, I knew if I snuck up and jumped him, I wouldn't land punch number one. I'm only human, and I can't compete with someone who could easily arm wrestle a bear. Or is a bear. But not every creature I might come up against would have super strength, and I was tired of getting wiped with the floor. I was still getting wiped with the floor now, but at least I was learning. Not fast enough, though. Brannoc had assigned Sean as my bodyguard until further notice. Good to know everyone had faith in my ninja skills.

After a thorough examination of my injuries, Bran declared

me alive and told me to get back into the clearing. Sean was doing the sort of warm-up jog I'd seen boxers do before a match. I didn't think he needed the warm-up. I considered mimicking him, but figured I'd just look stupid. He rolled his neck quickly to each side, a small crack coming from his adjusted vertebrae. I got into position across from him.

He pulled at a chunk of his auburn hair, which made me think of his sister. Of the siblings, Sean resembled Brid the most. He shook his head as if he'd followed my train of thought.

"You got a twig in your hair there, lover boy."

I shrugged, settling into a crouch. "Just going to get more, I'm sure."

Sean grinned. "That's the spirit." He stopped his warm-ups and mirrored me.

Bran stood in the center, a somber referee. "Sam, this time I'd like you to concentrate on how you fall."

"I've had plenty of practice on that."

"Apparently not," Bran said. "You're still not rolling into it. Learning to fall is every bit as important as learning to fight. A seasoned fighter knows how to take a tumble, lessen the possibility of injury, and turn it to his or her advantage. The way you're doing it, you're going to get hurt."

I was already hurting, so I didn't feel I could argue with him. Instead I listened as he glossed over the technique again, telling me how to go with the impact.

Good thing, too, since twenty seconds later, I was tumbling back toward the base of that tree. This time I tried to roll with it. I was so shocked when I rolled back up on my feet that I almost lost any advantage I'd gained. Sean came barreling toward me. I twisted to the side and sprinted along the tree line. Brannoc's whooping laughter followed me as I ran, but it didn't sound mocking. Not that I cared if it was. There's a time for pride and then there's a time for self-preservation.

The evening sun was slicing through the trees, leaving patches of shadow on the ground. I knew the only reason I'd managed to dodge Sean was because he was moving slowly for me. At his normal speed, I didn't stand a chance. Running wouldn't solve anything, but I kept doing it anyway. I was tired of ending up on the ground.

I ran until I got a stitch in my side. It took longer than you might think. I may not be able to fight, but I've been skateboarding for a long time, and it's very aerobic. And the first thing you learn is how to run. Cops and security guards don't appreciate skaters.

Brannoc's voice filtered through the trees. "Stay along the tree line. You'll get lost if you cut into the woods."

"Or eaten by something," Sean shouted helpfully.

Holding my side, I cut back toward the clearing. I walked slowly and tried to even out my breath. Sean and Bran were waiting patiently for me when I arrived? When I got close, I stopped and sat down, waving my hand in a circular motion to let Brannoc know I was ready for my lecture. Instead, his mouth twitched in what was almost a smile.

"That's actually the smartest fighting you've done so far."

"I ran," I said, panting.

He shook his head. "You were facing an opponent who out-classed you. You were thrown and got back up. Instead of being proud and stupid, you were smart. In a real fight, you only win if you live. Running was your best option."

"Sean would have caught me if he'd tried."

It was Bran who answered me this time. "Yes, he would have. But you won't always be up against Sean."

I picked a blade of grass and twisted it between my finger and thumb. "Running isn't going to work forever."

Bran sighed, rubbing a hand through his brutally cropped hair. Bran's looks were as somber as the rest of him, but I think most girls would still refer to him as "dreamy."

"No, it isn't. I know you're frustrated, Sam, but the reality is you're in a world now where the majority of the people you run into will be able to snap you like a twig."

"My world was like that before."

Sean coughed, but it sounded suspiciously like a laugh. I threw a pinecone at him. He caught it without looking and stuck it down his pants. Why? Because it would make me laugh, and while Bran was great at teaching, Sean was the master at keeping morale up.

Bran crossed his arms. "Bottom line? You've got to play to your strengths, and right now your strength is running like hell." He motioned for me to get up. "You don't have to like it. Just do it."

Brannoc stayed close to watch this time, his arms crossed and an amused look on his face. Bran stood to his left, a solemn reflection of his father.

Sean pointed to his head again.

"What," I said, "another twig?"

"You're bleeding a little."

I swiped at my forehead; my hand came back with a slight smear of red. Bleeding seemed to be my biggest strength. I certainly did a lot of it. I wiped my blood on the grass—and felt them as soon as my hand met the tickle of the grass blades.

When people think about necromancy, if they ever think about it at all, they envision dark rites, dead goats, guys in robes making spirits do their bidding. And this very well might be true. I was still pretty new to this sort of thing. The only other necromancer I'd ever met, Douglas, was one robe short of that stereotype. But I knew that wasn't the way it had to be. I couldn't even kill a goat to eat it (I'm vegetarian), and I absolutely never made ghosts do my bidding. The spirit I saw the most, Brooke, tended to order me around, if anything. And I didn't own a bathrobe, let alone a cloak or whatever. I generally spent my time in jeans and T-shirts, today's example sporting a very excited-looking Yoshi dinosaur. A far cry from the dark and brooding image of the typical necromancer.

My point being, there are a lot of stereotypes floating about when it comes to my kind. There are even more when it comes to what we do. As far as the undead go, people tend to visualize Hollywood-style zombies running amok and gnawing on brains. Or crawling out of graves and eating brains. Or, I don't know, dehydrating brains so they can snack on them during their next camping trip. Either way, brains are involved. But most of those movies feature the biological undead, where some sort of virus or toxic waste takes perfectly normal people and turns them into unstoppable killing machines. I've never actually seen that. The few times I've raised the dead, I don't remember anyone asking for brains at all. Like I said, I'm still new, but a zombie under control isn't going to bite anyone, and even if it did, the only infection you'd probably get is from the normal freakish bacteria found in the human mouth.

I guess I'm getting a little sensitive about the whole thing.

They always show zombies rising from a grave, too. I mean, that kind of makes sense, but what people don't seem to understand is that death is all around us all the time. When you drive down to the market, you pass squashed animals. In the store, you roll your cart by aisles and aisles of flesh. In fact, you're probably wearing bits of creatures right now. People are, and have always been, surrounded by death. We've learned, as a species, over the years, to ignore it.

The problem with me is that the part that sees death, the part that's supposed to be ignored and dormant, is—if you'll excuse the terminology—alive and thriving. And since I'd just spread my blood thinly on the grass, it was whispering to me exactly where each little piece of death was. I stared at the thin crimson smear and remembered that getting injured, while it seemed to be a hobby of mine, really wasn't my skill set.

Death was.

Maybe I couldn't toss Sean around, but that didn't mean I couldn't one-up him. Brannoc was right—I had to start fighting smart. I concentrated on each of those little islands of death, the tiny daily tragedies of smaller creatures that the human race was blind to. I gently woke them, pulled them aboveground. And it felt natural, good, like taking a deep breath of fresh air after hiding from monsters under your covers for an hour. By the time I got up, I was smiling. Relaxed. And surrounded by death.

Sean had started walking toward me but slowed when he saw what I'd done. He came to a stop and stared. I followed his eyes as he looked. Raccoons, squirrels, blue jays, and owls, all part of the normal collection of Pacific Northwest wildlife. But all very, very dead. I counted them in my head. About twenty all together. I think there was even a mole in there somewhere.

"You, uh." Sean paused and scratched his cheek. "You know I'm top of the food chain, right?"

I shrugged. Sean laughed, but I could see Bran staring at the creatures like I'd finally done something interesting.

Sean returned my shrug and came at me.

I didn't move—I didn't need too. Sean may be strong and fast, but the thing about the undead is that they can just keep coming. An owl swooped down at his eyes, making him swerve away from me. The raccoon jumped onto his back while the smaller birds began to dive-bomb. Sean stopped his forward assault, attempting to swat while he turned around and tried to get the raccoon. But for every bird or mole he swatted, another took its place. Pretty soon he was just spinning, a ball of flailing arms and feet.

And the squirrel? I watched as it slid up Sean's pant leg. Sean didn't seem to notice until the furry little guy hit about mid-thigh. The he stopped flailing and screeched, directing all his attention to swatting at his leg. I watched as the squirrel popped out of the hole in the knee of Sean's jeans. Sean swatted it off, and then, apparently having had enough, he ran off toward the house with tiny scratches dripping blood, the owl still dive-bombing his head and a constant torrent of curses flowing behind him. I think I heard him yell that he'd see us at dinner, but I'm not sure—Bran was laughing too hard for me to make it out. He had a good laugh. Most of us wouldn't laugh at seeing our sibling assaulted, but I'd learned that weres, and Bran especially, had very different senses of humor.

"I suppose you can call them off now," Brannoc said with a smirk.

I summoned them back, the squirrel getting to me first. It ran up my leg and sat on my shoulder. I reached over and scratched its head in thanks. "You think he learned his lesson?" I asked.

Brannoc came up and reached toward the squirrel, looking at me for permission before he gently patted its head.

"That depends," he said, his lip twitching in amusement. "What lesson were you trying to teach him?"

"Top of the food chain is nice, but there are a lot more things on the bottom."

Bran had regained control of himself and was nodding solemnly. "If he didn't, then it might be something we'll have to go over. There are others besides Sean who could use that lesson desperately."

I didn't say anything, but I agreed. I'd only known the pack a short time, but I'd started to notice that some of them acted like they were invincible. Powerful, yes. Strong? Most certainly. But invincible? That was a dangerous notion to cling to.

I gave the squirrel one last scratch on the head and then returned all the animals to the ground, my heartfelt thanks sending them into the abyss. Though I knew it was right, it always made me a little sad to send things back. I'd never been great with good-byes.

Brannoc slung his arms around Bran and me, pulling us into a loose hug. "You staying for dinner?"

He phrased it like a question, even though we both knew it was more of a statement. Even if I didn't want to, I'd be talked into staying. The pack seemed to take my scrawniness personally, taking any chance to fatten—or toughen—me up. I didn't mind. The pack had a damn good cook.